Re-visiting Angela Carter

Books by the same author

(Ed. with Stacy Gillis and Gillian Howie) *Third Wave Feminism: A Critical Exploration* (2004)

(With Stacy Gillis) *Feminism and Popular Culture: Explorations in Post-feminism* (forthcoming)

Decadent Daughters and Monstrous Mothers: Angela Carter and the European Gothic (forthcoming)

Re-visiting Angela Carter

Texts, Contexts, Intertexts

Edited by

Rebecca Munford
Lecturer in 20th and 21st Century Literature
University of Exeter

First published 2006 by
PALGRAVE MACMILLAN
Houndmills, Basingstoke, Hampshire RG21 6XS and
175 Fifth Avenue, New York, N.Y. 10010
Companies and representatives throughout the world

PALGRAVE MACMILLAN is the global academic imprint of the Palgrave
Macmillan division of St. Martin's Press, LLC and of Palgrave Macmillan Ltd.
Macmillan® is a registered trademark in the United States, United Kingdom
and other countries. Palgrave is a registered trademark in the European
Union and other countries.

ISBN-13: 978–1–4039–9705–0 hardback
ISBN-10: 1–4039–9705–5 hardback

This book is printed on paper suitable for recycling and made from fully
managed and sustained forest sources.

A catalogue record for this book is available from the British Library.

Library of Congress Cataloging-in-Publication Data

Re-visiting Angela Carter: texts, contexts, intertexts/edited by Rebecca
Munford.
        p.cm.
    Includes bibliographical references and index.
    ISBN 1-4039-9705-5 (cloth)
        1. Carter, Angela, 1940-1992-Criticism and interpretation. 2. Women
    and literature-England-History-20th century. I. Munford, Rebecca, 1975-
    II. Title: Re-visiting Angela Carter.

PR6053.A73Z84 2006
823'.914—dc22

                                                                    2006046251

10   9   8   7   6   5   4   3   2   1
15   14   13   12   11   10   09   08   07   06

Printed and bound in Great Britain by
Antony Rowe Ltd, Chippenham and Eastbourne

Contents

Foreword

Jacqueline Pearson

> Believe what you want to believe. What you want to
> believe is the truth.
>
> (Angela Carter, *Shadow Dance*)

In Angela Carter's first novel, *Shadow Dance* (1966), the ambiguous Honeybuzzard takes out a 'small, plastic rose on a coiling rubber stem attached to a bulb [...] he pressed the [...] bulb and an obscene, ridged, pink, tactile, rubber worm leaped out, quivered momentarily, and then sank back into the crimson nest of plastic petals, detumescent' (65). In a novel so full of scraps of literary quotation, it is easy to recognize this as a joke-shop literalization of William Blake's warning of sexuality corrupted by 'the invisible worm' in "The Sick Rose" (1795). This is entirely appropriate to the ersatz world of the novel where sexual desire is twisted by violence or futility, and where literature and art are transposed into their most fragmentary and meaningless forms. In *Shadow Dance*, Carter creates through quotations a blackly hilarious demotic version of T.S. Eliot's *The Waste Land* (1922), where allusions, explicit and implicit, jostle to be recognized and to gain priority in the novel's competing realities. Morris sees the world through a cascade of imperfectly remembered and understood echoes: 'A quotation floated from a vague corner of his mind. "Besides, that was in another country, and the wench is dead." Who said that?' (17); '"Revenge is a wild kind of justice" [...] Who said that?' (33).[1] Cut adrift from any aesthetic, political or moral context, fragments of Dante, Charles Dickens, Fyodor Dostoevsky, *Gulliver's Travels* (1726), *King Lear* (ca. 1605), *Through the Looking Glass* (1871), "Goblin Market" (1862), *Lady Chatterley's Lover* (1928), Henry Vaughan and Thomas Traherne emphasize the fundamental incoherence and moral bankruptcy, but also the wildly imaginative fertility, of the novel's world.

These intertextual strategies provide a comically exact textual equivalent of the junk-shop run by Honeybuzzard and Morris where false faces, junk of all kinds, dismembered bodies and dismembered phrases, imply a culture in collapse. In *Shadow Dance*, and elsewhere in Carter's early novels, the fragments of high culture create not a nostalgic yearning for better, more ordered times, as in *The Waste Land*, but a vigorous and abrasive celebration of ambiguity. The security of our knowledge totters in the face of 'the fictionality of realism' (Gamble 23). The reality of reality becomes problematic, with Morris uncertain of whether he is dreaming or not, even whether he really exists or not, and Honeybuzzard explicitly denying the availability of objective truth: 'Believe what you want to believe. What you want to believe is the truth' (125). Again this seems to echo Blake, this time the Blake of *The Marriage of Heaven and Hell* (ca. 1790–93), apparently now adopted by Honeybuzzard as the patron of total moral relativism.[2] While for earlier highly allusive writers, for John Webster, Alexander Pope or Eliot, the ability to deploy intertextual reference marked our knowledge of and our ability to control the world, for Carter it is part of a project which combines a lively appreciation of the literature of the past with a radical 'demythologising' project ("Notes from the Front Line" 71) which challenges our confidence in our social, cultural and psychic structures and the nature of reality itself.

From earliest to latest work, Carter plays with allusions from literature, art and film. From Shakespeare to Sade, from Baudelaire to the Brothers Grimm, from Proust to Poe, from Jean-Jacques Rousseau to Le Douanier Rousseau, from John Ford the seventeenth-century dramatist to John Ford the film-director, all is grist to her mill. For Carter, though, intertextual processes and the knowledge they encode seem always two-edged. At the end of *The Magic Toyshop* (1967), with the toyshop burning in an apocalyptic conflagration and losing her family for the second time, Melanie escapes on to the roof with Finn. An absolute break with the past is indicated: as Carter herself commented, the toyshop burns and 'adult life begins' (Sage 190) – though, ironically, even this scene merely replays the past, for Melanie has 'already lost everything, once' (199). Finn and Melanie can now 'only be like ourselves' (199): metaphors, allusions, and images can no longer be appropriate, for mature identity depends on multiple renunciations of the past (a literary as well as a psychological past). But, of course, this return to the womb of a pre-literate existence cannot really happen. Carter herself acknowledged the expulsion of Adam and Eve from Eden as a crucial intertext here (Haffenden 80), and there are others. 'At night, in the garden, they faced each other in a wild surmise' (200). This quotation, from John Keats's "On first looking into Chapman's Homer" (1816), picks up and completes a quotation begun on the first page of the novel, where Melanie is seen exploring herself, 'a physiological Cortez' (1). In repudiating art (Finn's paintings are burned) and allusion in favour of a grittier, more mature knowledge and individualism, Carter's characters can do so here only in the intertextual language of allusion.

If for Carter allusion helps to provide a language for ambiguity, one way of achieving this is to tell and retell certain central narratives. I have in mind especially her use of fairy tales. *The Bloody Chamber* (1979) contains three engagements with "Little Red Riding Hood" (in which respectively the grandmother, the hunter, and the girl herself prove to be the wolves)[3] and two radically different retellings of "Beauty and the Beast". In "The Courtship of Mr Lyon", the cosiness of the fairy story happy ending is so exaggerated, the underlying theme of emotional blackmail so naked, that irony is inescapable. In the last lines, Mr and Mrs Lyon, the ordinary bourgeois married couple who were once Beauty and the Beast, walk 'in a drift of fallen petals' (51), evoking at once the garden of Oscar Wilde's Selfish Giant and the Garden of Eden, overblown images of transience which challenge the very fairy tale security they seem to affirm. "The Tiger's Bride", Carter's exhilarating recreation of "Beauty and the Beast", concludes not, by contrast, in the socialization and humanization of the Beast, but in her accepting her inward, deepest, essential Beastly nature and becoming transformed herself: 'each stroke of his tongue ripped off skin after successive skin, all the skins of a life in the world [...] I shrugged the drops of my beautiful fur' (67).

Carter's practice with allusion changes over the course of her career. In *Shadow Dance* especially, but also to some degree in other early novels like *The Magic Toyshop*, *Heroes and Villains* (1969), and *Love* (1971), a prodigal, apparently unstructured stream of allusions evokes lives, families or cultures, that have collapsed into fragments. (Conversely, in *Several Perceptions* an apparently chaotic world and narrative may come into a newly, though perhaps ironically, clear form when we see it through the prism of its main intertext, *Alice's Adventures in Wonderland* [1865]).[4] The later novels tend to limit or at least to redirect this lush undergrowth of allusion. In her last novel, *Wise Children* (1991), the whole work is structurally shaped by its intertexts. As a novel 'about English culture' and about Shakespeare 'as one of the originating myths of English culture' (Day 95), *Wise Children* simultaneously demythologizes and remythologizes. English culture is depicted as saturated with commodified, fetishized versions of Shakespeare, evoked by the repeated reference to Shakespeare's head on a £20 note (ibid.). But at the same time Carter appreciated Shakespeare, and not only as the apotheosis of low culture, 'the intellectual equivalent of bubble-gum' (Sage 186). Self-confessedly a 'rather booksy person' (Haffenden 85), she acknowledges the continuing power of his narratives, and their ability to shape both the legitimate culture of the great Shakespearean actors and the illegitimate, both literally and metaphorically, culture embodied by Dora and Nora Chance. The story of Shakespearean actors takes on the form of Shakespearean comedy, with its multiple pairs of identical twins evoking *The Comedy of Errors* (ca. 1594) and numerous other Shakespearean allusions. Dora and Nora Chance's lives are even comically overdetermined by their residence in Bard Road, Brixton.

The earlier *Nights at the Circus* (1984) mimics, feminizes and makes strange the Dickensian biographical novel, and continues to be rich in allusions, to *Gulliver's Travels*, *The Tempest* (ca. 1610–11), Charles Baudelaire, W.B. Yeats, *Hamlet* (1599), Lord Byron, Leo Tolstoy and *As You Like It* (1599). The sense however is 'Ludic' (99) rather than sinister, and its structure, although wildly episodic, evokes not so much fragmentation as luxurious excess, to some extent disciplined by an allegedly 'straightforward allegorical' framework (Haffenden 87). Questions continue to be asked about the reality of reality – 'Is she fact or is she fiction?' (7) – but the novel ends with Fevvers's triumph over reality, her triumphant assertion that she has 'fooled' not only Walser but us readers. Fevvers, the larger-than-life heroine, appropriates both Mae West and the Kristevan woman who is 'outside naming and ideologies' (Kristeva 21; qtd. in Moi 163).

It is now fourteen years since Carter's tragically premature death, and her influence is still discernible on much contemporary fiction, and on those of us who read her so avidly, and delighted in her scepticism about all orthodoxies, including feminism itself. We are now ripe for a reassessment of her work, and a full-scale examination of her intertextual strategies is a promising way forward. This volume examines Carter's intertextual practices in relation to film (Jean-Luc Godard) and literature (Marcel Proust, William Shakespeare, Jonathan Swift, Charles Dickens and Edgar Allan Poe), and also allows her to be contextualized within broader cultural movements (gender politics, surrealism, Orientalism). These essays will challenge our assumptions about Carter and her world and enlarge our understanding of her political and literary preoccupations. Carter's 'fiction is often a kind of literary criticism' (Haffenden 79), with representation itself thematized through quotation, allusion and intertextuality. Until the end she challenged the reality of the real, the truthfulness of literary texts, and the scope of our ability to know the real world. The reader might, finally, discern tension between Carter's 'committed materialism' ("Notes from the Front Line" 70) and her delight in 'the shop-soiled yet polyvalent romance of the image' or allusion (*Nights at the Circus* 107). But ambiguity is Carter's most distinguishing feature, the 'ambiguity of the mirror' (*Nights at the*

Circus 8) one of her favourite images, and the two-edged quality of her literary allusiveness and appropriation constitutes a key strategy for embodying that ambiguity.

Notes

1. The answers, of course, are Christopher Marlowe in *The Jew of Malta* (ca. 1592 and 1633) and Francis Bacon in the *Essays* (1625) respectively.
2. 'Everything possible to be believ'd is an image of the truth' (184).
3. These are "The Werewolf", "The Company of Wolves" and "Wolf-Alice".
4. For a fuller account, see Pearson (252–53).

Works cited

Blake, William. *The Nonesuch Blake*. Ed. Geoffrey Keynes. 4th ed. London: Nonesuch Press, 1975.

Carter, Angela. *The Bloody Chamber*. 1979. London: Vintage, 1995.

———. *The Magic Toyshop*. 1967. London: Virago, 1981.

——— *Nights at the Circus*. 1984. London: Vintage, 1994.

———. "Notes from the Front Line." *On Gender and Writing*. Ed. Michelene Wandor. London: Pandora Press, 1983. 69–77.

———. *Several Perceptions*. 1968. London: Virago, 1995.

———. *Shadow Dance*. 1966. London: Heinemann, 1966.

———. *Wise Children*. 1991. London: Chatto and Windus, 1991.

Day, Aidan. *Angela Carter: The Rational Glass*. Manchester: Manchester University Press, 1998.

Gamble, Sarah, ed. *The Fiction of Angela Carter: A Reader's Guide to Essential Criticism*. Basingstoke: Palgrave Macmillan, 2001.

Haffenden, John. "Angela Carter." *Novelists in Interview*. London: Methuen, 1985. 76–96.

Kristeva, Julia. "La femme, ce n'est jamais ça." *Tel Quel* 59 (1974): 19–24.

Moi, Toril. *Sexual/Textual Politics: Feminist Literary Theory*. London: Routledge, 1985.

Pearson, Jacqueline. "'These Tags of Literature': Some Uses of Allusion in the Early Novels of Angela Carter." *Critique: Studies in Contemporary Fiction* 40.3 (1999): 248–56.

Sage, Lorna. "Angela Carter Interviewed by Lorna Sage." *New Writing*. Ed. Malcolm Bradbury and Judy Cooke. London: Minerva Press, 1992. 185–93.

Acknowledgements

I would like to thank the contributors for their correspondence about Angela Carter's work – not to mention their quick responses to editorial queries. Thanks also to Michelle Parslow for her assiduousness in preparing the index, to Paula Kennedy for her support of the project, and to Joanna O'Neill for kindly granting permission to use her artwork for the cover. Lastly, thanks to Paul Young for his sagacity and enthusiasm.

Notes on Contributors

Charlotte Crofts is a Senior Lecturer in Digital Film and Video at London South Bank University and an independent filmmaker. She is the author of *'Anagrams of Desire': Angela Carter's Writing for Radio, Film and Television* (2003) and has published on Neil Jordan's *Company of Wolves* and Terence Malick's *Days of Heaven*. She has also made a number of short films, one of which, "Bluebell", was inspired by Carter's reappropriation of the "Little Red Riding Hood" fairy tale and rape narrative.

Robert Duggan is a Teaching Fellow in English at Keele University and holds a doctorate from the University of Kent. He has written on the works of Ian McEwan and Martin Amis, and is currently working on cinematic representations of the terrorist and a book on contemporary British fiction.

Anna Watz Fruchart is a doctoral student at Uppsala University, where she is currently working on a thesis on Angela Carter, surrealism and the 1960s. She was awarded an MA from the University of East Anglia in 2000, and worked in publishing in London before starting her doctoral studies. Her research interests include 1960s literature and avant-garde art and writing.

Sarah Gamble is a Senior Lecturer in English and Gender at the University of Wales, Swansea. She is the author of *Angela Carter: Writing From the Front Line* (1997) and *Angela Carter: A Literary Life* (2005), and the editor of *Angela Carter: A Reader's Guide to Essential Criticism* (2001). She has also published essays on a range of twentieth-century writers, including Carol Shields, Charlotte Haldane and Pat Barker.

Anna Hunt is a doctoral student in the School of English at the University of Exeter, where she previously completed an MA in Critical Theory and co-organized the Feminist Research Network. Her current research examines abjection and aesthetics in contemporary women's fiction, focusing on constructions of femininity and femaleness in literature from Australia, New Zealand, Canada and the Caribbean.

Rebecca Munford is a Lecturer in 20th and 21st Century Literature at the University of Exeter. She is the co-author of *Feminism and Popular Culture* (2007) and the co-editor of *Third Wave Feminism: A Critical Exploration* (2004). She has published articles on Angela Carter, the Gothic and third wave feminism and is currently completing a mono-graph entitled *Decadent Daughters and Monstrous Mothers: Angela Carter and the European Gothic* (2008).

Jacqueline Pearson is a Professor of English Literature at the University of Manchester. Although she works primarily in the seventeenth century, with special interests in gender, writing and reading, she has also pub-lished on eighteenth-, nineteenth- and twentieth-century women writers. She is the author of an article on uses of allusion in the early novels of Angela Carter (*Critique*, 1999).

Julie Sanders is a Professor of English Literature and Drama at the University of Nottingham. She is the author of *Novel Shakespeares: Twentieth-Century Women Novelists and Appropriation* (2001) and has recent-ly published a volume in the New Critical Idiom series on *Adaptation and Appropriation* (2005).

Maggie Tonkin is a sessional teacher in the English Department at the University of Adelaide, where she has recently completed a doctoral the-sis on Angela Carter's revisionary readings of the Decadent tradition. She has published on Carter and contemporary Australian fiction, and also writes dance criticism. She is currently working on an interdiscipli-nary project which examines the representation of cancer in literary texts, the popular media and self-writing, as well as the reception of these representations.

Gina Wisker is a Professor and Head of the Centre for Learning and Teaching at the University of Brighton. Her research interests are in postcolonial women's writing and women's genre writing, in particular horror and the Gothic. Her most recent books are *Horror: An Introduction* (2005), *Postcolonial and African American Women's Writing* (2000), and beginners' guides to *Virginia Woolf, Sylvia Plath, Angela Carter* and *Toni Morrison* (2000–2003).

Angela Carter and the Politics of Intertextuality

Rebecca Munford

> [M]y fiction is very often a kind of literary criticism, which is something I've started to worry about quite a lot. I had spent a long time acquiescing very happily with the Borges idea that books were about books, and then I began to think: if all books are about books, what are the other books about? Where does it all stop? [...] Books about books is fun but frivolous.
>
> (Angela Carter in interview with John Haffenden)

Angela Carter's œuvre is characterized by its extraordinary range of literary and cultural references. Christina Britzolakis, for example, refers to 'the voracious and often dizzying intertextuality' of Carter's writing (50), while Linden Peach argues that intertextuality is a 'boldly thematised part of her work' (4). From fairy tale to French decadence, from medieval literature to Victoriana, and from cookery books to high theory, Carter's narratives are littered with allusions and references drawn from a wide range of cultural spheres.[1] As Carter herself puts it in an interview with John Haffenden:

> I have always used a very wide number of references because of tending to regard all of western Europe as a great scrap-yard from which you can assemble all sorts of new vehicles...*bricolage*. Basically, all the elements which are available are to do with the margin of the imaginative life, which is in fact what gives reality to our own experience, and in which we measure our own reality. (92)

It is owing to the suggestive image of the scrap-yard from which Carter irreverently loots and hoards that her 'distinctively magpie-like relation to literary history' (Britzolakis 50) and iconoclastic approach to canonicity have most often been framed in relation to a postmodern aesthetic. Undoubtedly, Carter's promiscuous use of citation, appropriation and literary resonance dismantles the boundaries between 'high' and 'low' cultural forms and unsettles the workings of power, legitimacy and the sacred. In this respect, it shares postmodernism's challenge to mimetic assumptions about representation by promoting narrative uncertainty, heterogeneity and dispersal. Nevertheless, this straightforward understanding of Carter's eclectic intertextual citation in terms of the formal textual qualities associated with postmodernism is held in tension with her self-declared 'absolute and committed materialism' – her frank and steadfast 'investigation of the social fictions that regulate our lives' ("Notes from the Front Line" 70). In short, her oft-cited claim that she is in the 'demythologising business' (ibid. 71).

One of the most recurrent and mordant charges levelled at Carter is that her fiction thematizes – even fetishizes – the surface so that words and images are divorced from their context. In his interview with Carter, Haffenden, for example, questions whether 'the highly stylized and decorative apparatus' of her novels 'might appear to be disengaged from the social and historical realities' she wishes to illuminate in them (85). Similarly, in her reading of Carter's 'unabashed fetishism,' Britzolakis proposes that

> [f]or a certain purist tradition of Marxism, as much as for liberal humanist criticism, Carter is a deeply embarrassing figure, adopting as she does a postmodern aesthetic which, it has been argued, privileges style over substance, eroticizes the fragment and parasitically colludes with consumer capitalism. (44)[2]

In its articulation of the 'rift between politics and pleasure, between allegory and fantasy', that has come 'to inhabit Carter criticism, as indeed [...] it inhabits Carter's writing' (44), Britzolakis's analysis thus brings into focus the supposed tension between the aesthetic and the political which frequently haunts Carter criticism. The literary scavenging to which Carter herself alludes is recapitulated as parasitic and predatory; the figure of the vampire, one of her most favoured motifs, becomes a metaphor for her textual practice.

What seems to be at stake in such understandings of Carter's use of intertextuality as both vampiric and sybaritic is the issue of pleasure. This is an issue which, especially in early readings of her work, is tied to notions of the 'proper' position of the feminist author and the politics of authorship – the notion that Carter's writing 'could do with a dose of social realism' (Haffenden 91).[3] Such assumptions about the appropriate position of the 'feminist' author are epitomized by Robert Clark's well-known critique of Carter's fiction which appeared in *Women's Studies: An Interdisciplinary Journal* in 1987. Here Clark proposes that Carter's 'writing is often feminism in a male chauvinist drag' (158). He moves on to attribute this designation to Carter's 'primary allegiance' to a postmodern aesthetics – an allegiance which, he argues, 'precludes an affirmative feminism founded in referential commitment to women's historical and organic being' (158). He continues:

> The brilliant and choice lexicon, the thematization of surfaces and odours, of beauty, youth, and power, the incantatory rhythms and tantalizing literariness, are strategies that bind the reader poetically, give the illusion of general significance without its substance, and put the reason to sleep, thereby inhibiting satire's necessary distancing of the reader from both the text and the satirized illusions. (158–59)

For Clark, the response to Haffenden's questioning of the potential dissonance between the heavily stylized décor of Carter's novels and socio-historical contexts is unambiguous: Carter's 'incantatory' and 'tantalizing' literariness necessarily prohibits political commitment – and, in particular, any commitment to a rational *feminist* politics. Most troublingly, Clark's analysis rests on an essentialist assumption about women's 'organic' being, so that Carter's stylistic heresy is cast as an affront to the 'reality', or 'authenticity', of women's experience.

Elaine Jordan proposes, with an air of Carteresque mischief, that Clark's criticism of Carter 'reads like a sinister piece of female impersonation' in its blatant disregard for Carter's unequivocal and repeated statements about her 'allegiance' to political and cultural analysis – albeit an analysis derived from 'specific experiments rather than from a single assured base towards a single Utopian goal' ("Enthralment" 26). Not only a sardonic riposte to Clark's condemnation of Carter's 'male chauvinist drag', Jordan's remark here also, of course, echoes Carter's own comments about the element of the 'male impersonator' which characterized some of her early writing.[4] The tension in Carter's work, then, issues from the uncomfortable position she occupies in relation to a dominant model of second wave Anglo-American feminist literary criticism and its notion of the role – and responsibility – of the 'woman author'. Of especial concern for Carter detractors has been her fervent critique of the mystification of female virtue and victimhood within certain strands of second wave feminist discourse and, in particular, her apparently tolerant dialogue with the Marquis de Sade and the possibilities of 'moral pornography' as a mode of social critique in *The Sadeian Woman: An Exercise in Cultural History* (1979).[5] As Lorna Sage puts it, Carter's writing 'unravels the romance of exclusion. And this means it's in an oblique and sometimes mocking relation to the kind of model of female fantasy deployed by Gilbert and Gubar in *The Madwoman in the Attic* – where fantasy is a matter of writing against the patriarchal grain' (*Women in the House* 168). Concerned as she is with entering the male-dominated territories of decadence, surrealism and pornography, the trouble with Carter is that she often writes against the *feminist* grain and, as Sage suggests elsewhere, becomes 'an offence to the modest, inward, realist version of the woman writer' ("Death of the Author" 248).

Nevertheless, as is explored in this collection, in spite of 'the fantastic and exotic surface' of Carter's fictions (Haffenden 91), and in spite of her refusal to 'repose securely in the bosom of the sisterhood' (Sage, "Death of the Author" 248), Western patriarchy remains an ongoing object of interrogation – and denunciation – in her writing. Carter's concerted and candid investigation of social fictions, including the 'social fiction' of femininity, comprises a painstaking (if, at times, painful) challenge to the stability and authority of male-authored canonical representations. She repeatedly described her fiction as 'very often a kind of literary criticism' (Haffenden 71) and was unequivocal in her alignment of the political and the aesthetic, and her belief in the social responsibility of the artist:

> Fine art, that exists for itself alone, is art in a final state of impotence. If nobody, including the artist, acknowledges art as a means of knowing the world, then art is relegated to a kind of rumpus room of the mind and the irresponsibility of the artist and the irrelevance of art to actual living becomes part and parcel of the practice of art. (*The Sadeian Woman* 6)

Thus, Carter's extensive and multifarious engagements with previous literary and cultural frameworks need to be reconsidered in light of a more complex understanding of her intertextuality as a feminist strategy – one that re-examines the correspondences between style and substance, between text and context, in her writing. Reading Carter's intertextuality merely in terms of a postmodernist textual procedure effaces its theoretical and political import. A re-examination of her textual and intellectual strategies – and their interrelationship – will provide an opportunity to re-visit the ambivalences, fissures and pleasures of her work.

Carter and intertextuality: 'the death of the author'

'Intertextuality' is an incredibly voluminous term – one that has been subject to various definitions, uses and, according to Graham Allen, misinterpretations (2). Coined by Julia Kristeva in her discussion of Mikhail Bakhtin's theories of dialogism and carnival in the late 1960s, the term intertextuality has since become a commonplace of contemporary critical vocabulary. In its most contracted appropriation, intertextuality posits an understanding of text as wanting in independent meaning; that is, to cite Kristeva's reading of Bakhtin, 'any text is constructed as a mosaic of quotations; any text is the absorption and transformation of another' (66). Rather than representing a field of intentional influence, allusion and quotation, or of generic equivalence, this theory of intertextuality maintains that a text (as signifying system) does not function as a closed system of meaning.[6] For Kristeva, Bakhtinian dialogism, the 'double-voiced' nature of language, posits a notion of 'the "literary word" as an *intersection of textual surfaces* rather than a *point* (a fixed meaning), as a dialogue among several writings: that of the writer, the addressee (or the character) and the contemporary or earlier cultural context' (65; emphasis in original). This conceptualization of (literary) structure as generated in relation to (or 'transposed' into) another structure thus disrupts notions of monologic meaning and truth – opening up a space for new understandings of the relationship between language, politics and subjectivity.

While an in-depth exposition of intertextuality and its various theoretical articulations and operations is outside the remit of this discussion, it is nonetheless important to locate Carter in relation to 'intertextuality' as, to cite Mary Orr, 'a critical term and catchphrase' that 'captured the mood of May 1968 in its spearheading of extensive cultural reappraisal' (1).[7] The term 'intertextuality' is one that is frequently employed to describe Carter's textual practices and processes, and Carter engaged with specific theories of textuality, representation and authorship – in particular, certain strands of French structuralist and poststructuralist thinking – in both her fiction and non-fiction. In an essay entitled "Death of the Author", published in *Granta*'s issue on "Biography" in 1992, Sage describes Carter as being 'of a generation nourished on the Death of the Author (Barthes, 1968 Vintage)' (235).[8] It is the case, certainly, that Roland Barthes – alongside other 'master' theorists (for example, Sigmund Freud, Claude Lévi-Strauss, Michel Foucault, Walter Benjamin and Theodor Adorno) – appears as a point of engagement for Carter in several interviews and essays, and his understanding of textuality is explicitly identified as a determining influence on her post-1968 novels. In an interview with Les Bedford for Sheffield University Television in 1977, for example, Carter discusses the ways in which her fourth novel, *Heroes and Villains* (1969), marked a turning point in her textual practice: 'I was beginning to regard the work that I was doing as external to myself [...] I was beginning to perceive text as text, as Barthes would say' (Bedford). This shift in her view of textuality, Carter continues, was vital to a notion of writing as no longer a place to work through 'personal situations', but a place where she could engage with 'ideas'.

Barthes' seminal essay, "The Death of the Author" (1968), offers one of the most well-known models of intertextuality and one that resonates with certain aspects of Carter's textual process. Challenging the ideology of authorial originality and consciousness, Barthes proposes a theory of (inter)textuality which implies a refusal of authority:

> We know now that a text is not a line of words releasing a single 'theological' meaning (the 'message' of the Author-God) but a multi-dimensional space in which a variety of writings, none of them original, blend and clash. The text is a tissue of quotations drawn from innumerable centres of culture. [...] the writer can only imitate a gesture that is always anterior, never original. His only power is to mix writings, to counter the ones with the others, in such a way as never to rest on any one of them. (146)

This frequently quoted passage from Barthes' essay, with its implicit renunciation of paternal power and ownership, is in many respects consonant with the feminist (and atheistic) challenge to patriarchal authority central to Carter's writing. In "Notes from the Front Line"

(1983), Carter famously recalls her experience of the late 1960s as one when

> truly, it felt like Year One, that all that was holy was in the process of being profaned and we were attempting to grapple with the real relations between human beings. [...] I can date to that time and to some of those debates and to that sense of heightened awareness of the society around me in the summer of 1968, my own questioning of the nature of my reality as a *woman*. How that social fiction of my 'femininity' was created, by means outside my control, and palmed off to me as the real thing. (70; emphasis in original)

Celebrating the late 1960s as a defining moment in terms of the development of her feminist consciousness, as well as 'various intellectual adventures into anarcho-surrealism' (70), Carter's dual pleasure in profanation and cultural reappraisal, read alongside her comment in the Bedford interview, points up a shared concern with 'the desacrilization of the image of the Author' proposed by Barthes (144).

On one hand, the Barthesian notion of text as 'made of multiple writings, drawn from many cultures and entering into mutual relations of dialogue, parody, contestation' has much in common with the textual patterns of Carter's fiction – the intersection of textual traces from 'an official past, specifically a literary past, but [...] paintings and sculptures and the movies and folklore and heresies, too' ("Notes from the Front Line" 73). However, in his explication of Kristeva's notion of 'intertextuality', Barthes states that '[t]he intertext is not necessarily a field of influences: rather it is a music of figures, metaphors, thought words; it is the signifier as *siren*' (*Roland Barthes* 145; emphasis in original). For Barthes, it is the pleasure-seeking reader, responding to the siren call of text, who emerges foremost in his theory of intertextuality. As he writes in "The Death of the Author":

> the reader is the space on which all the quotations that make up a writing are inscribed without any of them being lost; a text's unity lies not in its origin but in its destination. Yet this destination cannot any longer be personal: the reader is without history, biography, psychology; he is simply that *someone* who holds together in a single field all the traces by which the text is constituted. (148; emphasis in original)

While the question of gender remains markedly absent – or, perhaps, effaced – from Barthes' text, Carter offers a distinctly feminist inflection to the process of sacrilege. As is evident in the above quotation from "Notes from the Front Line", Carter is most often concerned with disentangling those social fictions from which the nature of her 'reality as a *woman*' is constructed – in other words, her intertextual strategies refuse the 'impersonality' proposed by Barthes in a move to consider the specific historical and socio-cultural contexts for the construction of *gendered* subjectivities.

The tension between the poststructuralist model of intertextuality represented by Barthes and Carter's refusal of impersonality is exemplified in the title story of *Black Venus* (1985), a collection of short stories focused on re-writing canonical authors and texts to give voice to silenced histories and biographies. Carter's "Black Venus" is an intertextual reworking of Charles Baudelaire's representation of Jeanne Duval, his Creole mistress and putative muse in the so-called 'Black Venus cycle' of *Les Fleurs du mal* (1857 and 1861).[9] The story is composed of re-presentations of and quotations from the opulent and fetishistic register of Baudelaire's poetry interspersed with imagined fragments of Duval's speech and inner narrative so that, Linda Hutcheon proposes, 'two discourses meet – and clash: the poetic language of male sublimated desire for woman (as both muse and object of erotic fantasy) and the language of the political and contextualizing discourses of female experience' (145). For example, an ironic allusion to "Le Serpent qui danse" allows Duval to reproach Baudelaire for his poetic idealization of her:

> He said she danced like a snake and she said, snakes can't dance: they've got no legs, and he said, but kindly, you're an idiot, Jeanne; but she knew he'd never so much as *seen* a snake [...] – if he'd seen a snake move, he'd never have said a thing like that. (6; emphasis in original)

Thus, although Duval ostensibly colludes with Baudelaire's poetic projections by performing the dance 'he wanted her to perform so much and had especially devised for her' (3), she takes up an ambiguous position in relation to his meticulously staged choreography. Carter's ironic re-contextualization of fragments of *Les Fleurs du mal* thus open up a space for Duval's realism and vernacular commentary to deflate Baudelaire's poetic by negating the role of inspiration and charm she is ascribed as muse in his poetry.

According to Britzolakis, Carter's 'stylistic investment in Baudelaire's text cannot help but to reinscribe [Duval], at least partially, within the iconic framework of the *Fleurs du Mal*' (52). Nevertheless, while Carter's language in this story might turn 'Baudelaire into a décor' (ibid. 51), another exotic surface, Duval is, in the end, reinstated firmly outside of the Baudelairean literary universe. Re-imagining the photographer and biographer Félix Nadar's closing account of Duval in her old age as toothless, hairless and 'hobbling on crutches along the pavement to the dram-shop' (12), Carter provides Duval with false teeth, new hair, and an elegant walking stick. Moreover, while in the later stages of syphilitic degeneration Baudelaire is left 'so far estranged from himself that [...] when he was shown his reflection in the mirror, he bowed politely, as to a stranger' (12), Duval is shown to have 'found herself; she had come down to earth, and with the aid of her ivory cane, she walked perfectly well upon it' (13). Standing proud with her cane, the symbol of the *flâneur*, she walks the streets not as a prostitute, but as an *arriviste* leaving her 'charming house to take last night's takings to the bank' (ibid.). 'Chugging away' on a steamer heading to the Caribbean, it is ultimately Duval who mobilizes the Baudelairean topos of the boat as a symbol of the poet's transcendental journey to return to her motherland. Thus, Carter demystifies and humanizes Duval by not only *re-presenting* her as a historical subject, but by *re-presencing* her as an agent in history – as a re-birthed Black Venus rising from the ashes of Baudelaire's poetic.

Carter's presentation of Jeanne as reader of the Baudelairean text foregrounds the specific contexts of her textual position as a Creole Woman silenced by 'the lapidary, troubled serenity of her lover's poetry' (9). In this respect, Carter's ironic recasting of the siren call has a particular resonance: 'Daddy paid no attention to what song his siren sang, he fixed his quick, bright, dark eyes upon her decorated skin as if, sucker, authentically entranced' (3). While the playful re/deconstruction of the Baudelairean text suggests a pleasure in the seductive qualities of language (of 'the signifier as siren'), "Black Venus" exposes the history of desire as the history of *male* desire. Carter's fictional biography of Jeanne Duval refuses the impersonality of the poststructuralist avowal of the 'death of the author' proposed by Barthes because, to draw on Patricia Waugh's discussion of the fraught relationship between feminist and poststructuralist thinking,

a conception of the self which involves the possibility of historical agency and integration of ego is necessary for effective operation in the world and must be experienced before its conceptual basis can be theoretically deconstructed. [...] In order to function effectively, as 'selves', we need to discover our histories (a sense of continuity in time), a sense of agency (how we can act upon the world), and to be able to reflect self-consciously upon what we take ourselves to be. (30–31)

In its representation of the distinct positions occupied by Duval and Baudelaire in relation to language and literary history/production Carter's story thus anticipates Nancy K. Miller's argument that '[b]ecause women have not had the same historical relation of identity to origin, institution, production that men have had' the 'postmodernist decision that the Author is Dead [...] prematurely forecloses the question of agency for them' (106).[10] In exposing the representational modes upon which constructions of identity and selfhood are contingent, Carter points up the possibilities of re-constructing identity. In this respect, the *specificity* of her textual engagements resists a Barthesian understanding of intertextuality as an equalizing of texts: she is concerned with the *re*-location, rather than the *dis*-location of the subject. Carter, Sage proposes, 'had a position on the politics of textuality. She went in for the proliferation, rather than the death, of the author' (*Angela Carter* 58).

Anxiety of influence: daddy's girl

In her recent study of the figure of the woman author in contemporary women's fiction, Mary Eagleton highlights how the question of authorship and authority was also being disputed in feminist literary criticism of the late 1960s and 1970s – with some critics seeking to instate alternative canons of women writers, while others challenged the possibility of a coherent or knowable subjectivity (2–3). Barthes' essay, she suggests, offered an ironic expression of this 'twin impulse both to give birth to the woman author and to bury her' (ibid. 3). As Eagleton goes on to highlight, 1977, the year in which "The Death of the Author" was made widely available to an Anglophone readership (owing to its publication in Stephen Heath's edited collection of Barthes' essays), was also the year in which Barbara Smith published "Toward a Black Feminist Criticism", Luce Irigaray the French edition of *This Sex Which Is Not One* and Elaine Showalter *A Literature of their Own*. These texts, she continues, indicate a curious contradiction in intellectual history, how one group of academics was declaring the 'death' of the author as a figure of origin, meaning and power at precisely the same moment as another group, from varying feminist positions, was looking for the 'birth' of the author in terms of a reclamation of women's literary history [...] Even if one believes with Samuel Beckett that we give birth astride a grave, no one expected birth and death to be quite so proximate. (3)

This latter set of texts, alongside Sandra Gilbert and Susan Gubar's *The Madwoman in the Attic*, published in 1979, offers an alternative model of intertextuality – one concerned with the issues of influence and source eschewed by Barthes and, centrally, with mapping relations between women writers within a specific literary tradition (in other words, a feminist re-working of the Bloomian model of influence). Linda Anderson, for example, highlights the relevance of the term 'intertextuality' for understandings of women's writing in relation to the repression of 'alternative stories, other possibilities, hidden or secret scripts' (vii), proposing that '[i]f women's texts point to other texts it is frequently with a sense of an imagined elsewhere, unacknowledged alternatives, other stories waiting silently to be told' (vii–viii). This, then, is a notion of intertextuality derived from the *resurgence* of the female author.

While Carter's textual practice might be focused on the recovery and recuperation of 'alternative stories' and 'hidden or secret scripts', as exemplified by "Black Venus", her writing, as suggested earlier in this essay, does not sit comfortably with the model of marginality and exclusion represented by the 'madwoman in the attic'. Very often, the women in Carter's fiction – for example, Ghislaine in *Shadow Dance* (1966) and Annabel in *Love* (1971) – are not uncomplicatedly '*virtuous* because they didn't construct their prison' (Sage, *Women in the House* 168; emphasis in original). Rather, their complicity with the structures and narratives of male desire is interrogated. At the same time, from the representation of Mother in *The Passion of New Eve* (1977) to her re-articulation of Eugénie's violent attack on her mother in *The Sadeian Woman*, Carter's narratives enact an unremitting assault on traditional images of the mother and maternal lineage. Indeed, one of the most contentious aspects of Carter's writing is her intertextual engagement with 'the rhetoric and iconography of a prominent, largely male-authored strand of European literary history' (Britzolakis 49). It is, of course, Carter's dialogue with the Marquis de Sade that has harnessed most feminist criticism (both in terms of analysis and condemnation), but from Perrault and the Brothers Grimm to Baudelaire and Poe, her textual liaisons are very often grounded in male-centred literary and cultural frameworks.

Nevertheless, Carter's textual investment in male-centred frameworks is not synonymous with a political investment in them. Her most frequently cited comment on her textual practice appears at the beginning of "Notes from the Front Line", and it is worth reiterating here because, however critically-worn it might be, it cuts to the heart of her writing strategies:

> I try, when I write fiction, to think on my feet – to present a number of propositions in a variety of different ways, and to leave the reader to construct her own fiction for herself from the elements of my fictions. (Reading is just as creative an activity as writing and most intellectual development depends upon new readings of old texts. I am all for putting new wine in old bottles, especially if the pressure of the new wine makes the old bottles explode.) (69)

Carter, like Fevvers in *Nights at the Circus* (1984), may at times occupy the position of the wayward daughter in relation to her feminist foremothers, but this does not mean that she is straightforwardly a 'daddy's girl'. Although her last novel, *Wise Children* (1991), is structured as a quest for paternal origin and influence, this is a search that ends with a comical debunking of paternal power. The sacred Melchior Hazard is finally held in view with 'an imitation look [...] like one of those great, big, papier-mâché heads they have in the Notting Hill parade, larger than life, but not lifelike' (230). In the end, the father is not figured as a point of (literary) origin, but as an image of endless recycling – a 'pulp fiction'. While concerned with destabilizing authorial discourse – and, in particular, the figure of the Author-God – Carter is nonetheless concerned with entering into dialogue with a specific literary and cultural past because, she proposes, '[t]his past [...] has important decorative, ornamental functions; further, it is a vast repository of outmoded lies' where you can check out what lies used to be à la mode and find the old lies on which new lies have been based' ("Notes from the Front Line" 73). As such, her work might best be understood in relation to the intersection between the two models of intertextuality outlined here – as occupying a position of in-betweenness which mirrors the dissonances and fissures between style and substance in her own texts.

At the end of the introduction to her collection of essays on Carter for the *New Casebooks* series, Alison Easton identifies the need for 'much, much more [...] close textual work on her sources and multi-layered meanings, the intricacies of tone and structure' as a key area for future Carter scholarship (16). *Re-visiting Angela Carter: Texts, Contexts, Intertexts* offers the beginnings of a response to Easton's appeal. Of course, the essays in this collection re-visit only some of the wide range of Carter's intertextual engagements: the scrap-yard within which Carter rummaged and looted is a vast one and, as Easton warns, 'Carter declared war on the myths of Western culture, and we need to be careful not to create new grand narratives out of favoured theorists' (7). The intention of this volume is not, therefore, to offer an exhaustive account of Carter's influences and intertexts – should such an unenviable task be possible. Nor is it to offer definitive readings of specific engagements with particular literary and cultural forms and frameworks. Rather, its aim is to open up new dialogues about Carter's imaginative procedures and writing strategies by offering concerted and sustained readings of some of her specific influences and intertexts. Vital to this endeavour is the re-contextualization of some of these key engagements. As Jacqueline Pearson points out in her foreword, Carter's intertextuality challenges both our confidence in our social, cultural and psychic structures and the nature of 'reality' itself. A fuller understanding of Carter's textual practice thus requires a reading of her work outside of the formal textual strategies of pastiche, bricolage, etc. – outside of an interpretation of intertextuality as synonymous with 'postmodernism' – and a reconsideration of the relationship between *text* and *context*.

It is for this reason that, for the most part, the essays in this volume focus on Carter's re-working of specifically androcentric literary and cultural frameworks.[11] Some of these essays address and re-visit specific texts; others explore themes as they manifest themselves more broadly in her œuvre. The first two essays, by Anna Watz Fruchart and Sarah Gamble, address Carter's early novels, novels which offer us 'the world of the second-hand trade, where the inherited stuff of the past – clothes, furniture, imagery, ideas – is reassembled in travesty' (Sage, *Women in the House* 169). It is in these early novels that Carter's sexual/textual politics are, perhaps, at their most perilous, especially insofar as they manifest what Jordan has described as the 'apparent contradiction between Carter's feminist "line" and her exploitation of a dangerous reactionary fascination – heterosexual desire in thrall to soft pornography and sado-masochism' ("The Dangers of Angela Carter" 123). Fruchart's essay takes as its focus Carter's first novel, *Shadow Dance* – undoubtedly one of Carter's most problematic texts in terms of her representation of gendered violence. Counter to dominant readings of the novel in terms of literary realism, Fruchart undertakes a re-reading of *Shadow Dance* as a simultaneous celebration and critique of surrealism's logic of transgression with particular reference to the German surrealist artist Hans Bellmer's series of child-woman dolls. Unpacking Carter's dialogue with surrealism, she highlights the tension between a project of transforming texts/worlds and the image of woman as disarticulated and deprived of voice. Gamble too is concerned with Carter's problematic depiction of sexual politics in her early writings, an issue she explores in relation to the French New Wave *auteur*, Jean-Luc Godard. Through a comparative reading of Godard's films and Carter's 'Bristol Trilogy' (Marc O'Day 25), Gamble examines congruencies in their narrative techniques apropos the representation of constructions of femininity. Focusing on the figure of the *femme fatale*, she reconsiders Godard and Carter's mutual interest in notions of the destructive power of female sexuality and their deployment of violence as a critique of society's exploitation of women.

The next two essays in the collection are concerned with constructions of Otherness. Maggie Tonkin's essay re-reads Carter's *The Infernal Desire Machines of Doctor Hoffman* (1972) in dialogue with Marcel Proust's *À la recherche du temps perdu* (1913–27) and some of the critical traditions it has generated. Challenging Elisabeth Bronfen's reading of the novel in terms of the foreclosure of interpretative ambivalence, Tonkin proposes that *The Infernal Desire Machines of Doctor Hoffman* unleashes interpretative ambivalence in the service of a specific intertextual critique – one that addresses itself not only to a specific intertext, but also more broadly to the dialectic of absence and presence that underpins the trope of the Muse-as-(Dead)-Beloved as it has been deployed in the male-authored literary canon. While Carter's 'decolonializing' project is most often taken up in relation to her demythologization of gender, the postcolonial dimensions of her writing remain a largely uncharted territory in Carter scholarship. This neglect is redressed by Charlotte Crofts in her essay on Carter's 'new fangled Orientalism'. Drawing on Carter's radio plays, journalism and the short story collection *Fireworks* (1974), Crofts explores the impact of her

formative experiences in Japan on her feminist and political consciousness as a writer. However, while considering the importance of Carter's
engagement with Japan in terms of her gendered and racialized identity, Crofts attends to the dangers of simply seeing Japan as an Orientalist
lens through which Carter was able to scrutinize her own culture.
Situating Carter's experiences in Japan within a post-1968 context, she
highlights the necessity of re-thinking these experiences in relation to
the racial and cultural power relations determining the Western intellectual's travel to another culture. In so doing, Crofts analyses the
tension in Carter's work between a 'decolonializing' project and the
remnants of the 'old-fashioned' Orientalism of her white male literary
influences.

The penultimate two essays in the collection – focusing on Carter's
engagement with William Shakespeare and Jonathan Swift respectively
– are concerned with notions of hybridity and marginality in her later
novels. In her essay on Carter's 'hybrid Shakespeare', Julie Sanders
examines Carter's ongoing intertextual relationship with 'Shakespeare'
– both in terms of his body of work and with his cultural agency as a
literary icon and commodity. Sanders's essay interrogates the political
and cultural contexts for particular appropriations and reinventions, in
particular the Victorian bowdlerization of Shakespeare, examining the
ways in which Carter melds early modern dramatic and textual practice
with the contemporary idiom of feminist and postcolonial theory.
Through close readings of Carter's allusions to and re-workings of the
figures of Ophelia and Marianna, Sanders explores the 'What if ...?'
intertextual games in which Carter engages her reader. Anna Hunt's
essay on the abject and the grotesque in Carter and Jonathan Swift similarly highlights Carter's 'textual teasing' and interpretative mockery.
Here she considers both writers' concern with the slipperiness of subjectivity through an analysis of their narratives of disorder and distortion. Examining the eighteenth-century fascination with freak shows
and its influence on narratives of self and spectacle in *Gulliver's Travels*
(1726) and *Nights at the Circus*, Hunt draws on the work of Mary
Douglas, Julia Kristeva and Mary Russo to consider Swift's and Carter's
aesthetics of abjection – their re-examination of 'the margins of the
imaginative life'.

The final two essays are concerned with questions of theatricality and
spectacle and with the tension between fantasy and social critique
which structures Carter's fiction. Robert Duggan returns to Charles
Dickens – and his critical reception – in order to re-open the tension
between 'fantasy' and 'reality' in Carter's writing. Drawing on the

notion of heteroglossia that Bakhtin saw as central to the tradition of the English comic novel, Duggan proposes that Dickens's fiction antic- ipates the coalescence of politics and fantasy characterizing Carter's later novels. The last essay in the collection by Gina Wisker is concerned with the theatricality of violence and power characterizing Carter's engagement with and re-working of Gothic horror and, especially, the themes and tropes of Edgar Allan Poe's tales. Re-visiting a selection of Carter's short stories – in *Fireworks, The Bloody Chamber* (1979) and *American Ghosts and Old World Wonders* (1993) – Wisker traces Carter's re-casting of horror motifs linking sex, beauty and death. She argues that, unlike those of Poe's imagining, many of Carter's beautiful dead, un-dead, or near dead women refuse to lie down forever but, like Fevvers in *Nights at the Circus*, fly in the face of patriarchal structures and discourses.

As the essays in this collection explore, Carter's work is multiple and unstable; it is concerned with offering new perceptions of wor(l)ds, new ways of knowing and seeing. Jordan, one of the most rigorous exponents of Carter's textual practice, avers that her writing 'worked a risky edge, political and literary' ("The Dangerous Edge" 189). That is not to say, however, that 'the political' and 'the literary' act independently in her work; it is, rather, from this 'dangerous edge' that the pleasures and ambivalences of her writing materialize. Be it the admiring evocation of a Baudelairean poetic in "Black Venus" or the playful recasting of the Sadeian interior in *The Infernal Desire Machines of Doctor Hoffman* and "The Bloody Chamber", the alluring literariness of Carter's writing is most often at work as part of a feminist analysis of the social fictions which shape identity and experience. If intertextuality is a 'thematized' part of her work, its thematization is part of a wider political examination of 'what certain configurations of imagery in our society, in our culture, really stand for, what they mean, underneath the kind of semireligious coating that makes people not particularly want to interfere with them' (Katsavos 12). Carter may be concerned with destabilizing the figure of the Author-God, but her demythologizing project also involves a debunking of certain feminist 'Ur-religions' (ibid. 13). For Carter, nothing is sacred. Susannah Clapp, Carter's literary executor, describes her work as 'voluptuous, political, fantastic, snarling, erot- ic, learned'. It is also, she adds, 'the work of a writer who was singu- lar in seeing no paradox in being a dandy as well as a socialist' (xvii). Carter's writing is both highly stylized and politically engaged. And it often involves negotiating the precarious border between duplication and duplicity, between complicity and critique.

Notes

1. Joseph Bristow and Trev Lynn Broughton remark that by the time Carter published *The Infernal Desire Machines of Doctor Hoffman* (1972) 'the allusiveness of her writing was so broad that one can only commiserate with the task facing future annotators of the novel' (9).
2. Robert Clark similarly describes Carter's writing as 'parasitic' in his article discussed below (156).
3. Haffenden is referring to Tom Paulin's review of Carter's *Nothing Sacred* (1982) which appeared in *London Review of Books*. Here Paulin remarks that 'the easy fluency and soft stylishness of Angela Carter's fictions is won at the expense of form and mimesis [...] It could be that her cerulean imagination would benefit from the constraints of the documentary novel' (19; qtd. in Haffenden 91). For more on Paulin's reading of Carter see Duggan's essay in this volume.
4. See, for example, "Notes from the Front Line" (71) and, specifically, the Afterword to the 1987 edition of *Love* in which Carter describes the novel's 'almost sinister feat of male impersonation' (113).
5. It is a tension between 'the literary' and 'the political' that is embedded in the two most well-known condemnations of Carter's engagement with de Sade. Andrea Dworkin, for example, denounces *The Sadeian Woman* as a 'pseudo-feminist literary essay' more concerned with celebrating de Sade than with tackling the implications of the gendered sado-masochistic relations underpinning the pornograph (84), while Susanne Kappeler charges Carter with wantonly elevating Sade 'as artist and writing subject' rather than decrying his position as a 'multiple rapist and murderer' (134).
6. For a succinct elaboration on this, see Still and Worton (1–2).
7. This essay is particularly concerned with Carter's engagement with specific theories of intertextuality and, especially, her repeated allusions to Barthesian notions of text. For a more detailed overview of various theories of intertextuality, see Allen and Still and Worton. For an in depth interrogation and re-mapping of the debates surrounding intertextuality and, especially, the marginalization of Kristeva in accounts of intertextual theory, see Orr.
8. Published shortly after Carter's death, Sage's "Death of the Author" offers both a posthumous biographical account of Carter's life and an exposition of her textual practice. The dual resonance of Sage's title is particularly pertinent for Carter as a writer who, perhaps more so than any of her contemporaries, has herself been simultaneously mythologized and essentialized in posthumous constructions of her literary career (see, for example, Margaret Atwood's description of Carter as a 'born subversive' [61]). As Aidan Day highlights, Carter's anti-realism has provoked a peculiar and particular form of mythologizing, one 'that confounds author and work' (2).
9. For an extended reading of "Black Venus", see Munford (*passim*).

10. See also Anja Müller who, in her study of Carter's de/constructive practices, proposes that 'the pluralism postmodernism likes to claim for itself is one based on masculine parameters. Its deconstructive strategies not only destroy the patriarchal reality and its subject but also the potential for a notion of femininity within it' (4).

11. That is not to say, however, that Carter's intertextual dialogues are exclusively located within the male-centred literary/cultural arena. There has been much valuable discussion of her literary debt to, for example, Virginia Woolf (see Armstrong), Djuna Barnes (see Russo) and the 'corrupting influence' of Colette (Sage, "Savage Sideshow" 55; see Ward Jouve).

Works cited

Allen, Graham. *Intertextuality*. London: Routledge, 2000.

Anderson, Linda. Preface. *Plotting Change: Contemporary Women's Fiction*. Ed. Linda Anderson. London: Edward Arnold, 1990. vi–xi.

Armstrong, Isobel. "Woolf by the Lake, Woolf at the Circus: Carter and Tradition." *Flesh and the Mirror: Essays on the Art of Angela Carter*. Ed. Lorna Sage. London: Virago, 1994. 257–78.

Atwood, Margaret. "Magic Token Through the Dark Forest." *The Observer* 23 Feb. 1992: 61.

Barthes, Roland. "The Death of the Author." 1968. *Image/Music/Text*. Trans. Stephen Heath. London: Fontana-HarperCollins, 1977. 142–48.

———. *Roland Barthes*. 1975. Trans. Richard Howard. New York: Farrar, Straus and Giroux, 1977.

Baudelaire, Charles. *Les Fleurs du mal*. 1857 and 1861. Intro. Claude Pichois. 2nd ed. Paris: Gallimard, 1996.

Bedford, Les. "Angela Carter: An Interview." Sheffield University Television. Feb. 1977.

Bristow, Joseph, and Trev Lynn Broughton. Introduction. *The Infernal Desires of Angela Carter: Fiction, Femininity, Feminism*. Ed. Joseph Bristow and Trev Lynn Broughton. Harlow: Addison Wesley Longman, 1997. 1–23.

Britzolakis, Christina. "Angela Carter's Fetishism." *The Infernal Desires of Angela Carter: Fiction, Femininity, Feminism*. Ed. Joseph Bristow and Trev Lynn Broughton. Harlow: Addison Wesley Longman, 1997. 43–58.

Carter, Angela. "Black Venus." *Black Venus*. 1985. London: Vintage, 1996. 1–14.

———. "Notes from the Front Line." *On Gender and Writing*. Ed. Michelene Wandor. London: Pandora Press, 1983. 69–77.

———. *The Sadeian Woman: An Exercise in Cultural History*. 1979. London: Virago, 1992.

———. *Wise Children*. 1991. London: Vintage, 1992.

Clapp, Susannah. Introduction. *The Curious Room: Collected Dramatic Works*. By Angela Carter. London: Vintage, 1997. vii–x.

Clark, Robert. "Angela Carter's Desire Machine." *Women's Studies: An Interdisciplinary Journal* 14.2 (1987): 147–61.

Day, Aidan. *Angela Carter: The Rational Glass*. Manchester: Manchester University Press, 1997.

Dworkin, Andrea. *Pornography: Men Possessing Women.* London: Women's Press, 1981.

Eagleton, Mary. *Figuring the Woman Author in Contemporary Fiction.* Basingstoke: Palgrave Macmillan, 2005.

Easton, Alison. "Introduction: Reading Angela Carter." *Angela Carter: Contemporary Critical Essays.* Ed. Alison Easton. Basingstoke: Macmillan, 2000. 1–19.

Gilbert, Sandra M., and Susan Gubar. *The Madwoman in the Attic: The Woman Writer and the Nineteenth-Century Literary Imagination.* Princeton, NJ: Yale University Press, 1979.

Haffenden, John. "Angela Carter." *Novelists in Interview.* London: Methuen, 1985. 76–96.

Hutcheon, Linda. *The Politics of Postmodernism.* London: Routledge, 1989.

Jordan, Elaine. "The Dangerous Edge." *Flesh and the Mirror: Essays on the Art of Angela Carter.* Ed. Lorna Sage. London: Virago, 1994. 189–215.

———. "The Dangers of Angela Carter." *New Feminist Discourses: Critical Essays on Theories and Texts.* Ed. Isobel Armstrong. London: Routledge, 1992. 119–31.

———. "Enthralment: Angela Carter's Speculative Fictions." *Plotting Change: Contemporary Women's Fiction.* Ed. Linda Anderson. London: Edward Arnold, 1990. 19–42.

Kappeler, Susanne. *The Pornography of Representation.* Cambridge: Polity, 1986.

Katsavos, Anna. "An Interview with Angela Carter." *The Review of Contemporary Fiction* 14.3 (1994): 12–17.

Kristeva, Julia. *Desire in Language: A Semiotic Approach to Literature and Art.* Trans. Thomas Gora, Alice Jardine and Leon S. Roudiez. New York: Columbia University Press, 1980.

Miller, Nancy K. *Subject to Change: Reading Feminist Writing.* New York: Columbia University Press, 1988.

Müller, Anja. *Angela Carter: Identity Constructed/Deconstructed.* Heidelberg: Universitätsverlag C. Winter, 1997.

Munford, Rebecca. "Re-presenting Charles Baudelaire/Re-presencing Jeanne Duval: Transformations of the Muse in Angela Carter's 'Black Venus'." *Forum for Modern Language Studies* 40.1 (2004): 1–13.

O'Day, Marc. "'Mutability is Having a Field Day': The Sixties Aura of Angela Carter's Bristol Trilogy." *Flesh and the Mirror: Essays on the Art of Angela Carter.* Ed. Lorna Sage. London: Virago, 1994. 24–58.

Orr, Mary. *Intertextuality: Debates and Contexts.* Cambridge: Polity, 2003.

Paulin, Tom. "In an English Market." *London Review of Books* 3–17 March 1983: 19.

Peach, Linden. *Angela Carter.* Basingstoke: Macmillan, 1998.

Russo, Mary. "Revamping Spectacle: Angela Carter's *Nights at the Circus*." *Angela Carter.* Ed. Alison Easton. Basingstoke: Macmillan, 2000. 136–60.

Sage, Lorna. *Angela Carter.* Writers and their Work. Plymouth: Northcote House, 1994.

———. "Death of the Author." *Granta 41: Biography* (1992): 233–55.

———. "The Savage Sideshow: A Profile of Angela Carter." *New Review* 4.39/40 (1977): 51–57.

———. *Women in the House of Fiction: Post-War Women Novelists.* London: Macmillan, 1992.

Still, Judith, and Michael Worton. Introduction. *Intertextuality: Theories and Practices*. Ed. Michael Worton and Judith Still. Manchester: Manchester University Press, 1990. 1–44.

Ward Jouve, Nicole. "'Mother is a Figure of Speech…'." *Flesh and the Mirror: Essays on the Art of Angela Carter*. Ed. Lorna Sage. London: Virago, 1994. 136–70.

Waugh, Patricia. *Feminine Fictions: Revisiting the Postmodern*. London: Routledge, 1989.

1
Convulsive Beauty and Compulsive Desire: The Surrealist Pattern of *Shadow Dance*

Anna Watz Fruchart

> It is this world, there is no other but a world trans-
> formed by imagination and desire. You could say it is
> the dream made flesh.
>
> > (Angela Carter, "The Alchemy of the Word")

Angela Carter's first novel, *Shadow Dance*, was published in 1966, the same year that André Breton, the founder and theoretician of the surrealist movement, died. The movement largely came to an end with his death, but its thought nonetheless informed and inspired the founding of the new avant-gardes of the period, such as the *nouveau roman*, Situationism and *Tel Quel*.[1] Susan Rubin Suleiman points out that

> [t]he idea of *rupture*, a radical break with the past, dominated both the aesthetic and the philosophical and political program of the *Tel Quel* group, for example, which for a few years (roughly, 1967 to 1977) came closest to espousing the doubly revolutionary project of the historical avant-gardes, notably of Surrealism: to transform both language (writing, reading, *text*) and the world, to transform the latter by transforming the former. (*Subversive Intent* 33–34; emphasis in original)

The idea of a break with the past runs through Carter's début novel too, as, in line with the avant-gardes of the time and the surrealists before them, it wages war against the static conventional values and accepted truths of Western patriarchy. In *Shadow Dance*, as in the work of the surrealists, the rigid structures of old are made to crumble and fluidity and mutability rule in the wreckage.

Shadow Dance is still one of Carter's least known novels. Partly a consequence of being out of print for a long time (until its reissue in 1994), its obscurity might also be due to the fact that it is one of her most shocking and violent books, in which the female characters become passive objects of male (often misogynistic) desires: while steadfastly being denied agency or voice, they become disfigured, violated or infused with meanings beyond their own control. Critics have tended to read *Shadow Dance* primarily as a work of realism, stressing its firm rootedness in 1960s counterculture.[2] As an alternative way of entering the novel, I propose here a reading which focuses on its intervention in the territory of surrealism.[3] I will argue that the novel presents a specifically surrealist version of woman, and engages in a dialogue with surrealist ideas of transgression and subversion of accepted values. In a characteristically Carteresque manner, however, *Shadow Dance* opts neither for an uncritical endorsement nor a flat rejection of surrealist ideology and aesthetics. I will suggest that the position the novel adopts vis-à-vis surrealism can best be described in terms of a 'double allegiance', a concept I borrow from Suleiman, and which she describes as 'on the one hand, an allegiance to the formal experiments and some of the cultural aspirations of the historical male avant-gardes; on the other hand, an allegiance to the feminist critique of dominant sexual ideologies, including the sexual ideology of those same avant-gardes' (*Subversive Intent* xvii).

The image of 'woman' played a crucial part in the surrealist aspiration of reshaping the world in the name of desire: to this end, the female body was played with, fragmentized and transgressed. In Gwen Raaberg's words, woman in surrealism was conceived of as 'man's mediator with nature and the unconscious, *femme-enfant*, muse, source and object of man's desire, embodiment of *amour fou*, and emblem of revolution' (2). The woman evoked in surrealist poetry tends to be idealized and elevated as 'embodiment of magic powers, creature of grace and promise, always close in her sensibility and behaviour to the two sacred worlds of childhood and madness' (Shattuck 25). The image of woman in the visual arts, on the other hand, is more marked by misogynistic attacks of sadism and mutilation as the female body is disarticulated or forced through disfiguring transformations.[4] Whether elevated or violated, however, 'woman' in surrealism remains a projection of the masculine heterosexual imagination, never granted a voice of her own. Despite appearing malleable and mutable, she is not so of her own accord as she has no agency to redefine her own image.[5] The surrealist version of woman, and particularly her representation in visual art, is conjured up in *Shadow Dance* in the characterization of Ghislaine.

Mutability and mutilation

The narrative point of view of *Shadow Dance* is provided by its principal character, junk-shop owner and amateur painter Morris. The novel opens as he meets Ghislaine, fresh out of hospital, in the local bar. Once a beautiful girl, Ghislaine is now cruelly disfigured after having been knifed by Morris's dandyish friend and business partner Honeybuzzard:

> The scar went all the way down her face, from the corner of her left eyebrow, down, down, down, past nose and mouth and chin until it disappeared below the collar of her shirt. The scar was all red and raw as if, at the slightest exertion, it might open and bleed; and the flesh was marked with purple imprints from the stitches she had had in it. (2)

Although it was Honeybuzzard who scarred Ghislaine, Morris is guiltily aware of his complicity in the crime, as, after a disastrous one-night stand with her, he gave her to Honeybuzzard to 'teach her a lesson' (34). The image of the scarred Ghislaine, inflected through Morris's tormented perception, is an ambiguous blend of sexiness, innocence, mutilation and provocation. She is a doll-like child-woman, 'like a young girl in a picture book, a soft and dewy young girl. [...] She had such a little face, all pale; and soft, baby cheeks and a half-open mouth as if she was expecting somebody, anybody, everybody she met to pop a sweetie into it' (2). Still, despite her apparent innocence, Ghislaine is highly sexually charged, 'a burning child, a fiery bud', gathering 'them up in armfuls, her lovers, every night, in the manner of a careless baby playing in a meadow, pulling both flowers and grass and nettles and piss-the-beds in a spilling, promiscuous bundle' (3), and she gives off a scent of 'contraceptives and her own sexual sweat' (5). With her once-perfect beauty shattered by Honeybuzzard's knife she is rendered all the more ambiguous, as the boundaries between innocence, eroticism and the grotesque uncannily dissolve. Her face is contradiction epitomized:

> The whole cheek was a mass of corrugated white flesh, like a bowl of blancmange a child has played with and not eaten. Through this devastation ran a deep central trough that went right down her throat under the collar of her coat. [...] But the other half of the face was fresh and young and smooth and warm as fruit in the sunlight. The two sides of the moon juxtaposed. (152–53)

Thus, juxtaposing contradictory characteristics, Ghislaine is suggestive of many of surrealism's portraits of mutilated women.

In this essay, I would like to examine Ghislaine's affiliation with the 'woman' of surrealist representation by considering her framed in relation to the sequence of child-woman dolls created and photographed by the German surrealist artist Hans Bellmer. Bellmer began constructing his first doll in 1933, inspired by Jacques Offenbach's opera *Tales of Hoffmann* (first performed in 1881), which contained an adapted version of E.T.A. Hoffmann's "The Sandman" (1816).[6] Made of a framework of wood and metal and covered by papier-mâché and plaster pieces, the doll could be assembled and reassembled like a machine. This doll was the subject of more than 30 photographs, of which ten appeared in Bellmer's 1934 book *Die Puppe*, with a short introduction by the artist entitled "Memories of the Doll Theme". Eighteen images were later reproduced in the surrealist journal *Minotaure* under the title "Poupée: Variations sur le montage d'une mineure articulée" (1934). In 1935, Bellmer constructed a second doll out of glue and paper (painted to resemble flesh) around a central ball joint. These hundred-something photographs exhibit an even more unstable body whose parts are often duplicated or substituted.[7]

As avatars of surrealism, Bellmer's automata share a number of characteristics with Ghislaine. Although not an inanimate construction like the dolls, Ghislaine nevertheless reveals the eerie attributes of an artificial being: 'She used to speak with the electronic, irresistible singsong of a ravishing automaton' and with her stitch-marks still showing summons up 'the bride of Frankenstein' (4). The dolls, patched up like Ghislaine, confuse and conflate categories such as sexiness and innocence, childhood and adulthood, beauty and its destruction, eroticism, mutilation and death in a manner characteristic of surrealism. The pubescent dolls are splayed and twisted into poses which project an image of woman as simultaneously passive victim and powerful seductress, in likeness with Lorna Sage's description of Ghislaine as 'the victim as predator' (10). One photograph from "Poupée: Variations sur le montage d'une mineure articulée", for instance, shows the doll partially dismembered and equipped with a long dark wig, dressed in a skimpy slip raised to expose her buttocks. In a half-turned pose she casts a coy yet martyrized glance at the observer. The surface of her face, like that of the rest of her body, is cracked and crumbling. The top of her left leg is showing in the photograph as a part wooden and part metal stick, reminding us of her inanimate and mechanized condition. As in the rest of the photographs, the doll, although arranged in an erotically suggestive manner, bears traces of violation, even death. In a number of images, the doll appears on a bed, disarticulated like a broken, yet eroticized, corpse.

The founding father of transgressive writing, the Marquis de Sade, was celebrated by the surrealists as one of their intellectual heroes, and Bellmer's manipulation of his dolls characteristically bespeaks an obsession with sadistic mastery and control.[8] His desire to dominate his dolls extends even beyond the contortion of their limbs: in "Memories of the Doll Theme" he speaks openly about his wish to control even their thoughts and desires. The first doll, he writes, was partially intended to 'lay bare suppressed girlish thoughts, so that the ground on which they stand is revealed, ideally through the navel, visible as a colorful panorama electrically illuminated deep in the stomach' (174). Honeybuzzard in *Shadow Dance* is spurred by a similar fantasy of power, which becomes especially evident in his relish for making jumping-jack caricatures of the other characters in the novel: he likes pulling people's strings in both a figurative and literal sense. He also dreams up a chess game with real men and women in which he controls everyone's moves: 'I would stand on a chair and call out my moves from a megaphone and they would click their heels and march forward' (117). Honeybuzzard's sadistic impulses are also, of course, translated into the erotic games he plays with Ghislaine.

Like the dolls, Ghislaine becomes manipulated in a sexually ambiguous and deathly manner. Inherently perverse, Honeybuzzard's love affair with her features innocent erotic play as well as mutilation and, eventually, murder. Seemingly harmless, the initial games include posing together in erotic photographs, in which the erect Honeybuzzard is masquerading with 'a wide variety of false noses, false ears, plastic vampire teeth etc.' (16). However, Honeybuzzard's erotic play can switch from innocuous games to sadistic aggression in an instant, and the pleasure invested in the making of the photographs is readily translated into his destruction of Ghislaine's beauty. His mutilation of her is an essentially erotic violation, as he creates with his phallic knife what Sarah Gamble has identified as a 'grotesque image of the female genitalia' in her face (55). With his act of transgression he participates in a surrealist aesthetic which, as Suleiman points out in her article on *The Infernal Desire Machines of Doctor Hoffman* (1972), delights in voyeuristically 'representing female orifices and body parts, and scenes of extreme sexual violence perpetrated on the bodies of women' ("The Fate of the Surrealist Imagination" 114).[9] Honeybuzzard's violent treatment of Ghislaine reaches its climax after she, in a final élan of masochism, has given herself to him to do with her as he likes. Honeybuzzard, drunk on his desire to master Ghislaine, takes her to one of the derelict Victorian houses he and Morris have earlier rummaged through for objects to sell in their junk-shop, and murders her.

Honeybuzzard's viciously playful and performative lifestyle echoes the outrageous behaviour of Jacques Vaché, one of the great sources of inspiration for Breton. The dandyish Vaché was 'the flamboyant pro-tagonist of a devastating form of wit which he designated *umor*' with a sense of the 'theatrical and joyless uselessness of everything' (Rosemont 10).[10] At the première of Guillaume Apollinaire's *Les Mamelles de Tirésias* (1917), in which the term 'surrealism' was first coined, Breton observed him coming into the theatre with a revolver in his hand, threatening to fire straight into the audience. Carter, in "The Alchemy of the Word" (1978), writes that Vaché 'exercised a far greater influence over surreal-ism than his exiguous life would suggest; ten years later, Breton would write in the *Second Manifesto of Surrealism*: "the simplest surrealist act consists of going out into the street revolver in hand and firing at ran-dom into the crowd as often as possible"' (510). Vaché's actions illus-trate the surrealist aspiration to transform the category of art into an intrinsic aspect of everyday life.

Like Vaché, Honeybuzzard lives his life like a work of art and, in many respects, he reads as a representation of a surrealist artist. He embodies to an extreme degree the surrealist project to make the Pleasure Principle triumph over the Reality Principle, and, like many of the libertines in Carter's subsequent books, acts according to his capricious desires.[11] Constantly in the process of ridiculing his friends and acquaintances, pulling rubber fried eggs, blackface soap, plastic snot and exploding cig-arettes out of his never-ending joke-bag, Honeybuzzard, as Sage observes, 'plays tirelessly and cruelly, like a big cat; anything and anyone is fair game' (11). He is a junk collector and bricoleur who, Alison Lee notes, has furnished his bedroom in the manner of a surrealist collage where anything and everything is crammed in and juxtaposed (26) – 'a crystallization of the personality Honeybuzzard presented to the world' (98).[12] Like the surrealists, 'breaking with the notion of unitary self that dominated post-Enlightenment thinking' (Chadwick 14), Honeybuzzard makes the dissolution of a unified self into a camp game as he role-plays: 'I like – you know – to slip in and out of me. I would like to be somebody different each morning. Me and not-me. I would like to have a cupboard bulging with all different bodies and faces and choose a fresh one every morning' (78).[13] He transforms art into life and life into art, and in the process he 'profan[es] all that is (supposed to be) holy' (Sage 13). Both he and the surrealists place eroticism at the heart of their project of cultural subversion, an eroticism which in Honeybuzzard's case is both playful and, eventually, murderous.

In his *Second Manifesto of Surrealism* (1930), Breton proposed that the primary motivating force of surrealism was to find and fix the point in the human mind 'at which life and death, the real and the imagined, past and future, the communicable and the incommunicable, high and low, cease to be perceived as contradictions' (123). The breakdown of boundaries is thus central to surrealist philosophy and the site the surrealists chose again and again for playing out their aesthetics of transgression was the female body, which they fragmentized into bits and pieces. Bellmer's dolls are a primary example since, as Hal Foster argues, the point where contraries meet 'is very charged in the *poupées*, for these tableaux force together apparently polar opposites – figures that evoke both an erotogenic body and a dismembered one, scenes that suggest both innocent games and sadomasochistic aggressions, and so on' (102). Similarly, the juxtaposition of contradictions in the characterization of Ghislaine produces an instability of meaning and points to a collapse of distinct categories: beauty, destruction, desire and horror dissolve into one another.[14]

Surreal perceptions

As Therese Lichtenstein argues, the distortion and contradictoriness of the bodies of Bellmer's dolls call forth a complicated anxiety, produced by 'a dramatic ambivalence between desire for and revulsion at the female body' (13). This ambivalence also permeates Morris's anxiety towards Ghislaine, for his fear of her is tinged with both desire and revulsion. Thus, the surrealist atmosphere of the novel, achieved through Honeybuzzard's 'creation' of the mutilated Ghislaine, is reinforced by the way in which Morris perceives her. The effect on him when faced with her 'exploded beauty' (154) and the dissipation of clear-cut boundaries which she represents is in fact the effect of *convulsive beauty*, a phrase which Breton coined in *Nadja* (1928) and further developed in *L'Amour fou* (1937). Often obscene, violent and pornographic, convulsive beauty 'located the disruptive force of Eros in the body of Woman' (Chadwick 14) and was a tool in the surrealist repertoire of assaults on normative culture. Convulsive beauty is closely related to two other key concepts of surrealism – *the marvellous*, and *objective chance* – and it is cryptically defined by Breton as 'veiled-erotic, fixed-explosive, magical-circumstantial' (*L'Amour fou* 19; qtd. in Foster 23).

Following this definition, Breton offers a sequence of images which stress contradiction and formlessness and provoke shock, mixing delight and dread (Foster 28). The experience of convulsive beauty is, in Carter's words, 'an abandonment to vertigo'; 'you *feel* it, you don't see it' ("The Alchemy of the Word" 512; emphasis in original). Louis Aragon described the bewildering and unexpected experience of the marvellous, and thus implicitly of convulsive beauty, as '[t]hose moments when everything slips away from me, when immense cracks appear in the palace of the world' (qtd. in Cardinal and Short 54).[15] Ultimately, the disturbing upheavals in psychological coherence of convulsive beauty bring the subject close to the point in the mind where Breton saw contradictions conflate. According to Rosalind Krauss, '[t]he experience of "convulsive beauty" shakes the subject's self-possession, bringing exultation through a kind of shock' (85), as it collapses the distinction between imagination and reality. The limits of the self start sliding and the subject is jolted out of its customary ways of thinking; a shaking up of the world which is both liberating and frightening. Like a surrealist work of art, the convulsive beauty of Ghislaine disturbs Morris's sense of identity as the real dissolves into the imaginary.

Honeybuzzard's erotic transgression reaches its climax as he murders Ghislaine, drunk on his desire to master her. The crime scene is an exhibition of eroticism and death bound up together in a mode crucial to surrealism. Ritualistically, Ghislaine has been arranged on an altar-like table in the abandoned church-house:

> Naked, Ghislaine lay on her back with her hands crossed on her breasts, so that her nipples poked between her fingers like the muzzles of inquisitive white mice. Her eyes were shut down with pennies, two on each eyelid, and her mouth gaped open a little. There were deep black fingermarks in her throat. (177)

Georges Bataille, a sometime surrealist who referred to himself as the movement's 'old enemy from within' (qtd. in Lichtenstein 43), opines that the transgressive experience of eroticism is by implication disorderly, excessive and wasteful, even murderous. The transgressive subject oversteps the borders of rational behaviour, which is structured by work and profit. 'Pleasure is so close to ruinous waste that we refer to the moment of climax as "little death". Consequently anything that suggests erotic excess always implies disorder. [...] Brutality and murder are further steps in the same direction' (Bataille 170). For Bataille, transgression is inseparable from the awareness of the taboo it violates; in fact, the transgression of a prohibition completes and reinforces it, and, as Suleiman argues, '[t]he characteristic feeling accompanying transgression is one of intense pleasure (at the exceeding of boundaries) *and* of intense anguish (at the full realization of the force of those boundaries)' (*Subversive Intent* 75; emphasis in original). This paradoxical combination of feelings is, according to Bataille, epitomized in eroticism, which, like any transgressive experience, makes the limits of the self unstable.

Although it is Honeybuzzard who mutilates and finally kills Ghislaine, it is Morris who most fully embodies the contradictory mix of anguish and pleasure infused in transgression. Cast as simultaneously double and other to Honeybuzzard, Morris is also motivated by a sado-erotic drive to mutilate and destroy Ghislaine, but he only unleashes his desires momentarily in symbolic repetitions of Honeybuzzard's transgressions in dreams, fantasies and paintings. Their desires are often in a complex entanglement, bound up in an erotic triangle with Ghislaine, and Morris himself, at the end of the novel, interprets his drive to hurt Ghislaine as fuelling Honeybuzzard's cruelties: 'But I wanted it. I am to blame, too' (178).[16] So, while it is Honeybuzzard who performs his acts of erotic transgression on the body of Ghislaine, Morris is driven by the same motivation, and although he guiltily attempts to suppress his desires, they nevertheless re-emerge in the scenes he dreams up about Ghislaine or his wife Edna, where he recreates Honeybuzzard's erotic violence.

Morris's initial desire to mutilate Ghislaine seems to emanate from the 'burning recollection' (17) of 'the disaster of their one time' (34): 'she so beautiful but never to be enjoyed, was that her fault? At the time, it had seemed so. And therefore Honey, who was as heartless as she, should have her, to show her what heartlessness meant' (34). In this way, Morris's cruelty becomes a measure of the rage he feels at being unable to possess her completely. His moral complicity in Ghislaine's mutilation translates into a haunting and all-pervasive feeling of guilt, which only exacerbates his rage. Likewise, Morris's contempt for his wife Edna is also fuelled by pangs of conscience: knowing that he can never provide Edna with what he thinks she wants (conventional marital stability, security and children), he feels at fault for disappointing her. Furthermore, although he desires other women he is too guilt-conscious to cheat on her. His desire for and rage towards both Ghislaine and Edna are thus inextricably entangled with his perceived sense of guilt, which simultaneously takes part in forming his compulsion to transgress the limits of morality *and* constrains him from doing so. In an act of symbolic violence, however, Morris repeats Honeybuzzard's mutilation of Ghislaine. With Edna sleeping in the next room, he, guiltily, as if in a 'fever' (15), gets out some erotic photographs he and Honeybuzzard took of Ghislaine before she was scarred. At the sight of the images he remembers how Ghislaine tirelessly 'contorted herself, spread herself wide, arrayed herself in a bizarre variety of accessories' (17), scenes which conjure up the arrangement and rearrangement of the doll in Bellmer's photographs. Intending to blot out Ghislaine's face with ink to eliminate the shameful memories of his affair with her ('decency dictated that she should be destroyed' [17]), he is instead overwhelmed by a desire to scar her and proceeds to stripe 'each image of her with a long scar from eyebrow to navel', not stopping 'until he had finished marking them all in' (17). After his symbolic mutilation of Ghislaine, he is overcome by anxiety and guilty revulsion at himself, in a manner characteristic of the experience of transgression.

Morris's anguished obsession with Ghislaine's scar colours the atmosphere of the entire novel. In his fear of losing psychological unity, Ghislaine's scar comes to represent a monstrous vagina, which threatens to 'absorb him, threshing, into the chasm in her face' (39). In Morris's imagination, Ghislaine has transformed into a 'vampire woman, walking the streets on the continual qui vive' (39), evocative of the praying mantis, whose female devours the male after copulation, which so fascinated the surrealists. The surrealist comparison of woman to a mantis, as Xavière Gauthier has argued, draws on the myth of the *vagina dentata*, as the mouth of the mantis/woman comes to stand for the vagina and the eaten male to symbolize the castrated penis (170–71). As with the mantis, Ghislaine's scar/vagina poses the threat of both a loss of self and of castration for Morris. Simultaneously, the scar/vagina signifies the bleeding wound left by woman's putative castration, which again reminds Morris of the threat of his own castration. Ghislaine's castrative state elicits in him both fear and a desire to punish her for her condition. Her scar/vagina is exposed in a manner reminiscent of the obsessively investigated sex of Bellmer's dolls, as they also, as Foster points out, seem to embody a sadistic punishment against the image of woman as emblem of castration (106).[17] The image of the castrated woman, posing a threat to the patriarchal subject, thus draws forth a desire to violate, dominate and disarm her in order to securely lock her in her position of passive victim.

In this way, the myth of the castrated woman fuels Morris's sadistic feelings towards Ghislaine. As Carter writes in *The Sadeian Woman* (1979),

[t]he whippings, the beatings, the gougings, the stabbings of erotic violence reawaken the memory of the social fiction of the female wound, the bleeding scar left by her castration [...] Female castration is an imaginary fact that pervades the whole of men's attitude towards women and our attitude to ourselves, that transforms women from human beings into wounded creatures who were born to bleed. (23)

Shadow Dance, like many of Carter's subsequent books, exposes the fiction of the wounded and suffering woman. According to Sage, this was a spectacle Carter both 'feared and loathed and found hilarious', and her cruel treatment of this image 'is a measure of her fear' (32–33). Although Ghislaine at first might seem to be sexually liberated, she shares with Edna a self-imposed submissiveness, which makes passive martyr-victims out of them both. The two women, who in many ways appear to be one another's opposite, represent aspects of the stereotypically feminine – woman as either dangerously and insatiably sexual or motherly and asexual – and they both embody a myth of feminine passivity that has disastrous consequences in the realm of sexual politics.

Woman in surrealism is similarly confined by the shackles of her passivity. Whether idealized and elevated, or a victim of violation and manipulation in tableaux of erotic display, the surrealist representation of woman nevertheless remains a category devoid of subjecthood. Carter too finds this problem at the heart of surrealism:

The surrealists were not good with women. That is why, although I thought they were wonderful, I had to give them up in the end. They were, with a few patronised exceptions, all men and they told me that I was the source of all mystery, beauty, and otherness, because I was a woman – and I knew that was not true. I knew I wanted my fair share of the imagination, too. Not an excessive amount, mind; I wasn't greedy. Just an equal share in the right to vision.

When I realised that surrealist art did not recognise I had my own rights to liberty and love and vision as an autonomous being, not as a projected image, I got bored with it and wandered away. ("The Alchemy of the Word" 512)

Ghislaine, like so many surrealist images of woman before her, lacks the agency to break away from Honeybuzzard's puppeteering games. As Gamble points out, because they are excluded from the formation of discourse, the women in *Shadow Dance* 'are rendered figments of a fevered male imagination, and [...] become silent receptacles for male desires' (54).[18] Ghislaine is the novel's *femme-enfant*, doll, devouring mantis and erotic object, locked into the surrealist imagination as a projected image, and never allowed the agency to become a subject.

Although the mature Carter's feminist politics are only nascent in *Shadow Dance* (she claimed herself that at the beginning of her career she 'didn't see the point of feminism' [Clapp 26; qtd. in Gamble 54]), the text, while endorsing surrealism's antipatriarchal and antitraditional claims, nevertheless exposes the version of woman dreamed up by the surrealist imagination as nothing more than a projected image. As I have suggested, *Shadow Dance*'s dialogue with surrealism is characterized by what Suleiman has called a 'double allegiance', an ambivalent position which incorporates both endorsement and critique. On the one hand, the text celebrates 'the parodic perversions of Surrealism [which] were meant to be understood as (among other things) a strategy for radical political and cultural change' (*Subversive Intent* 148). The surrealist manner of juxtaposing contradictions effects a disturbance and questioning of reality as we perceive it and, in Carter's own words, 'extend[s] our notion of the connections it is possible to make'. 'In this way', she adds, 'the beautiful is put at the service of liberty' ("The Alchemy of the Word" 512). On the other hand, *Shadow Dance* holds up a mirror to surrealism's sexist and passifying images of woman, which, like the dolls, often appear (at least to a contemporary audience) misogynistic in their end result. The feminist critique infused in this depiction is achieved through a type of *mimicry*, as the text self-consciously repeats or exposes the male surrealist version of woman.[19] As Luce Irigaray argues, '[o]ne must assume the feminine role deliberately. Which means already to convert a form of subordination into an affirmation, and thus begin to thwart it' (76). In drawing Ghislaine as a stereotype of the surrealist woman, and by extension as a projection of male desires, the text, 'by an effect of playful repetition' (ibid. 76), discloses the misogyny of the surrealist discourse and its failure to imagine and allow feminine subjecthood into its revolutionary project. More than that, *Shadow Dance* offers an image of Ghislaine that exaggerates her dollishness even beyond that of Bellmer's dolls, as she deliberately assumes her submissive role and renounces her own agency. Having been mutilated and discarded by Honeybuzzard, she comes back for more, exclaiming: 'I've learned my lesson, I can't live without you, you are my master, do what you like with me' (166). Despite all its horror, Ghislaine's exaggerated masochism and subordination appear almost parodic, and Honeybuzzard's reaction to her offering of herself makes him laugh, a gesture which contains both relish (at the thought of his forthcoming transgressions) and sheer amusement (at her ridiculousness). Thus, by exposing, and sometimes overdoing, stereotypical images of the feminine within surrealist discourse, the text seeks to undermine them.[20]

It is impossible, however, to ascertain where Carter's promotion of surrealism ends and her mocking mimicry of its logic begins. Although surrealism presents a version of woman that she cannot accept, the fundamental aim of its philosophy is nevertheless to question and transform the structures that make up reality, and with it the fixed gender roles of Carter's reality as a woman. Moreover, the surrealist discourse itself participates in an aesthetic of exaggeration and excess in which Ghislaine's extreme masochism could be read as provocation.[21] In addition to this, *Shadow Dance* could be flirting with the 1960s avant-garde literary mode, which, influenced by Bataille, metaphorically equates 'the violation of *sexual* taboos and the violation of *discursive* norms' (Suleiman, *Subversive Intent* 74; emphasis in original). Thus, the references to and evocations of surrealist aesthetics do not point to a unified stance towards surrealism and cannot be reduced to single meanings, not even in obvious instances of surrealist misogyny or violence towards women.[22] In its ambivalent dialogue with surrealism, *Shadow Dance* oscillates between positions, making signification slippery and any unequivocal interpretation of its standpoint impossible.

In likeness with the surrealist version of woman, neither Ghislaine nor Edna, as I have argued, have a voice or agency to escape the passivity the text forces upon them. Instead, the actions they are assigned invite this passivity, as they both participate in reducing themselves to joints of meat ready for consumption. This is also how they are perceived by Morris in his dreams and fantasies, where he compulsively re-enacts Honeybuzzard's cruelties in a manner which results in a confusion between the female body and meat. The meat imagery is first introduced as Morris thinks of Edna as 'a poor flat fillet on the marble slab of her bed' (13), and he later dreams of slicing her open on the very same bed. However, the dream begins with Morris cutting up the face of Ghislaine:

> He dreamed he was cutting her face with a jagged shard of broken glass [...] And then he and Ghislaine were in his own bed and her head rolled on the pillows and all the yellow hair went brown, as if it was blighted, and then it was Edna he saw that he was slicing open and there was blood everywhere, on her and on his hands and in his eyes and mouth. (18)

In this dream, as in other instances, predatory Ghislaine and martyr-like Edna become amalgamated, as Morris's desire to violate Ghislaine becomes projected onto his wife. The confusion between the female body and meat, of course, anticipates Carter's discussion of the workings of power in sexuality in *The Sadeian Woman*, as it signifies woman in her ultimate state of passivity (see 138).

The theme of Morris's first nightmare finds its way back into another one of his recurring dreams in which he cuts Ghislaine's face with a blunt kitchen knife: 'Her head came off in his hands, after a while, and he cut her into a turnip lantern, put a candle inside and lit it through her freshly carved mouth' (39). His fear of her dominates his daily activities too: the memory of Ghislaine follows Morris everywhere he goes, 'clutching him with her white legs and her long, slender arms' (37). Her ambiguity and convulsive beauty make her uncontrollable and uncontainable, as she threatens to disrupt Morris's subjectivity. He himself claims that

> [h]e could best accommodate the thought of Ghislaine as the subject for a painting, a Francis Bacon horror painting of flesh as a disgusting symbol of the human condition; that way, she became somehow small enough for him to handle [...] Yet he could only think in this way, never execute; never paint the painting which would justify treating her as a thing and not a human being. (19–20)

Towards the end of the novel, however, Morris does execute a painting of this kind – 'a decaying female form, dead' which he 'disliked [...] intensely' – but he identifies the 'woman-shaped lump' (122) as being Edna and not Ghislaine, showing once again that the two women are to some extent interchangeable in his imagination. Reminiscent of a dismembered corpse, the surrealist motif of Morris's painting, and also the mutilated female bodies of his dreams, point to his desire to master and contain woman by 'meatifying' her and thereby reducing her to a passive object. However, as Gamble has pointed out, her passive and subordinate state paradoxically renders woman all the more dangerous (54), and incites in Morris a desire to violate her further.

The association between woman and inert lumps of meat in Morris's imagination strengthens the affinity between the image of woman in *Shadow Dance* and her representation within surrealist discourse. As I have argued, Bellmer's corpse-like and disarticulated dolls are a case in point, but also relevant in this context is the series of photographs Bellmer took in 1958, which show a naked female body which has been bound with string to force cruel confinement onto her. One of the images seems to provide a visual analogue for the association between

the female body and meat in *Shadow Dance*. The photograph exposes
the female body resting on a bed, reinforcing the sexual undertones
already present in the image. It has been bound and manipulated to
show only her back and buttocks, and resembles, not a woman, but a
joint of meat. As Alyce Mahon observes, the female in the photograph
is 'fresh, bound and ready for consumption' (264). Like Edna 'on the
marble slab of her bed', she is perceived as totally inert and lifeless.
Bellmer's image was published in the spring edition of *Le Surréalisme,
même* in 1958 with the disturbing title "Tenir au frais" ("Keep in a Cool
Place"), overtly playing with the double meaning of the German word
Fleisch as referring to both flesh and meat.

Reducing woman to an object, unable to make words, is Morris's strategy to master his feelings of guilt, contempt and fear. Woman is dangerous
and must be dominated, and even in her guise as passive object she must
be annihilated. Morris's destructive urges, like those of Honeybuzzard, are
essential to the surrealist aesthetic, for, as Foster argues, 'it is fundamental
to surrealism, perhaps evident in its very mandate, in painting, collage,
and assemblages alike, to destroy the object as such' (13). Consequently,
Morris is not free from the uncanny spell cast by Ghislaine until he sees
her dead body; only then can he perceive how harmless she in fact is:

> With pity and tenderness, for the first time unmixed with any other
> feeling, Morris saw how her fingernails were bitten down to the
> quick and how shadows smoothed out the cratered surface of her
> cheek and how the chopped tufts of golden hair had grown no far-
> ther than an inch or so below her ears and how there was soft,
> blonde down on the motionless flesh of her stomach. (177)

At this point he finally faces up to the desires he has tried to suppress
throughout the narrative, but which have nonetheless returned in his
dreams and art. In murdering Ghislaine, Honeybuzzard has merely
done 'what Morris had always wanted but never defined': 'choking out
of Ghislaine her little-girl giggle [...] filling up her voracity once and for
all by cramming with death the hungry mouth between her thighs,
keeping her little bitten hands for ever from picking and stealing.
Putting her to sleep' (177–78).

Perversion and surrealist play

It is quite obvious that Honeybuzzard would have murdered Ghislaine
even without Morris's misogynistic intentions. After the murder, the
delirious Honeybuzzard continues to play with the dead girl, as he

proceeds to include a plaster Christ in his ultimate piece of blasphemous performance art. Ghislaine has been revealed to be the daughter
of a clergyman, which makes Honeybuzzard's cruel debasement of her
throughout the novel all the more an act of profanation. Upon finding the plaster Christ in an earlier scene in the same house, he muses:
'chaining her to that symbol of her father over there and raping her –
now, that would really be something' (132). Aidan Day has read
Honeybuzzard's incorporation of the crucifix in Ghislaine's murder as
a statement of his allegiance to the 'attitudes of religious patriarchy'
(16). Although there is no doubt about the misogyny inherent in
Honeybuzzard's victimization of the female, there is, however, more at
work in this image. I would venture that his inclusion of the symbol
of Christianity signifies, at least on one level, the very opposite of the
conclusion reached by Day. Honeybuzzard's murder of Ghislaine is
doubtlessly a horrific crime, but the killing of the clergyman's daughter and the desecration of the crucifix simultaneously become the final
revolt against the Western patriarchal tradition the surrealists so fer-
vently attacked in their art and writing. In this way, Honeybuzzard's
subversive violence comes to symbolize the perverse aspects of surrealism. Perversion, as Janine Chasseguet-Smirgel has argued, 'is one of
the essential ways and means [man] applies in order to push forward
the frontiers of what is possible and to unsettle reality' (293; qtd. in
Suleiman, *Subversive Intent* 148).[23] As Suleiman observes, this 'is a pretty good definition of Surrealist aesthetics [...] as well as of Surrealist
philosophy and cultural politics' (ibid. 148). The law (of the father)
aims to maintain distinctions and categorizations. The pervert, as he
attempts to 'free himself from the paternal universe and the law',
favours mixture and the hybrid: 'The man who does not respect the
law of differentiation challenges God. He creates new combinations of
new shapes and new kinds [...] Notice that the word *hybrid* comes
from *hybris*, which means violence, excess, extremeness, outrageous-
ness' (Chasseguet-Smirgel 298; qtd. in Suleiman, *Subversive Intent* 149).
Perversion, thus, becomes an aesthetic trope employed in surrealism
to challenge the law of the father as it promotes ideas of radical inno-
vation and play. Honeybuzzard's sadistic games, then, become liberating when his perversion is read as a symbol of his rebellion against
norm and convention.

In parallel to this, however, Honeybuzzard, in murdering Ghislaine,
has finally completely transgressed the boundaries of sanity, and in his
madness 'fallen through a hole in time into a dimension of pure horror'
(178) where reality and meaning have collapsed. The seductive aspects

of transgression and playing with versions of the self are thus, as Gamble aptly points out, accompanied in the text by an awareness of 'the risk of the obliteration of an independent subjectivity altogether' (48). The text seems to argue for a continuous re-evaluation of the 'real', but without losing a firm footing in the material world in the process. The surrealists were grappling with a similar problem; as Sadie Plant argues:

> [t]he paradoxical 'rational disordering of the senses' with which they were working meant that they wanted to voyage into the unknown while at the same time returning to tell the tale, expressing their adventures in the terms of existing structures of language and meaning. This desire to straddle madness and sanity, chaos and poetry, formed a central tension of surrealist activity. (51)

This tension is very pronounced in *Shadow Dance*. Although questioning and deconstructing the structures and categories that make up 'reality' is crucial to bring about the change which Carter and the surrealists strive for, a complete shift into a dimension where all meaning is lost results not in liberation but in utter narcissism and madness. Like Honeybuzzard, Morris too, at the end of the novel, abandons the 'real' and vanishes into a 'dimension outside both time and space' where he does not have to acknowledge the real world's 'authority over him' (181) and where Honeybuzzard's murder of Ghislaine can be seen as the climax of his transgressive creativity. However, in the 'real world' of the novel, it must not be forgotten, Ghislaine is really dead and Honeybuzzard's crime a gruesome act of sadistic misogyny.

The surrealist pattern of *Shadow Dance* is woven of four different threads: the characterization of Ghislaine, Honeybuzzard's transgressive play, Morris's transgressive dreams and imagination, and his surrealist perception of reality. As I have argued, the engagement with the surrealist logic of transgression in the text contains a simultaneous celebration and critique of this logic. The novel adopts, adapts, responds to and rejects the iconography and mythology elaborated by the male surrealists, enacting a dialogue I have referred to as a double allegiance on Carter's part. Through exposing the surrealist image of woman as nothing more than a projection of the male imagination, the text seeks to disclose the power structures hidden in the surrealist discourse. However, although the text contains elements of critique of surrealism's misogyny and implication in patriarchy, Honeybuzzard's playfulness is nonetheless also a homage to the 'energy, the inventiveness, the explosive humor and sheer proliferating brilliance of much male avant-garde "play"' (Suleiman, *Subversive Intent* 162). Sometimes in line with surrealist goals of unshackling reality and creating a new liberated world – which would contain a new liberated version of woman – and sometimes criticizing the surrealist inability to imagine subjecthood for such a liberated woman, Carter's dialogue with surrealism nevertheless shows her conviction that our perception of the world and its constraining 'truths' can be changed. Like the surrealists, she knows that 'struggle *can* bring something better' ("Alchemy of the Word" 507; emphasis in original).

Notes

1. Specifically, the writings of fringe surrealist Georges Bataille have had a major influence on the theories of cultural subversion articulated by the *Tel Quel* group, and many highly influential postmodernist theorists and philosophers – Roland Barthes, Jacques Derrida, Philippe Sollers and Michel Foucault, to name a few – published articles about Bataille around the time that *Shadow Dance* was written and published.

2. See, for example, Marc O'Day's argument that *Shadow Dance*, *Several Perceptions* (1968) and *Love* (1971) stand out in Carter's oeuvre, and 'invite readings in terms of quite traditional realism' (24).

3. Jane Hentges has similarly identified a surrealist theme in *Shadow Dance*. However, the focus of her analysis and the conclusions she reaches about Carter's engagement with surrealism are different from mine. Alison Lee also briefly touches upon the connection between *Shadow Dance* and surrealism (see 26, 27 and 29).

4. This distinction between the woman of surrealist poetry and that of visual art was originally identified by Xavière Gauthier in her pioneering feminist critique of surrealism, *Surréalisme et sexualité* (1971). She states: 'Dans la poésie surréaliste, la femme est bonne et aimée. Dans la peinture surréaliste, la femme est mauvaise et haïe' (331). While Gauthier's distinction is a generalization, she is nevertheless right in identifying a significant difference in surrealism's literary and visual representation of 'woman'.

5. The question of surrealist sexism has been hotly debated by feminists since the seventies, with works such as Gauthier's *Surréalisme et sexualité* seeking to expose surrealist misogyny. More recently, Rosalind Krauss has made a case for reading the fragmentation and mutability of woman in surrealist art as a proto-feminist critique of gender stereotypes (95).

6. "The Sandman" is a well-known source of inspiration for Carter too. As she writes in her Afterword to *Fireworks* (1974), she had always been fond of Hoffmann, and the puppet theme of "The Sandman" is echoed in, for example, *The Magic Toyshop* (1967) and "The Loves of Lady Purple" (1974). In *The Infernal Desire Machines of Doctor Hoffman* (1972), as Suleiman has pointed out, Hoffmann's tales provide a structural model for the entire novel ("The Fate of the Surrealist Imagination" 104).

7. As Sue Taylor writes: 'With the first doll, Bellmer had initially employed photography to document the stages of its construction and later to create

various still-life arrangements with lacy fabrics and fetishistic props such as a long-stem artificial rose and eyelet underlinen. As is often noted, there is a significant shift in strategy with his hundred-some photographs of the second doll, which date from 1935 to 1938. The differences are essentially twofold: the second series is more narrative and sinister in mood than the first. In addition, Bellmer hand-colored a number of photographs in the latter group, heightening both the emotive possibilities and the apparent artifice in many instances, and referencing nineteenth-century picture postcards and erotica that he and [Paul] Eluard each collected' (73–74).

8. Several critics have pointed out that the dolls were a response on Bellmer's part to the rise of Nazism in Germany, and an attack on Nazi stereotypes of normalcy (see, for example, Lichtenstein and Mahon). Hal Foster has suggested that the sadism infused in the dolls be read as both an allegory of and an attack on Fascist/Nazi sadism (directed at 'the feminine') and simultaneously an instance of Bellmer's own sadistic drives and fantasies (114–22).

9. Suleiman identifies references in *The Infernal Desire Machines of Doctor Hoffman* to surrealist works of art exhibiting mutilated female figures, such as Duchamp's *Etant Donnés*, which was completed in 1966 and made available to the public in 1969.

10. Influenced by Vaché's *umor*, black humour, both rebellious and anti-commonsensical, was to become an essential part of surrealist aesthetics.

11. The most extreme of Carter's libertines is the character of the Count in *The Infernal Desire Machines of Doctor Hoffman*, who is to a great extent modelled on the Marquis de Sade.

12. One might see in Honeybuzzard and Morris's love of junk a reference to the surrealist cult of the found object (*objet trouvé*). Often spotted in flea markets, the found object 'is one which when seen among a large number of other objects possesses an attraction [...] It is usually an old-fashioned manufactured object, whose practical function is not evident and about whose origins nothing is known' (Alexandrian 141).

13. As critics such as Sage and Gamble have argued, Honeybuzzard is himself a representation of a camp sensibility, of 'Being-as-Playing-a-Role.' See Sage (8–9 and 12) and Gamble (39–41 and 52–53).

14. Like Ghislaine, the androgynous Honeybuzzard is also an embodiment of transgressed boundaries, his name alone implying, as Gamble writes, 'an irreconcilable combination of the sweet and the predatory' (52).

15. Aragon's words are echoed by Joseph in *Several Perceptions*, who 'now and then [glimpses] immense cracks in the structure of the real world' (2–3).

16. Although it is nowhere explicitly stated in the novel, there are hints that Morris and Honeybuzzard's friendship is intensified by homoerotic desire, tied into their mutual desire for Ghislaine.

17. Both Foster and Krauss have argued that the aggressive manipulation of the dolls – 'construction *as* dismemberment' – is a kind of castration in its disconnection of body parts (see Foster 103 and Krauss 86).

18. As Sue Roe has argued, Annabel in *Love* – a novel she calls 'Angela Carter's Surrealist poem for the forlorn daughter' – is similarly denied subjecthood, except as surrealist 'peinture-poésie, photomontage, *cadavre exquis*, collage' (62).

19. As Suleiman suggests in an article on surrealist black humour, the strategy of mimicry implies a double allegiance on the part of the woman artist ("Surrealist Black Humour" 5).
20. Edna is, of course, also a caricature of the stereotypically feminine (albeit not of a typical surrealist woman) and her characterization similarly an instance of mimicry. As Irigaray points out, mimicry should only be an initial strategy for woman when inserting herself into discourse. *Shadow Dance*, Carter's first novel, does not elaborate on the possibilities beyond mimicry; in order to discover how Carter imagines her own version of woman we will have to turn to her later explorations in the field of sexuality in texts such as *The Passion of New Eve* (1977) and *Nights at the Circus* (1984).
21. As I have argued above, surrealism was heavily influenced by the writings of de Sade.
22. Moreover, as Foster points out, the motivation behind many surrealist misogynistic images is not always easily identifiable, as they are 'often ambiguously reflexive about male fantasies, not merely expressive of them' (13).
23. The affinity between Carter's concerns in *Shadow Dance* and Chasseguet-Smirgel's definition of perversion has also been noted by Hentges (53).

Works cited

Alexandrian, Sarane. *Surrealist Art*. 1970. Trans. Gordon Clough. London: Thames and Hudson, 1985.

Bataille, Georges. *Eroticism*. 1962. Trans. Mary Dalwood. London: Penguin, 2001.

Bellmer, Hans. "Memories of the Doll Theme." 1934. *Behind Closed Doors: The Art of Hans Bellmer*. By Therese Lichtenstein. Berkeley: University of California Press, 2001. 169–74.

Breton, André. *L'Amour fou*. Paris: Gallimard, 1937.

———. *Second Manifesto of Surrealism*. 1930. *Manifestoes of Surrealism*. 1969. Trans. Richard Seaver and Helen R. Lane. Ann Arbor: University of Michigan Press, 1972. 117–94.

Cardinal, Roger, and Robert Stuart Short. *Surrealism: Permanent Revelation*. London: Studio Vista, 1970.

Carter, Angela. "The Alchemy of the Word." 1978. *Shaking a Leg: Collected Journalism and Writings*. Intro. Joan Smith. Ed. Jenny Uglow. London: Vintage, 1998. 507–12.

———. *The Sadeian Woman: An Exercise in Cultural History*. 1979. London: Virago Press, 2000.

———. *Several Perceptions*. 1968. London: Virago, 1997.

———. *Shadow Dance*. 1966. London: Virago, 1997.

Chadwick, Whitney. "An Infinite Play of Empty Mirrors: Women, Surrealism, and Self-Representation." *Mirror Images: Women, Surrealism, and Self-Representation*. Ed. Whitney Chadwick. Cambridge, MA: MIT Press, 1998. 2–35.

Chasseguet-Smirgel, Janine. "Perversion and the Universal Law." *International Review of Psycho-Analysis* 10 (1983): 293–301.

Clapp, Susannah. "On Madness, Men and Fairy-Tales." *The Independent on Sunday* 9 June 1991: 26–27.

Day, Aidan. *Angela Carter: The Rational Glass*. Manchester: Manchester University Press, 1998.

Foster, Hal. *Compulsive Beauty*. Cambridge, MA: MIT Press, 1993.

Gamble, Sarah. *Angela Carter: Writing from the Front Line*. Edinburgh: Edinburgh University Press, 1997.

Gauthier, Xavière. *Surréalisme et sexualité*. Paris: Éditions Gallimard, 1971.

Hentges, Jane. "Painting Pictures of Petrification and Perversion: Angela Carter's Surrealist Eye in *Shadow Dance* and *The Magic Toyshop*." *Études britanniques contemporaines* 23 (2002): 43–53.

Irigaray, Luce. *This Sex Which Is Not One*. 1977. Trans. Catherine Porter and Carolyn Burke. Ithaca: Cornell University Press, 1985.

Krauss, Rosalind. "Corpus Delicti." *L'Amour Fou: Photography and Surrealism*. Ed. Rosalind Krauss and Jane Livingston. Washington: Corcoran Gallery of Art, 1985. 54–111.

Lee, Alison. *Angela Carter*. New York: Twayne Publishers, 1997.

Lichtenstein, Therese. *Behind Closed Doors: The Art of Hans Bellmer*. Berkeley: University of California Press, 2001.

Mahon, Alyce. "Hans Bellmer's Libidinal Politics." *Surrealism, Politics and Culture*. Ed. Raymond Spiteri and Donald LaCoss. Aldershot: Ashgate, 2003. 246–66.

O'Day, Marc. "'Mutability is Having a Field Day': The Sixties Aura of Angela Carter's Bristol Trilogy." *Flesh and the Mirror: Essays on the Art of Angela Carter*. Ed. Lorna Sage. London: Virago, 1994. 24–58.

Plant, Sadie. *The Most Radical Gesture: The Situationist International in a Postmodern Age*. London: Routledge, 1992.

Raaberg, Gwen. "The Problematics of Women and Surrealism." *Surrealism and Women*. 1990. Ed. Mary Ann Caws, Rudolf Kuenzli and Gwen Raaberg. Cambridge, MA: MIT Press, 1991. 1–10.

Roe, Sue. "The Disorder of *Love*: Angela Carter's Surrealist Collage." *Flesh and the Mirror: Essays on the Art of Angela Carter*. Ed. Lorna Sage. London: Virago, 1994. 60–97.

Rosemont, Franklin. Introduction. *What is Surrealism? Selected Writings*. By André Breton. New York: Monad Press, 1978. 1–147.

Sage, Lorna. *Angela Carter*. Writers and their Work. Plymouth: Northcote House, 1994.

Shattuck, Roger. "Introduction: Love and Laughter: Surrealism Reappraised." *The History of Surrealism*. Ed. Maurice Nadeau. Trans. Richard Howard. Cambridge, MA: Harvard University Press, 1989. 11–34.

Suleiman, Susan Rubin. "The Fate of the Surrealist Imagination in the Society of the Spectacle." *Flesh and the Mirror: Essays on the Art of Angela Carter*. Ed. Lorna Sage. London: Virago, 1994. 98–116.

———. *Subversive Intent: Gender, Politics and the Avant-Garde*. Cambridge, MA: Harvard University Press, 1990.

———. "Surrealist Black Humour: Masculine/Feminine." *Papers of Surrealism* 1 (2003): 1–11. <http://www.surrealismcentre.ac.uk/publications/papers/journal1/acrobat_files/Suleiman.pdf.>

Taylor, Sue. *Hans Bellmer: The Anatomy of Anxiety*. Cambridge, MA: MIT Press, 2000.

2
Something Sacred: Angela Carter, Jean-Luc Godard and the Sixties

Sarah Gamble

Although Angela Carter could not see the point of religion, firmly believing that 'atheism [...] is the most honourable course a human person can take' (Appignanesi), she had a noticeable tendency to fall into quasi-devout rhetoric whenever she talked of the cinema. This is exemplified in *Angela Carter's Curious Room*, the *Omnibus* documentary made shortly before her death in 1992, in which she asserted her belief that 'there is something sacred about the cinema, which is to do with it being public, to do with people going together, with the intention of visualizing, experiencing the same experience, having the same revelation' (Evans). As if to underline that contention, in the same programme she chose to be shown watching one of her favourite films, the 1935 version of *A Midsummer Night's Dream*, directed by Erich von Stroheim. Moreover, she is not viewing it alone, but – in a particularly poignant touch – with her husband and son, in a scene that acts as an exemplar of her opinion that cinema is a medium that demands communal participation, uniting individuals within a shared imaginative experience. Carter had nothing against television as an art form – she admitted to watching 'anything that flickers' (qtd. in Clapp ix) – but she was of the opinion that television as a medium performs precisely the opposite function to cinema. Firstly, because television 'has extraordinary limitations as a medium for the presentation of imaginative drama of any kind' by possessing 'an inbuilt ability to cut people down to size' ("Acting it Up" 405), it cannot create the larger-than-life iconic figures that arise out of the alchemy of screen and dream. Furthermore, in contrast to the cinema's capacity for bringing people together in a shared public event, television watching is an essentially solitary activity, enabling individuals to carve out islands of isolation within the domestic space.[1]

But as Carter's own writing demonstrates, she did not work on a small scale, and the isolated vision did not interest her in the least. Instead, her heart lies with the exaggerated, the overblown and the iconic, and with the kind of art that demands response, discussion and active engagement. She loved to cast her critical demythologizer's eye over the Hollywood star system and the pretensions of directors; but she also, quite simply, loved cinema. Two of her novels in particular – *The Passion of New Eve* (1977) and *Wise Children* (1991) – are specifically about the creation of movie stars and cinematic myths, but they are merely overt manifestations of a fascination that underlies almost all of her writing. It is the intention of this debate to contend not only that cinema constitutes a seminal influence on Carter's art, but also that it did so from the very beginning of her career. Her early novels, while less obviously full of cinematic allusions compared to some of her later texts, draw on her fascination with film not only in terms of what she wrote about, but also *how* she wrote, for they show Carter experimenting with translating techniques developed for the visual representation of action on the screen onto the page. In this sense, it is her indebtedness to film that influences the development of her own highly visual, descriptive and distinctive style.

In the beginning: the National Film Theatre

When Carter began work on what was to be her first published novel in 1963, she was a mature student at Bristol University. She described herself at this stage of her life as a 'wide-eyed provincial beatnik' who was desperate to publish a book 'for reasons of psychological compulsion, to validate myself' (Sage, "The Savage Sideshow" 54). But by the time *Shadow Dance* eventually appeared in print in 1966 Carter was convinced that, at the ripe old age of 26, she was 'a has-been [...] because when I was growing up it was the era of the child prodigy' (ibid. 55). In actuality, of course, *Shadow Dance* launched what was to become a distinguished and prolific career, leading to Carter's posthumous status as one of the most important British novelists of the late twentieth century. What is remarkable, though, about her first novel is the way in which it is instantly, recognizably, Carteresque: no tentative piece of juvenilia, but a text that showcases influences and ideas that Carter was to continue to work through in all the fiction she wrote subsequently. James Wood, for example, notes that *Shadow Dance* introduces, fully-fledged, Carter's beautifully mannered, baroque style. In an otherwise rather equivocal review, he praises Carter's language in this text as '[a]lready [...] rich and brightbuttoned. One marvels at the confidence with which she rolls up the old heavy carpet of detailed narration and dangles instead her own brighter mat' (20). It was a 'polish' Carter attributed to her familiarity with French, and although she deplored that she would 'never be able to write in French', she said that 'the structure of sentences' and the 'subtle grammar' of that language had influenced her own writing (Sage, "The Savage Sideshow" 55).

But the French influences on *Shadow Dance* extend beyond the linguistic. Although one of the hallmarks of Carter's art is the extravagance of her prose, which highlights her evident love of language (she once described herself as being 'cursed a bit by fluency' [Haffenden 38]), this text also shows how her inspiration very often came from visual media. Carter's fascination with the cinema dated, she said, from her earliest years, and childhood outings with her father to the Granada cinema in Tooting. It was here that she was introduced to 'the big-screen experience'; although she claimed to 'scarcely remember the movies I watched with my father, only the space in which we sat to watch them' ("The Granada, Tooting" 400). But it was in her 'lonely, brooding, gloomy adolescence' that Carter became an aficionado of 'a completely different kind of concrete bunker than the Granada Tooting', the National Film Theatre, and the films she saw there were far more specifically memorable (Evans). As she was to recall in later life, it was here she was introduced to Louise Brooks in *Pandora's Box* (1929), Marlene Dietrich in *The Blue Angel* (1930) and, perhaps most significantly, the work of Jean-Luc Godard and other *auteurs* of the French New Wave.

All these films came to exert an incontrovertible influence over Carter's view of the world and her artistic method, but she singled out Godard in particular as the figure who epitomized the intellectual promise of the 1960s. Writing in 1983, she maintained that:

> Godard's movies uniquely crystallise the vertigo of that decade. The vertigo that had nothing to do with the ephemeral pop mythology of the Beatles or mini-skirts, but with Vietnam, with the Prague spring, culminating in the events of May in Paris, '68, when, however briefly, it seemed imagination might truly seize power. Vertigo that came from the intoxicating, terrifying notion that the old order was indeed coming to an end, vertigo of beings about to be born. ("Jean-Luc Godard" 381)

Carter held Godard personally responsible for nothing less than influencing an entire generation of British adolescents by inducting them into 'the great international conspiracy of the disaffected' (ibid.) that was spreading across Europe. In her essay "Truly, It Felt Like Year One" (1988), Carter eulogized the 1960s as a period seemingly poised on the edge of unimaginable change, during which '[t]hings were becoming accessible to me [...] that I'd never imagined – ways of thinking, versions of the world, versions of history, of ways for societies to be' (211). For Carter personally, films such as *Breathless* (1961), *Vivre sa vie* (1962) and *Weekend* (1967) became not only a significant medium through which such ideas were communicated, but also provided a framework within which she could make sense of the freewheeling cultural anarchism of the period. Godard's films became, she claimed, the 'touchstone' against which her 'whole experience of the next decade can be logged' (ibid.).

Given such ringing endorsements, it is surprising that the extent to which Godard's cinematic oeuvre may have influenced Carter's own work has been so little investigated. Yet, reading Carter's early writing alongside the films Godard produced during the 1960s raises some highly interesting interpretive possibilities, since it provides us with both a means of assessing the narrative techniques she utilizes within many of the novels she published during this decade, and a new angle from which to understand her often problematic depiction of sexual politics, a dilemma thrown up particularly acutely in her early writing. It is true that Carter did subsequently appear to disassociate herself somewhat from her younger self's intentions in this regard. In "Notes from the Front Line", written in her forties, she describes herself twenty years earlier as someone 'in the process of becoming radically sceptical, that is, if not free, then more free than I had been', but nevertheless still 'suffering a degree of colonialisation of the mind. [...] So there was an element of the male impersonator about this young person as she was finding herself' (71). It was a caveat Carter reiterated in the Afterword to *Love* (1971) on its reissue in 1987, in which she comments on the novel's 'almost sinister feat of male impersonation' (113).

Stop, start, stop: destroying the illusion

As Elaine Jordan has argued, there is certainly an 'apparent contradiction between Carter's feminist "line" and her exploitation of a dangerous reactionary fascination – heterosexual desire in thrall to soft pornography and sado-masochism' (123), but it is my contention that this contradiction can be better comprehended when aligned with what Godard was doing at around the same time. Novels such as *Shadow Dance* and *Love* echo Godard's tactic in films like *Vivre sa vie* – that of showing female victimization in the process of its construction and, in so doing, laying the mechanisms of oppression open to subversion and revision. The mannered presentation that is the hallmark both of the French New Wave and of Carter's fiction results in a portrayal of female subjectivity that is entirely devoid of naturalism, so that the audience is kept in a state of constant awareness that what they are seeing or reading is an invention formed out of an assemblage of artfully-arranged allusions and literary or cinematographic representational techniques. In refusing to allow their art to imitate life, both Carter and Godard suggest that what we take to be our essential, real, *inescapable* selves are just as much inventions as anything with which they present us – products of choice and circumstance that could, if conditions were different, be constructed in quite another way.

One of the principal ways in which this is achieved by both author and *auteur* is through an abandonment of continuity, the effect of which is to deprive their characters of motivation. The loss of a back-story flattens them: lacking any sense of a history, they become little more than two-dimensional representations. In his first film, *Breathless*, Godard pioneered his use of the 'jump cut', discarding frames from the reel at random so that the connections between one event and the other are simply lost. While *Vivre sa vie* does not include jump cuts, a similar effect is achieved by dividing the action up into a series of twelve tableaux, scenes in the life of the central character Nana. The gaps between the scenes are not filled in – no explanation is provided as to how Nana has got from one episode to the next – with the result that the action proceeds in the same disconnected fashion as those films that utilize the jump cut. As Susan Sontag has argued in her essay on *Vivre sa vie*, 'the whole point' of the film 'is that it does not explain anything. It rejects causality. (Thus, the ordinary causal sequence of narrative is broken in Godard's film by the extremely arbitrary decomposition of the story into twelve episodes – episodes which are serially, rather than causally, related)' (199).

Sontag's description of Godard's eschewal of the 'total sensuous whole' in favour of 'techniques that would fragment, dissociate, alienate, break up' (ibid. 200) could also be applied to a recurring feature of a great deal of Carter's early work. In fact, perhaps Lorna Sage had this very analogy in mind when she described Carter's first three books as sharing 'plots [that] move from one tableau to another, "still" after "still", quickened into movement by a kind of optical illusion – as in a flicker book, or of course a film' (*Women in the House* 169). Novels such as *Shadow Dance, Several Perceptions* (1968) and *Love*, in particular – a triumvirate that have been termed 'the Bristol trilogy'[2] – are characterized by a disorientating sense of discontinuity, which is only accentuated by the inclusion of bizarre episodes that lack any rational explanation within the storyline of the novel.[3] *Shadow Dance*, for example, centres on the interactions of Morris and Honeybuzzard, who run a ramshackle junk shop in a bombed-out area of Bristol. Early one morning, for no good reason that appears in the narrative, the shop is besieged by 'a crazy, silent, dancing crew' (114) who 'as if at a signal […] shouting […] surged across the road at the very moment when the streetlamps went out […]. Morris thought he caught the flicker of a knife' (115). Nothing is known of this mob or its motivation for the attack on the shop, and it all peters out anyway as soon as a 'ponderous bicycle of a patrolling policeman rolled majestically down the road' (115). The anti-naturalism of the event is deliberately confronted within the episode, during which Carter describes one of the female participants as 'paus[ing] theatrically and thr[owing] back her head, pealing with ringing laughter' (115). *Several Perceptions*, Carter's third novel, contains a similarly staged scene, in which a fight breaks out in a bar between an anonymous man and woman, figures in no way connected with the narrative, and that appear in it only momentarily. We appear to be witnessing a moment of high emotion, yet this impression is undercut by the dramatic metaphors that are threaded through the episode: the girl performs a dance that conveys 'the freezing menace of a dance in an Elizabethan tragedy' (51), 'her demonic red lips […] stretched in a flamenco dancer's artificial smile' (53). Her male companion, in contrast, 'seem[s] content to play a passive prop in this scene she was acting' (51).

It can therefore be seen that in these surreal, discontinuous fragments of action inserted into both *Shadow Dance* and *Several Perceptions* one of the ways in which Carter points at the artificiality of her fictional construct is by habitually attaching theatrical tropes to the female participants. In *Several Perceptions*, this linking of artificiality with femininity is writ particularly large in the text: not just through anonymous and marginal characters, but in the spectacular, substantial figure of Mrs Boulder, who, 'painted like a holy statue' (48), wears a mask of youth that is wholly false. Anti-naturalism becomes, by implication, a condition of femininity, precisely because it is primarily through the women in the scene that the breaking of the fictional illusion is foregrounded. And it is at this point that Godard's and Carter's portrayal of the female figure becomes remarkably synchronous; a claim that can be supported through a parallel reading of *Shadow Dance* and *Vivre sa vie*, the film that Carter picked out for special mention in her promotion of Channel Four's Godard season in 1983.

Framing the woman: *Vivre sa vie* and *Shadow Dance*

In an interview given in 1962 to mark the screening of *Vivre sa vie* at the London Film Festival, Godard said that the film was very different from earlier works such as *Breathless*, demonstrating that he was 'beginning, gradually, to make more realistic films' (Milne 5). Yet his notion of 'realism' is a paradoxical one, for he argued that the film's claim to reality actually resides in the extremity of its theatricality:

> [T]here is documentary realism and there is theatre, but ultimately, at the highest level, they are one and the same. What I mean is that through documentary realism one arrives at the structure of theatre, and through theatrical imagination and fiction one arrives at the reality of life. (ibid. 4)

This is very close to Carter's view that the use of non-realistic literary forms is perfectly fine so long as they do not attempt to seduce an audience into belief. In an interview Carter gave in 1984, she admiringly described:

> a Museum of Atheism in Leningrad which has all these miracle workings exposed – so you can see how the blood flows out of the spear wound, so you can see how the tears come out, so you can see how the mechanism worked. That's how I regard my work sometimes. (Harron 10)

The blood and tears shed all too frequently by Carter's heroines, even in the early novels, can be regarded as functioning in this manner. Although it is an uncomfortable conclusion that is difficult to arrive at without some hesitation, I do not believe that Carter intends the extremity of their experiences to be taken at face value. Instead, through such figures, the theatrical illusion is displayed in all its artifice and it is in the act of acknowledging it *as* an illusion that we arrive at the reality of life. By her own admission, Carter, like Godard, intended her work to stand – to quote Susan Sontag on Godard – as 'an exhibit, a demonstration' (199). She was contemptuous, for example, of romanticized notions of 'character', believing 'the idea that the characters can take over a novel and run away with it' to be 'utterly self-indulgent on the part of a writer'. In contrast, her characters, 'however lively they might appear, however full of spontaneous creation and invention,' have 'always got a tendency to be telling you something' (Evans).

proceeds to use her corpse to satisfy his own necrophilic desires. Moreover, as Morris has sufficient insight to realize, in 'choking out of Ghislaine her little-girl giggle' (177–78), Honeybuzzard is acting out Morris's own darkest, barely-acknowledged, ambition. Even at this point, his primary identification is with Honeybuzzard, not Ghislaine: 'I am to blame, too, I should have guessed, *I should have protected him*' (178; emphasis added).

For both Nana and Ghislaine, therefore, obliteration lies at the end of their idealistic search for love, for they are trapped in a landscape in which, like one of Escher's optical illusions, every avenue of escape only brings them right back to where they started. Their sexual power over men is actually no power at all, since it does not bring them security, autonomy or a secure sense of self. Instead, their peculiar form of passive-aggressive sexuality becomes the very means by which they are destroyed, in a punishment for daring to be sexual beings – even though that is the only context in which they can attain any kind of visibility or recognition. This cruel paradox is emphasized because the only way in which we are enabled to know either Nana or Ghislaine is through their relation to men, for in neither film nor novel are any other motives ascribed to them. Both are beautiful figures cast in two dimensions, existing as exquisitely desirable bodies, but denied any comprehensible inner life.

In *Vivre sa vie*, this is shown through the film's persistent inquiry into the nature of the self. It opens with a quotation from Montaigne – 'Lend yourself to others, but give yourself to yourself' – which is superimposed upon Nana's face. What the audience is subsequently shown, of course, is precisely the opposite: the chronicle of a subject who gives herself to others without reserve, and who suffers as a consequence. It is a point further underlined at the end of the first tableau, when Paul tells Nana an anecdote related to him by his father, a school teacher, concerning an essay written by one of his pupils on the topic of their favourite animal: 'One little girl of eight chose a bird. It went: "A bird is an animal with an inside and an outside. Remove the outside, there's the inside. Remove the inside and you see the soul"'. Nana, though, conveys no sense of interior life or essence. Instead, she becomes the sum of her actions – or, perhaps, *re*actions – for what goes on in her head is a mystery. Precisely because Godard tells us nothing of her motivations, the whole notion of an 'inner self' is thus placed in question. This does not mean that Godard rejected the concept altogether – indeed, he argued that the best way 'to render the inside' is '[p]recisely by staying prudently outside' (qtd. in Sterritt, *Films of Jean-Luc Godard* 65). What that 'inside' may consist of, however, is left ambiguous: as David Sterritt proposes, it remains 'a "something else" that can only be approached through oxymoronic genres like *theatre-vérité* and eccentric creative processes' (ibid. 66). Yet, as Carter was aware, Godard remained insistent that Nana's story, whatever the manner of its ending, was one of 'a prostitute who sells her body but retains her integrity' ("Jean-Luc Godard" 381) – a view that would appear to mark a distinct point of departure from *Shadow Dance*.

Carter presents Ghislaine, too, solely from the outside: the point of view throughout is deliberately limited to that of the male voyeur. But her staunch atheism precludes her from embracing the notion of an inner spiritual 'essence' of any kind, with the result that Ghislaine remains bereft of any kind of discernable integrity. However sympathetic we are disposed to be towards this figure she remains alienated from us, for throughout *Shadow Dance* she is only viewed through the slewed perspective of Morris, who is murderously antagonistic towards the sexual threat he perceives her to represent. He is not interested in Ghislaine as an individual, but sketches her into his narrative in crude outlines – she is 'a horror-movie woman' (4), 'a vampire woman' (39); and, in one particularly telling dream, 'a turnip lantern' he has carved out with a blunt knife, and 'put a candle inside and lit it through her freshly carved mouth' (39–40). She is, in other words, nothing more than a piece of *animé*, resembling Nana in her opacity, lack of interiority and malleability. Carter never gives Ghislaine a point of view, nor allows her any kind of veracity within a narrative in which her only role is to undergo a steady process of destruction.

Nevertheless, that is not to say that Ghislaine is intended to stand for womanhood as a whole in this novel. *Vivre sa vie* is obsessively focused on Nana: the camera rarely leaves her, and other female characters in the film remain shadowy. Carter, on the other hand, offers more than one version of femininity in *Shadow Dance*, where Ghislaine's awful moral vacuity is counterbalanced by Emily, the female figure who does not lose herself in Honeybuzzard's world. Where Ghislaine is malleable, Emily is solid, possessing 'a firm sense of occupancy inside her clothes and her strong, well-made body and the firm features of her quiet face. She was always at home in herself' (98). Emily's firm sense of self-worth means that she remains untainted and incorruptible, eventually turning Honeybuzzard in to the police in order to save not only herself, but also her unborn child, thus providing some small glimmer of hope in the otherwise uncompromisingly bleak ending of the novel.

The contradictions posed by Nana – a girl who retains some kind of personal rectitude even while she is exploited to her death – are thus divided in *Shadow Dance* between Ghislaine and Emily. But it is interesting to note that by Carter's fiction of the 1970s the two have united, resulting in girl–women whose contradictory mixture of naïvety and corruption becomes an increasingly strong ground upon which to build a sense of autonomy. In one of Carter's most well-known short stories, "The Company of Wolves" (1979), Little Red Riding Hood has sex with the wolf-man who has ambushed her in her grandmother's house, having made the pragmatic decision that 'since her fear did her no good, she ceased to be afraid' (117). Such a refusal to be cast in the role of victim is her salvation, enabling her to end the story sleeping 'sweet and sound [...] in granny's bed, between the paws of the tender wolf' (118). Robert Clark argues of this episode that '[t]he point of view is that of the male voyeur; the implication may be that the girl has her own sexual power, but this meaning lies perilously close to the idea that all women want it really, and only need forcing to overcome their scruples' (149); but, read on Carter's terms, this absolutely characterizes the concept put forward by films such as *Vivre sa vie*: that women can be exploited, yet retain a fundamental core of integrity. There is an important difference to be discerned here, though, for while Nana's integrity remains shadowy because it does not result in any kind of action that would enable her to escape, it gives Carter's later heroines the motivation to survive by any means necessary.

Victor or victim?: the *femme fatale*

The combination of toughness and vulnerability exhibited by Ghislaine and Emily together does not originate out of Carter's interest in Godard alone, although it emerges from a source on which Godard also drew. Nana and Ghislaine, in particular, are bound together through a common progenitor: one of the earliest, and greatest, of the cinematic *femmes fatales*. Louise Brooks was an American actress who achieved iconic status through her role in G.W. Pabst's *Pandora's Box*, itself an adaptation of a play by Frank Wedekind. Carter viewed Lulu 'as one of the key representations of female sexuality in twentieth-century literature' ("Barry Paris" 388), and it is difficult not to draw the conclusion that Lulu was one influence over Carter's own portrayals of female sexuality. *Pandora's Box* is the tale of a sexual adventuress whose allure attracts both men and women like moths to a flame. And like moths to a flame they are all destroyed, for Lulu's liaisons inevitably end in tragedy and disaster. Lulu herself becomes subject to the same cruel fate conventionally meted out to 'loose' women, ending her days as a prostitute and one of Jack the Ripper's victims.

Godard's Nana explicitly constitutes a visual homage to Brooks, most particularly in her adoption of Brook's distinctive bobbed haircut. The fact that it was known in France as the 'Joan of Arc' haircut adds another layer of allusion to the scene in the cinema when Nana watches Dreyer's film, which is already, as Carter observes, a '[c]omplex homage, connecting the erotic magic of Brooks to the martyrized virgin of Dreier's [sic.] imagery' ("Jean-Luc Godard" 381). The scene Nana sees represents the moment when Joan is told she is to be burned at the stake, to which her response, though anguished, is also triumphal, as indicated by her proclamation 'My deliverance, death'. This is a moment of significant foreshadowing and cinematic echoing, since for Nana, as for Lulu before her, death is her salvation, 'delivering' her from the downward cycle of exploitation in which she is trapped. As Carter says of Lulu, by the end of the film Nana 'can only hope, now, to accede to death as if it were some kind of grace' ("Femmes Fatales" 353). Carter regards Lulu's fate as inevitable: the victim of her own unrestrained sexual energy, she 'must die because she is free' (ibid.).

In her introduction to the anthology *Wayward Girls and Wicked Women* (1986), Carter comments that:

> on the whole, morality as regards woman has nothing to do with ethics; it means sexual morality and nothing but sexual morality. To be a wayward girl usually has something to do with pre-marital sex; to be a wicked woman has something to do with adultery. This means it is far easier for a woman to lead a blameless life than a man; all she has to do is avoid sexual intercourse like the plague. What hypocrisy! (x)

It is statements such as this that provide an opportunity to view characters such as Ghislaine in a different light by bringing her symbolic aspect to the fore. If we regard her as a product of Carter's interest in figures such as Pabst's Lulu and Godard's Nana, she is no longer just a lonely lost girl, or an irremediable victim, but a manifestation of the *femme fatale*. And, as Carter argues, *femmes fatales* are not just women gone to the bad: by 'expressing an unrepressed sexuality in a society which distorts sexuality' ("Femmes Fatales" 353), they act as potent symbols, if not of liberation per se, at least of the recognition of the existence of repression. 'This is the true source of the fatality of the *femme fatale*; that she lives her life in such a way her freedom reveals to others their lack of liberty. So her sexuality is indeed destructive, not in itself but in its effects' (ibid.).

Of all the novels in the Bristol Trilogy, it is *Several Perceptions* that offers a particularly interesting take on the figure of the *femme fatale* through the character of Mrs Boulder, who represents the fate of the fatally seductive woman now past her prime. An aging prostitute who cultivates a *faux* gentility, she dresses up 'in dazzling white on steel heels as high as a kite' (72) in order to entertain her gentlemen friends. But Mrs Boulder's extra years have not brought her either security or strength. In fact, she resembles Ghislaine and Annabel more than is at first apparent, for her façade of paint and powder and her power-dressing only imperfectly mask the fearful girl who remains beneath:

An ill-cemented curl began to tumble from her Martello tower of hair; maybe the whole painfully assembled fortification of sophistication was about to collapse entirely now she had revealed how fragile her defences were. She put her hand up to her hair; an expression of terror crossed her face. (73)

When, subsequently, she sleeps with her son's best friend Joseph, he learns her story, one which recalls that of both Nana and Lulu: 'I'd started out in showbusiness, as a dancer. I had a nice figure, nice legs [...] Mum and dad had high hopes for me, but first a fellow let me down and then one thing and another' (117–18). As if to point out the possibility of Godardian antecedents, Joseph imagines himself, after the act, as 'a pretty boy in a French film smoking a faintly perfumed cigarette in a harlot's bed while its owner sat before a mirror working on her face' (116).

But Mrs Boulder does not share the fate of her predecessors, even though, worn out by the constant battle to resist the aging process, she has contemplated suicide as a real possibility. However, she tells Joseph, she changed her mind because 'I don't know whether it is a vein or an artery you are supposed to cut. And there was no hot water for a bath, anyway' (108). So, although it seems to be more through lack of opportunity rather than deliberate decision, Mrs Boulder survives, however tenuously; diligently, doggedly, transforming herself into an 'icon' (119), a vaudevillian 'white queen' (131), because she cannot envisage herself as anything other than a sexual being who has no function other than to arouse male desire. But in an economy that values youth over experience, she is fast losing her market value. Nevertheless, Mrs Boulder is neither an unsympathetic nor a wholly pitiable figure, for viewed through Joseph's eyes she embodies a kind of masochistic heroism. Even if we do not approve of the woman she strives to be, we are still invited to admire the determination with which she continues to cultivate the *femme fatale* persona, however grotesque the result. And of all the women of her type in the Bristol trilogy she alone gets her man: 'an enormous African' who plays 'black king' (131) to her white queen. It is an appropriate ending to the most optimistic and carnivalesque of Carter's early novels – the (albeit momentary and provisional) redemption of the *femme fatale*. In this context, Mrs Boulder represents the future denied to all the girls who die too young – Nana, Lulu, Ghislaine and Annabel amongst them – and stands defiantly against the tradition of cinematic and literary representation which demands that the whore pay her moral dues and be brought to a bad end.

Obscene for a reason: Godard as moral pornographer

If Carter does become a kind of male impersonator with regard to the depiction of women in her early work, then it is at least focused through the gaze of men who themselves possess the capacity to critique the female condition. In "Femmes Fatales", Carter describes *Pandora's Box* as a film that improves upon its dramatic original, with Brooks and Pabst colluding in depicting the 'cultural myth of the femme fatale [...] irresistibly in action while, at the same time, offering evidence of its manifest absurdity' (350–51). While in Wedekind's 'Lulu' plays, Lulu is portrayed as nothing more than 'the passive instrument of vice', in the film version she becomes a figure of 'negative virtue [... that] illuminates the spiritual degradation of every single other character in the movie' (351). Though not nearly so destructive, Godard's Nana also shares this trait of 'negative virtue', for her beauty, her suffering and her eternal, hopeless, optimism all combine to form an explicit denunciation of a society in which women such as she possess no other way of making a living. As Wheeler Winston Dixon argues:

> Although the film's very premise objectifies the feminine corpus within the text of the film as a whole, Godard is aware of the level of scrutiny he subjects Nana to, and is uncomfortable with the idea of woman-as-victim, woman-as-object-to-be-saved, woman-as-prostitute, all of which are gender constructions of the feminine self as defined by patriarchal commerce. (32)

Dixon draws attention to the highly contradictory position Godard occupies *vis-à-vis* his subject. Not only does he create Nana precisely in order to suffer – she has absolutely no function otherwise – but he also projects

;ration onto the big screen for the voyeuristic con-
To carry on the Joan of Arc metaphor, Nana is
m, burnt at the stake of his artistic vision. Yet it is
ieously acts as his justification, for *Vivre sa vie* does
..ate the inequities of gendered representation, but
..iiibits them for the purpose of inspection and critique.

In discussions of Carter's portrayal of sexual politics, the most com-
monly cited intertextual influence is the work of the Marquis de Sade,
the subject of her polemical text *The Sadeian Woman* (1979). Carter
claimed not to have encountered de Sade until the late 1960s, yet her
depiction of characters such as Ghislaine in *Shadow Dance* and Annabel
in *Love*, another beautiful, corrupt innocent who comes to a tragic end,
corresponds to an extraordinary degree with her definition of Justine in
The Sadeian Woman as perpetually 'the dupe of an experience that she
never experiences *as* experience; her innocence invalidates experience
and turns it into events, things that happen to her, but do not change
her' (51; emphasis in original). This description also, of course, fits both
Nana and Lulu, who never learn from experience either. Nana and Lulu,
Ghislaine and Annabel – all are female figures who fulfil Justine's narrative role as 'the heroine of a black, inverted fairy-tale...[whose] subject
is the misfortunes of unfreedom' (39). In *Love*, Annabel is an innocent
before she meets her boyfriend Lee, who 'wipe[s] away the blood' (15)
that marks his taking of her virginity. From then on, it is downhill all
the way for Annabel, who comes to use sex and masochism as weapons
in a relationship in which only voluntary subjugation gains her a
warped sense of dominance. On one occasion, for example, she and Lee
play chess and she hits him when he takes her queen – solely, it seems,
to engineer Lee's violent response, which is to:

> tie her wrists together with his belt, force her to kneel and beat her
> until she toppled over sideways. She raised a strangely joyous face to
> him; the pallor of her skin and the almost miraculous lustre of her
> eyes startled and even awed him. He was breathless with weeping, a
> despicable object.
> 'That will teach you to take my queen,' she said smugly. (40–41)

Female pain validates the female self – Ghislaine and Honeybuzzard may
be dead and gone by the end of *Shadow Dance*, but the *danse macabre* of
sexual politics goes on. And, like Ghislaine, when Annabel's flirtation with
self-destruction results in actual suicide, her body is transformed into
an erotic iconic object for male contemplation: in this case Lee and his

brother Buzz. Underlining Lee's complicity in Annabel's death (although conveniently glossing over his own), Buzz only half-ironically proposes that Lee should stand with his 'foot on her neck': 'Then I would take your picture with your arms crossed [...] Like, in a victorious pose' (112).

How can we justify Carter's representation of such grotesque victimization? The answer is to be found in *The Sadeian Woman*, the whole point of which is to investigate whether the Marquis de Sade himself is capable of fulfilling the hypothetical role of what Carter terms 'the moral pornographer', whose 'business would be the total demystification of the flesh and the subsequent revelations, through the infinite modulations of the sexual act, of the real relations of man and his kind' (19). Shocking though this statement might be (indeed, is deliberately *intended* to be), Carter's apparent fascination with pornographic sex is, it seems to me, somewhat of a red herring: the real focus of her interest in this statement is the attempt to depict reality accurately and unflinchingly through whatever means necessary, no matter how unconventional or controversial. And she had found a precedent for this even before she encountered de Sade's work; Godard's assertion that 'I shall write old verses on top of new forms' (qtd. in Kreidl 22) finds its echo in Carter's own oft-cited statement that 'I am all for putting new wine in old bottles, especially if the pressure of the new wine makes the old bottles explode' ("Notes from the Front Line" 69). Both Godard and Carter are concerned with stretching the limits of the sayable, with shocking an audience out of their comfortable preconceptions; and both, no matter how avant-garde they might seem, have motivations beyond the purely aesthetic.

In the *Omnibus* documentary, Carter described herself as believing that: 'all art is political [...] I think my work is very, very deeply political [...] I like creeping up on people from behind and sandbagging them with an idea that maybe they haven't thought of for themselves' (Evans). Yet, in accordance with her belief that 'fiction should be open-ended; you bring your own history to it and read it on your own terms' (Watts 163), her work is never overtly polemical, but depends on its unconventionality to force a reaction from its audience. In the same way, Sterritt has described how:

> Godard enjoys the prospect of jarring, jolting and generally shaking up his audience. Some of his reasons are political, based on a desire to portray our world in unfamiliar ways that stimulate active thought rather than passive emotionalism. Others are personal, reflecting a mischievous streak that delights in frustrating ingrained expectations. (*Films of Jean-Luc Godard* 12)

Godard and Carter therefore unite in their conviction that a good piece of fiction or of film is, in Godard's words, 'not only to have a story, but to have a *subject* – a meaning, a belief in something' (qtd. in Sterritt, "Ideas, Not Plots" 177; emphasis in original). They share, in other words, the very attributes that Carter was later to attach to her theoretical 'moral pornographer': a habit of forcing representation to its limits; a disregard for the niceties of taste; a desire to shock their audience into a new, radicalized, awareness.

There is far more to be said about what Carter might have taken from Godard's art, as well as about the many other intertexts upon which Carter drew at this early stage in her career. She was much too complex and intelligent an author to absorb her influences wholesale, and it would be a gross oversimplification to maintain that Carter modelled her artistic agenda upon Godard in a manner that was unqualified and uncritical. But, as I hope this debate has shown, there are grounds for maintaining that Godard's artistic approach, which combined aesthetic experimentation and social critique, and which openly displayed its own intertextuality, found a receptive audience in the young woman who was to use precisely these strategies in the development of her distinctive literary voice. Moreover, the influence of Godard is most discernible in Carter's contradictory, controversial portrayal of women. It is from him that she seems to have learnt the potential of the avant-garde in furthering the risky tactic of exhibiting exploitation for the very purpose of its deconstruction.

Notes

1. Carter claimed, for example, that to 'retreat into the television' could constitute the only means of creating 'a little privacy from time to time' in the midst of one's family ("The Box Does Furnish a Room" 412).
2. See Marc O'Day, who argues that the novels are linked not only by their shared use of Bristol as a setting, but also because they all 'offer realist representations of the 1960s "provincial bohemia" which Carter herself inhabited' (25).
3. For further analysis of Carter's use of the jump cut in the Bristol trilogy, see Gamble (63–69).

Works cited

Appignanesi, Lisa. "Angela Carter in Conversation." London: ICA Video, 1987.
Carter, Angela. "Acting It Up on the Small Screen." 1979. *Shaking A Leg* 405–409.
———. "Barry Paris: Louise Brooks." 1990. *Shaking A Leg* 387–92.
———. "The Box Does Furnish a Room." 1979. *Shaking A Leg* 409–12.
———. "The Company of Wolves." *The Bloody Chamber and Other Stories.* 1979. London: Vintage, 1995. 110–18.

62   *Re-visiting Angela Carter: Texts, Contexts, Intertexts*

————. "Femmes Fatales." 1978. *Shaking A Leg* 350–54.
————. "Godard: History: Passion." *Visions*. Large Door Productions Ltd. Channel 4. 11 May 1983. [Collected as "Jean-Luc Godard" in *Shaking A Leg* 380–81.]
————. "The Granada, Tooting." 1992. *Shaking a Leg* 400.
————. Introduction. *Wayward Girls and Wicked Women*. Ed. Angela Carter. London: Virago Press, 1986. ix–xii.
————. "Jean-Luc Godard." *Shaking A Leg* 380–81.
————. *Love*. 1971. Rev. ed. London: Vintage, 1987.
————. "Notes from the Front Line." *On Gender and Writing*. Ed. Michelene Wandor. London: Pandora Press, 1983. 69–77.
————. *The Sadeian Woman: An Exercise in Cultural History*. 1979. London: Virago, 2000.
————. *Several Perceptions*. 1968. London: Virago, 1995.
————. *Shadow Dance*. 1966. London: Virago, 1994.
————. *Shaking a Leg: Collected Journalism and Writings*. Intro. Joan Smith. Ed. Jenny Uglow. London: Chatto & Windus, 1997.
————. "Truly, It Felt Like Year One." *Very Heaven: Looking Back at the 1960s*. Ed. Sara Maitland. London: Virago, 1988. 209–16.
Clapp, Susannah. Introduction. *American Ghosts and Old World Wonders*. By Angela Carter. London: Chatto & Windus, 1993. ix–xi.
Clark, Robert. "Angela Carter's Desire Machine." *Women's Studies: An Interdisciplinary Journal* 14.2 (1987): 147–61.
Dixon, Wheeler Winston. *The Films of Jean-Luc Godard*. Albany: State University of New York Press, 1997.
Evans, Kim, dir. *Angela Carter's Curious Room*. Omnibus. BBC 1. 15 Sept. 1992.
Gamble, Sarah. *Angela Carter: A Literary Life*. London: Palgrave Macmillan, 2006.
Godard, Jean-Luc, dir. *Vivre sa vie*. Panthéon Distribution, 1962.
Godard on Godard: Critical Writings by Jean-Luc Godard. Trans. Tom Milne. Ed. Jean Narboni and Tom Milne. New York: Viking, 1972.
Haffenden, John. "Magical Mannerist." *The Literary Review* Nov. 1984: 34–38.
Harron, Mary. "'I'm a Socialist, Damn It! How Can You Expect Me to Be Interested in Fairies?'" *The Guardian* 25 Sept. 1984: 10.
Jordan, Elaine. "The Dangers of Angela Carter." *New Feminist Discourses: Critical Essays on Theories and Texts*. Ed. Isobel Armstrong. London: Routledge, 1992. 119–31.
Kreidl, John. *Jean-Luc Godard*. Boston: Twayne Publishers, 1980.
Milne, Tom. "Jean-Luc Godard and *Vivre sa vie*." *Jean-Luc Godard: Interviews*. Ed. David Sterritt. Jackson: University Press of Mississippi, 1998. 3–8.
O'Day, Marc. "'Mutability is Having a Field Day': The Sixties Aura of Angela Carter's Bristol Trilogy." *Flesh and the Mirror: Essays on the Art of Angela Carter*. Ed. Lorna Sage. London: Virago, 1994. 24–58.
Sage, Lorna. "The Savage Sideshow: A Profile of Angela Carter." *New Review* 4.39/40 (1977): 51–57.
————. *Women in the House of Fiction: Post-War Women Novelists*. London: Macmillan, 1992.
Sontag, Susan. "Godard's *Vivre sa Vie*." *Against Interpretation*. London: Eyre and Spottiswoode, 1967. 196–207.
Sterritt, David. *The Films of Jean-Luc Godard: Seeing the Invisible*. Cambridge: Cambridge University Press, 1999.

———. "Ideas, Not Plots, Inspire Jean-Luc Godard." *Jean-Luc Godard: Interviews.* Ed. David Sterrit. Jackson: University Press of Mississippi, 1998. 175–78.

Watts, Helen Cagney. "An Interview with Angela Carter." *Bête Noir* 8 Aug. 1985: 161–76.

Wood, James. "Bewitchment." *London Review of Books* 8 Dec. 1994: 20–21.

Youngblood, Gene. "Jean-Luc Godard: No Difference Between Life and Cinema." *Jean-Luc Godard: Interviews.* Ed. David Sterritt. Jackson: University Press of Mississippi, 1998. 9–49.

3
Albertine/a the Ambiguous: Angela Carter's Reconfiguration of Marcel Proust's Modernist Muse

Maggie Tonkin

Feminism has killed the Muse. According to Arlene Croce, the feminist argument against the Muse runs something like this:

> Like Nekrasov, who said, 'I'd rather be a citizen than a poet,' today's woman says, 'I'd rather be a citizen than a Muse.' We know the arguments: Muses are passive, therefore passé. Muses are a fantasy rooted in wrongheaded notions of biological 'essentialism' (i.e., femininity). Most degradingly, Muses do not choose to be Muses; they are chosen. Since the nineteen-seventies, modern feminism has based its appeal to women on the premise that all barriers to the dream of self-realization are political. Whatever can't be acquired for oneself, invoking one's civil rights, isn't worth having, and who wants to be a symbol anyway? The Muse is only a man speaking through a woman, not the woman herself. What male artists call Woman is a construct designed to keep real women in their place. (164)

For Croce, the feminist case against Musedom is in error because it is premised upon anti-essentialist ideas about gender with which she disagrees, and the feminist 'murder' of the Muse is a crime that threatens the very basis of artistic production – the relation of male artist to female Muse. Given her declared project of demythologizing cultural myths of gender, it is not surprising that Angela Carter also has something to say about the Muse. Nor is it surprising that her view is the antithesis of that of Croce. In a 1985 interview with Kerryn Goldsworthy, Carter was quite emphatic on the subject of this most explicitly gendered of literary tropes:

> I think the Muse is a pretty fatuous person. The concept of the Muse is – it's another magic Other, isn't it, another way of keeping women

out of the arena. There's a whole book by Robert Graves dedicated to the notion that poetic inspiration is female, which is why women don't have it. It's like haemophilia; they're the transmitters, you understand. But they don't suffer from it themselves. (11–12)

Carter's remarks arose in response to Goldsworthy's question about how the idea of the Muse fits in with her representation of two real Muses: Jeanne Duval, Baudelaire's much-maligned mistress, and Dorothy Wordsworth, sister of the poet. To date, discussions of the Muse in Carter's fiction have been almost exclusively concerned with her attempt to 'de-Muse' Duval, and to reinstate her as a real historical subject in "Black Venus" (see Matus and Munford) although her parodic restaging of Poe's maternal Muse in "The Cabinet of Edgar Allen Poe" has recently been examined (see Tonkin).

In this essay I wish to skew the discussion away from Carter's treatment of real Muses to that of an 'unreal' Muse; in fact, to a Muse so phantasmic as to have almost no reality status at all: the enigmatic Albertina in *The Infernal Desire Machines of Doctor Hoffman* (1972). It seems to me that Carter's representation of Albertina as an over-determined signifier of hyperbolic ambiguity can only be understood if *Infernal Desire Machines* is read as an ironic parody of that master text of sexual and gender ambiguity, Marcel Proust's *À la recherche du temps perdu* (1913–1927). Several critics have noted the allusions to the *Recherche* in Carter's novel but none have as yet elaborated upon them (see Peach 103 and Suleiman, "The Fate of the Surrealist Imagination" 104). However, a consideration of *Infernal Desire Machines* as a revisionary re-reading of the *Recherche* opens up multiple interpretative possibilities because, although Proust's monumental novel is but one of *Infernal Desire Machines*'s multitudinous intertexts, it is *the* most significant in respect to the politics of gender. After all, the *Recherche* is considered one of the foundational texts for gender and queer studies, given that, as Eve Kosofsky Sedgwick argues, it presents 'the definitive performance of the presiding incoherences of modern gay (and hence nongay) sexual specification and gay (and hence nongay) gender' (213). Just such a focused intertextual reading also offers a way to test the claim Carter repeatedly made that her fiction 'is very often a kind of literary criticism' (Haffenden 79). The question that interests me here is to which aspect of the *Recherche*'s representation of gender Carter addresses her fictional critique.

It may seem paradoxical to read *Infernal Desire Machines* as a critique of the gender politics of a secondary text, given that the dominant reading has eschewed issues of gender in favour of the terms set out by Carter herself, who described her novel as a 'dialectic between reason and passion, which it resolves in favour of reason' (Sage 34).[1] For the most part, issues of gender have been considered as secondary to the consideration of how this dialectic is played out. Ricarda Schmidt and David Punter, for example, have both asserted that this novel is not concerned with gender.[2] The few explicitly feminist analyses of the novel are divided over its representation of gender. Cornel Bonca argues that it is exclusively concerned with masculine power, masculine Eros and masculine civilization (61). Paulina Palmer concurs, contending that 'the point of view is chauvinistically male', and that the male narrator's representation of 'sexual atrocities' is an instance of Carter's vaunted 'male impersonation' (190).

A more sympathetic approach to Carter's project underpins the distinct yet complementary readings of Sally Robinson and Elisabeth Bronfen. Robinson draws on Teresa De Lauretis' analysis of Oedipus as an intrinsically gendered myth in which the female characters have no story of their own but function as 'figures or markers of positions – places and topoi – through which the hero and his story move to their destination and to accomplish meaning' (109). Robinson reads Desiderio as a paradigmatic Oedipal subject, and claims that Carter uses a masculine narrative voice to articulate male sexual fantasies of the domination and objectification of women in order to politicize desire. According to Robinson, Woman is everywhere in *Infernal Desire Machines* but women as fully human subjects are absent; Carter's text constructs subject positions for the female reader that enable her to adopt either a very uncomfortable identification with Desiderio, or an almost impossible identification with either the female 'sexual appliances' of the text or its elusive phantom, Albertina (104). The implicit corollary of Robinson's argument is that the text produces interpretative ambivalence, which provokes reflection about its representation of gender.

Bronfen similarly regards Carter's 'Woman' as a highly self-conscious inscription of women as the paradigmatic non-agents in narrative, arguing that *Infernal Desire Machines* is a

> feminist re-reading of the cultural cliché that Woman is man's symptom, the phantom of his desires. Her text performs the theme of the dead beloved as Muse, with the heroine functioning as a free floating signifier, absent in any actual sense from the text she inspires. (420)

But Bronfen takes the opposite tack from Robinson with her claim that Carter's deconstruction of the dead beloved as Muse does not *produce* interpretative ambivalence but actually *eliminates* it:

> In a tale about a man who finds his desires made explicit at the body of a beautiful woman, she renders the cliché explicit, attaches univocal explanatory meanings to gestures otherwise read as ambivalent. This elimination of ambivalence by virtue of explanatory commentary [...] assures that we interpret the events in the book as the critique she means her narrative to be. (421)

There is an obvious rejoinder to Bronfen's claim. If Carter's narrative commentary eliminates ambivalence and forces a univocal interpretation of her text, how can feminist objections to its gender politics, such as those of Bonca and Palmer, be explained?

Finding Albertine again

In contradistinction to Bronfen, I contend that *Infernal Desire Machines* does not eliminate interpretative ambivalence but rather strategically unleashes it in the service of a specific intertextual critique. I will argue here that Carter's spectacular restaging of the ambiguity of Proust's Muse Albertine – she of the 'famously floating gender' (Schmid 109n) – does not foreclose interpretative ambivalence but rather produces it. I will demonstrate that Carter's strategy is to unsettle representations of gender through ironic parody of its high canonical intertext, and the tradition of representation inscribed therein. There are a number of links between the two texts, such as the stylistic echo of Proust in Carter's long and heavily qualified sentences and extravagant use of metaphor. There are, in addition, a number of understated references to the *Recherche*: the hawthorns in the Mansions of Midnight section; the hallucination of naked *fin-de-siècle* women parading 'as if they had been in the Bois de Boulogne' (19); the narrator's recurring vision of a young woman being trampled by horses. However, the key to Carter's critique of Proust's representation of gender lies in her reinscription of the Muse–Narrator dyad. Not only is the name 'Albertina' an unmistakeable Proustian signifier, but the name of Carter's narrator, Desiderio – 'desire' in Italian – literalizes Proust's concept of the narrator's desire as the engine of narrative.

That Desiderio is a reinscription of Proust's narrator is made clear in the Introduction. Nothing could be more calculated to simultaneously reflect and deflate the whole Proustian enterprise than Desiderio's opening line: 'I remember everything. Yes. I remember everything perfectly' (11). The madeleine flies, figuratively at least, out of the window. But although at the outset Desiderio eschews the need for a trigger in order to conjure up the past, thus overturning the notion of involuntary memory that underpins Proust's narrative, this assurance is undercut on the first line of chapter one with the admission 'I cannot remember exactly how it began' (15). Desiderio's oscillation between remembering and forgetting is a calculated echo of the endless 'dialectic of remembering and forgetting' (Collier xxii) in Proust's text, as is his notion of memory and narrative as means to construct or resurrect the past, rather than as an unmediated record of the past. But his heroism, which distinguishes him from his Proustian model, is the paradoxical result of his disaffection and ambivalence, rather than of any heroic impulse:

> But, when I was a young man, I did not want to be a hero. [...] I became a hero only because I survived. I survived because I could not surrender to the flux of mirages. I could not merge and blend with them; I could not abnegate my reality and lose myself for ever as others did, blasted to non-being by the ferocious artillery of unreason. I was too sardonic. I was too disaffected. (11–12)

As Susan Rubin Suleiman argues, Desiderio is 'ambivalence itself, a perfect emblem of the Romantic, but also no doubt the postmodern subject' ("The Surrealist Imagination" 534). The Proustian conjunction of desire and ambivalence fuels his narrative. He is lured on by his desire for Albertina, yet his ambivalence renders him immune to the barrage of images unleashed by Doctor Hoffman, including, at the dénouement, the image of Albertina herself.

Carter's ironic and excessive refiguring of Proust's Albertine as Albertina is the vehicle for her investigation into how the cultural trope of the Muse-as-Beloved has been deployed in narrative. By definition, the Muse is the artist's Other; however, Albertine's otherness is accentuated to the point that it becomes her defining attribute. Despite (or perhaps because of) the thousands of words Proust expends upon her, Albertine is rendered as an inscrutable mystery whose contradictory thoughts and desires are, in the end, unreadable; a fragmented, constantly evolving being that the artist can never conclusively capture. Proust's rendition of his Muse as essentially unknowable reflects the Modernist drive to find new ways of depicting the unfathomability and complexity of character, which is exemplified by Virginia Woolf's call for modern writers to find new tools for presenting characters of 'unlimited capacity and infinite variety' ("Mr Bennett and Mrs Brown" 128), and for the development of an art worthy of this task. Woolf asks: 'Is it not the task of the novelist to convey this varying, this unknown and uncircumscribed spirit, whatever aberration and complexity it may convey?' ("Modern Fiction" 108). Proust's singularly Modernist invocation of the unlimited, infinite character as Muse is essential to Carter's purpose because its ambiguity allows her to explore and explode the contradictions inherent in the trope. To this end, Carter's Albertina literalizes and foregrounds the critical controversies engendered by Proust's Albertine.

Desiderio's description of Albertina in the Introduction as 'the heroine of my story, the daughter of the magician, the inexpressible woman to whose memory I dedicate these pages...the miraculous Albertina' (13) signals her status as Muse. That Albertina is the product of memory and desire, rather than an objective woman, is apparent from the first:

> if Albertina has become for me, now, such a woman as only memory and imagination could devise, well, such is always at least partially the case with the beloved. I see her as a series of marvellous shapes formed at random in the kaleidoscope of desire. (13)

This conception of Albertina as fluid, multiple, and fantasmically generated by the narrator's desire literalizes Proust's Modernist Muse. In order to trace how Carter refigures Albertine as Albertina, it is necessary not only to recapitulate her role in Proust's text, but also to give an outline of the critical tradition that has read the *Recherche* as a *roman à clef*, and has sought the model for Albertine in Proust's personal history. As we shall see, Carter's parody exploits both the *Recherche* itself and the psychobiographical tradition that effectively strips the ambiguity from its Muse by reading the novel reductively as a mirror of its author's life: in other words, as mimesis.

Albertine makes her first appearance in the *Recherche* on the beach at the seaside resort of Balbec where the narrator is holidaying, but their fledgling romance is aborted when she refuses his kiss. At an unspecified later date, it is re-established in Paris, and continues during a further visit to Balbec. However, the narrator's feelings towards Albertine are perpetually fluctuating, until he begins to suspect her of secret lesbianism, which engenders such jealousy that he takes her back to Paris where he keeps her in his house as a virtual prisoner. Here begins the economy of spying and lying that henceforth characterizes their relationship. The narrator's obsessive surveillance of Albertine and his paranoid attempts to control her every movement are thwarted by what he interprets as her innate deceit. His feelings for Albertine now oscillate between boredom and the wish to be rid of her, and desire intensified by jealousy. Finally, although he has threatened to break with her several times, the narrator is devastated when Albertine takes the initiative by fleeing his house. His attempts to induce her to return are cut short by the news that she has been killed in a horse-riding accident. But far from ending his torments, Albertine's death triggers a paroxysm of grief, guilt and unremitting self-analysis on the part of the narrator. Finally, the passage of time enables him, if not to forget Albertine, then at least to remember her without anguish.

   This bare plot summary does little to suggest what qualifies Albertine to be called Muse; nor does it convey how Proust uses the figure of Albertine to destabilize the realist conception of character and advance a thoroughly Modernist notion of the other as plural, mutable and unknowable. As J.E. Rivers says:

> Proust uses Albertine to redefine conventional conceptions of literary character. Etymologically the word 'character' denotes an impress, a distinctive mark, a well-defined outline. That is what it meant to Theophrastus in his *Characters,* and this is what it has traditionally meant in literature. Proust dismisses this concept and shows that except on the most superficial levels of understanding there is no well-defined outline for human identity. Proust depicts the unlimited, the limitless personality. (249)

Whilst Proustians concur with Rivers' view of Albertine as an exemplary Modernist character, she is not usually considered in terms of the Muse. Proust himself, towards the end of *Finding Time Again,* identifies time and involuntary memory as the two Muses of his work. However, as Jean-Yves Tadié points out, with the exception of the narrator, Albertine is the most important single character in the *Recherche.* She is, he argues, '[t]he woman in *À la recherche du temps perdu,* since the name of Albertine is mentioned in it 2360 times [...] No other heroine comes close to matching this figure, nor does any hero; only the narrator intervenes more frequently' (606; emphasis in original).

Whilst the narrator never calls Albertine 'Muse', he nonetheless adumbrates her narrative function in the terms of this trope when he signals the crucial role she plays in the generation of his text:

> it was actually quite clear that the pages I would write were some-thing that Albertine, especially the Albertine of those days, would not have understood. That is precisely why (and this is a recommen-dation not to live in too intellectual an atmosphere), because she was so different to me, that she had fertilized me through grief, and even at the beginning through the sheer effort of imagining something different from oneself. If she had been capable of understanding these pages then, for that very reason, she would not have inspired them. (*Finding Time Again* 225)

As is always the case with the Muse, Albertine inspires the text, but she is not commensurate with it. It always exceeds her: she is the germ, the seed, the fructifying force that 'fertilizes' the artist, in this case, 'through grief', by virtue of her sexual difference and the mystery of her desires. This narrative focus on the enigma of female desire has led critics such as Lisa Appignanesi to consider Albertine as a manifestation of the fem-inine archetype, the so-called 'Eternal Feminine' (157–215). But the problem with the archetypal approach is that in its exclusive concern with the universal, it fails to attend to the particular, and so fails to explicate what is novel about Proust's invocation of the Muse.

This novelty resides in part in the deconstructive analysis to which the Muse–narrator relation is subjected. The narrator's self-conscious-ness about his invocation of the Beloved, and subsequent realization that the unhappiness she caused him has 'fertilized' his book, is a kind of self-reflexive meta-commentary on the origin of the text, and an alle-gory of the narrative function served by the Muse in the male-authored literary canon. In the figure of Albertine, Proust simultaneously inscribes and deconstructs the trope of the Muse, and this simultaneous inscription/deconstruction is the key to Carter's parody. For instance, Proust bodies Albertine forth as a Muse-as-Beloved in the Petrarchan sense, then proceeds to lay bare the workings of this trope. Just as Petrarch never gives a coherent picture of Laura, but represents her synecdochically, the narrator fixates on certain parts of Albertine's body to the exclusion of the rest. Her face, in particular, is the hub of a series of associations that generate reverie and self-reflection within the artist, and is hence pivotal to the germination of his book:

Of course, it is with that face, as I had seen it for the first time by the sea, that I associated certain things which I should no doubt be writing about. In a sense, I was right to associate them with her, because if I had not walked along the sea-front that day, if I had not met her, all these ideas would not have been developed (unless they had been developed by another woman). (*Finding Time Again* 225)

However, the synecdochical reinscription of the Muse-as-Beloved is immediately undercut by self-conscious narrative commentary. Not only does the narrator subvert the notion that the Muse is a singular, incomparable being by hinting that the choice of the Beloved is arbitrary, but also, more importantly, he claims her as an aspect of his own consciousness: 'I was also wrong, though, because this generative pleasure which we try retrospectively to situate in a beautiful feminine face comes from our own senses' (ibid.).

Proust destabilizes the idea that the face, or the fragmented female body, generates reflection with the repeated assertion that Albertine's face, and indeed Albertine *in toto*, is a projection. The Beloved, he claims, is 'a product of our temperament, an inverted image or projection, a negative, of our sensitivity' (*In the Shadow* 471–72). The artist or narrator as desiring subject produces his ideal object, and this object functions as a mirror in which his desires are refracted. The individual woman is forced to simulate 'Woman':

It is the wicked deception of love that it begins by making us dwell not upon a woman in the outside world but upon a doll inside our head, the only woman who is always available in fact, the only one we shall ever possess, whom the arbitrary nature of memory, almost as absolute as that of the imagination, may have made as different from the real woman as the real Balbec had been from the Balbec I imagined; a dummy creation which little by little, to our own detriment, we shall force the real woman to resemble. (*The Guermantes Way* 368)

Here Proust inverts the convention that the Muse inspires the artist's reverie, which ultimately triggers the production of art, with the assertion that the artist's reverie produces the Muse. The Muse is a 'dummy creation'. The 'generative pleasure' essential to both romantic love and the production of art is dependent upon the woman successfully mimicking the 'doll' inside the artist's head.

The ontological status of the Muse is further destabilized by Proust's invocation of Albertine as both multiple and in flux. Even physically, she is always in process, never a finite product, as is evidenced by the narrator's claim: 'I was always surprised when I caught sight of her; she changed so much from day to day' (*The Guermantes Way* 350). From her first appearance in the text, his image of a singular Albertine gives way to a vertiginous proliferation of Albertines:

> It was almost certain that Albertine and the girl going to her friend's house were one and the same. And yet [...] if I wind in the clew of my memories of her, I can follow the same identity from one to the other, find my way through the labyrinth and come back always to the same person, on the other hand if I try to find my way back to the girl I passed when I was with my grandmother, I lose my way. (*In the Shadow* 425)

This protean being is a fugitive, an *être de fuite*, in the figurative sense in that in her flux and evolution she eludes the narrator's knowledge and definition. But she is also a literal fugitive, a being in constant motion, in flight, always associated with modes of transport: the bicycle, the automobile, the aeroplane, and finally, fatally, the horse. The association of Albertine with speed and motion suggests that she is not simply the ground or topoi of the narrator's quest, but that she herself is a questing subject, albeit one whose quest remains obscure.

The enigma of Albertine's quest is, of course, bound up with the enigma of her desires. And her desires are enigmatic precisely because *she* does not articulate them: they are the products of the narrator's discourse, of *his* imagination, of *his* desire. He imagines her desires as sexually transgressive because, although Albertine is outwardly compliant with his normative project of heterosexual monogamy, he suspects that she harkens for more exotic pleasures. Proust uses the Biblical term 'Gomorrah' to encompass the polymorphously perverse desires and pleasures that the narrator believes Albertine and her female friends enjoy, and attributes his exclusion from Gomorrah, his inability to experience or know Albertine's pleasures, to sexual difference: 'the rival was not of my own kind, their weapons were different, I could not give battle on the same terrain, or afford Albertine the same pleasures, or even conceive of them accurately' (*Sodom and Gomorrah* 512). However, if we reframe Albertine's enigma within the terms of the Muse-as-Beloved trope, it is clear that her enigmatic quality is as much a structuring principle of the trope as a product of sexual difference per se. The inability of the Poet to 'know' the Beloved/Woman/Muse in any definitive sense is built into the structure of the Poet–Muse dyad, for whilst the masculine narrating subject has direct access to discourse, the Muse occupies the silent position of the object. He enunciates; she is enunciated. She cannot articulate her desire; in effect, because 'she' is merely the product of his discourse, 'she' does not exist and consequently *has* no desire, other than that imagined and depicted by the masculine artist.

Albertine, then, is an oxymoronic Muse. Caught between the iteration and the deconstruction of the trope, she both exceeds, and is ultimately constrained by, its conventions. She is simultaneously desiring, questing subject and silent object: the topos of the narrator's quest, in Oedipal terms. On the one hand, the overarching paradox of Proust's invocation of the Muse trope is that in the end it is Albertine's refusal to mirror the narrator's desire, to mimic the 'doll' inside his head, and to act out the codes of the 'dummy creation' of the Muse-as-Beloved, that instates her as the Muse of the *Recherche*. For the corollary of Albertine's purportedly myriad desires is that she is irreducible to 'Woman', or the narrator's ideal erotic object. The realization that Albertine is not only an object, but also a subject of desire generates the narrator's quest to know her desires and hence, in part, his narrative. On the other hand, despite the ironic turn Proust brings to bear on his Muse, she is ultimately subsumed to the all-consuming project of the narrating 'I', which is to explore the experience of the narrating, masculine self to its farthest reaches. The aberrant subjectivity of the Muse becomes, in the end, the instrument of the narrator's self-knowledge and the vehicle for his meditation on the ultimate unknowability of the Beloved. There is a degree of ironic self-consciousness in the narrator's claim that 'one is forced to be thankful that famous authors have been kept at a distance and betrayed by women when their humiliations and sufferings have been, if not the actual goad to their genius, then at least the subject matter of their writings' (*The Guermantes Way* 466). Seen in this light, Albertine's death is the fortuitous, indeed the essential, precondition for the narrator's experience of grief, and his subsequent narrativization of that experience. It is the means whereby Albertine, the oxymoronic Muse-as-Beloved, is recuperated as a fully-fledged Muse-as-Dead-Beloved.

Garçon or garçonne?

If we are to understand how Carter pushes Proust's paradoxical embodiment of the Modernist Muse to the limits of its coherence, we must turn from his text to the history of its reception; for Carter's Albertina draws her critical signification not only from Albertine, the figure *in* the text, but also from how Albertine has been figured *extra-textually*. As we shall see, critics have drawn on biographical material to explain the singularity with which Proust bodies forth the figure of Woman. Carter's re-reading of Proust engages with the critical traditions surrounding his text as much as the text itself. In this respect, *Infernal Desire Machines* functions as a kind of meta-commentary on both its intertext and the critical traditions that have determined that intertext's reception. A brief survey of the critical reception given to Proust's Albertine reveals that, in their recourse to the biographical, critics have disambiguated his Muse and fixed her as the Dead-Beloved in his closet.

'Proust [has] made of an Albert an Albertine' (Crevel 65). The words of the surrealist René Crevel, written in 1925, foreshadow what was to become an enduring concern of Proustian scholarship: the enigmatic sex of Albertine. This long-standing fascination with Albertine's sex is inextricable from Proust's posthumous outing as a homosexual. As with Poe, assumptions about Proust's sexuality have frequently determined how his text is read. The rumour that Proust was a denizen of Sodom, which began to circulate after the publication of *Sodome et Gomorrhe I* in 1921, soon entered the public domain. Despite Proust's repeated avowals that his novel was not a *roman à clef*, those determined to read it as such sought the model for Albertine in his personal history. Robert Vigneron was the first to publicly assert that Albertine was modelled on Proust's chauffeur-secretary, Alfred Agostinelli (*passim.*). Vigneron's claim underpins one of the most influential essays in Proust criticism, Justin O'Brien's "Albertine the Ambiguous: Notes on Proust's Transposition of Sexes," published in 1949. O'Brien's so-called 'transposition theory' also draws sustenance from the conversations with Proust recounted in André Gide's *Journals*, in which Proust allegedly confessed to transposing some of the masculine objects of desire in his novel into the feminine sex (265–67). O'Brien asserts that Proust's narrator is literally Proust got up in heterosexual drag: 'By creating a near-replica of himself as center and narrator of the action and endowing him with heterosexual characteristics, Proust had simply to transpose his own recollections *à l'ombre des jeunes filles*' (937). O'Brien claims that Proust transposed the sex, not just of Albertine, but of many of the other 'ambiguous' female characters in the *Recherche*. According to the logic of his argument, *les jeunes filles en fleurs*, those barely differentiated young girls who become the objects of the narrator's desires at Balbec, are literally a bunch of pansies.

Despite the paucity of textual evidence to support the transposition theory, it has nevertheless spawned two antithetical interpretations of the *Recherche*. The homophobic interpretation exemplified by O'Brien claims that the putative transposition of the sexes, along with the introduction of homosexuality as a major theme, undermines the *Recherche*'s claim to universality. On the other hand, gay-affirmative critics such as Edmund White regard what has come to be known as the 'Albertine strategy' as the necessary disguise of a gay writer in a homophobic culture, and the canny circumvention of the interdiction of the expression of homosexual desire (22–23; see also Russell 129). In typical Proustian metafictional fashion, the *Recherche* anticipates, and indeed, sanctions, this gay-positive reading: '[t]he writer must not take offence when inverts give his heroines masculine faces. This mildly deviant behaviour is the only means by which the invert can proceed to give full general significance to what he is reading' (*Finding time Again* 219). But, as Elisabeth Ladenson points out, regardless of whether it is advocated by homophobes or homophiles, or even by Proust himself, the transposition theory effaces arguably the 'queerest aspect' of the *Recherche*, which is 'the narrator's preoccupation with lesbianism' (17). Furthermore, as Rivers argues, the transposition theory is predicated on a fundamental misrecognition, in that it fails to recognize that Albertine's resistance to the dominant gender codes of the period mark her not as a 'boy-in-drag', but as a representation of the New Woman, as a *garçonne* rather than a *garçon* (244). Finally, as I stated previously, O'Brien's theory paradoxically confounds its own title of 'Albertine the Ambiguous' by *disambiguating* Albertine.

Setting fire to the object: desire, death and the production of text

Carter's inferential walk through lost time flamboyantly re-ambiguates Proust's Muse. Not only does *Infernal Desire Machines* parody the critical tradition that reads Albertine as Albert, but it also reveals the contradictions inherent in Proust's invocation of the oxymoronic Muse. Carter's strategy is one of excess, inversion and literalization, which works by making Albertina excessively mobile, dramatically enigmatic, and, finally, explosively dead. When read through the prism of the Muse trope, Carter's revisionary re-reading of the *Recherche*, and the transposition theory it has inspired, demonstrates that even when the sex of the Muse is arguably male, her gender is inherently feminine. Carter reminds us that the trope is a convention of representation, and that according to its grammar, the gender of the artist and the Muse is determined, not by the respective sex of each actant, but by how they are positioned by the politics of enunciation. According to the dominant patriarchal construction of gender, the Muse, as the silent product of another's discourse, occupies an inherently feminized position.

Infernal Desire Machines literalizes the critical tug-of-war over Albertine's sex by bodying Albertina forth as fantastically mutable: as variously inanimate, bestial, and human; and as serially androgynous, masculine and feminine. She first appears as a persistent hallucination of a transparent woman with a heart of flames; then as the Black Swan in Desiderio's dreams; then as the androgynous Ambassador of her Father, Doctor Hoffman. Later, Desiderio catches a glimpse of her in the eyes of Mary Anne, the beautiful somnambulist; in the decapitated head in the set of samples hiked around by the travelling showman; and in the face of Nao-Kurai, the Amerindian river man who saves his life after his escape from the Determination police. Still later, Albertina appears in the guise of the masked Madam of the House of Anonymity and travels under the disguise of the Count's much-abused boy valet Lafleur before, finally, shedding her disguises. Even when she is not disguised, Albertina is not static but continues to evolve from the relatively helpless victim of the centaurs to the authoritative and briskly efficient Generalissimo of her father's army.

This excessively mobile and protean re-figuring of Albertine as Albertina restores the erotics of ambiguity to the Muse, in direct retort to the transposition theorists. Nowhere is this more evident than in Albertina's manifestation as the Ambassador, whose indeterminate sex is extravagantly oversignified. Eyes painted with 'thick bands of solid gold cosmetic,' nails 'enamelled dark crimson' to match those on his feet encased in 'gold thongs', and garbed in 'flared trousers of purple suede' with 'several ropes of pearl for a belt around his waist', the Ambassador is not merely sexually ambiguous, no simple androgyne, but rather a hyper-ambiguous hybrid of human, phantom, and beast who seems to 'move in soft coils' and whose gestures are 'instinct with a self-conscious but extraordinary reptilian liquidity' (32). In Desiderio's eyes, the Ambassador's desirability is inextricable from both his ontological indeterminacy and the sense of threat he exudes:

> I think he was the most beautiful human being I have ever seen – considered, that is, solely as an object, a construction of flesh, skin bone and fabric, and yet, for all his ambiguous sophistication,

indeed, perhaps in its very nature, he hinted at a savagery which had been cunningly tailored to suit the drawing room, though it had been in no way diminished. He was a manicured leopard patently in complicity with chaos.

[...]Certainly I had never seen a phantom who looked at that moment more shimmeringly unreal than the Ambassador, nor one who seemed to throb with more erotic promise. (32, 36)

The throbbing is amplified when Desiderio examines the exquisite handkerchief left behind by the Ambassador and finds the name 'Albertina,' previously seen only in his dreams, embroidered upon it. Henceforth 'Albertina' functions as a fabulous signifier of desire which

seemed to shelter three magic entities, the glass woman, the black swan and the ambassador. The name was a clue which pointed to a living being beneath the conjuring tricks, for such tricks imply the presence of a conjurer. I was nourishing an ambition – to rip away that ruffled shirt and find out whether the breasts of an authentic woman swelled beneath it; and if around her neck was a gold collar with the name ALBERTINA engraved upon it. (40)

The metaphor of drag parodically inverts the critical tradition that seeks to rip open Albertine's bodice to reveal the flat chest of Proust's rent-boy. This inversion is reiterated when Albertina, disguised as the Count's valet Lafleur, is stripped by the soldiers of the Cannibal Chief, and reveals not the 'lean torso of a boy but the gleaming curvilinear magnificence of a golden woman' (164). But whilst it highlights the reductive effect of the transposition theory, which disambiguates Proust's Muse by seeking the singular model for Albertine in Proust's sexual history, the substitution of a 'girl-in-drag' for a 'boy-in-drag' is not in itself reductive because it is never definitive or final but is always undercut by Albertina's next manifestation.

When each disguise is stripped away, what is revealed is not the 'authentic' being within but simply the next layer of an onion-like enigma. The impenetrability of the enigmatic Muse is foreshadowed in the hallucination of Albertine as the glass woman: despite her 'quite transparent flesh' which reveals the 'exquisite filigree of her skeleton' and the 'knot of flames' that stands in place of her heart (25), Desiderio recognizes that she is a manifestation of a 'language of signs which utterly bemused me because I could not read them' (25). Despite her transparency, the Muse remains illegible, always eluding the narrator's knowledge. However, *Infernal Desire Machines*'s parody is directed not only at Proust's critics but also at the *Recherche* itself. Clearly, Albertina's seemingly limitless disguises mimic Proust's vertiginously proliferating Muse that is not *one*. At the same time, the notion that there is an 'authentic woman' lurking behind her various embodiments parodies Proust's narrator's fixed belief that there is an authentic truth to be uncovered about Albertine's sexuality.

This relentless parody of the desire to penetrate the enigma of the Muse is but one aspect of the novel's treatment of the theme of desire. Albertina's cry – 'Oh Desiderio! never underestimate the power of that desire for which you are named!' (167) – gives voice to the notion of desire as an all-pervasive and overwhelming force which lies at the heart of this text. Desire is everywhere in the novel: from the title to the name Desiderio; the peep-show proprietor's exhortations to 'objectify your desires' (110); the Acrobats of Desire; the representation of the Count as a terrorist of desire; Doctor Hoffman's Cogito, 'I DESIRE THEREFORE I EXIST' (211); and so forth. Desire is the motor of Desiderio's quest, and the desire to liberate desire is the driving force behind the Doctor's project, although he seems to Desiderio to be, paradoxically, 'a man without desires' (211).

The debt to Proust is evident not just in this thematization of desire, but also in the deployment of his narrative dynamics of desire to structure the novel. Carter foregrounds and hyperbolically literalizes the central conceit of the Proustian iteration of the Muse: the notion that she is the product of the subject's desire. Her whole text hinges on the 'gnomic utterance' of the peep-show proprietor: 'Objectify your desires' (110). Both Desiderio's quest and Doctor Hoffman's project are structured by this injunction, as Desiderio proleptically informs us in his Introduction:

> Rather, from beyond the grave, her father has gained a tactical victory over me and forced on me at least the apprehension of an alternate world in which all the objects are the emanations of a single desire. And my desire is, to see Albertina again before I die.
>
> But, at the game of metaphysical chess we played, I took away her father's queen and mated us both for though I am utterly consumed with this desire, it is as impotent as it is desperate. My desire can never be objectified, and who should know better than I? (13–14)

Of course, his lament notwithstanding, prior to her murder at his hands and for the greater part of the narrative, Albertina *is* the objectification of Desiderio's desires. At the dénouement she forestalls Desiderio's sexual advances with the revelation: 'You have never yet made love to me because, all the time you have known me, I've been maintained in my various disguises only by the power of your desire' (204). Her revelation is all of a piece with her father's theory that, since the set of samples had been lost or destroyed in the earthquake, 'all the subjects and objects we had encountered in the loose grammar of Nebulous time were derived from a similar source – my desires; or hers; or the Count's, for he had lived on closer terms with his own unconscious than we' (186). Doctor Hoffman's theory that the desires of the subject can affect concrete changes on the body of the object is a fantastic, hyperbolic rendering of Proust's axiom that the lover sees only what he desires to see in the beloved, that his particular Muse is a projection of his particular temperament.

Proust's solipsistic notion of the subject–object relation is given more concrete expression in Exhibit Two in the peep-show proprietor's set of samples, 'THE ETERNAL VISTAS OF LOVE', which reflects the viewer's eyes back to himself in 'a model of eternal regression' (45). This ironically titled pictorial depiction of the self-regarding subject sets up a model of love, or rather desire, as *mise en abyme* – eternal, narcissistic regression in lieu of reciprocity. The 'Eternal Vista of Love' is ironically titled for the subject sees not the other but a mirror in which the subject and his desires are endlessly refracted. Love is imaged here as displaced narcissism. This model of desire as eternal, narcissistic regression is played out in the text through the notion of the double. The ludicrously narcissistic Count and his nemesis the Black Pimp/Cannibal King (surely an echo of Proust's Baron Charlus and his flagellator) represent this notion *in extremis*. But the notion of the double is also played out in the affirmative, romantic pairing of Desiderio and Albertina. Their physical likeness is repeatedly stressed, and, after dressing himself in Hoffman's castle, Desiderio looks in the mirror and observes: '[n]ow I was entirely Albertina in the male aspect. That is why I know I was beautiful when I was a young man. Because I know I looked like Albertina' (199). Albertina, he claims, is his perfect object 'my Platonic other, my necessary extinction, my dream made flesh' (215). Albertina reframes their doubling in terms of the mirror: '[o]urs is a supreme encounter, Desiderio. We are two such disseminating mirrors' (202).

Carter mimics Proust in sundering this narcissistic economy through the figure of the aberrant, desiring Muse. In the first five chapters, Albertina is a discontinuous, mutating phantom, 'a ghost born of nothing but my longing' (140) in Desiderio's words, and as such she functions as the mirror of *his* desire. But when she sheds her disguise and assumes ontological solidity as Hoffman's daughter Albertina, Desiderio – and, by implication, the reader – is confronted with the problem of interpreting her desire. This problem emerges in the incident of Albertina's rape by the centaurs. Although Desiderio, under the influence of the peep-show proprietor's injunction 'Objectify your desires!', is convinced that he is 'somehow, all unknowing, the instigator of this horror' (180), Albertina attributes her torments to her own unconscious desire, 'for she was convinced that even though every male in the village had obtained carnal knowledge of her, the beasts were still only emanations of her own desires, dredged up and objectively reified from the dark abysses of the unconscious' (186). Desiderio tries to refute Albertina's belief in the omnipotence of her desire, but he is silenced by the appearance of the rescuing helicopter at the very moment the pair are about to be tattooed by the centaurs, simultaneous with the spontaneous combustion of the centaurs' sacred-horse tree. The latter event seems to bear out the quotation from de Sade written in Albertina's hand, which Desiderio had found earlier in his coat pocket: 'My passions, concentrated on a single point, resemble the rays of a sun assembled by a magnifying glass; they immediately set fire to whatever object they find in their way' (97).

But Albertina's desire becomes problematic to Desiderio, not when it reveals its propensity for orgiastic masochism, but when it fails to mirror his own. After their escape from the centaurs, when Albertina puts 'away all her romanticism' (193) and assumes the role of her father's Generalissimo, Desiderio recoils. For the first time, he feels an 'inexplicable indifference to her' (193). Her primary desire, he now realizes, is to be her father's accomplice. His endlessly deferred union with her is to be harnessed to her father's grand project of liberating desire; he discovers that the 'grotesque dénouement' of their 'great passion' (216) is not to be sexual liberation but sexual slavery in Doctor Hoffman's love pens. Her desire will indeed set fire to its object; it is to be the instrument of not only her father's megalomaniacal project, but also of Desiderio's annihilation as an autonomous subject. This double-edged, instrumental desire is the crux of Albertina's ambiguity, for she represents both the promise of ecstasy and the threat of the annihilation of the narrating subject.

Even before he learns of his projected fate in the love pen, Desiderio has come to the realization that sex with Albertina will never fulfil his overblown expectations: 'as I pared my dessert persimmon with the silver knife provided, I was already wondering whether the fleshly possession of Albertina would not be the greatest disillusionment of all' (201).

Had Desiderio consented to be shackled to Albertina in the love pen till he expires (surely an analogy for marriage, if ever there was one), he could not, of course, have penned the narrative. Byron, it might be remembered, said something similar in *Don Juan* (1821), when he acidly observed: 'Think you, if Laura had been Petrarch's wife/He would have written sonnets all his life?' (111.8.63–64). Desire might be the engine of narrative, as critics such as Peter Brooks claim (*passim*), but consummated desire, Carter hints, is the death of it. Here Carter satirizes Robert Graves' thesis that '[a] poet cannot continue to be a poet if he feels that he has made a permanent conquest of the Muse, that she is always his for the asking' (444). The poet stops being a poet, he argues, when he loses his sense of the Muse, the 'White Goddess':

> the woman whom he took to be a Muse, or who was a Muse, turns into a domestic woman and would have him turn similarly into a domesticated man. Loyalty prevents him parting company with her, especially if she is the mother of his children and is proud to be reckoned a good housewife; and as the Muse fades out, so does the poet. [...] The White Goddess is anti-domestic, she is the perpetual 'other woman', and her part is difficult indeed for a woman of sensibility to play for more than a few years, because the temptation to commit suicide in simple domesticity lurks in every maenad's and Muse's heart. (449)

Desiderio's murder of his Muse not only forestalls on the inevitable disappointment of consummation, but also saves him from 'domestic suicide' and enables his transformation into hero and narrator.

Albertina's murder literalizes and brings to the reader's realization the fate of the Muse in Proust's *Recherche*. Whereas Albertine dies 'offstage' by a narrative sleight-of-hand, so that the narrator, although grief-stricken and remorseful, bears no direct responsibility for her death, Carter has her narrator literally stick the knife in. *Infernal Desire Machines* thus parodically anatomizes the transformation of the Muse-as-Beloved into the Muse-as-*Dead*-Beloved in Proust's text, a transformation that is the precondition both for his narrator's career in melancholia, and for the realization of his vocation of writer. Killing off the Muse enables the narrative turn to elegy. *Infernal Desire Machines*'s introductory dedication – 'I, Desiderio, dedicate all my memories to Albertina Hoffman with my insatiable tears' (14) – ironically foregrounds the elegiac subtext to the final volumes of Proust's novel. Furthermore, Carter's move to make the narrator own his murder of the Muse demystifies the ostensible separation between the masculine narrator and the masculine author of the

Recherche. By fusing the author and the narrator in the figure of Desiderio, Carter shows that the death of the Muse is a plot device that serves as the precondition to narrative.

Carter's revisioning of the *Recherche* makes obvious the analogous function of the Muse's death in Proust's text, for the death of Albertine reinstates the Petrarchan dyad of male desiring subject and unattainable female object in which distance is the *sine qua non* of textual production. Killing the Muse simultaneously eradicates the threat of domesticity and creates the distance necessary for writing. Albertine's narrative function tends to disappear in the sheer voluminousness of the *Recherche*; but through its critical restaging *Infernal Desire Machines* exposes the paradoxical role she plays as Muse: essential to the generation of the text, yet ultimately redundant to the vocation of the writer. Thus Carter's revision might well be said to parodically reprise Byron: 'Think you, if Albertine had been Marcel's wife/He would have written the *Recherche* all his life?'

Infernal Desire Machines, then, is a critical fiction that addresses itself not only to a specific intertext, but also more broadly to the dialectic of absence and presence that underpins the trope of the Muse-as-(Dead)-Beloved as it has been deployed in the male-authored literary canon. Carter's text restages the singularly Modernist aspects of Proust's Muse – that is to say, her mutability and the notion that she is the product of the narrator's desire – and simultaneously, through its rendition of Albertina as hyperbolically ambiguous, literalizes the critical dispute over Albertine's sex advanced by transposition theorists. But this fantastical refiguring of Albertine's mutability and ambiguity is ironic and strategic, for, as Albertina's murder by the narrator illustrates, the politics of enunciation determine that she occupies a fixed position in relation to discourse, which transposition theory only serves to obfuscate. For all her ambiguity, the Modernist Muse is reined in at the end by what we might term her tropological grammar; she is first enunciated and then murdered by the narrator in the service of narrative. Because *Infernal Desire Machines* offers no other point of identification other than with Desiderio, the reader is forced into an uncomfortable complicity with the murderous project that subsumes the Muse to the vocation of the writer and the production of the text. I contend that such a discomforting reading position generates ambivalence, and it is this ambivalence, rather than Carter's explicit narrative commentary, as Bronfen suggests, which provokes an examination of the novel's restaging of the gender politics of the Muse–Poet dyad. One of the singular achievements of Carter's masterful intertextual play here is her demonstration that it is not, after all, feminism that killed the Muse, as Croce claims, but, rather, those very writers who apostrophize her, eulogize her, and feed off her corpse.

Notes

1. Carter's characterization of the novel is reflected in most critical readings of the text. For instance, Cornel Bonca writes that the mythic conflict at the heart of the text is 'as old as the hills – Dionysus vs. Apollo, Orc vs. Urizen, Eros vs. Civilization' (57), while Andrzej Gasiorek reads the novel as a sustained critique of Plato's *The Republic* (128–29). Finally, Elaine Jordan describes the novel as one in which 'Carter traces the history of reason and desire in literary and philosophic representation' (34).
2. Both Schmidt and Punter consider the novel as explicitly intervening in the political debates about desire and liberation that were current in the 1960s, specifically the theories of Wilhelm Reich and Herbert Marcuse, which ignored the issue of gender (see Schmidt 56–57 and Punter 209–11).

Works cited

Appignanesi, Lisa. *Femininity and the Creative Imagination: A Study of Henry James, Robert Musil and Marcel Proust*. London: Vision, 1973.

Bonca, Cornel. "In Despair at the Old Adams: Angela Carter's *The Infernal Desire Machines of Doctor Hoffman*." *The Review of Contemporary Fiction* 14.3 (1994): 56–62.

Bronfen, Elisabeth. *Over Her Dead Body: Death, Femininity and the Aesthetic*. New York: Routledge, 1992.

Brooks, Peter. *Reading for the Plot: Design and Intention in Narrative*. Cambridge, MA: Harvard University Press, 1984.

Byron, Lord. *Don Juan*. 1821. *The Complete Poetical Works*. Ed. Jerome J. McGann. Vol. 5. Oxford: Clarendon Press, 1986.

Carter, Angela. *The Infernal Desire Machines of Doctor Hoffman*. 1972. Harmondsworth: Penguin, 1982.

Collier, Peter. Translator's Introduction. *The Fugitive*. Trans. Peter Collier. London: Allen Lane, 2002. Vol. 5 of *In Search of Lost Time*. By Marcel Proust. Ed. Christopher Prendergast. xviii–xxv.

Crevel, René. *Mon corps et Moi*. Paris: Pauvert, 1925.

Croce, Arlene. "Is the Muse Dead?" *New Yorker* 26 Feb.– 4 Mar. 1996: 164–69.

De Lauretis, Teresa. "Desire in Narrative." *Alice Doesn't: Feminism, Semiotics, Cinema*. Bloomington: Indian University Press, 1984. 103–57.

Gasiorek, Andrzej. *Post-War British Fiction: Realism and After*. London: Edward Arnold, 1995.

Gide, André. *The Journals of André Gide: Vol. 11: 1914–1927*. Trans. Justin O'Brien. London: Secker & Warburg, 1948.

Goldsworthy, Kerryn. "Angela Carter." *Meanjin* 44.1 (1985): 4–13.

Graves, Robert. *The White Goddess*. New York: Octagon, 1972.

Haffenden, John. "Angela Carter." *Novelists in Interview*. London: Methuen, 1985. 76–96.

Jordan, Elaine. "Enthralment: Angela Carter's Speculative Fictions." *Plotting Change: Contemporary Women's Fiction*. Ed. Linda Anderson. London: Edward Arnold, 1990. 19–40.

Ladenson, Elisabeth. *Proust's Lesbianism*. Ithaca: Cornell University Press, 1999.

Matus, Jill. "Blonde, Black and Hottentot Venus: Context and Critique in Angela Carter's 'Black Venus'." *Studies in Short Fiction* 28 (1991): 467–76.

Munford, Rebecca. "Re-presenting Charles Baudelaire/Re-presencing Jeanne Duval: Transformations of the Muse in Angela Carter's 'Black Venus'." *Forum for Modern Language Studies* 40.1 (2004): 1–13.

O'Brien, Justin. "Albertine the Ambiguous: Notes on Proust's Transposition of Sexes." *PMLA* 64.5 (1949): 933–52.

Palmer, Paulina. "From 'Coded Mannequin' to Bird Woman: Angela Carter's Magic Flight." *Women Reading Women's Writing*. Ed. Sue Roe. Brighton: Harvester, 1987. 179–205.

Peach, Linden. *Angela Carter*. Basingstoke: Macmillan, 1998.

Proust, Marcel. *Finding Time Again*. 1927. Trans. Ian Patterson. London: Allen Lane, 2002. Vol. 6 of *In Search of Lost Time*. Ed. Christopher Prendergast. 6 vols.

———. *The Guermantes Way*. 1920. Trans. Mark Treharne. London: Allen Lane, 2002. Vol. 3 of *In Search of Lost Time*. Ed. Christopher Prendergast. 6 vols.

———. *In the Shadow of Young Girls in Flower*. 1918. Trans. James Grieve. London: Allen Lane, 2002. Vol. 2 of *In Search of Lost Time*. Ed. Christopher Prendergast. 6 vols.

———. *Sodom and Gomorrah*. 1922. Trans. John Sturrock. London: Allen Lane, 2002. Vol. 4 of *In Search of Lost Time*. Ed. Christopher Prendergast. 6 vols.

Punter, David. "Angela Carter: Supersessions of the Masculine." *Critique: Studies in Contemporary Fiction* 25.4 (1984): 209–21.

Rivers, J. E. *Proust and the Art of Love: The Aesthetics of Sexuality in the Life, Times, and Art of Marcel Proust*. New York: Columbia University Press, 1980.

Robinson, Sally. *Engendering the Subject: Gender and Self-Representation in Contemporary Women's Fiction*. New York: SUNY Press, 1991.

Russell, Paul. *The Gay 100: A Ranking of the Most influential Gay Men and Lesbians, Past and Present*. Secaucus, NJ: Citadel Press, 1996.

Sage, Lorna. *Angela Carter*. Writers and their Work. Plymouth: Northcote House, 1994.

Schmid, Marion. "The Disembodied Intertext: From Baudelaire's *Passante* to Proust's Albertine." *Corporeal Practices: (Re)figuring the Body in French Studies*. Ed. Julia Prest and Hannah Thompson. Oxford: Peter Lang, 2000. 107–20.

Schmidt, Ricarda. "The Journey of the Subject in Angela Carter's Fiction." *Textual Practice* 3.1 (1989): 56–75.

Sedgwick, Eve Kosofsky. *Epistemology of the Closet*. Harmondsworth: Penguin, 1994.

Suleiman, Susan Rubin. "The Fate of the Surrealist Imagination in the Society of the Spectacle." *Flesh and the Mirror: Essays on the Art of Angela Carter*. Ed. Lorna Sage. London: Virago, 1994. 98–116.

———. "The Surrealist Imagination in Postmodernist Fiction: Angela Carter's *The Infernal Desire Machines of Doctor Hoffman*." *ICLA '91 Tokyo: The Force of Vision*,

III: Powers of Narration; Literary Theory. Ed. Earl Miner *et al*. Tokyo: International Comparative Literature Association, 1995. 531–39.

Tadié, Jean-Yves. *Marcel Proust: A Life*. New York: Penguin, 2000.

Tonkin, Maggie. "The 'Poe-etics' of Decomposition: Angela Carter's 'The Cabinet of Edgar Allan Poe' and the Reading-Effect." *Women's Studies: An Interdisciplinary Journal* 33.1 (2004): 1–21.

Vigneron, Robert. "Genèse de Swann." *Revue d'Histoire de la Philosophie et d'Histoire de la Civilization* (1937): 67–115.

White, Edmund. *Proust*. London: Phoenix, 1999.

Woolf, Virginia. "Modern Fiction." 1919. *The English Modernist Reader, 1910–1930*. Ed. Peter Faulkner. Iowa: Iowa University Press, 1986. 105–11.

———. "Mr. Bennett and Mrs Brown." 1924. *The English Modernist Reader, 1910–1930*. Ed. Peter Faulkner. Iowa: Iowa University Press, 1986. 112–28.

4
'The Other of the Other': Angela Carter's 'New-Fangled' Orientalism

Charlotte Crofts

In 1969 Angela Carter used the proceeds of her Somerset Maugham Award to travel to Japan where, she claims, she 'learnt what it is to be a woman and became radicalised' (*Nothing Sacred* 28). Carter states that she chose Japan because she 'wanted to live for a while in a culture that is not now nor has ever been a Judaeo-Christian one, to see what it was like' (ibid.).[1] In "Notes from the Front Line" (1983) she discusses how her encounter with Japanese culture also troubled and denaturalized her racial identity (72). Given Carter's self-professed interest in 'decolonialising' existing hegemonic structures it is surprising that Carter scholarship has not engaged more extensively with postcolonial theory.[2] Whilst there has been a great deal of exploration of Carter's 'decolonialising' project in terms of her demythologizing of gender, there has been less extensive exploration of the racial dynamics in Carter's work.[3] Drawing on her journalism, radio plays and short fiction, this chapter explores the impact of Carter's formative experiences in Japan on her feminist and political consciousness as a writer. However, whilst Japan can be glossed as the source of Carter's feminist and political enlightenment, it is important to examine both the risks of eliding sexual and racial difference, and the dangers of straightforwardly situating Japan as an intellectual playground for the development of Carter's Western aesthetic. Thus, this chapter considers both the strengths and the limitations of Carter's political strategies in relation to her engagement with Japan.

Lorna Sage's *Angela Carter* (1994) has become the bedrock for critical interpretations of Carter's time in Japan and its impact on her work. Sage sees Carter's journey to Japan as a 'rite of passage,' 'the place where she lost and found herself' (24) and 'discovered and retained a way of looking at herself, and other people, as unnatural' (28). Sage continues her argument in her edited collection *Flesh and the Mirror*

(1994), itself named after one of Carter's Japanese short stories, asserting that in Japan 'Carter was compounding, multiplying and confronting her sense of the artificiality of her own "nature"' (8). Sarah Gamble draws on Sage's argument to support her valuable thesis about Carter's politics of marginality, suggesting that 'Oriental culture offered Carter the experience of alienation writ large' (16). Linden Peach similarly argues that 'the influence of Japan on the later novels is evident in their more pronounced sense of the artificiality of culture and of the self as a product of social and cultural processes' (21), offering an illuminating discussion of the Japanese references in *The Infernal Desire Machines of Doctor Hoffman* (1972). Susan Fisher extends these arguments drawing on theories of performativity and the 'other,' themes which she notes were already present in Carter's earlier writing, suggesting that 'the experience of living in a different culture gave her new ways to explore them' (165).

I concur with Gamble, Peach and Fisher that Carter's engagement with Japan, in both her fiction and non-fiction writing, offers important insights into the rest of her work. In addition to *The Infernal Desire Machines of Doctor Hoffman*, several of the short stories published in the *Fireworks* collection (1974), written whilst she was living in Japan, and extensive journalism which she sent back to *New Society* from 1970–72, collected in *Nothing Sacred* (1982) and *Shaking a Leg* (1997), all overtly explore Carter's experiences as a foreigner in Japan. As Gamble points out, Carter retains her sense of being 'foreign' in her cultural critique of Britain: 'she did not only regard the truly foreign country, Japan, with the eyes of the anthropologist or travel writer; returning, Carter subjects her own country to the same kind of scrutiny' (94–95). However, it is necessary to highlight the dangers of simply seeing Japan as an Orientalist lens through which Carter was able scrutinize her own culture. There is, I think, sometimes too straightforward an analysis of Carter's experience of Japan in existing criticism that needs to be re-explored. For example, Sage configures Carter's relationship with Japanese culture as a new sort of Orientalism:

> At the time, in Tokyo, whatever she was looking for, she found out the truthfulness *and finality* of appearances, images emptied of their usual freight of recognition and guilt. This was not, in other words, old-fashioned orientalism, but the new-fangled sort that denied you access to any *essence* of otherness. (*Angela Carter* 26; emphasis in original)

Sage's take on Carter's engagement with Japan as 'new-fangled' Orientalism sets up a number of interesting questions about the nature of Orientalism: how, precisely, is 'new-fangled' Orientalism different from the 'old-fashioned' sort? And is it ever possible for the Western imagination to operate outside Orientalist discourse?

White male Orientalism

A useful starting point for this analysis is Carter's critique of 'old-fash-ioned' white male Orientalism in her radio play *Come Unto These Yellow Sands* (1979), in which she deconstructs the life of patricidal Victorian painter, Richard Dadd. In the play, Dadd's madness is precipitated by a tour of the Middle East accompanying his patron, Sir Thomas Phillips. With an exaggerated RP accent, Phillips describes himself as an 'inde-fatigable tourist' (40). Having '"done" Europe' (ibid.) he charts his onward journey, reeling off a list of exotic locations brought to life with dramatic spot effects: we hear waves, desert bells and hooves, which cre-ate a vivid aural landscape. Meanwhile, Dadd's fragile voice is intercut with this itinerary, acting as a counterpoint to Phillips' self-satisfied, Eurocentric discourse:

> DADD: … I, all unprepared for the stark light, the wild people, was pre-cipitated into a landscape not dissimilar to that of the infernal regions …
> PHILLIPS: … to Beirut, to Damascus …
> *(Muezzin which brings in background of Damascus.)*
> DADD: […] nothing was as I could have imagined it, all threw my nerves into a state of tremendous agitation. Can men truly live in such a different way to us? (40–41)

Both Dadd and Phillips are trapped within the Orientalist mode of see-ing the other as exotic spectacle. But where Phillips is complacent in his own subjectivity as tourist, Dadd's worldview is irrevocably shaken by contact with what he sees as an overwhelmingly 'alien' culture. With pastoral England as his only point of reference, Dadd is unable to see the Eastern landscape as anything but 'wild', 'infernal' and 'strangely troubling' (41).

Carter situates Dadd's transformative experiences in the East firmly in the context of nineteenth-century British imperialism. When Dadd vis-its an Egyptian bazaar, she has one of the merchants step out of the play and deliver a caustic lecture on Orientalism, whilst masquerading as the deferential subaltern:

> SHOPKEEPER: Effendi?
> DADD: The meanest merchant in the bazaar looks like a Sultan in an eastern fairy tale ...
> SHOPKEEPER: I knew immediately I saw him that this young man would buy anything I chose to sell him. (42)

It is worth commenting on the double meaning of 'buy' here – as in either 'believing' or 'buying into' the Orientalist construction of Egypt via buying souvenirs – and Carter emphasizes these commercial power relations with the sound effect of a ringing cash register:

> (*Cash register.*)
> [SHOPKEEPER:] What's this? (*To inaudible* voice over his shoulder.) What? You want my lecture on Orientalism?
> (*Coughs, clears throat. Crossfade to rustling of lecture theatre audience.*) My lecture on Orientalism ... are you attending? Very well. (43)

The Shopkeeper goes on to delineate the history of middle class tourism as a by-product of imperialism, the Industrial Revolution and the rise of the bourgeoisie. 'They wanted to be taken out of themselves, you understand, but *not for long*. So tourism was born' (44; emphasis in original). Whilst exotic travel may have started off as escapism, the Shopkeeper argues, it quickly became a matter of aesthetics: 'they soon realised they could hire their artists to do their travelling for them, and so need not hazard the flies, the heat, the diarrhoea and so forth. The European middle class drank deep of the savage splendours of the East ... without stirring a step from their drawing-rooms' (44).

Carter situates Dadd's travels within a long history of artistic, intellectual and sexual tourism through the mouth of the Shopkeeper, who illustrates how the East has been constructed as the forbidden other by the European sexual imagination,[4] disagreeing vehemently when Oberon (a character in one of Dadd's paintings) interrupts his lecture to suggest a more innocent reading:

> OBERON: ... a compensatory ideology of innocence ...
> SHOPKEEPER: (*Tetchy.*) No, no, no, no! Innocence? Never! These were the lands of the harem, of the assassin, of the naked blonde slave-girl in the market ... the cult of the exotic was a compensatory ideology

of sensuality, of mystery, of violence. Of the *forbidden*, which the customers of my customers could enjoy vicariously, without any danger
of their souls. (44; emphasis in original)

In an article on Carter's radio drama, Guido Almansi takes issue with
this scene: 'This reminds me a bit too closely of certain lectures of a
sociological nature which I had the misfortune to hear thirty years
ago, plus the distant echo of a perfunctory reading of Edward W. Said's
Orientalism' (228). I would argue, however, that Carter's allusion to
Said's *Orientalism* (1978) is not a 'distant echo', as Almansi suggests,
but an explicit engagement with postcolonial discourse. Whilst Said's
theories of Orientalism are being troubled by more recent theories of
'cosmopolitanism' and the possibility of a positive identification with
difference, to dismiss these debates, as Almansi appears to do, seems
to be a fundamental misreading both of Carter's project, and of the
wider political arena.[5] Said's theories clearly remain pertinent and he
himself went on to actively revise and extend his ideas.[6] Furthermore,
Almansi misses both the humour and the politics of the Shopkeeper's
lecture. By situating postcolonial theory in the mouth of the
Shopkeeper the colonized subject is given a voice, recalling Gayatri
Spivak's article, "Can the Subaltern Speak?". As the Shopkeeper points
out, the subaltern is more often a construction of the Western imagination: 'We were not responsible for their fantasies about us' (45).
Carter is aware of, and seeks to foreground, the complicated nexus of
power, domination and exploitation implicit in the capitalist con-
sumer culture of tourism. However, the fact that Almansi does not 'get'
the irony of Carter's inversion of the 'imperial gaze' suggests that it is
a risky strategy that is open to misreadings.[7]

In *A Self-Made Man* (1984), her radio play about novelist Ronald
Firbank, Carter also explores the central character's attitudes to travel and
cultural difference. Once again situating Western tourism within in a specific socio-historical context, the play begins and ends with Firbank's
death in a 'hotel room full of valises' (123), the culmination of a life of
luxury middle class travel. Significantly, Firbank was born in 1886, the
year Dadd died, and Carter clearly situates him as the product of the
Industrial Revolution and the imperialism that she critiques in *Come Unto
These Yellow Sands*. But, unlike Dadd, Firbank's relationship with travel is
more self-conscious. Firbank holds no illusions about the fact that the
places he visits are filtered through his own fantasies, enjoying travel not
for travel's sake, nor for the sake of arrival, but for 'that fleeting moment
when the ecstatic elsewhere of the imagination is near at hand yet

unachieved' (123–24). As with the Shopkeeper's lecture on Orientalism, Carter uses the device of a seminar series entitled 'Elementary Structures of Ronald Firbank'. In each seminar, both male and female narrators, commentators, experts, characters and Firbank himself compete to comment on Firbank's life, sometimes offering contradictory versions of events. As I argue in *'Anagrams of Desire'* (2003), the use of multiple narrators in both of these 'artificial' biographies works to formally destabilize dominant white/male subjectivity by playing with narrative point of view (86). In the section on 'Ragtime', introduced with a jazz drum roll, Carter has the 'Male Narrator' compare the syncopated rhythm of Firbank's prose with the greats of white jazz: 'Bix Beiderbecke, Eddie Condon, Mezz Mezzrow, white jazz played by white boys who loved it so much they wanted to simulate, synthesise, make it their own music' (148). The next seminar on 'Elsewhere' explores Firbank's fictional worlds and his penchant for exotic travel, including Lotus Land, Arcadia, Haiti, the West Indies and Carthage, 'where the young men bathing in the sea [...] wore diamonds in their navels flashing in the sun' (149), foregrounding the homoerotics of Firbank's tourism.[8]

Firbank's attraction to the other can be linked to his marginalized position, both as an artist and in terms of his homosexuality, because it provides an alluring alternative to the dominant culture. Exploring the notion of 'cosmopolitan modernity', Mica Nava alludes to:

> the urban and often feminized worlds of entertainment, commerce, the arts and the emotions in metropolitan England during the first decades of the 20th century, in which an interest in abroad and cultural 'others' increasingly signalled an engagement with the new. ("Cosmopolitan Modernity" 81)

Nava goes on to suggest that this cosmopolitan interest in abroad constitutes a counter-cultural position – 'cultural difference and the foreign constituted a source of interest, pleasure and counter-identification that existed in tension with more conservative outlooks' – and includes 'jazz dance in the interwar period' among her points of reference (ibid. 86). She proposes that this 'alternative culture of modernity' can be seen as 'a revolt against the constraints of the parental culture' and suggests that this 'cannot be understood as another form of orientalism through which the west dominates the east', citing the specifically gendered and positive identification with the other as undermining a straightforward postcolonial thesis ("Visceral Cosmopolitanism" para. 5). Firbank's yearning for the 'other', whether it is the modernity of jazz or 'some fabulous Indies of the imagination' (149), can be read in terms of a positive engagement with the foreign. However, whilst this clearly differs from the unconscious 'old-fashioned' kind of Orientalism of Phillips and Dadd, in exoticizing the other, Firbank nevertheless perpetuates the binary opposition between East and West. So, how does this relate to Carter's 'new-fangled' Orientalism?

Feminism and Orientalism

The profound effect of the East on Dadd and Firbank's passion for the 'ecstatic elsewhere of the imagination' can be parallelled with Carter's own radically transformative experience in Japan. Like Dadd, Carter's experience of the 'East' threw her own culture into relief, but in Carter's case this challenge to her Western worldview is experienced as positive.[9] As Sage suggests, in Japan 'her size – and her colour – made her utterly foreign. She compounded her oddity when she stepped into the looking-glass world of a culture that reflected her back to herself as an alien' (*Angela Carter* 26). Dislocated into another cultural environment, Carter connects the experience of being seen as alien, other and foreign with the experience of being viewed as a sex object, as man's Other. In "Poor Butterfly" (1972) she describes this reverse Orientalism: 'Such bars will employ Caucasian girls as exotic extras, like a kind of cabaret' (47). Becoming an 'exotic extra' has the affect of radicalizing her as a woman in relation to her own culture by amplifying the gender dynamics implicit in Western culture to such an extent as to make them recognizable as cultural constructions. Carter's Japanese experience, then, defamiliarized Western societal relationships by putting them into an alien context and exaggerating them: 'Japan is just the same as everywhere else, only more so' (ibid.).

Carter is amongst many feminist writers and artists who have found Orientalism a useful paradigm for deconstructing white male subjectivity. As Mary Ann Doane points out in her discussion of Leslie Thornton's film *Adynata* (1991), '[i]t is not surprising that the "otherness" of orientalism would be aligned by Thornton with the culturally determined otherness of femininity. Both partake of the exotic; both function to stabilize the identity of the Western male subject' (182). But it could be claimed that Carter is in danger of eliding the differences between the experience of being seen as racially other, alien and foreign, with the experience of being viewed as man's sexual 'other'. As many black feminists have pointed out, this too easy conflation of racial and sexual oppression has been a problem within white feminism since its inception.[10] However, Carter's time in Japan not only 'radicalised' her as a woman, it also forced her to examine her own cultural identity. In "Notes from the Front Line", for example, she emphasizes the impact of her experience in Japan on her nascent political consciousness:

> My female consciousness *was* being forged out of the contradictions of my experience as a traveller, as, indeed, some other aspects of my political consciousness were being forged. (It was a painful and enlightening experience to be regarded as a coloured person, for example; to be defined as a Caucasian before I was defined as a woman, and learning the hard way that most people on this planet are not Caucasian and have no reason either to love or respect Caucasians). (72; emphasis in original)

A prominent theme of black feminist theory's critique of white feminism has been the call to see whiteness from the perspective of the 'other', through the 'black gaze'. Carter's experiences in Japan indeed enabled her to see herself through the gaze of the other. In the short story "A Souvenir of Japan" (1974), the first person narrator describes herself as 'the mysterious other' to her Japanese lover:

> I had become a kind of phoenix, a fabulous beast; I was an out-landish jewel. He found me, I think, inexpressibly exotic. But I often felt like a female impersonator. [...] I wore men's sandals because they were the only kind that fitted me [...]. My pink cheeks, blue eyes and blatant yellow hair made of me, in the visual orchestration of this city in which all heads were dark, eyes brown and skin mono-tone, an instrument which played upon an alien scale. (7)

As Susan Rubin Suleiman suggests, for Carter Japan was 'both a link to Europe and a country of absolute otherness – not only because she saw it as Other in relation to what she knew, but because she herself was seen, in the "completely Japanese environment" in which she lived, as an unassimilable Other, a foreigner, "*Gaijin*"' (99).

There is a striking similarity between Carter's experience of being looked at as 'other' in Japan and Julia Kristeva's account of the 'countergaze' of Chinese women: 'myself, an eternal stranger, frozen in my thwarted desire to be recognized as one of them, happy when they lost themselves in con-templation of my face and when only my bell-bottomed trousers made the old peasant woman at the Great Wall cry out "aiguo ren!" (foreign woman)' (57).[11] For both Carter and Kristeva, it seems, the encounter with another culture destabilizes white subjectivity. Su-lin Yu argues that the returning look of the Chinese women exposes the instability of Kristeva's Western imperialist position:

> Being among the first foreigners to visit the village of Huxian, Kristeva is conscious of how the gaze of Chinese women queries her very 'strangeness.' For Kristeva, that the Chinese women return her gaze immediately exoticizes her and triggers a crisis of her identity as a sovereign imperialist. (para. 18)

Similarly, Sage asserts that Carter's experiences in Japan 'confirmed her in her sense of strangeness' (*Angela Carter* 29), reinforcing her existing sense of alienation as an existential stance: 'alienated is the only way to be after all' ("The Mother Lode" 16). However, whilst contact with another culture can have a disturbing effect (as in Dadd's case, triggering his schizophrenia), or, for Carter, an equally destabilizing but profoundly liberating effect, either way, it is still white subjectivity which is the central focus. As Dick Pels argues, the notion of marginality has become 'a cognitive plaything of the educated elite' (69) whereby the position of the alienated subject is seen as a privileged space from which the intellectual can observe and comment on dominant culture. This is clearly problematic in terms of the upwardly mobile Western traveller straightforwardly aligning themselves with the less privileged, economically and politically marginalized 'other'.

Still, it is crucial to acknowledge that Carter's journey to Japan took place in a specific cultural, social and historical context. The relationship between Japan and the West is not easily categorized in terms of European colonialism or the postcolonial paradigms of US slavery. Clearly, the Second World War and post-war US cultural imperialism, as well as early Western contact with Japan, can be read in an Orientalist light, but Japan is not a Third World country, has never been directly colonized by the West and indeed has its own history of aggressive imperialism. It is also important to point out that Carter went to Japan post-1968 when the Vietnam War had generated a huge countercultural movement in both Europe and the US. In "Truly, It Felt Like Year One" (1988), an essay in a collection looking back at the 1960s, Carter cites Vietnam as a defining moment:

> Wars are great catalysts for social change and even though it was not specifically *our* war, the Vietnam war was a conflict between the First

World and the Third World, between Whites and Non-Whites and, increasingly, between the American people, or a statistically signifi- cant percentage thereof, and Yankee imperialism. And the people won, dammit. (211–12; emphasis in original)

This reading signals an active and positive identification with the other, rather than 'straightforward' or unconscious Orientalism, recalling Nava's 'progressive cosmopolitanism'. Indeed, Carter goes on to enquire why so much felt at stake for Britain in the Vietnam War, citing 'an internationalism that wasn't in the least superficial' (212). It is clear, then, that Carter's trip to Japan was not simply a wish to follow in the footsteps of her mainly nineteenth-century white male literary prede- cessors, nor a nostalgia for a pre-lapsian life 'outside the Judaeo- Christian tradition' (Fisher 174). It was also part of a constructive and politically motivated attempt to engage with a non-Western culture in the aftermath of the Vietnam War.

Empire of signs

Carter's travel to Japan needs to be situated in the context of the intel- lectual tourism of the French theorists of the *Tel Quel* group in the early 1970s, who were also looking to the East in 'search for solutions to Western political and cultural problems' (Yu para. 26). As Sage attests, 'another kind of travelling [Carter] had been doing was mental travel- ling – particularly in the realms of theory and, more particularly still, structuralist anthropology and deconstruction' (Introduction 11). In her chapter "Travelling White Theorists," E. Ann Kaplan cites Lisa Lowe's argument that 'Western theorists travel to other cultures when seeking ways out of dilemmas at home', suggesting that this is 'the intellectual equivalent to literal imperial travel intended to refresh tired European markets and feed increasingly exotic desires' (141).[12] In these terms, then, Carter's formative experiences in Japan could be read as just another narcissistic imperial conquest.

Significantly, Carter and Barthes travelled to Japan at around the same time and there appears to be a great deal of congruence between Carter's Japanese writings and Barthes' semiotic analysis of Japan in *Empire of Signs* (1970). As Sage highlights, '[t]he coincidence between Barthes' Japan and Carter's is striking: they visited the same country of the skin, no question, and its topography derives from their very Western wants' (*Angela Carter* 27). Both Barthes and Carter experience

Japanese culture as a semiotic and sexual playground: Barthes discovered his homosexuality; Carter her feminism. However, it is clearly no coincidence that they both travelled to Japan to seek an alternative to the Western symbolic order in the context of post-1968 disillusionment with the establishment. Barthes makes it clear from the outset that he is not interested in the 'real' or 'essential' Japan:

> If I want to imagine a fictive nation, I can give it an invented name, treat it declaratively as a novelistic object, create a new Garabagne, so as to compromise no real country by my fantasy [...]. I can also – though in no way claiming to represent or to analyze reality itself (these being the major gestures of Western discourse) – isolate somewhere in the world (*faraway*) a certain number of features (a term employed in linguistics), and out of these features deliberately form a system. It is this system which I shall call: Japan. (3; emphasis in original)

Like Carter, Barthes was attracted to Japan because it represents a culture completely outside of the Judaeo-Christian tradition: 'I am not lovingly gazing toward an Oriental essence – to me the Orient is a matter of indifference, merely providing a reserve of features whose manipulation – whose invented interplay – allows me to "entertain" the idea of an unheard-of symbolic system, one altogether detached from our own' (3).[13] As Doane suggests, 'Barthes's writing about his trip to Japan is evidence of an impossible desire for *absolute* and irreducible otherness – with no point of contact with the West' (179; emphasis in original).[14]

It is at the point of language that Barthes' and Carter's experiences in Japan most closely coincide. In a piece entitled "Without Words", Barthes suggests that 'the murmuring mass of an unknown language constitutes a delicious protection, envelops the foreigner (provided the country is not hostile to him) in an auditory film which halts at his ears all the alienations of the mother tongue' (9). Similarly, Carter finds that the inaccessibility of the language forces her to look at things at face value: 'since I kept on trying to learn Japanese, and kept on failing to do so, I started trying to understand things by simply looking at them very, very carefully, an involuntary apprenticeship in the interpretation of signs' (*Nothing Sacred* 28). For Carter, this lack of linguistic understanding enables her to conduct semiotic analyses of the Japanese art of body tattooing, *irezumi*, in "People as Pictures" (1970) and pornographic *manga* comics in "Once More into the Mangle" (1971): 'What is actually going on in the pictures often looks rather odd to me because I cannot read Japanese. When a translation is provided, it usually turns out to be worse than I could have imagined' (41). Carter repeatedly comments on the foreignness of Japanese language both in her fiction and non-fiction. In "Tokyo Pastoral" (1970), she sketches the soundscape of a Tokyo suburb, including the 'clickety-clackety rattle of chattering housewives, a sound like briskly plied knitting needles, for Japanese is a language full of Ts and Ks' (29). She reuses almost the exact same phrase in the short story "The Loves of Lady Purple" (1974): 'When the Professor spoke, nobody could understand him for he knew only his native tongue, which was an incomprehensible rattle of staccato k's and t's' (25–26). Indeed Carter's journalism and fiction about Japan is littered with clichés and stereotypes about Japanese people and culture, the very language in fact of 'old-fashioned' Orientalism: she comments on the 'clatter of demotic Japanese' (7) and the 'hypocrisy' (10) of the Samurai in "Souvenir of Japan", and describes her Japanese lover as 'inscrutable' (68) in "Flesh and the Mirror" (1974). Whilst it is not my project to offer an exhaustive list of these here, nor indeed to castigate Carter for being politically incorrect, it is interesting to note how these stereotypes find their way into her writing – how they become recycled in effect.

Fisher suggests that there is a 'dimension of nostalgia in Carter's travel to Japan' – that although she was clearly travelling there for the first time 'she was not going there without preconceptions. She was seeking something that she felt nostalgia for, an experience she felt was lost or unavailable in England and that she believed she might encounter somewhere else' (173). Fisher relates this 'longing' to the 'image of the literary traveller', including Firbank and the 'nineteenth-century tradition of French exoticism' (174) amongst Carter's influences. But whilst Fisher argues that Carter went to Japan with a 'nostalgia for the idea of the writer as exotic traveller, and her desire to experience these kinds of imaginative transports for herself' (174), it is also important to acknowledge that, even in the earliest of her Japanese writings, "A Souvenir of Japan", Carter explicitly foregrounds her own Western literary and cultural baggage, knowingly alluding to Gauguin (6) and Baudelaire (10) amongst others in the context of her own encounter with another culture.[15] As Fisher points out, '[t]he Orientalist tradition they represent is not a very respectable one, but Carter seems to be acknowledging its role in forming her own *idées reçues* about Japan' (173).

In her later writing, Carter is more overtly critical of both the Eurocentrism of figures such as Baudelaire, Dadd and Firbank and the wider colonial culture from which they herald. In several articles about her development as a writer, Carter recognizes the hegemony of white feminism, describing 'the notion of a universality of female experience' as 'a clever confidence trick' (*The Sadeian Woman* 12), and drawing attention to the 'fictive quality about the notion of a universality of "women only" experience' ("The Language of Sisterhood" 231). In "Notes from the Front Line", Carter acknowledges that 'white women can't get out of our historic complicity in colonialism, any more than the white working class can' (73), and identifies the 'slow process of decolonialising our language and our basic habits of thought' as crucial for 'the creation of a means of expression for an infinitely greater variety of experience than has been possible heretofore, to say things for which no language previously existed' (75). Carter's words echo those of bell hooks who identifies the need for 'counterhegemonic' narratives to challenge 'the conventional structures of domination that uphold and maintain white supremacist capitalist patriarchy' (*Reel to Real* 3). Elsewhere, hooks calls for 'the holders of hegemonic discourse' to 'dehegemonize their position and themselves learn how to occupy the subject position of the other' (*Black Looks* 177). There is, therefore, clearly a central paradox and conflict that fuels Carter's writing about Japan. She is torn between an anti-colonial impulse to renounce Western hegemony and a deep sense of being indebted to her white male predecessors.[16] This ambivalent view of Western culture as both an oppressive and creative force is at the core of Carter's position as a writer and as a feminist.

Flesh and the mirror

It is in light of this paradox that I offer a re-reading of Carter's short story "Flesh in the Mirror". In "Occidentalism", a review of Rana Kabbani's *Europe's Myths of Orient* (1986), Carter suggests that realizing 'we are the Other of the Other' is 'an existentially uncomfortable position' (9). It is this 'uncomfortable position' from which she writes, particularly in this short story, collected in *Fireworks* (1974).[17] "Flesh and the Mirror" chronicles Carter's self-reflexive journey from a traditional Orientalist perspective to one in which the relationship with another culture is rendered more complicated. As Sage asserts, this is one of a series of short stories in the *Fireworks* collection that 'most uncharacteristically, are hardly fictionalized at all' (*Angela Carter* 26). The story maps the narrator's/Carter's developing recognition of her own gaze as Eurocentric. At the beginning of the story the narrator searches the streets of Tokyo looking for her lover after he fails to meet her off the ferry at Yokohama dock. The first-person narrator describes herself as a tragic figure 'walking through the city in the third person singular, my own heroine, as though the world stretched out from my eye like spokes from a sensitised hub that galvanized all to life when I looked at it' (68). Note the distance between the moment of narration and the narrated here, in which the narrator explicitly draws attention to the mechanics of narration, stating that her past 'self', the character in the story, saw herself in the 'third person singular', which in turn suggests that the narrator is now speaking/writing from a position of a different kind of knowledge:

> I think I know, now, what I was trying to do. I was trying to subdue the city by turning it into a projection of my own growing pains. What solipsistic arrogance! The city, the largest city in the world, the city designed to suit not one of my European expectations, this city presents the foreigner with a mode of life that seems to him to have the enigmatic transparency, the indecipherable clarity, of dream. And it is a dream he could, himself, never have dreamed. The stranger, the foreigner, thinks he is in control; but he has been pre-cipitated into somebody else's dream. (68–69)

In "Notes from the Front Line", Carter characterizes this slippage (into using the masculine pronoun as universal) as a youthful tendency towards 'male impersonation': 'I was, as a girl, suffering a degree of colo-nialisation of the mind. Especially in the journalism I was writing then, I'd – quite unconsciously – posit a male view as a general one' (71). As mentioned above, in the same article Carter specifically states that her experiences as a traveller in Japan contributed to the development of her 'female consciousness' (72). But, as we have seen, Carter's experi-ence in Japan also caused her to question her white subjectivity. It is in "Flesh and the Mirror" that the process of 'decolonialisation', or becom-ing 'radicalised', both in terms of feminism and her political conscious-ness, is most apparent.

The narrator extends the tendency to think of herself in the 'third person singular' to the metaphor of the puppet theatre, casting herself as both puppet and puppet master, with Tokyo acting as an exotic set-ting for her own self-dramatization:

> There I was, walking up and down, eating meals, having conversa-tions, in love, indifferent, and so on. But all the time I was pulling the strings of my own puppet; it was this puppet who was moving

about on the other side of the glass. [...] So I attempted to rebuild the city according to the blueprint in my imagination as a backdrop to the plays in my puppet theatre, but it sternly refused to be so rebuilt; I was only imagining it had been so rebuilt. (69–70)

Doane argues that Thornton's *Adynata* actively investigates 'the *mise-en-scène*' of Orientalism through the use of cliché and exaggeration. This is clearly what Carter's narrator is doing here in drawing attention to Tokyo as a 'location' or set. Carter had already used the puppet idea with Uncle Philip's sinister 'Marionette Microcosm' in *The Magic Toyshop* (1967), published prior to her travels in Japan, returning to the theme in "The Loves of Lady Purple", in which the Asiatic Professor dexterously manipulates the inanimate Lady Purple, bringing her to uncanny life: 'the more lifelike his marionettes, the more godlike his manipulations and the more radical the symbiosis between inarticulate doll and articulating fingers' (24).[18] As Fisher points out, 'the style of puppetry practised by the Asiatic Professor' is clearly '*bunraku*, performed to the accompaniment of "the delirious *obbligato* of the [...] samisen"' (168). *Bunraku* is the ancient Japanese art of puppet theatre which utilizes three-quarter life-sized puppets, each manipulated by three puppeteers who are clearly visible on stage. All the puppeteers wear black. The face of the master puppeteer is visible, whilst the others wear hoods concealing their faces. The master puppeteer works the right arm, head and upper torso of the puppet whilst the other two handle the rest of the body. To either side of the stage sit the narrators and musicians who accompany the performance with text and music.

Significantly, three of the pieces in Barthes' *Empire of Signs* are devoted to *bunraku*. Barthes is fascinated by the concurrent but separate performances of the puppet master, the puppet and the narrator: '*Bunraku* thus practices three separate writings, which it offers to be read simultaneously in three sites of the spectacle: the puppet, the manipulator, the vociferent: the effected gesture, the effective gesture, the vocal gesture' (49). Barthes goes on to discuss *bunraku* in terms which are not dissimilar to those of Sergi Eisenstein's dialectical montage, in which the narrator's voice is given a 'counterpoise, or better still, a countermove: that of gesture' (49) in contrast to the movement of the puppets. There is a doubling of this gesture with 'the emotive gesture on the level of the doll' and the 'transitive action on the level of the manipulators'. Barthes claims that *bunraku* 'separates action from gesture: it shows the gesture, lets the action be seen, exhibits simultaneously the art and the labour, reserving for each its own writing' (54).

Up until this point in the story, Carter has utilized a first person narrator, but in the next sentence there is a sudden shift into the third person which is precipitated by the narrator's chance encounter with a beautiful stranger whom she accompanies back to an 'unambiguous' love hotel: 'On the night I came back to it [Tokyo], however hard I looked for the one I loved, she could not find him anywhere and the city delivered her into the hands of a perfect stranger' (70). They make love and the hotel's mirrored ceiling acts as a catalyst through which the narrator is able to view both herself and the world differently: 'The magic mirror presented me with hitherto unconsidered notion of myself as I' (71):

> Women and mirrors are in complicity with one another to evade the action I/she performs that she/I cannot watch, the action with which I break out of the mirror, with which I assume my appearance. But this mirror refused to conspire with me; it was like the first mirror I'd ever seen. (70–71)

The allusion to Jacques Lacan's 'mirror stage' and Lewis Carroll's *Through the Looking Glass* (1871), combined with the extended puppet metaphor, allows Carter to operate a complex shift in person that disrupts the realist illusion of the narrative and allows a space for the reader's imagination. The mirror destabilizes the three Aristotelian unities that Rosemary Jackson argues traditionally uphold Western hegemonic order (176): 'the mirror annihilated time, place and person' (64). It is apposite to return to Barthes' exploration of *bunraku* in this connection. As Barthes points out, 'all this connects, of course, with the alienation effect Brecht recommends' (54). Barthes goes on to suggest that *bunraku* troubles the dialectic between the animate and the inanimate, arguing that it 'jeopardizes it, eliminates it without advantage for either of its terms' (58), dismissing 'the concept which is hidden behind all animation of matter, and which is, quite simply, "the soul"' (60).[19] For Barthes, *bunraku's* rejection of simulation for 'sensuous abstraction' (60) creates a Bretchtian distancing effect through which the audience can retain a critical distance, rather than identifying with characters and events, as in naturalistic theatrical forms. Whereas Western theatre's function is to 'manifest what is supposed to be secret [...] while concealing the very artifice of such manifestation (machinery, painting, makeup, the sources of light)' (61), in *bunraku* this 'artifice' is clearly on display.

Whilst Fisher also notes the Brechtian possibilities of the art form, she predominantly discusses *bunraku* in terms of 'gender as performance' theory (166). But whilst she fully explores Carter's use of puppets in "The Loves of Lady Purple", and *The Magic Toyshop*, she misses the opportunity to elaborate on them in her discussion of the more autobiographical story "Flesh and the Mirror", where Carter's use of the puppet/puppet master metaphor also seeps into the formal construction of the story. Not only does Carter use *bunraku* as a metaphor in "Flesh and the Mirror", but her writing method itself mimics its formal properties, revealing the mechanics of storytelling by making visible, and drawing attention to, the shift in person/voice. Carter's artifice is clearly on display. There are three separate 'writings' of the central character: the puppet (third person), the puppet master (first person) and the narrator (who operates a shift in narration between the two). By making the mechanisms of the narrative visible Carter achieves a Brechtian 'defamiliarizing' effect similar to that proffered by Barthes.[20]

The following morning, the narrator is reunited with her original lover. Carter then extends the puppet/performance metaphor to include a range of filmic reference:

> I no longer understood the logic of my own performance. My script had been scrambled behind my back. The cameraman was drunk. The director had a *crise de nerfs* and had been taken away to a sanatorium. And my co-star had picked himself up off the operating table and painfully cobbled himself together again according to his own design. All this had taken place while I was looking in the mirror. (75)

The two lovers quarrel until nightfall, finding their way to another hotel, which is 'in every respect a parody of the previous night' (76). The relationship ends a few days later: 'Then the city vanished; it ceased, almost immediately, to be a magic and appalling place. I woke up one morning and found it had become home' (77). Carter foregrounds the Eurocentric perspective of the narrator at the beginning of the story, using cliché and the *mise-en-scène* of Orientalism, but by the end of the story the narrator's experience of another culture has been transformed. Tokyo has ceased to be 'unheimlich' or foreign and has become simply 'home'.[21] The narrator, I/she, is with hindsight able to deconstruct her self-dramatization as the forlorn lover on the desolate stage of Tokyo. Finding that she is no longer able to 'pull the strings of myself and so take control of the situation' (74), the city ceases to function as an exotic backdrop for the narrator's puppet theatre and takes on a life of its own. Fisher maintains that Carter 'ultimately remains a performer, controlled by her received ideas about Japan and by the script that they dictate. She is condemned to perform because she cannot find an authentic way to be in Japan' (169). However, it seems clear that a shift in the narrator's perspective has indeed occurred by the end of the story and the narrator's self-awareness suggests that a very different subject position has been arrived at from the 'solipsistic arrogance' at the beginning of the tale.

A Souvenir of Japan

Whilst it is important to explore the impact of Carter's experiences in Japan on her later writings, it is equally important to situate those experiences within a specific historical, cultural and social context. Rather than unproblematically constructing Japan as a privileged marginal space from which Carter could critique her own culture, it is crucial to acknowledge the racial and cultural power relations inherent in the Western intellectual's travel to another culture. As I have demonstrated, there is a paradoxical tension in Carter's work between her self-defined 'decolonialising' project and the remnants of the 'old-fashioned' Orientalism of the white male literary heroes whose work she admired. Like the 'male impersonation' which she claims characterized her juvenile work, Carter's early Japanese writings are, to a certain degree, perhaps inevitably, inflected by the discourses of unreconstructed Orientalism. However, to suggest that it is eternally impossible for the Western imagination to engage with another culture without being simply Orientalist seems to be a self-defeatist reinscription of the dichotomy between East and West – a dilemma with which postcolonial studies continues to struggle. Carter's extended stay in Japan forced her to become aware of her white subjectivity and challenged her received ideas about Japan, leading to a different kind of knowledge. This transition from unconscious Orientalism to the position of political consciousness which informs her later writings is played out in "Flesh and the Mirror" on both a formal and a thematic level. In her later radio plays on Dadd and Firbank, and in critical writings reflecting on her emerging feminism and development as a writer, Carter explicitly engages with postcolonial discourse. As I've highlighted in this essay, these hitherto neglected engagements are vital to an understanding of Carter's writing strategies. It is crucial, therefore, that Carter scholarship pursues the avenues for discussion opened up here to further address the racial politics of Carter's work.

Notes

1. Carter's attraction to a culture outside of the Judaeo-Christian tradition is interesting in the light of Richard Dyer's arguments about the relationship between Christianity and 'whiteness'. In his deconstruction of white hegemony in *White* (1997), Dyer suggests that white power has legitimized itself through the discourse of Christianity in which the ideal of bodily transcendence becomes synonymous with the ideal of whiteness itself. Carter's critique of white Christianity is evidenced in her controversially 'blasphemous' TV programme, *The Holy Family Album* (1991), which I discuss in my book *'Anagrams of Desire'* (168–93).
2. In "Notes from the Front Line", Carter maintains that her appropriation of literary sources 'is part of the slow process of decolonialising our language and our basic habits of thought' (75). The act of reappropriating language to express experience outside the dominant culture is also the project of much postcolonial literature. In fact, Carter sees herself as linked to such postcolonial writers as Gabriel Garcia Marquez and the black South African writer Bessie Head, 'who are transforming actual fictional forms to both reflect and to precipitate changes in the way people feel about themselves' (76).
3. There has been some discussion of Carter's representation of blackness, such as Jill Matus' analysis of Carter's depiction of Baudelaire's mistress, Jeanne Duval.
4. A large section of the Shopkeeper's monologue (which is cut from the recorded performance) is devoted to a list of his famous clientele, including Victor Hugo, Pierre Loti, Gérard de Nerval, Edward Lear and Lord Leighton: 'You would have thought the East had turned their brains' (43).
5. See, for example, E. Ann Kaplan's work on the 'imperial gaze' and Mica Nava's research on 'progressive cosmopolitanism' in "The Cosmopolitanism of Commerce and the Allure of Difference" and "Visceral Cosmopolitanism". Both critics suggest ways out of the double bind of the East/West Orientalist dichotomy by suggesting that cross-cultural looking and identification is not always necessarily a negative power relation.
6. See *Culture and Imperialism* and "East isn't East".
7. Kaplan's research into the 'imperial gaze' is a response to the critique of 1970s and 1980s white feminist film theory's neglect of race in its emphasis on Laura Mulvey's theory of the 'male gaze'. Kaplan explores inter-racial looking relations in film, specifically focusing on discussion of films about travel, which are clearly pertinent to both Carter's critique of Dadd's experiences in the East, and her own experiences as a traveller.
8. For more on this see Boone.
9. It is important to point out that this 'positive' experience can be seen as being in line with hegemonic Orientalist discourse. It is equally important not to conflate the Middle East with Japan, a move which runs the risk of reinscribing Orientalist discourses of the East as one homogenous Other.
10. Black feminist critics have challenged white feminism's claims to universality, questioning the over emphasis on psychoanalytical models as being ill-equipped to deal with the representation of race (see Gaines); drawing attention to the importance of denaturalizing whiteness (see Carby); and

calling for white feminists to see their whiteness and acknowledge invisible white privilege (see hooks, *Black Looks*).

11. It is interesting to note that in both cases it is the Western women's clothing that appears to be the signifier of cultural difference.

12. Lowe cites Julia Kristeva's recourse to Chinese femininity in *About Chinese Women* (1974) as exploitative and Roland Barthes' semiotic deconstruction of Japan in *Empire of Signs* (1970) as reinscribing difference (22–44). See also Yu, who suggests that Kristeva's cultural curiosity is as much about her own cultural specificity as it is about that of Chinese women (para. 20).

13. Barthes' declaration of 'indifference' and anti-essentialism will have alarm bells ringing for some Marxist materialists. Philip Hammond notes a danger of conflating 'cultural difference' with racial difference, warning that 'an ahistorical conception of culture which tends to naturalize difference is a problem in Cultural Studies [...] not despite but because of its anti-essentialist, anti-universalist and anti-humanist approach' (para. 1).

14. The first piece in *Empire of Signs* is entitled "Faraway," and Barthes' yearning for a space outside of Western discourse is reminiscent of Firbank's longing for that 'forever unattainable, non-existent Eden' in *The Self-Made Man* (150).

15. Carter is of course highly critical of Baudelaire's exploitation of his 'mulatto' mistress Duval in "Black Venus" (1985).

16. Yu makes a similar point about Kristeva's inability to divorce herself from the very Orientalist hegemony she seeks to subvert in *About Chinese Women*: 'Undoubtedly, in her account of her journey to China Kristeva was affected by Orientalist ideology and involved in postcolonial relations. [...] Throughout the text she both consciously and unconsciously affirms the West's previous knowledge and representations about the nature of Chinese women and culture. [...] At other times, she has to acknowledge that China can only be readable through the Western lens. [...] Ultimately, the dynamics of imperial discourse could not but enter and structure her work – even if her relationship to some imperialist ideologies was self-consciously oppositional' (para. 37). However, there are important differences between Kristeva's three-week visit and Carter's years living and working in Japan. Furthermore, Carter does not specifically identify with Japanese women in the way that Kristeva could be said to essentialize Chinese women.

17. It is worth noting that the stories from the *Fireworks* collection were written between 1970 and 1973 and are ordered in chronological order. "Flesh and the Mirror" is the sixth story and the last to be set in Japan.

18. Both Uncle Philip and the Asiatic Professor are male puppet masters, pulling the strings of patriarchy. In "Flesh and the Mirror", however, the female narrator is her own puppet master, foregrounding the process by which women conspire/collude unconsciously in their own subjugation.

19. See also the 1986 screen adaptation of *The Magic Toyshop*, which uses old-fashioned film techniques to intercut between life-size marionettes and actors, creating an uncanny effect, whereby the spectator is unable to differentiate between animate and inanimate (see Crofts 127–55).

20. Barthes similarly locates Japan as a place that unsettles his Western subjectivity, referring to himself in the third person: 'Japan has afforded him [the author] a situation of writing. This situation is the very one in which

a certain disturbance of the person occurs, a subversion of earlier readings, a shock of meaning lacerated, extenuated to the point of its irreplaceable void [...] writing is after all a *satori* [...] which causes knowledge or the subject, to vacillate: it creates an emptiness of language' (4).

21. In an article on the redefinition of the 'foreigner' in the context of globalization, Rebecca Saunders calls on Freud's definition of the 'uncanny' as a way to explore the concept of the foreign: 'Freud not only associates the uncanny with the operations of the unconscious but with the foreign, signaling the degree to which the German word unheimlich [uncanny] connotes foreignness. It is, he writes, "obviously the opposite of 'heimlich' [homely], 'heimish' [native] (or belonging to the home), and we are tempted to conclude that what is 'uncanny' is frightening precisely because it is not known and familiar"' (90).

Works cited

Almansi, Guido. "In the Alchemist's Cave: Radio Plays." *Flesh and the Mirror: Essays on the Art of Angela Carter*. Ed. Lorna Sage. London: Virago, 1994. 216–29.

Barthes, Roland. *Empire of Signs*. 1970. Trans. Richard Howard. New York: Hill & Wang, 1982.

Boone. Joseph A. "Vacation Cruises; or The Homoerotics of Orientalism." *Edward Said, Part 1: Intellectuals and Critics: Positions and Polemics*. Ed. Patrick Williams. Thousand Oaks, CA: Sage, 2001. 89–107.

Carby, Hazel. "White Woman Listen! Black Feminism and the Boundaries of Sisterhood." *Black British Feminism: A Reader*. Ed. Heidi Safia Mirza. London: Routledge, 1997. 45–53.

Carter, Angela. "Black Venus." *Black Venus*. 1985. London: Vintage, 1996. 1–14.

———. *Come Unto These Yellow Sands*. Dir. Glynn Dearman. BBC Radio 3. 7 April 1979. [Collected in *The Curious Room: Collected Dramatic Works*. Ed. Mark Bell. London: Chatto & Windus, 1996. 33–59.]

———. "Flesh and the Mirror." *Fireworks: Nine Profane Pieces*. 1974. London: Virago, 1987. 67–77.

———. *The Holy Family Album*. Dir. Jo Ann Kaplan. Large Door Productions. Channel 4. 3 Dec. 1991.

———. *The Infernal Desire Machines of Doctor Hoffman*. 1972. Harmondsworth: Penguin, 1982.

———. "The Language of Sisterhood." *The State of the Language*. Ed. Leonard Michaels and Christopher Ricks. Berkeley: University of California Press, 1980. 226–34.

———. "The Loves of Lady Purple." *Fireworks: Nine Profane Pieces*. 1974. London: Virago, 1987. 24–40.

———. *The Magic Toyshop*. 1967. London: Virago, 1980.

———. *The Magic Toyshop*. Dir. David Wheatley. Granada TV/Palace Pictures, 1986.

———. "The Mother Lode." 1976. *Nothing Sacred* 3–19.

———. "Notes from the Front Line." *On Gender and Writing*. Ed. Michelene Wandor. London: Pandora Press, 1983. 69–77.

————. *Nothing Sacred: Selected Writings*. London: Virago, 1982.

————. "Occidentalism: Angela Carter on Euromythologies." Rev. of Rana Kabbani, *Europe's Myths of Orient: Devise and Rule*. London: Macmillan, 1986. *The Guardian* 3 April 1986: 9.

————. "Once More into the Mangle." 1971. *Nothing Sacred* 38–44.

————. "People as Pictures." 1970. *Nothing Sacred* 33–38.

————. "Poor Butterfly." 1972. *Nothing Sacred* 44–50.

————. *The Sadeian Woman: An Exercise in Cultural History*. 1979. London: Virago, 1992.

————. *A Self-Made Man*. Dir. Glynn Dearman. BBC Radio 3. 4 May 1984. [Collected in *The Curious Room: Collected Dramatic Works*. Ed. Mark Bell. London: Chatto & Windus, 1996. 121–51.]

————. *Shaking a Leg: Collected Journalism and Writings*. Intro. Joan Smith. Ed. Jenny Uglow. London: Chatto & Windus. 1997.

————. "A Souvenir of Japan." *Fireworks: Nine Profane Pieces*. 1974. London: Penguin, 1987. 1–13.

————. "Tokyo Pastoral." 1970. *Nothing Sacred* 29–33.

————. "Truly, It Felt Like Year One." *Very Heaven: Looking Back at the 1960s*. Ed. Sarah Maitland. London: Virago, 1988. 209–16.

Crofts, Charlotte. *'Anagrams of Desire': Angela Carter's Writing for Radio, Film and Television*. Manchester: Manchester University Press, 2003.

Doane, Mary Ann. *Femmes Fatales: Feminism, Film Theory, Psychoanalysis*. London: Routledge, 1991.

Dyer, Richard. *White*. London: Routledge, 1997.

Fisher, Susan. "The Mirror of the East: Angela Carter and Japan." *Nostalgic Journeys: Literary Pilgrammages Between Japan and the West*. Ed. Susan Fisher. Vancouver: Institute for Asian Research, University of British Colombia, 2001. 165–74.

Gaines, Jane. "White Privilege and Looking Relations: Race and Gender in Feminist Film Theory." *Cultural Critique* 4 (1986): 59–79.

Gamble, Sarah. *Angela Carter: Writing from the Front Line*. Edinburgh: Edinburgh University Press, 1997.

Hammond, Philip. "The Mystifications of Culture: Western Perceptions of Japan." Globalizing Cultural Studies? Pacific Asia Cultural Studies Forum Conference. Goldsmiths College, University of London. June 1998. <http://myweb.lsbu.ac.uk/philip-hammond/1999c.html>.

hooks, bell. *Black Looks: Race and Representation*. Boston: Southend Press, 1992.

————. *Reel to Real: Race, Sex and Class at the Movies*. New York: Routledge, 1996.

Jackson, Rosemary. *Fantasy: The Literature of Subversion*. London: Routledge, 1981.

Kaplan, E. Ann. *Looking For the Other: Feminism, Film and the Imperial Gaze*. New York: Routledge, 1997.

Kristeva, Julia. *About Chinese Women*. 1974. Trans. Anita Barrows. New York: Marion Boyars, 1977.

Lowe, Lisa. "Heterogeneity, Hybridity, Multiplicity: Marking Asian American Differences." *Diaspora* 1.1 (1991): 24–44.

Matus, Jill. "Blonde, Black and Hottentot Venus: Context and Critique in Angela Carter's 'Black Venus'." *Studies in Short Fiction* 28 (1991): 467–76.

Nava, Mica. "The Cosmopolitanism of Commerce and the Allure of Difference: Selfridges, the Russian Ballet and the Tango 1911–1914." *International Journal of Cultural Studies* 1.2 (1998): 163–96.

———. "Cosmopolitan Modernity: Everyday Imaginaries and the Register of Difference." *Theory, Culture and Society* 19.1–2 (2002): 81–99.

———. "Visceral Cosmopolitanism: The Specificity of Race and Miscegenation in the UK." *Politics and Culture* 3 (2003). <http://aspen.conncoll.edu/politicsand-culture/>.

Peach, Linden. *Angela Carter.* Basingstoke: Macmillan, 1998.

Pels, Dick. "Privileged Nomads: On the Strangeness of Intellectuals and the Intellectuality of Strangers." *Theory, Culture and Society* 16.1 (1999): 63–86.

Said, Edward. *Culture and Imperialism.* London: Chatto & Windus, 1993.

———. "East isn't East: The Impending End of the End of Orientalism." *Times Literary Supplement* 4792. 3 Feb. 1995: 1–3.

———. *Orientalism.* London: Routledge and Keegan Paul, 1978.

Sage, Lorna. *Angela Carter.* Writers and Their Work. Plymouth: Northcote House, 1994.

———. Introduction. *Flesh and the Mirror: Essays on the Art of Angela Carter.* Ed. Lorna Sage. London: Virago, 1994. 1–23.

Saunders, Rebecca. "Uncanny Presence: The Foreigner at the Gate of Globalization." *Comparative Studies of South Asia, Africa and the Middle East* 21.1–2 (2001): 88–98.

Spivak, Gayatri. "Can the Subaltern Speak?" *Marxism and The Interpretation of Culture.* Ed. Cary Nelson and Lawrence Grossberg. Urbana: University of Illinois Press, 1988. 271–313.

———. *The Post-Colonial Critic: Interviews, Strategies, Dialogues.* New York: Routledge, 1990.

Suleiman, Susan Rubin. "The Fate of the Surrealist Imagination in the Society of Spectacle." *Flesh and the Mirror: Essays on the Art of Angela Carter.* Ed. Lorna Sage. London: Virago, 1994. 98–116.

Yu, Su-lin. "'Reconstructing Western Female Subjectivity: Between Orientalism and Feminism in Julia Kristeva's *About Chinese Women.*" *Jouvert: A Journal for Postcolonial Studies* 7.1 (2002). <http://social.chass.ncsu.edu/jouvert/v7is1/slyu.htm>.

5
Bubblegum and Revolution: Angela Carter's Hybrid Shakespeare

Julie Sanders

Angela Carter's Shakespeare was undoubtedly a many splendoured thing. Throughout her career, she persistently invoked, reworked, adapted, and appropriated Shakespeare's texts and the very idea of the national poet. The plurality and hybridity of her approach to 'Shakespeare' – those quotation marks deliberately signal the element of camp in her allusions to the playwright[1] – function as a version in microcosm of her approach to literary intertextuality as a whole: one that embraced multiplicity over singular influence, *bricolage* as opposed to deferential citation.[2] Carter's penchant for *bricolage* is frequently equated with a postmodernist assertion of the 'death of the author', but a fuller understanding of her engagement with Shakespeare serves to challenge any simplistic identification of her approach with postmodernist techniques of fragmentation and dispersal.[3] Both Shakespeare and the Shakespearean canon provide particularly solid vertebrae to Carter's allusive body of work and in turn reveal much about the political dimension to her personal brand of intertextuality. Carter is alert to the politics of Shakespearean citation in the late twentieth century, and to the critical perspectives on his texts mobilized by feminism and postcolonialism. This aspect to her work further subverts conventional notions of postmodernist fragmentation operating as a form of political disengagement.

In numerous interviews Carter stressed the significance of 'the Bard', simultaneously reclaiming him from what she saw as the stifling confines of high culture and asserting the manifold ways in which his work had been adapted and reinterpreted by alternative ages and cultures:

> The extraordinary thing about English literature is that actually our greatest writer is the intellectual equivalent of bubblegum, but can

make 12 year-old girls cry, can foment revolutions in Africa, can be translated into Japanese and leave not a dry eye in the house. (Sage, "Angela Carter" 187)[4]

This quotation, from a 1992 interview with Lorna Sage, has significance for Carter's intertextual deployments of Shakespeare. The stress on Shakespeare as an icon of popular culture as much as a mechanism for the élite articulations of high culture is inescapable; he is for Carter the 'intellectual equivalent of bubblegum'. Shakespeare as popular cultural commodity recurs in several of her texts, reaching a zenith in her final novel *Wise Children* (1991), where as well as becoming the overt symbol of cultural capital via his presence on the English £20 note in the 1980s – 'not just on any old bank note but on a high denomination one, to boot' (191) – the playwright's work becomes the subject and object of reinterpretation in genres and domains as wide-ranging and juxtaposed as music-hall, vaudeville, television game-show, advertising, and Hollywood talking pictures.

Jean Baudrillard's highly influential theory of simulacra suggests that in the postmodern era many objects and ideas, aesthetic, cultural, and architectural, are effectively 'hyperreal', mere simulacra and simulations of the traditions from which they evolve (see also Malpas 121). In recognizing the fragmentation of Shakespeare into a series of evacuated cultural icons in the modern era, Carter appears to endorse Baudrillardian theory and yet for her this endless reworking of Shakespearean material was not necessarily devoid of political content. In fact, she registered considerable political and cultural force at play in the seemingly tireless reinvention of Shakespearean texts and language in a global context.

Carter's Shakespeare and cultural context

Carter's versions of Shakespeare were in part produced by her own cultural context and studies of her work must as a result engage with the dominant critical theories of the time-period in which she operated. Feminism and postcolonialism are clearly informing discourses and her fictional style pays regular lip-service to postmodernism, while also mischievously challenging its central premises. For a writer so frequently associated with theories of performativity in both social and gendered terms, it is perhaps not surprising that she also responded to the dominant theatrical and performance theories of her day. The 1960s to 1980s witnessed an upsurge of interest in 'World Shakespeares' and intercultural performances of his plays deploying techniques from, for example,

Japanese Noh and Kabuki theatre, Indian Kathakali dance-drama, and Zulu or West African performance.[5] The experimentation of theatre directors such as Peter Brook, Yukio Ninigawa, and Ariane Mnouchkine, alongside the film work of Akira Kurosawa and Satayjit Ray, among others, created a precedent for the global account of Shakespeare that Carter offered in the 1992 interview.

There are several important ways in which Shakespeare became representative for Carter of theatre in general. In *Wise Children*, there is no doubting that theatre, and performance in its widest social context, becomes a means of societal levelling and cultural encounter. Shakespeare, as a shared cross-cultural as well as intra-cultural discourse, provides the perfect vehicle to facilitate this move. Gérard Genette has stressed the necessity of familiarity on the part of readers of intertextual or hypertextual writings with the source being alluded to or adapted (381). Such familiarity enables a form of lexical shorthand. In the preface to her fictional biography of Marilyn Monroe, Joyce Carol Oates declares that 'synecdoche is the principle of appropriation' (ix). Carter seems to share this understanding of appropriation when she deploys Shakespearean plotlines, dialogue, and characters. A single phrase ('To be or not to be,' 'All the world's a stage') or image (a woman on a balcony, someone distributing flowers) is often sufficient to connote a far larger scenic context, from *Hamlet* to *As You Like It*, from Juliet's romantic encounter with Romeo to Ophelia's tragic madness.[6] So much so that when in the 1992 interview Carter implicitly links Shakespeare's global impact to the quintessential theatrical cliché 'not a dry eye in the house' she quietly effects the equation of Shakespeare with performance more generally.

This same phrase, 'not a dry eye in the house', is mobilized in one of the short stories in the 1985 *Black Venus* collection, where it describes the impact of the theatrical performances of Edgar Allan Poe's mother: 'She had a low, melodious voice of singular sweetness, an excellent thing in a woman. When crazed Ophelia handed round the rosemary and rue and sang: 'He is dead and gone, lady,' not a dry eye in the house, I assure you' ("The Cabinet of Edgar Allan Poe" 33). This short extract is further indication of Carter's densely allusive aesthetic: the literary in-joke is that Poe's mother's exquisite voice is described in terms lifted directly from the description of Cordelia in *The Tragedy of King Lear*: 'Her voice was ever soft,/Gentle, and low, an excellent thing in a woman' (5.3.247–48). The ironies of this embedded allusion proliferate when we remember that these lines are spoken over Cordelia's corpse; the play has effectively silenced her for ever, a tragic fate for a character associated with careful deployment of speech and silence in the earlier flattery-soaked scenes of the text. This is synecdoche in operation, since Carter is able by means of these brief allusions to bring into the framework of her short story a whole context of supposedly aberrant or transgressive women in literature and society, the category into which Poe's unconventional mother is clearly placed by her contemporaries.

Carter is able to use the Shakespearean allusions to effect a deft shift of tone or register in her short story. The allusions to Ophelia and Cordelia, and by extension to *Hamlet* and *King Lear*, achieve a generic shift from comedy to tragedy, the same trajectory that Mrs Poe undergoes during her life. She dons the chemise from Ophelia's mad scenes for her final performance, but this piece of theatre does not take place on any commercial stage; she is dying for real. It is no coincidence that the theatrical clichés that encapsulated her stage career resurface in the context of her ritualized, stage-managed funeral:

> They told her children that now she could come back to take no curtain-calls no matter how fiercely all applauded the manner of her going. Lovers of the theatre plied her hearse with bouquets: 'And from her pure and uncorrupted flesh May violets spring.' (Not a dry eye in the house.) (35)

As a collection of short stories *Black Venus* is dedicated to adopting new perspectives on canonical authors, texts, and events, ranging from Poe to Lizzie Borden to Charles Baudelaire to Shakespeare's plays. In "Overture and Incidental Music for *A Midsummer Night's Dream*", Carter offers an iconoclastic 'behind-the-scenes' view of one of Shakespeare's best-known romantic comedies. By according the first-person narration of the early part of her story to the sexually ambiguous 'Golden Herm', the offstage Indian Prince warred over by the fairy king and queen in the play, Carter adopts a strategy now familiar from many self-consciously appropriative texts such as Jean Rhys's *Wide Sargasso Sea* (1966) of voicing the otherwise silenced or marginalized figures of canonical literature. Rhys's experimental novel rewrites Charlotte Brontë's *Jane Eyre* (1847) from the perspective of Rochester's first wife, Bertha, who was consigned in the nineteenth-century source to the role of 'madwoman in the attic'. That phrase has become seminal in feminist discourse, providing the title as it does for Sandra Gilbert and Susan Gubar's canonical text of literary criticism on nineteenth-century women's writing, and Carter's approach to Shakespeare is clearly informed by this larger critical context. But as well as being written from a feminist perspective, Carter's postcolonial vision of the character of the Golden Herm in her short story enables a deconstruction of many of the most abiding, and constrictive, notions of Shakespeare's *A Midsummer Night's Dream* in performance. Not for her the gauzy child-fairies of innumerable nineteenth-century and early twentieth-century stage productions of the play. Her Titania is a buxom giantess attended by sarcastic, muttering, rain-sodden creatures: 'poor dears, their little wings all sodden and plastered to their backs, so water-logged they can hardly take off and no sooner airborne than they founder in the pelting downpour' (43).

Of course, all this allows a comic sideswipe at proverbial English midsummer weather but Carter also has in her sights the hijacking of Shakespeare and his texts by high cultural forces. In her account this move was promulgated by the Victorians, who bowdlerized Shakespeare, censored him, and tidied his playtexts up for public consumption in accordance with the repressed, and repressive, morality of their age:

> The wood we have just described is that of nineteenth-century nostalgia, which disinfected the wood, cleansing it of the grave, hideous and elemental beings with which the superstition of an earlier age had filled it. Or, rather, denaturing, castrating these beings until they came to look just as they do in those photographs of fairy folk that so enraptured Conan Doyle. It is Mendelssohn's wood. ("Overture and Incidental Music" 46–47)

This extract is typically dense in its references. The 'fairy folk' that so enraptured Sir Arthur Conan Doyle, a ready believer in the paranormal, were fakes; these were the so-called Cottingley fairies, a photographic deception dreamt up by two schoolgirls.[7] The Athenian wood of Shakespeare's comic drama has in turn become 'Mendelssohn's wood' because productions of the play, both theatrical and balletic, are inextricably associated in the public consciousness with Mendelssohn's composition. Not only did this symphony feature in many mainstream theatrical productions of *Dream* throughout the twentieth century but it provided the evocative soundtrack to the first speaking picture version, made at vast expense in Hollywood during the economic depression of the 1930s.

That 1935 film, directed by Max Reinhardt and Willem Deiterle, resurfaces wholesale in the central chapter of *Wise Children* (the novel is structured in terms of five chapters or 'acts' in a self-conscious nod to its dramatic provenance) when the twin protagonists, Nora and Dora Chance, travel to Hollywood to star as Peaseblossom and Mustardseed in a cinematic spectacular of Shakespeare's play: 'The wood near Athens covered an entire stage and was so thickly art-directed it came up all black in the rushes' (124; see also Hackett 64–66). In the context of the novel the film becomes an extravagant example of the adaptation and shameless commodification of Shakespeare by the modern era, a 'masterpiece of kitsch' according to some (*Wise Children* 111). Through the nostalgic narrative of her first-person narrator, Dora, Carter seems to espouse regret for the demise of Shakespeare and theatre: 'What I missed most was illusion. That wood near Athens was too, too solid for me [...] there wasn't the merest whiff about of the kind of magic that comes when the theatre darkens, the bottom of the curtain glows' (125); and yet elsewhere in her work she was clearly fascinated by the power and seduction of cinema as an art-form.[8] Indeed, in one of her later short stories in *American Ghosts and Old World Wonders* (1993) she links Shakespeare to the history of film: in "The Merchant of Shadows" an embedded allusion to Orson Welles's failed attempt to film *The Merchant of Venice* may exist in what constitutes another of Carter's fictional ruminations on the iconic, yet spectral, quality of cinematic stardom.

The problem with celluloid versions of Shakespeare for Carter, as with fixed Victorian notions of what productions of *A Midsummer Night's Dream* should look and sound like, was the ossification of his works into one rigid and unchanging interpretation. What she implicitly sought to celebrate is Shakespeare's plurality rather than his fixity, his endless textual reinvention and reanimation in the context of different media, eras, and cultural contexts. Her penchant for parody and pastiche in relation to Shakespeare rarely, then, if ever, constitutes a direct attack. Indeed, in the specific case of *A Midsummer Night's Dream* she once declared that she liked the play 'almost beyond reason, because it's beautiful and funny and camp – and glamorous, and cynical' (Sage, "Angela Carter" 186–87). It would be erroneous to suggest that Carter was embarked on a journey of deification and blind homage. Her objective was to defamiliarize 'Shakespeare', both in terms of direct textual and intertextual inheritances and his artistic legacy as the national poet. For political reasons, Carter questioned Shakespeare's positioning as the poet of empire and establishment. Her methodologies were again shaped by contemporary dramatic practice. Parallel to the interest in intercultural performance cited earlier, the 1960s and subsequent decades witnessed a Brechtian-inspired determination to politicize and defamiliarize the conventions of mainstream British theatre.[9] Chief exponents of this theatrical agenda included several playwrights who looked directly to early modern drama for inspiration and influence: Edward Bond and Howard Barker, among others. These playwrights and practitioners looked to Shakespeare and his contemporaries for direct intertexts – witness Bond's *Lear* (1972) or Barker's *Women Beware Women* (1986), a savage riff on Thomas Middleton's early modern city tragedy. They also recognized early modern drama's capacity to mobilize realism and artifice in a series of complex shifts and modulations within a single production or performance, leading to their labelling in the media as the 'neo-Jacobeans'. As Benedict Nightingale has noted, '[t]he Elizabethans and Jacobeans in particular ask you to suspend disbelief in the existence of titanic feelings and absolute values' (qtd. in Saunders 18). Carter seems to have recognized something very similar to contemporary theatre practitioners in this respect.

Melding the modern, the postmodern, and the early modern

Carter references a number of early modern dramatists other than Shakespeare. At the beginning of *Several Perceptions* (1968), Joseph identifies in the mirror a troubling image of ambiguous villainy (5) that calls to mind the complicated audience responses evoked by characters such as De Flores in Thomas Middleton and William Rowley's *The Changeling* (1622) and Flamineo in John Webster's *The White Devil* (1612). Elsewhere in that novel there are echoes of Christopher Marlowe's *The Jew of Malta* (1589–90) and in a much later short story, 'John Ford's 'Tis Pity She's a Whore' (1993), Carter effects a brilliant parallel between two geographically, culturally, and temporally distanced John Fords: the Caroline playwright, best known for his 1629 play of incestuous sexual encounter, and his twentieth-century namesake, the director of US film Westerns such as *The Searchers* (1956): 'In the old play, one John Ford called them Giovanni and Annabella; the other John Ford, in the movie, might call them Johnny and Annie-Belle' (21).

Carter was undoubtedly drawn to the capacity of early modern drama to activate fantasy and reality simultaneously, and to blur, sometimes irreparably, the boundaries between the two. This dynamic is a driving force in early novels, such as *Several Perceptions*, where, as Linden Peach has indicated, David Hume's notion of the 'theatre of the mind' serves as an epigraph and helps to introduce a destabilizing air of unreality to events (23).[10] A similar concept informs the entire fifth 'act' of *Wise Children*, where characters return on a magical wind (or tempest) and in clouds of butterflies. These are self-conscious allusions to Shakespeare's

fantastic late plays, where the lines between art and reality are deliberately blurred, as well as to the vogue for magical realism inspired by
South American fiction in the latter half of the twentieth century.[11]
Carter once declared that 'Shakespeare, like Picasso, is one of the great
Janus-figures that sum up the past as well as opening all the doors
towards the future' (Sage, "Angela Carter" 186–87) and it seems clear
that in the self-aware melding she effects between early modern dramatic and textual practice, the 'past historical' as it were, and the more
contemporary idiom of movements such as feminism, postcolonialism,
or magical realism, to name just a few, she sought to deploy Shakespeare
as just such a 'hinge-figure' in her own narrative *bricolage*. In re-vision-
ary texts such as "Overture and Incidental Music for *A Midsummer
Night's Dream*", Carter re-reads *Dream* from a feminist and postcolonial
perspective and strives to reinsert a darker magic and sexuality. This
serves to restore Shakespeare to popular culture in the same way that
Wise Children seeks to restore him to his 'pre-canonized self' (Sage,
Angela Carter 56). It is no small coincidence that in that novel Dora and
Nora Chance reside at 49, Bard Road, Brixton, in South London, the
location of the Liberties where many of Shakespeare's plays were first
staged to distinctly non-élite audiences.

One further appeal for Carter of Shakespearean plays and early modern drama more generally is undoubtedly their generic hybridity. The
early modern era was an epoch of theatre that consciously juxtaposed
the tragic with the comic, and the grittily realistic with the magical and
fantastic, within the dramaturgy of a single playtext and performance. At
times *Wise Children* seems like a positive experiment in the writing of
tragicomedy in prose, although the same mixed generic register is identifiable in earlier works such as *Shadow Dance* (1966) and *The Magic
Toyshop* (1967). Undoubtedly, however, it is in Shakespeare's experimental late plays, in particular *The Winter's Tale* and *The Tempest*, that she
found the most influential exposition of this generic hybridity. These
plays persistently inform the fantastical events of *Wise Children*. All the
happenings of that novel, which takes place on a single day – 23 April,
Shakespeare's birthday – are framed by a magical tempest: 'the kind of
wind that blows everything topsy-turvy' (3). The single day's setting that
nevertheless traverses times and cultures can obviously be read as
Modernism-inflected, reworking as it seems to do the early twentieth-
century narrative experimentation of Virginia Woolf and James Joyce in
texts such as *Mrs Dalloway* (1925) and *Ulysses* (1922) which unfold within the controlling parameters and timeframe of a single day (Dora's twin
may even be named Nora in an intertextual gesture towards Joyce). But

in her notebooks Woolf proclaimed that *Mrs Dalloway* was an attempt to rework the dramatic unities in a fictional context, so perhaps here again Carter is evoking Shakespeare as a 'hinge-figure'.[12] By overtly linking *Wise Children's* temporal structure to Modernist narrative experimentation and to the idea of the dramatic unities adhered to and subverted by early modern theatre, she achieves a suggestive melding of the modern, postmodern, and distinctly early modern in her all-encompassing narrative sweep that emulates the version of Shakespeare as a connective between past and present which she found so attractive.

In attending to the magical elements in *Wise Children*, however, we must retain an operative sense of how debunking 'Shakespeare' provides much of the comedy in the novel, from the music hall and pantomime revisions that punctuate the Chance twins' stage careers to the superb kitsch of the Hollywood *Dream* and the ridiculous pomposity of Melchior Hazard's Globe theatre birthday cake on his 100th birthday (also the momentous day on which the events of the novel take place). The festive and carnivalesque forces at play here are undeniable. All the significant happenings of the novel are structured around festive events, from birthdays to weddings to Twelfth Night fancy-dress parties (Shakespearean costume required, of course). Specific characters such as Estella and Perry import a carnivalesque dynamic into the narrative. Carter's interest in the carnivalesque has been discussed by many critics and the common point of reference is usually the ideas of early modern carnival promulgated by Russian theorist Mikhail Bakhtin.[13] She, however, consistently resisted drawing too close an alliance between her approach and Bakhtin's utopian account of the potential for plebeian protest latent in carnival festivity (see Peach 142). Her notion of festive potential, tied so closely as it was to the pre-modern agricultural calendar and hinge-dates such as the midsummer and winter solstices, appears in actuality to have more kinship with the structuralist accounts of Shakespearean drama that pre-date Bakhtinian theory's circulation in English academic circles, in particular the work of Northrop Frye and C.L. Barber (see Peach 145).[14] In this way, a fuller examination of Carter's engagement with Shakespeare in her writing unsettles, or at the very least opens out, previously dominant readings of her work as 'carnivalesque' in a purely twentieth-century sense of the term.[15]

The quasi-hallucinatory events of Christmas Eve and Christmas Day in *Several Perceptions*, which involve topsy-turvy sexual encounters, miraculous medical cures, and much intermittent confusion, undoubtedly make great comic capital of their festive setting: 'It was the time of the winter solstice, one of the numinous hinges of the year' (143). Much later in

Carter's canon, the festive happenings or 'hinge-dates' of *Wise Children*, including a Hollywood wedding with substitute brides, a fire at a Twelfth Night gathering that quite literally brings the house down, and that fifth-act spectacle of reunions and revelations at the multiple birthday party, provide the structure to both the day on which the novel is ostensibly set and the memories which come flooding back to the narrator, Dora. In the final act of carnivalesque confusion the impulse for this recollection appears multiple: at the beginning of the novel Dora seems to be sorting though her memoirs at home, but later we are apparently in the hands of a pub raconteur who is '[d]runk in charge of a narrative' (158): 'Well, you might have known what you were about to let yourself in for when you let Dora Chance in her ratty old fur and poster paint [...] accost you in the Coach and Horses and let her tell you a tale' (227).

Shakespeare, his shifting and contradictory history in performance, and his multivalent reception in twentieth-century literary criticism cohere to provide a complex and revealing series of intertexts in Carter's *oeuvre*. The tendency in Shakespearean drama for plotlines of cross-dressing and multiple identities provided a particularly rich seam for her to mine in her fiction. From *The Passion of New Eve* (1977) to the twinned and constantly swapped identities of *Wise Children*, Carter was fascinated by the constructed nature of social and gendered identity. Her interest in these topics and its complex working out in the context of her plotlines has been related by several critics to the work of another prominent theorist of the late twentieth century, critic Judith Butler, whose seminal study *Gender Trouble* (1990) and its companion volume *Bodies That Matter* (1993) cast a long shadow over intellectual work in the spheres of literature, language, drama, and social theory. Once again, however, Carter's genuine interest in the issues of constructed or performed identity that Butler's work disseminates has its roots not only in twentieth-century theories of performativity but also in the early modern context of Shakespearean drama, with its tradition of boy actors in female roles; witness the account of masquerade she offers in *The Passion of New Eve*: 'I was a boy disguised as a girl and now disguised as a boy again, like Rosalind in Elizabethan Arden' (132).

Unstable identities pervade the text of the Shakespeare-soaked *Shadow Dance* where the morally ambivalent and sexually androgynous figure of Honeybuzzard appears in the guise of the mad Ophelia towards the sinister close of the novel. These cross-dressings reach their zenith in the deliberately proliferating plotlines of *Wise Children* where we encounter numerous stage cross-dressers, including the carnivalesque Estella who plays Hamlet 'in drag' (12), and the identity-swapping of the identical twins, Dora and Nora. The twins' 'performances' rework the plotlines of several Shakespearean plays: from the impersonation of a supposedly adulterous Hero by the servant Margaret in *Much Ado About Nothing* which leads to disrupted nuptials and a feigned funeral, to the bed-swaps of *All's Well that Ends Well* and *Measure for Measure*. Dora's account of losing her virginity to Nora's boyfriend in the guise of her more assertive twin – 'I smelled the unfamiliar perfume on my skin and felt voluptuous. As soon as they started to call me Nora, I found that I could kiss the boys and hug the principals with gay abandon' (84) – directly recalls the confidence Rosalind finds to assert herself in doublet and house in the Forest of Arden exchanges with her erstwhile suitor Orlando in *As You Like It*, although here the cross-dressing is achieved at the level of substituted scent.

Carter's Ophelia complex

As well as overarching motifs such as festive culture and cross-dressing, Carter was drawn throughout her career to specific figures and events in the Shakespearean canon. Sometimes her intertextual games occur at the level of posing the question 'What if ...?', drawing readers' attention to marginalized or disenfranchised characters within canonical plays such as *King Lear* – 'Speaking of which, has it ever occurred to you to spare a passing thought as to the character of the deceased *Mrs* Lear?' (*Wise Children* 224)[16] – as well as the possibility of alternative endings. The absence of certain significant female characters from canonical plays such as *King Lear* and *The Tempest* is directly questioned by passages such as this, but such challenges in Carter's narratives also serve to highlight the wider deployment of Shakespeare's texts to endorse patriarchal or conservative values. For example:

> 'Don't worry, darlin', '*e*'s not your father!'
> What if Horatio had whispered that to Hamlet in Act 1 Scene i? And think what a difference it might have made to Cordelia. On the other hand, those last comedies would darken considerably in tone, don't you think, if Marina and, especially, Perdita weren't really the daughters of ... (*Wise Children* 213)

or:

> As if, when the young king meets up again with Jack Falstaff in *Henry IV, Part Two*, he doesn't send him packing but digs him in the ribs, says: 'Have I got a job for you!' (ibid. 222)

It is revealing that Carter chooses in the latter extract to rewrite the ultimate Shakespearean scene of rejection – that of Falstaff by the newly-
crowned Henry V. By means of such comic subversions, not least in *Wise
Children*, a novel all about illegitimacy and confused patronage, Carter
seeks to disturb the conservative or 'patriarchal version' of Shakespeare
promoted by certain critics.[17] What should be stressed, however, is that in
doing so she does not simply reject 'Shakespeare'; rather, she reclaims him
from a cultural and critical stranglehold. Hers is a gesture of liberation as
opposed to eschewal; it is an act of reanimation rather than rejection.

More often than not Carter traces the complex textual and cultural
afterlives of Shakespearean protagonists in her hybrid allusions to them.
The remainder of this essay will concentrate on just two such examples:
the tragic Ophelia from *Hamlet* and *Measure for Measure*'s abandoned
fiancée Mariana. What these case studies reveal is that, as with the theoretical deployments of Shakespeare, be they in the form of cross-dressing motifs and attendant debates about gender and performance, or the
mobilization of festive and carnivalesque cultural possibilities in her
narratives, Carter offers a hybrid version of 'Shakespeare' and his plays.
This hybrid version is filtered through a complex afterlife of adaptation
and appropriation, and the ongoing mediation of critical and performative reception and interpretation.

It was Lorna Sage who first suggested a special interest in Carter's writing in the figure of Ophelia, Hamlet's rejected lover:

> One of the images that haunts her fiction, one of her most poignant
> and persistent borrowings, is the image of crazy, dying Ophelia, as
> described by Gertrude in Shakespeare's *Hamlet*, and (possibly even
> more) as painted by Millais: waterlogged, draped in flowers, drifting
> downstream to her virgin death. (*Angela Carter* 33)[18]

It is undoubtedly the image of Ophelia in her most distracted state that
Carter is compelled to recreate. In addition to the previously cited
example of Poe's actor mother in "The Cabinet of Edgar Allan Poe",
performing the role of Ophelia on her deathbed, we see Honeybuzzard
performing a sinister version of the same in the Gothic house in which
the nightmarish actions of the latter sections of *Shadow Dance* take
place: 'Cap and dark glasses were mislaid or lost. His hair trailed like
mad Ophelia's [...] Under his breath, he sang a song they could not
hear' (179). The gender politics of this staging are intriguing since they
effectively align Honeybuzzard with the character of Ghislaine, who
elsewhere performs the stereotypical part of Gothic heroine, not least in
her iconographic death-scene.

A related fascination with Ophelia's bawdy songs, sung in her state of distraction and distress, emerges in the sequence in *Wise Children* where a pregnant and abandoned Tiffany performs her grief live on national television as part of her unfaithful lover's tawdry game-show, *Lashings of Lolly*:

> There was a bit of wallflower stuck in her hair, over her ear, and her hands were full of flowers, daffs, bluebells, narcissi, she must have picked them out of the front gardens and the window boxes and the public parks that she'd passed by on her way to the studio during that long walk from Bermondsey. (43)

The passage is typical of Carter in its highly material interpretation of the flower scene at 4.5 of *Hamlet*, where Ophelia gives flowers symbolic of personal qualities to her onstage interlocutors, and in its comic physical and verbal echo of other lines and moments from the play: 'She scored a palpable hit with the second [shoe]' (43).[19] Tiffany's onscreen return of Tristram's ill-judged gift of a Number 69 American Football shirt – 'My lord, I have remembrances of yours/That I have longed long to redeliver.' (3.1.95–96) – literally strips her pregnant body bare. In the midst of the comic slapstick, this remains a poignant portrayal of the deflowering, literal and psychological, of the trusting Tiffany.

What Sage's account of Carter's spectral haunting by the idea of Ophelia suggests, however, is that it is the *offstage* events of the play that fill her imagination as much as staged scenes such as the flower-giving. Ophelia's death (whether it is suicide or not remains poignantly unclear) is, of course, related with great poetic beauty by Gertrude at 4.7 of the play:

> There is a willow grows aslant a brook
> That shows his hoar leaves in the glassy stream.
> Therewith fantastic garlands did she make
> Of crow-flowers, nettles, daisies, and long purples,
> [...]
> There on the pendent boughs her crownet weeds
> Clamb'ring to hang, an envious sliver broke,
> When down the weedy trophies and herself
> Fell in the weeping brook. Her clothes spread wide,
> And mermaid-like awhile they bore her up;
> Which time she chanted snatches of old tunes,
> As one incapable of her own distress ...(4.7.138–41; 144–50)

Gertrude's speech describes how the mermaid-like serenity of Ophelia's journey cannot endure and she is dragged by her water-sodden garments to a 'muddy death' (4.7.155), but in the visual arts' representation of this offstage event the choice is frequently taken to freeze the moment earlier in the narrative, before Ophelia drowns or becomes fully conscious of her watery fate.

One of the best-known examples of this is alluded to by Sage in the above quotation as an equal influence, possibly even a greater influence, on Carter's fascination with this described moment in the play. In ca. 1851–52 John Everett Millais, a member of the so-called Pre-Raphaelite Brotherhood which exhibited a sustained interest in visual allusions to canonical texts of drama, poetry, and prose, painted Ophelia as described at this very moment in Gertrude's monologue. Describing the image, Tim Barringer notes '[t]he pale body of Ophelia, laid out like a corpse, but still singing her songs of madness' (62). Adrian Poole has observed how Gertrude's description as much as the Pre-Raphaelite representation aestheticizes Ophelia: 'The painting echoes the suspended quality of Gertrude's speech. The curious rivalries of light, colour, and texture begin to find visual equivalents for its verbal complexity – the obscure and the lucid, the evanescent and the spiny-sharp' (68). Reinforcing the supposition that Carter is entranced by the Millais image, a private letter of 1989 describes a London canal boat trip Carter had undertaken with her family and the new vantage point it provided her with, both on the city and its capacity for natural fecundity in the midst of the urban:

> the canals are wonderful.... You get this Ophelia-style view of the canal-bank; huge juicy plants & flowers & grasses; and we saw herons, & a king-fisher, and it was that frail, chilly early spring that is so English, & the East End – we went through Hackney – is now really one vast nature reserve, mile after mile of abandoned factories returning to the wild. (qtd. in Sage, *Angela Carter* 57)

Carter appears to rework Millais's own careful relocation of the Shakespearean heroine's death in a quintessentially English rural landscape (in his case the landscape of Ewell in Surrey where he and William Holman Hunt were painting in the early 1850s),[20] relocating Ophelia to an urban milieu. This is the process of adaptation and appropriation laid bare for us; a series of filtered mediations, relocations, and recontextualizations, that owe as much to the intertextual afterlife of texts as to their moment of composition.[21]

Carter's fascination with the Pre-Raphaelites is confirmed by a return to the narrative of her first novel, *Shadow Dance*, which is permeated by an awareness of the visual arts and the way in which traces of particular paintings in memory inform and shape our social performances. In the world of constructed identities that pervades the novel (its opening line is, tellingly, 'The bar was a mock-up, a forgery, a fake' [1]), and where repeated moments and gestures are viewed through the prism of artistic composition, several Pre-Raphaelite paintings and stances are directly evoked: Morris's wife Edna, a conscious reworking of the entrapped loyal wife of much Victorian fiction and painting, sits 'in the Pre-Raphaelite glow' of a single lamp (45); and the hideously scarred Ghislaine resembles a Millais painting:

> 'Compassion', Millais would have called her, with her upturned face and incandescent eyes [...] In a pompous gilt frame, she would have been exhibited at the Royal Academy and afterwards reproduced in the *Illustrated London News*, to subsequently grace a thousand humble walls up and down the country. (50)

There is a separate study to be written of Carter's evocation of the Victorian representation of femininity and female sexuality, but it is sufficient to observe in this context that it is the infinite reproduction of these images that fascinates her as much as the objectification of the female subject that they imply. This in turn serves as a model for her reworkings and revisions of Shakespeare as an unstoppable series of cultural reproductions and reinterpretations.

The Pre-Raphaelite allusions in *Shadow Dance* are not confined to a female frame of reference. Honeybuzzard, who, as we have seen, later performs the role of the distract Ophelia, attempts at one point, with the help of theatrical prosthetics, to appear 'doomed' in the manner of a Pre-Raphaelite painting: 'From the neck up, he suddenly became Janey Morris as Guinevere, mouth like a sad pomegranate, cheeks hollowed, shadowed with infinite weariness, infinite experience' (78). It is telling that it is not literally as Guinevere that he appears but as Janey Morris performing that role for the artist. As ever in Carter the reader stands at several stages' remove from the original intertext, able to assess its deployment with a degree of critical detachment because of the defamiliarization of the image. This detachment need not, however, be read as proof of political disengagement or evacuated postmodern parody. The facilitating parallel is again to be found with theatrical practice. Brechtian aesthetics revisited early modern dramatic conventions and performance techniques precisely because they mobilized, often in swift succession, both identification and detachment on the part of watching audiences, encouraging the fullest possible critical and intellectual response to what was being observed. Once again it proves revealing to subject Carter's technique to an early modern as well as a postmodern interrogative frame. If her work strives to 'reclaim' Shakespeare from modern, repressive versions, a willingness to see beyond postmodern conventions when analysing Carter may prove similarly insightful.

Carter was certainly interested in freezing the frame of reference at canonical moments of Shakespearean drama to enable the kinds of 'What if ...?' questions we identified previously as an impulse in her writing. This is perhaps most clearly seen in the instance of Tiffany in *Wise Children*, a novel whose narrative self-consciously plays with the notion of freeze-frame on film and the potentiality of the pause button on the VCR machine. For the reader alert to Ophelia intertexts, the expectation following the game-show flower scene must be that Tiffany will drown herself offstage, whether of her own volition or as the result of a tragic accident.[22] And yet this is a novel that consciously resists tragic expectation, rewriting several Shakespearean endings in the process. In fact, Tiffany returns as part of the fifth act's/chapter's evocation of the miraculous reunions and resurrections of the late plays, effecting a generic shift of her own in the process of moving away from the tragic to the romance plot. The statue scene of *The Winter's Tale* and Hermione's 'return' to life is lovingly and comically recalled in this version of pulling the rabbit from the hat: 'Out of that trunk stepped our little Tiff, as fresh as paint, not a tad the worse for wear except her eyes were no longer those of a dove, stabbed or whole, and she looked sound in mind and body almost to a fault' (210). Tiffany also proactively rewrites her ending in life as in death by refusing the execrable Tristram's proposal of marriage: '"I wouldn't marry you if you were the last man in the world. Marry your auntie, instead." A palpable hit' (211).

Interdisciplinary combinations; or, Mariana in the moated grange

Ophelia is, of course, a highly recognizable Shakespearean female protagonist, but Carter is equally interested in marginalized or minor figures of Shakespearean drama. One salient example is Mariana in *Measure for Measure*. The most obvious female role to mobilize from this play about sexual and social morality is Isabella, the novice nun threatened with rape by Angelo in return for saving her brother's life from his appointed day of execution. Carter chooses, however, to reanimate in her fiction the intertextual memory of the woman Angelo had already abandoned before the beginning of the play: Mariana, whose dowry drowned along with her brother in a merchant trading ship.[23] Her socially ascribed value lost, Angelo abandoned her, justifying his selfish action by besmirching her reputation:

> Left her in her tears, and dried not one of them with his comfort; swallowed his vows whole, pretending in her discoveries of dishonour; in few, bestowed her on her own lamentation, which she yet wears for his sake; and he, a marble to her tears, is washed with them, but relents not. (3.1.227–32)

In Shakespeare's play we first see Mariana onstage as a figure of melancholy and despair in 4.1. She is residènt in a moated grange on the land of St Luke's, a convent which has shown charity to her in her outcast condition (3.1.265–67). There are all sorts of observations to be made about this scene in the context of the wider play. The placing of Mariana in this space of confinement and sexual prohibition links her in important ways to Isabella who will prove so influential in her plot trajectory. It is Isabella who agrees to the duke's suggestion of engineering the bed-swap with Mariana, enabling the latter to spend a night of sexual intercourse with the hypocritical Angelo rather than Isabella herself, thereby consummating the previously intended union between them. The sexual morality of this action and its defining features are not to be debated here: neither the secret garden in which this significant offstage encounter is staged to take place ('He hath a garden circummured with brick,/Whose western side is with a vineyard backed;/And to that vineyard is a plankèd gate', 4.1.27–29);[24] nor the strategist duke's questionable reputation as 'the old fantastical Duke of dark corners' (4.3.152–53); nor Isabella's extreme reaction to the Duke's description of Mariana's plight that this woman would be better off dead (3.1.233–34). Nor is Mariana's questionable, if seemingly welcomed, fate to be married off to Angelo at the end of the play our concern. Instead, it is the frozen frame of Mariana's melancholy and sexual frustration, confined as she is in her moated grange at the start of 4.1., that we will focus on, since this is the moment in the play that the Victorian author Alfred, Lord Tennyson, chose to animate in poetic form and which in turn inspired yet another of Carter's potent reanimations of Shakespeare.

Tennyson's "Mariana" (1830) is a study in sexual frustration and solitude. The quasi-choric refrain that ends each stanza breathes out Mariana's despair – 'She said, 'I am aweary, aweary,/I would that I were dead!' – and, in a virtual exercise in pathetic fallacy, her surroundings echo and underline her mood:

> With blackest moss the flower-plots
> Were thickly crusted, one and all:
> The rusted nails fell from the knots
> That held the pear to the garden-wall.
> The broken sheds look'd sad and strange:
> Unlifted was the clinking latch; (ll. 1–6)

The poem moves between morning and evening and interior and exterior space, although Tennyson's Mariana, always beheld in the third person, seems entrapped by all states within her 'lonely moated grange' (l. 32). The stanzas, with their twelve-line format and interwoven rhyme scheme, function as symbolically truncated sonnets, echoing the foreshortened romance of Mariana's past.

In one of the later stanzas, Mariana's monotonous existence within the 'dreamy house' is described. Intriguingly, that stanza provided the raw material for another well-known painting by John Everett Millais:

> All day within the dreamy house,
> The doors upon their hinges creak'd;
> The blue fly sung in the pane; the mouse
> Behind the mouldering wainscot shriek'd,
> Or from the crevice peer'd about. (ll. 61–65)

Millais's "Mariana" visualizes this stanza, down to the detail of the mouse which can be viewed corner right in his 1851 oil painting, adding a certain symbolism of his own in the form of fading autumn leaves that appear to have been blown into the room, suggestive of the melancholic season but also of the sexual fall that Shakespeare's play, Tennyson's own intertextual source, relates. Millais's depiction of Mariana at a stained glass window is ostensibly a Pre-Raphaelite aestheticized vision of the Middle Ages. Yet, in many ways the blue velvet clad protagonist with her symbolic and dutiful embroidery and her tense body language (the way in which she holds the small of her back in a gesture of soothing an aching pain has been read in terms of sexual longing, although it is also connotative of menstrual pain which in turn underscores her childlessness) is entirely suggestive of a Victorian social scenario.[25] Marion Shaw has indicated the significance of Mariana's story as an archetype of loneliness to Victorian women; Elizabeth Barrett Browning made a direct comparison between herself and Mariana in her letters, though noticeably not with Shakespeare's Mariana but rather the frustrated heroine depicted by Tennyson and Millais: 'I am like Mariana in the moated grange ... and sit listening to the mouse in the wainscot' (qtd. in Shaw 105). For Lynne Pearce, Millais's evocative painting cannot exist separately from Tennyson's poem; she describes both in terms of an 'inter-disciplinary combination' (59). I would suggest that the Shakespearean pre-text or *avant-texte* to both is equally significant and that it is a deep knowledge of all three reconfigurations that animates Carter's reworking of Mariana's story in "The Smile of Winter" (1974).

"The Smile of Winter" first appeared as part of the *Fireworks* collection which is informed throughout by Carter's experiences in Japan and the feeling of otherness this inculcated.[26] The narrator of this short story is a figure both excluded and self-excluding ('after all, I came here in order to be lonely' [42]) from the coastal environment in which she finds herself. The wintertime setting – this is a 'Decembral littoral' (43) – sits on a cusp between old year and new, seasonal demise and springtime renewal. The coastal setting is equally suggestive of a life lived on the margins. This story takes place in an evocative borderland, a hinterland between land and sea and Carter plays on these coastal associations in her choice of words such as 'littoral', underlining the importance of margins and thresholds by means of the narrative's complex interplay between interior and exterior space, a feature itself imitative of Tennyson's poem and the liminal stance of Millais's pictorial protagonist at her stained glass window.

Sarah Gamble notes the indebtedness of this short story to Tennyson's "Mariana", suggesting that Carter portrays her version of the lovelorn woman, alone in a coastal Japanese fishing village, 'in such a way as to recall not the character in *Measure for Measure*, but Tennyson's extravagantly love-lorn Victorian heroine' (107). I want to nuance this slightly in light of the arguments made elsewhere in this essay that Carter's Shakespeare is always a hybridized form of Shakespearean playtext placed alongside its numerous cultural and literary afterlives. In "The Smile of Winter", Carter's first-person narrator is a complicated and self-aware amalgam of Shakespeare's play, Tennyson's poem, and Millais's painting: a full realization of this 'interdisciplinary combination', to use Pearce's phrase, helps us to understand the constructed nature of the isolation presented by the narrative. The narrator performs the role of melancholy, choosing her location, her 'stage', and her seasonal setting carefully – 'This is, after all, the season of abandonment' (44) – and striking a 'picturesque attitude' (that particular phrase is self-consciously repeated three times in one short passage to emphasize this point [45]). Pathetic fallacy, as in Tennyson's poem and Millais's art, is the informing convention: 'Everything combines with the forlorn mood of the châtelaine to procure a moving image of poignant desolation' (43).[27]

The direct intertext of Mariana is highlighted in "The Smile of Winter": 'I have read about all the abandoned lovers in their old books eating their hearts out like Mariana in so many moated granges.' (43) In addition, the narrator defines her location in intertextual terms, 'Outside my shabby front door, I have a canal, like Mariana in a moated grange' (44). This is entirely fitting for a narrative in which life constantly mutates into art, and in which natural phenomena are repeatedly described in aestheticized terms: the sea becomes Art Nouveau stained glass (48); waves become lace cuffs (49). The narrator is even able to catalogue the stage properties she has deployed in the process of creating her story:

> Do not think I do not realise what I am doing. I am making a composition using the following elements: the winter beach; the winter moon; the ocean; the women; the pine trees; the riders; the driftwood; the shells; the shapes of darkness and the shapes of water; and the refuse. (49–50)

This passage, towards the close, revisits all the central tropes and images of the preceding pages. As Gamble notes: 'The final twist is that the narrator reveals herself to have been all along perfectly aware of the paradoxes of her narrative position, suspended as it is between involvement and detachment.' (107) Carter's story encourages a similar vein of involvement and detachment in her readers. Respondents to the story are seduced by the sensory perceptions and cultural poetics of the narrator's descriptions and yet alert to the manipulations of pathetic fallacy.

There is self-conscious performativity implicit here as suggestive as any of the sub-Shakespearean cross-dressing Carter deploys elsewhere in her work. There is also the unavoidable self-consciousness created by an awareness of literature and the visual arts that Carter sees as both the curse and the great gift of the contemporary writer who works in the wake of such traditions. Nowhere more so does she play out this traumatic self-awareness in her writing than in her responses to

Shakespeare. Carter's postmodernism rests not in a wholesale rejection or eschewal of a canonical author such as Shakespeare, then, but in her willingness to acknowledge that we receive the past, textual or otherwise, mediated by numerous cultural and critical forces, and that we should use that knowledge to question the values which have come to be associated with certain texts or authors.

Genette has written persuasively of the pleasure that is involved in intertextuality, in the reading of texts alongside each other and in the sharing of references between writer and reader involved in literary forms such as imitation, homage, parody, burlesque, and pastiche (399). These are all forms associated with Carter's *oeuvre* and narrative technique, but it is a mark of the complexity and depth of her responses to Shakespeare throughout her work that none of these labels seems quite sufficient to describe the process. Her 'hybrid Shakespeare' is one who has been adopted, harnessed, even hijacked, for a diverse range of cultural and political positions and who Carter seeks to explore in the light of those re-readings from her own politicized vantage point. He is a playwright whose works have been restaged by subsequent cultures and in multiple media to very different ends and effects. Carter is both intrigued and disturbed by that endless redispersal, reinvention, and redissemination of Shakespeare, and she enacts a parallel redispersal of his influence in her own *oeuvre* as part of an ongoing investigation into the phenomenon that is the Shakespeare industry. In the end, 'hybridity' as a term can only begin to gesture at the numerous and numinous ways in which she borrows, alludes to, cites, critiques, revises, and appropriates Shakespeare, and in which she is in turn influenced, haunted, possessed, and obsessed by his texts and their seemingly unstoppable afterlife.

Notes

1. For more on this see Sontag (*passim*) and Gamble (39–41 and 178–79).
2. For Carter's own definition of *bricolage* in terms of treating the canon of Western literature as a huge salvage yard, see Munford's introduction to this volume.
3. Simon Malpas usefully defines postmodernism in terms of 'fracturing, fragmentation, indeterminacy, and plurality' (5).
4. The notion of fomenting revolution in Africa seems fanciful but Carter may well have been aware of the copy of Shakespeare's *Complete Works* that circulated among the inmates of Robben Island, South Africa, who had been jailed for their anti-apartheid activities. Passages were marked up for their significance. The inmates included Nelson Mandela, ANC leader and future South African president, who picked out a passage from *The Tempest* for special attention.

5. See, for example, Kennedy. On intercultural performance more generally, see Pavis.

6. All references to Shakespeare in this essay are taken from *The Oxford Shakespeare: The Complete Works*, Ed. Stanley Wells and Gary Taylor (Oxford: Oxford University Press, 1998).

7. For more on this see Bown (*passim*) and Purkiss (284–93).

8. On Carter and cinema, see, for example, Gamble in this volume.

9. Linden Peach has suggested that Bertolt Brecht is a particular influence on Carter due to his explorations of the theatre of Asia, in particular Japan and China: 'the work of [...] Brecht prepared her for, and in some ways helped shape, her response to oriental theatre; and perhaps most important of all to Shakespearean and Renaissance drama' (140). For Brecht's most explicit account of the influence of Chinese acting techniques on his theatrical practice, see "Alienation Effects in Chinese Acting".

10. Peach makes explicit a link between this and Shakespeare's ambiguous late plays, especially *The Winter's Tale*, 'in which the distinction between reality and illusion is blurred in potentially stunning pieces of experimental theatre' (23–24).

11. For more on this see Sanders (59) and also Bowers (*passim*).

12. In a notebook entry on her manuscript for *Mrs Dalloway*, Woolf observes: 'The book is to have the intensity of a play; only in narrative' (qtd. in Tomalin xx).

13. For an extension of this argument to the theatricality of Dickens and his influence on Carter, see Duggan's essay in this volume.

14. Bakhtin's *Rabelais and his World*, although first produced as a doctoral thesis under the Stalinist regime in the Soviet Union in the 1930s, was initially censored and was not translated into English until 1968. As a result, the full impact of theories of the carnivalesque, both in narrative and dramatic literary criticism, was not felt until the 1970s and 1980s in the US and the UK. For the structuralist account of Shakespeare's festive drama, see Frye and, especially, Barber. These ideas have been expanded upon more recently by Laroque.

15. For a Freudian-inflected analysis of Carter's version of carnival, see Chedgzoy's chapter "Wise Children and Foolish Fathers: Carnival in the Family" in *Shakespeare's Queer Children*.

16. Again, there are clear critical precedents for Carter's interests: see, for example, Kahn and Orgel.

17. The phrase is a direct quotation from Carter, "Overture and Incidental Music" (44).

18. On Ophelia representations more generally, see Showalter, *The Female Malady* (10–13 and 90–92) and "Representing Ophelia" (*passim*).

19. Compare *Hamlet*, 5.2.231.

20. For more on this see Barringer (61).

21. Carter would have been well aware that Millais's painting of Ophelia was reworked in a cinematic context by Laurence Olivier for his 1948 film version of *Hamlet*. For a discussion of this parallel see Bate (265).

22. For more on this see Berry and Du Plessis.

23. 'She should this Angelo have married, was affianced to her oath, and the nuptial appointed; between which time of the contract and limit of the

solemnity, her brother Frederick was wrecked at sea, having in that perished vessel the dowry of his sister' (*Measure for Measure*, 3.1.215–19).
24. On the spatial signifiers of this play, see Chedgzoy, *Measure for Measure* (*passim*).
25. Barringer describes the painting as 'a Tennysonian recreation of the Middle Ages' (43).
26. For a more detailed exposition of Carter's responses to and rewritings of her Japanese experiences, see Crofts's essay in this volume.
27. Carter's deliberate choice of the term 'châtelaine', with its medieval connotations of a lady of the castle but also the chains attached to a woman's belt to hold keys, underlines the confinement, both imposed and embraced, that is a theme of all the versions of Mariana's story from Shakespeare onwards.

Works cited

Barber, C.L. *Shakespeare's Festive Comedy: A Study of Dramatic Form and its Relation to Social Custom*. Newark, NJ: Princeton University Press, 1972.
Barringer, Tim. *The Pre-Raphaelites: Reading the Image*. London: Weidenfeld and Nicolson, 1998.
Bate, Jonathan. *The Genius of Shakespeare*. London: Picador, 1997.
Baudrillard, Jean. *Simulacra and Simulation*. Trans. Shelia Faria-Glasier. Ann Arbor: University of Michigan Press, 1981.
Berry, Philippa. *Shakespeare's Feminine Endings: Disfiguring Death in the Tragedies*. London: Routledge, 1999.
Bowers, Maggie Ann. *Magic(al) Realism*. London: Routledge, 2005.
Bown, Nicola. "'There are Fairies at the Bottom of our Garden': Fairies, Fantasy and Photography." *Textual Practice* 10 (1996): 57–82.
Brecht, Bertolt. "Alienation Effects in Chinese Acting." *Brecht on Theatre: The Development of an Aesthetic*. Ed. and trans. John Willets. New York: Hill and Wang, 1992. 91–99.
Carter, Angela. "The Cabinet of Edgar Allan Poe." *Black Venus*. 1985. London: Vintage, 1996. 32–42.
———. "John Ford's *'Tis Pity She's a Whore*." *American Ghosts and Old World Wonders*. 1993. London: Vintage, 1994. 20–42.
———. "The Merchant of Shadows." *American Ghosts and Old World Wonders*. 1993. London: Vintage, 1994. 66–85.
———. "Overture and Incidental Music for *A Midsummer Night's Dream*." *Black Venus*. 1985. London: Vintage, 1996. 43–53.
———. *The Passion of New Eve*. 1977. London: Virago, 1982.
———. *Several Perceptions*. 1968. London: Virago, 1995.
———. *Shadow Dance*. 1966. London: Virago, 1995.
———. "The Smile of Winter." *Fireworks*. 1974. Harmondsworth: Penguin, 1987. 41–50.
———. *Wise Children*. 1991. London: Vintage, 1992.
Chedgzoy, Kate. *Measure for Measure*. Writers and their Work. Plymouth: Northcote House, 2000.

———. *Shakespeare's Queer Children: Sexual Politics and Contemporary Culture.* Manchester: Manchester University Press, 1995.

Du Plessis, Rachel Blau. *Writing Beyond the Ending: Strategies of Twentieth-Century Women's Writing.* Bloomington: Indiana University Press, 1985.

Frye, Northrop. *A Natural Perspective: The Development of Shakespearean Comedy and Romance.* New York: Columbia University Press, 1965.

Gamble, Sarah. *Angela Carter: Writing from the Front Line.* Edinburgh: Edinburgh University Press, 1997.

Genette, Gérard. *Palimpsests: Literature in the Second Degree.* 1982. Trans. Charna Newman and Claude Doubinsky. Lincoln: University of Nebraska Press, 1997.

Gilbert, Sandra M., and Susan Gubar. *The Madwoman in the Attic: The Woman Writer and the Nineteenth-Century Literary Imagination.* New Haven, CT: Yale University Press, 1979.

Hackett, Helen. *A Midsummer Night's Dream.* Writers and their Work. Plymouth: Northcote House, 1997.

Kahn, Coppélia. "The Absent Mother in *King Lear.*" *Rewriting the Renaissance: The Discourse of Sexual Difference in Early Modern Europe.* Ed. Margaret W. Ferguson, Maureen Quilligan, and Nancy J. Vickers. Chicago: University of Chicago Press, 1986. 33–49.

Kennedy, Dennis. *Looking at Shakespeare: A Visual History of Twentieth-Century Performance.* Cambridge: Cambridge University Press, 1993.

Laroque, François. *Shakespeare's Festive World: Elizabethan Seasonal Entertainments and the Professional Stage.* Cambridge: Cambridge University Press, 1991.

Malpas, Simon. *The Postmodern.* London: Routledge, 2005.

Oates, Joyce Carol. *Blonde: A Novel.* London: Fourth Estate, 2000.

Orgel, Stephen. "Prospero's Wife." *Rewriting the Renaissance: The Discourse of Sexual Difference in Early Modern Europe.* Ed. Margaret W. Ferguson, Maureen Quilligan, and Nancy J. Vickers. Chicago: University of Chicago Press, 1986. 50–64.

Pavis, Patrice, ed. *The Intercultural Performance Reader.* London: Routledge, 1996.

Peach, Linden. *Angela Carter.* Basingstoke: Macmillan, 1998.

Pearce, Lynne. *Woman/Image/Text: Readings in Pre-Raphaelite Art and Literature.* Hemel Hempstead: Harvester Wheatsheaf, 1991.

Poole, Adrian. *Shakespeare and the Victorians.* London: Methuen, 2004.

Purkiss, Diane. *Troublesome Things: A History of Fairies and Fairy Stories.* Harmondsworth: Allen Lane, 2000. 284–93.

Sage, Lorna. *Angela Carter.* Writers and their Work. Plymouth: Northcote House, 1994.

———. "Angela Carter Interviewed by Lorna Sage." *New Writing.* Ed. Malcolm Bradbury and Judy Cooke. London: Minerva Press, 1992. 185–93.

Sanders, Julie. *Novel Shakespeares: Twentieth-Century Women Novelists and Appropriation.* Manchester: Manchester University Press, 2001.

Saunders, Graham. *'Love Me or Kill Me': Sarah Kane and the Theatre of Extremes.* Manchester: Manchester University Press, 2002.

Shakespeare, William. *The Oxford Shakespeare: The Complete Works.* Ed. Stanley Wells and Gary Taylor. Oxford: Oxford University Press, 1998.

Shaw, Marion. *Alfred, Lord Tennyson.* Hemel Hempstead: Harvester Wheatsheaf, 1988.

Showalter, Elaine. *The Female Malady: Women, Madness and English Culture, 1830–1930*. London: Virago, 1987.

———. "Representing Ophelia: Women, Madness, and the Responsibilities of Feminist Criticism." *Shakespeare and the Question of Theory*. Ed. Patricia Parker and Geoffrey Hartman. London: Routledge, 1991. 77–94.

Sontag, Susan. "Notes on 'Camp'." *Against Interpretation*. New York: Dell, 1996. 275–92.

Tennyson, Alfred. "Mariana." 1830. *Tennyson: A Selected Edition*. Ed. Christopher Ricks. Harlow: Longman, 1989. 3–6.

Tomalin, Claire. Introduction. *Mrs Dalloway*. By Virginia Woolf. Oxford: Oxford University Press, 1992. xii–xxxii.

6
'The Margins of the Imaginative Life': The Abject and the Grotesque in Angela Carter and Jonathan Swift

Anna Hunt

In pungent parodies of the Roman myth, Jonathan Swift's Yahoos – 'the most filthy, noisome, and deformed animal which nature ever produced' – evolve from 'the ooze and froth of the sea' (299–300) in *Gulliver's Travels* (1726) and 'goddess' Celia rises daily from the 'stinking ooze' (1. 132) of "The Lady's Dressing Room" (1732). Two centuries later, in *Nights at the Circus* (1984), Angela Carter conceives a very different kind of Venus whose origins are more avian than aquatic and who ascends, with 'the portly dignity of a Trafalgar Square pigeon' (17), from the 'bloody froth' (12) of pots of rouge and the tepid fizz of champagne to the dizzy heights of the circus tent: Fevvers, the infamous winged *aerialiste*, the 'Cockney Venus' (7). These playful mutations to the myth suggest a shared satirical interest in imploding cultural forms. Carter's texts at least, writes Jill Matus, relish 'the so-called freaks excluded from the Western pantheon of Venuses and relegated to circuses and sideshows' (165). Similarly, these spectacles of the unexpected, headlining the fairgrounds of Swift's eighteenth-century London, people the peculiar landscapes of Gulliver's far-flung destinations as well as the more domestic settings of Swift's poetry. The desire to peer beyond the glossy veneer unites these authors and their texts: from the Yahoos to Celia, from Fevvers to Madame Schreck's museum of woman monsters, these texts assemble a viewing gallery of anti-Venuses, a collection which questions idealized ideas of femininity.

Julia Kristeva's theory is becoming a familiar terrain in Carter criticism[1] and its presence seems apposite in a collection as hybrid as this one, credited as Kristeva is with the coining of the term 'intertextuality' (see Orr 1). As Graham Allen has summarized, intertextuality positions the literary work 'not as the container of meaning but as a space in which a potentially vast number of relations coalesce' (12). This spilling over of 'the container of meaning' seeps through Carter's narratives of self and spectacle into what Christina Britzolakis has called 'the voracious and often dizzying intertextuality of her writing' (50). Indeed, *Nights at the Circus* positively mocks interpretation with its propagation of lofty metaphor and textual teasing. It is a '*bricolage*', explains Carter, assembled from 'a great scrap-yard' of references to ancient European folklore, eighteenth-century fictional devices and nineteenth-century discourses; fundamentally, from 'all the elements which are available [...] to do with the margins of the imaginative life, which is in fact what gives reality to our own experience, and in which we measure our own reality' (Haffenden 92). It is, then, with these 'margins of the imaginative life' that this discussion is intrigued. The first section of this essay will examine the eighteenth-century fascination with freak shows and its influence on narratives of self and spectacle in *Gulliver's Travels* and *Nights at the Circus*. Acknowledging the theoretical beginnings of Mary Douglas, borrowing Kristeva's theory of abjection and drawing on Mary Russo's concept of the female grotesque, the latter part of the essay will then delve beyond the spectacle to uncover unabashed displays of disorder, distortion and excess which revel in the margins created by the abject and the grotesque. Here, Kristeva's theory will be examined alongside Swift and Carter's texts, initiating a dialogue between ideas which spans two centuries of imaginative thought. Indeed, the discussion of the abject and the grotesque will form a sort of sandwich filling for the chapter – 'the strips of rusty meat slapped between the doorsteps of white bread' in Fevvers's bacon butty (53).

The glamour of deformity

Gulliver's Travels is a gallimaufry of the weird and the wonderful. Indeed, as William Eddy exclaims, it would be tricky to find a literary list of marvellous races equal to those discovered by Gulliver: 'six-inch pygmies, seventy-foot giants, the flying island Laputa, deathless Struldbrugs, the magicians and the departed spirits of Glubdubdrib, and finally a race of speaking, thinking, and self-governing horses' (27). This focus on the fabulous tapped into what was, in Swift's time, a fervent English fascination with the curious contradictions of nature. London fairgrounds brimmed with exhibitions of 'monsters' and 'freaks': 'giants, midgets, dwarfs, bearded ladies, hermaphrodites, and Siamese twins' were frequent exhibits, while more unusual entertainments featured 'a boneless girl, only eighteen inches tall, who had seven sets of teeth' and 'a boy with a live bear growing out of his back' (Todd 5). This last exhibit represents what Dennis Todd, in his detailed discussions of monster viewing in eighteenth-century England, lists as 'the third most popular attraction at the

Fair': 'creatures which blurred the distinction between men and beasts' (147). Embodying an unsettling but alluring ambiguity, these humans who seemingly verged on the realms of animality included 'a boy who was covered with fish scales from his neck downward' and the famous 'Northumberland Monster', who boasted the head, mane, neck and forefeet of a horse on his otherwise human body (ibid.). These anomalies of nature and the monstrous births which created them fuelled the imagination of eighteenth-century society. Fascinating cases like the one around which Todd's discussion centres – that of Mary Toft of Surrey who reputedly gave birth to seventeen rabbits in 1726 – stretched the margins of accepted truth and acceptable entertainment.

Swift's reactions to these fairground spectacles of the (un)desirable unusual are documented in his poetry, most notably in the short poem "In Pity to the Emptying Town" (ca. 1709). Here, Swift exposes the 'corrupted taste' (l. 4) of fairgoers as such innocent pleasures as 'frisking lambs/Or song of feathered quire' are shunned for the contrived diversions of 'a dog dancing on his hams/And puppets moved by wire' (ll. 13–16). Indeed, the fair is painted as an artificial, even stifling, distortion of nature:

> So are the joys which nature yields
> Inverted in May Fair;
> In painted cloth we look for fields,
> And step in booths for air. (ll. 9–12)

And yet, Swift seemingly includes himself amongst the lured fairgoers: the poem speaks through a confessional 'we', rather than an accusatory 'you' or 'they'. For Swift, despite displaying an often scornful indifference to the popular playground of the fair, seemed to harbour a fascination with the human oddities of the sideshows. A disdainful attitude towards these fairs was, explains Todd, common in the early eighteenth century: enticing but ultimately empty pleasures satisfied the hunger for spectacle whilst demanding little intellectual engagement (148). Dramatized in Gulliver's own 'unquiet dance of attraction and avoidance, of desire and distance' (Todd 155), Swift's is a contradictory approach, articulated in Gulliver's admission that 'although I abhorred such kind of spectacles, yet my curiosity tempted me to see something that I thought must be extraordinary' (124–25). For, whilst sharing the distaste towards such shallow entertainment, Swift draws frequently from the imaginative cast provided by the fairground, most significantly in his writing of *Gulliver's Travels*. 'The objects of Swift's attention', writes Edward Said, are 'exhibits that shock, amuse, or fascinate'; and 'when we think of the human "content" of Swift's work, [...] we realize with some discomfort that we have before us a show of freaks and horrors' (75). Any indulgence by Swift in popular culture, however, is laced with a sharply satirical edge and, as Todd notes, we are prey to Swift's dry humour from the start. The extraordinary inhabitants encountered by Gulliver in his travels could in fact have been viewed for a penny in those very sideshows of the May Fair: *Gulliver's Travels* is consciously and overtly 'filled with the sights, shows, and diversions of London' (Todd 143). Parodying and playing with audience assumption, Swift's derision reveals that 'what purports to be a chronicle of several excursions to remote nations turns out to be a satiric anatomy of English attitudes and values' (ibid. 140).

Carter's fiction features a plethora of references to *Gulliver's Travels* from isolated asides, such as feeling 'as gross as Glumdalclitch' (8) in "A Souvenir of Japan" (1974), to the widely recognized literary debt of the society of centaurs in *The Infernal Desire Machines of Doctor Hoffman* (1972) to Swift's Houyhnhnms. *Nights at the Circus* similarly plays with several direct references to Swift's text – the 'high-stepping and contemptuous horses' of the circus ring, for example, 'who could spot a Yahoo when they saw one' (174) – but perhaps more interesting and less recognized are the shared narrative and thematic concerns of these novels. Like *Gulliver's Travels*, Carter's texts are peopled with the peculiar. By reincarnating and revamping the landscape of the May Fair, Carter's fiction delights in 'a diaspora of the amazing', a colourful backdrop for a puppet-act predecessor of the Cockney Venus: '*Lady Purple, the Shameless Oriental Venus*' (28). Carter's remarkable short story, "The Loves of Lady Purple", is set amidst a 'universal cast of two-headed dogs, dwarfs, alligator men, bearded ladies and giants in leopard-skin loin cloths'; a motley crew who 'share the sullen glamour of deformity, an internationality which acknowledges no geographic boundaries' (27). As Gulliver crosses multiple geographic boundaries, then, assembling his own international play list of human oddities, so *Nights at the Circus* adopts this 'universal cast' and follows the 'glamour of deformity' from London to Petersburg to Siberia. And centre-stage of this drama is the ultimate fairground exhibit, Fevvers. 'Rumoured to have started her career in freak shows' (14), the star of Captain Kearney's Grand Imperial Circus is an impressive representative of those composite 'creatures which blurred the distinction between men and beasts'. Her defining feature is a pair of polychromatic wings, 'fully six feet across' (15), which seemingly sprout from between her shoulder blades. Coupled with her 'six inches of false lash' (7), peroxide hair and layer of greasepaint, this 'fabulous bird-woman' (15) exists solely as 'the kind of spectacle people pay good money to see' (185); excelling 'in *being looked at* – at being the object of the eye of the beholder' (23; emphasis in original).

We are introduced to the Cockney Venus through the scribbled jottings of Jack Walser, the young Californian foreign correspondent whose interview with the feathered trapeze artist opens the narrative. In Walser we can read a nineteenth-century Gulliver. Both present a travelogue of their – albeit rather different – adventures on their journey to selfhood and knowledge. As a restless Gulliver sets sail on a voyage to the South-Sea, so Walser, as a 'scapegrace urchin [...], stowed away on a steamer bound from 'Frisco to Shanghai' (9). And, while Gulliver finds himself at the mercy of a violent storm and shipwreck, cast away on an unknown shore, so Walser is thrown from the wreckage of a train, stranded in the snowy wastes of the Siberian wilderness. Indeed, Walser's journalistic account of his 'picaresque career' (9) has persuasive echoes of Gulliver's travel tales. Discussing Swift's text within the genre of the Philosophic Voyage, Eddy suggests that such tales 'were written primarily to expound a philosophical position, [...] in which the narrative is simply a vehicle for instruction' (9). These fictional accounts, he writes, 'borrow the popular forms of travel literature in order that they may attract readers to a serious theme' (ibid.). Although the narrative of *Nights at the Circus* indisputably indulges itself beyond the constraints of 'a vehicle of instruction', it nevertheless inherits the discourse of prescription. Carter states that 'the idea behind *Nights at the Circus* was very much to entertain and instruct' and confirms that she 'purposely used a certain eighteenth-century fictional device – the picaresque, where people have adventures in order to find themselves in places where they can discuss philosophical concepts without distractions' (Haffenden 87). This 'mingling of adventure and the discussion of what one might loosely call philosophical concepts' (ibid.) weaves its way through *Gulliver's Travels* and *Nights at the Circus*, addressing the concepts of spectacle and self in both.

Walser's journalistic discourse places him in the interrogatory position of spectator; a position from which he observes his interviewee, through 'eyes the cool grey of scepticism', with a decidedly Swiftian slant (10). Fevvers, with her 'Is she fact or is she fiction?' slogan (7), embodies the eighteenth-century intrigue in the authenticity or otherwise of fabulous freak shows, and thus provokes a dichotomous response in Walser very similar to that of Swift. Gulliver's 'unquiet dance of attraction and avoidance, of desire and distance' is mirrored by Walser who is struck both by enchantment and revulsion at the physicality of Fevvers. And, while Gulliver 'shunts his desire' to delve into the unfamiliar 'into the comfortable parameters of scientific observation' (Todd 155) so Walser relies on his own grasp of logic to evade Fevvers's beguiling spell. Secure in the anonymity of the audience, witnessing Fevvers's larger-than-life performance, Walser assumes a position of knowing superiority:

> Walser whimsically reasoned with himself, thus: now, the wings of the birds are nothing more than the forelegs, or, as we should say, the arms, and the skeleton of a wing does indeed show elbows, wrists and fingers, all complete. So, if this lovely lady is indeed, as her publicity alleges, a fabulous bird-woman, then she, by all the laws of evolution and human reason, ought to possess no arms at all, for it's her arms that ought to be her wings! (15)

Smugly satisfied, Walser sits back 'with a pleased smile on his lips' and concludes his ponderings with a mathematical flourish: 'wings without arms is *one* impossible thing; but wings *with* arms is the impossible made doubly unlikely – the impossible squared' (15–16; emphasis in original). The confidence of the detached onlooker in the security of the theatre box dwindles considerably, however, in the overwhelming presence of Fevvers herself. Perched on a horsehair sofa in the stifling atmosphere of Fevvers's dressing room, Walser 'gave his mind a quick shake to refresh its pragmatism' (30). His musings have become less certain: 'Shall I believe it? Shall I pretend to believe it?' (28). This move to destabilize and make vulnerable the role of objective observer is a device employed by both Carter and Swift. During their philosophical voyages 'to find themselves', Walser and Gulliver experience an imbalance in the power relationship between onlooker and object as, at various stages in their travels, they are shifted uncomfortably from the position of spectator to spectacle. For Walser, this occurs most dramatically when, signing away his identity as foreign correspondent, he joins Captain Kearney's Ludic Game as the newest member of Clown Alley and finds himself on the more vulnerable side of the circus ring.

Gulliver too plays both the curious and the curiosity; he is an outsider in remote regions where, says Eddy, 'the traveller himself is the only monstrosity and his conception of life alone eccentric' (28). The 'Emptying Town' of Swift's May Fair poem is recreated in Lilliput, where 'prodigious numbers of rich, idle, and curious people' flock to see 'the Great Man-Mountain', so that 'the villages were almost emptied' (24–27). Later, in Brobdingnag, Gulliver is subjected to the scrutiny of 'three great scholars', who, with the aid of a magnifying-glass, variously conclude that he 'could not be produced according to the regular laws of nature', that it was not possible for him 'to be a dwarf, because [his] littleness was beyond all comparison', and even that he 'might be an embryo, or abortive birth' (106–7). Suffering further humiliation, Gulliver is exhibited on market-day in Brobdingnag, billed as 'a strange creature [...], not so big as a *splacknuck* (an animal in that country very finely shaped, about six foot long) and in every part of the body resembling an human creature' (100). Riddled with references to the fairgrounds of London, this episode sees Gulliver tormented by the 'ignominy of being carried about for a monster' and 'exposed for money as a public spectacle to the meanest of people' (99).

Size matters

Swift's satire in *Gulliver's Travels* is what Eddy calls a 'satire of proportion' (48). Playing with scale, Swift exploits the interest surrounding optical developments of his time to construct what has been widely read as a narrative of misanthropy. In *The Body in Swift and Defoe* (1990), Carol Houlihan Flynn tracks the influence on literature of eighteenth-century discourses of scientific progress. The arrival of the microscope promised the potential to reveal the mysteries of nature. The results, however, were not always as lucid or accurate as many claimed. 'Early microscopes', Flynn writes, 'led observers to construct elaborate theories from incomplete evidence' as scientists struggled both 'to see correctly through a lens subject to an average distortion of 19 percent' and 'to interpret what met the eye' (17). There was more distortion than clarity as a pertinent quotation cited by Flynn illustrates: 'As late as the end of the eighteenth century, a medical lecturer informed his class that "they could see anything they fancied in the objects examined through the microscope ... microscopic anatomy was essentially based on imagination"' (18). Gulliver both peers through and is put under the lens of this imaginative microscope in his travels to Lilliput and Brobdingnag, with the effect of 'first reducing and then magnifying the proportions of life to reveal its pettiness and its ugliness together' (Eddy 48). Again drawing on a popular diversion of London fairgrounds – the peepshow – Swift creates a miniaturized landscape in Lilliput into which Gulliver quizzically gazes. And what he gazes upon is Swift's staged representation of the literal pettiness of humankind. For in the actions and behaviour of the Lilliputians, Swift employs what Eddy has recognized as 'the allegorical device of representing the life of the Western world under a disguise' (43). There are notable episodes – such as when Gulliver is required to swear compliance to the conditions of his liberty: 'to hold my right foot in my left hand, to place the middle finger of my right hand on the crown of my head, and my thumb on the tip of my right ear' (37) – which, whilst told in sober tones of factual commentary, verge on farcical slapstick. In a show of mimicry and mockery, Swift's Lilliputians present a shrunken version of humankind, a display designed to parody 'man's exaggerated conception of his own importance' (Eddy 113).

In a relatively undiscussed episode of Carter's tale, Fevvers herself undergoes a process of Lilliput-like miniaturization. The Russian Grand Duke plays the part of the fairground compère, a curator of the curious whose lavish home is decorated with spectacles of all varieties. His exhibits include a clockwork orchestra and, most uncannily, a slowly melting, life-size ice-sculpture of Fevvers herself. On a personal quest to unravel the fact/fiction legend of Fevvers's physicality, the Duke wants not only to look at the infamous *aerialiste*, but to touch. Seducing her with diamonds, he presents the biggest threat to Fevvers so far and the first explicitly sexual scene of contact with the 'only fully-feathered intacta in the history of the world' (294). Whilst distracting Fevvers with his collection of bejewelled and enamelled eggs – a haunting tribute to her own '*hatched*' beginnings – the Duke 'run[s] his hands over her breasts and round beneath her armpits', blissfully 'agitat[ing] the plumage rustling under the red satin' (190). Not content, however, with demystifying the fabulous bird-woman, the Duke has endeavoured to detain her; to diminish her to more manageable proportions and reduce her solely to the status of spectacle. For, within the gallery of eggs in glass cases, the Duke has created his own unique variety of peepshow. Fevvers gazes upon an egg of pink enamel unfurling its Russian doll layers 'to reveal an inner carapace of mother-of-pearl which, in turn opens to reveal a spherical yolk of hollow gold. Inside the yolk, a golden hen. Inside the hen, a golden egg.' Entranced by this miniature marvel which has now 'diminished to the scale of Lilliput', Fevvers gawps at what the golden egg discloses: 'inside the egg there is the tiniest of picture frames, set with minute brilliants. And what should the frame contain but a miniature of the *aerialiste* herself, in full spread as on the trapeze and yellow of hair, blue of eye as in life' (189). Fevvers 'did not shrink; but was at once aware of the hideous possibility that she might do so' as, with a 'wet crash and clatter', the melted ice-sculpture collapses (192): the life-size idol of the winged giantess has succumbed to the egg-bound Lilliputian Fevvers.

As Fevvers flees from the optical oppression of the Russian Grand Duke, so Gulliver makes his escape from Lilliput and embarks on his next expedition. Swinging the scale of proportion, Gulliver's second voyage refocuses from the triviality of the Lilliputians to the magnified physical-ity of the Brobdingnagians. Amidst these 'monsters' (86) he is struck with an alarming sense of vulnerability as he 'reflected what a mortification it must prove to me to appear as inconsiderable in this nation as one single Lilliputian would be among us' (87). Gulliver has become the Lilliputian and, like Fevvers, is reduced to a spectacle within his own miniature peepshow. Confronted with the physical enormity of this race of giants, the spotlight seems not to be on the idiosyncrasies of ideology but rather on the sheer corporeal grossness of humankind. Far from discovering the wonders of nature, then, the Swiftian microscope reveals its flaws. Overwhelmed by sights and smells, Gulliver beholds in Brobdingnag some of 'the most horrible spectacles that ever an English eye beheld' (117). The body, as illustrated by the impoverished Brobdingnagian beg-gars, is portrayed as diseased and dirty: 'There was a woman with a can-cer in her breast, swelled to a monstrous size, full of holes, in two or three of which I could have easily crept, and covered my whole body' and 'a fellow with a wen in his neck, larger than five wool-packs' (ibid.). However, 'the most hateful sight of all', Gulliver recalls, 'was the lice crawling on their clothes. I could see distinctly the limbs of these vermin with my naked eye, much better than those of an European louse through a microscope, and their snouts with which they rooted like swine.' The overall impression of these Brobdingnagians was 'so nau-seous, that it perfectly turned my stomach' (ibid.).

As Gulliver's travels continue, the image of humanity viewed by Swift becomes increasingly distorted. From the pygmean Lilliputians to the giant Brobdingnagians, Gulliver encounters yet another extreme in the Yahoos, the brutish inhabitants of Houyhnhnms Land. Here, however, it is not actual size which has been distorted; rather, it is the repulsiveness of human nature itself that has been blown beyond proportion. The Houyhnhnms, a race of speaking, civilized horses governed by the principle virtues of 'friendship and benevo-lence', tolerate and tame the savage Yahoos (296). Fuelled by what Eddy has called 'the fires of misanthropy' (189), this fourth voyage is devoid of the gentle mockery of Lilliput. Rather, Swift concludes his narrative with a coup de grâce of 'devastating imaginative originality' that has, says Said, 'haunted all his readers' (89). Most insulting to readers was – and arguably still is – the 'strange disposition' of the Yahoos 'to nastiness and dirt': revelling in their own excrement, smelling 'very rank', exhibiting a 'filthy way of feeding' and following a 'custom of wallowing and sleeping in the mud' (291–93). The unsavoury physicality of the Brobdingnagian surpassed, the Yahoo is reduced to its base bodily functions. And yet, to Gulliver's 'horror and astonishment', within the 'singular and deformed' shape of this 'ugly monster' he recognizes the mirrored image of 'a perfect human figure' (245–53). More than in any other part of the text, observes Said, 'we can see in the Houyhnhnms and the Yahoos – with Gulliver between them – a measure of Swift's general intellectual disenchantment with society' (89); what Eddy describes as an 'illustration of man in a state of *complete* degradation' (189; emphasis in original). Polluted both with pessimism and the bodily filth of the Yahoos, this fourth voyage wallows in the disorder of humanity. If one is going to look, Swift seems to say, one should look properly. In an atavistic narrative of deconstruction, Swift strips society of all adornments of spectacle, leaving it naked, exposed and utterly abject. And it is this insalubrious intrigue with the corporeal – with, in short, 'what is behind things' – that exposes Swift and Carter's shared 'fondness for the filth of the body with its odors, excrements, and pollutions' (Eddy 46) and brings us to Kristeva's theory of abjection.

Theorizing filth

'The activity of classifying', states Mary Douglas in a recently written preface to her 1966 text *Purity and Danger*, 'is a human universal' (xvii). Providing the groundwork for Julia Kristeva's later work on abjection, Douglas constructs a theory of defilement that revolves around ideas of 'separating, purifying, demarcating and punishing transgressions' (5). Creating categories of classification is, she says, a positive attempt to 'impose system on an inherently untidy experience' (3); to 'make unity' (5) from the 'chaotic jumble' of existence (201). Avoidance of ambiguity is the endeavour – for ambiguity, defying definition, signals a threat to conformity and containment. And it is within that same ambiguous domain inhabited by the freaks and monsters of *Gulliver's Travels* and *Nights at the Circus* that dirt resides. In fact, Douglas insists, 'there is no such thing as dirt': amidst the disciplined classification of matter, dirt, or pollution, is simply 'matter out of place' (xvii), the 'by-product' of a system which privileges unity and discards inappropriate and unruly elements (44). 'There is hardly any pollution', however, 'which does not have some primary physiological reference' (202) continues Douglas and, as such, this network of ideology is mapped from the social body onto the individual body, creating a corporeal cartography of order/disorder.

As Heather Nunn has summarized, 'Douglas's thesis is that pollution behaviour highlights the inter-relationship of the body's margins and the boundaries of the cultural and the social'; the territorialized body creates a 'social topography' in which 'the boundaries of the body become the limits of the social' (18). This symbiotic set-up is scrutinized by Douglas who insists that we 'see in the body a symbol of society' and 'see the powers and dangers credited to social structure reproduced in small on the human body' (142). Regulating this microcosm are the dividing lines between pure and clean and dangerous and dirty that are clearly defined as internal and external:

> Any structure of ideas is vulnerable at its margins. We should expect the orifices of the body to symbolise its specifically vulnerable points. Matter issuing from them is marginal stuff of the most obvious kind. Spittle, blood, milk, urine, faeces or tears by simply issuing forth have traversed the boundary of the body. So also have bodily parings, skin, nail, hair clippings and sweat. The mistake is to treat bodily margins in isolation from all other margins. (150)

These bodily secretions and shavings are innately marginal and ambiguous – 'their half-identity still clings to them' (ibid. 197). The outlines of the (social) body, endowed by Douglas with the power to reward conformity and repulse attack, are in fact perforated, porous, permeable and leaky. 'It is', says Kristeva – writing fifteen years after Douglas – 'as if the skin, a fragile container, no longer guaranteed the integrity of one's "own and clean self" but, scraped or transparent, invisible or taut, gave way before the dejection of its contents' (53). Acknowledging Douglas's earlier work, Kristeva reiterates the borderline status of dirt, stating that 'filth is not a quality in itself, but it applies only to what relates to a *boundary* and, more particularly, represents the object jettisoned out of that boundary, its other side, a margin' (169; emphasis in original). Retracing the boundaries of Douglas's image of society, Kristeva views defilement as that which is discarded by the '*symbolic system*': 'that logical order on which a social aggregate is based' (65). Kristeva's abject is what upsets this symbolic system: 'what disturbs identity, system, order. What does not respect borders, positions, rules. The in-between, the ambiguous, the composite' (4). And, as Kristeva notes that 'Douglas seems to find in the human body the prototype of that translucid being constituted by society as symbolic system' (66), so her own concept of the abject is represented by those jettisoned contents of corporeality that blur the dividing lines between internal and external.

Powers of Horror (1980) details Kristeva's fascinating theories on the construction of social identity, tracing the necessary stage of separation that enables subject formation and unpicking the complex relationship between longing and loathing. In the pre-symbolic union of mother and infant the boundary between self and object is as yet unformed and the mother–child bond is omnipotent. To ensure separation and subjectivity the infant must initiate steps to expel or reject the mother. It is this process of rejection that Kristeva calls abjection: the subject must endeavour to rid itself of those objects which blur the boundaries between self and (m)other. These objects are the 'marginal stuff' of Douglas's analysis, that which imperils the *'clean and proper'* body. These polluting objects can be classified into two broad categories: food and corporeal waste; the latter subdividing into two: excrement and signs of sexual difference.[2]

Food appears as a polluting object that crosses the oral boundary of the self's clean and proper body and is, says Kristeva, perhaps the most elementary and most archaic form of abjection' (2). Corporeal waste, meanwhile, includes all the 'marginal stuff' issuing from the orifices of the body in Douglas's description. Kristeva distinguishes between polluting and non-polluting bodily waste products. The polluting objects fall into two types: excremental and menstrual. 'Excrement and its equivalents (decay, infection, disease, corpse, etc.)', represent 'the danger to identity that comes from without: the ego threatened by the non-ego, society threatened by its outside, life by death' (71). Within this category the corpse represents 'the most sickening of all wastes' (3) and poses the ultimate threat to subjectivity. Menstrual blood – representing the horror of the signs of sexual difference – conversely 'stands for the danger issuing from within the identity (social or sexual); it threatens the relationship between the sexes within a social aggregate and, through internalisation, the identity of each sex in the face of sexual difference' (71).

In short, the abject stands for the slipperiness of subjectivity, the messiness of existence which the social subject must attempt to delineate and disavow. By its very nature, however, abjection defies the neat ordering and segregation of identity; for the crux of Kristeva's theory of abjection is the assertion that whatever the corporeal seeks to expel, it can never expel completely: 'while releasing a hold, it [abjection] does not radically cut off the subject from what threatens it – on the contrary, abjection acknowledges it to be in perpetual danger' (9). It proves impossible for the subject to gain absolute separation from its polluting objects, which necessarily constitute the self. Rather, the abject is pushed to the very margins of identity, hovering as a continual threat of disarray. This 'constant risk' of regression is also a persistent temptation for there is, significantly, an element of alluring surrender in the ambiguity of the margins of abjection. In 'a vortex of summons and repulsion' (1) the abject 'simultaneously beseeches and pulverises the subject' (5), replicating the narrative of desire and disgust which runs through Swift and Carter's texts. It is not, Douglas acknowledges, 'always an unpleasant experience to confront ambiguity' (46); indeed, as we will see in a discussion of Carter's clowns, 'there is a whole gradient on which laughter, revulsion and shock belong at different points and intensities. The experience can be stimulating' (46).

Corporeal clowning

From the early introduction of Gulliver's master Bates, to the pelting of Gulliver with Yahoo dung and the examination of excrement by the Lagado professor, *Gulliver's Travels* exhibits an undercurrent of 'bodily' humour. A widely documented literary debt to Rabelais suggests a source for this crudeness, though Eddy highlights some differences in style: 'Rabelais writes with the queer turns of wit peculiar to the drunken man [...] but Swift is always sober' (47). Lacking the exuberance of Rabelais then – perhaps, as the Lagado professor believes, 'because men are never so serious, thoughtful, and intent, as when they are at stool' (209) – Swift nevertheless delights in bodily matters. Several of his obscene incidents are direct descendents from Rabelais's own work, including Gulliver's innovative method of extinguishing the fire at Lilliput's palace – dousing the flames with vast quantities of his urine – and the physician at the Academy of Lagado who tests his hypothesis of forcibly 'discharging' disease by applying bellows to the anus of a dog.[3]

This Rabelaisian element is continued in *Nights at the Circus*, where a narrative of the comic grotesque haunts Clown Alley. Although unread by Carter prior to writing her novel, Mikhail Bakhtin's important work *Rabelais and His World* (1968) constructs a concept of the grotesque that seems inherent to Kristeva's theory of abjection and that casts ripples of recognition throughout *Nights at the Circus*. Inherited, perhaps, from Swift rather than Bakhtin himself, the grotesque forms an intriguing, interbred intertext for Carter's novel. Like the abject, Bakhtin's grotesque is 'contradictory and double-faced' (23), both positive and negative, regenerating and degrading. Moreover, it is concerned to turn the 'subject into flesh' to 'transfer to the material level, to the sphere of earth and body' (Bakhtin 19–20). Again reminiscent of those vulnerable outlines exposed by Douglas's corporeal topography, Bakhtin emphasizes the blurriness of body boundaries:

> It is not a closed, completed unit; it is unfinished, outgrows itself, transgresses its own limits. The stress is laid on those parts of the body that are open to the outside world [...]. This means that the emphasis is on the apertures or the convexities, or on various ramifications and offshoots. (26)

And it is the abject waste oozing from these 'apertures or convexities' that fuels Carter's corporeal clowning.

The circus at the centre of *Nights at the Circus* epitomizes the now familiar dichotomy of longing and loathing which permeates Carter's and Swift's texts and underpins Kristeva's theory of abjection, providing a stage for a socially abjected group of people: the misfits, the runaways and the bizarre. Subsequently, this collaboration of the abjected exists on the fringes of society; exiled but never completely expelled. A touring spectacle of the outcast and the outlandish, such a group is essential in defining a societal norm, in maintaining what Michel Foucault calls the 'power of normalization' (196). Our ideas of normality and 'power', says Douglas, 'are based on an idea of society as a series of forms contrasted with surrounding non-form' (122). It is in this 'non-form', then, in the currency of 'the inarticulate area, margins, confused lines' (ibid.), that we find Carter's clowns. Their performance, their comedy, is wholly immersed in the corporeal – the human body made vulnerable and ridiculous. In this way, *Nights at the Circus* takes the disparate episodes of dry humour which inject Swift's text and dramatizes them into a staged spectacle of the abject.

The clown, declares Carter's Master Clown, Buffo the Great, is 'a wonder, a marvel, a monster, a thing [...] invented [...] to teach little children the *truth* about the filthy ways of the filthy world' (122; emphasis in original). From the 'restrained' tones of Swift's grotesque humour, there is a dramatic shift to the overt 'violent slapstick' of the clowns. In routines including the 'Clowns' Christmas Dinner' and 'The Clown's Funeral' abjection reigns as the horrors of digestion and death are played out in a show of 'convulsive self-dismemberment' (117). And Buffo himself, a 'giant' of Brobdingnagian proportions, performs the abject grotesque by wearing 'his insides on his outside, and a portion of his most obscene and intimate insides, at that': he sports 'a wig that does not simulate hair. It is, in fact, a bladder [...]; so that you might think he is bald, he stores his brains in the organ which, conventionally, stores piss' (116). In a performance of defilement, of the 'filthy ways' jettisoned to the margins of acceptance, the clowns exist, says Bakhtin, 'on a borderline between life and art, in a peculiar mid-zone as it were' (8). The masks which, for Bakhtin, reveal 'the essence of the grotesque' (40) visualize this ambiguity. In Carter's circus ring, the 'impenetrable disguises of wet white' (119) dictate the regurgitation of a mechanical sequence of comedy. And the response of the spectators, encompassing 'laughter, revulsion and shock', is a nervous snigger: a morbid fascination mixed with gratitude for the boundary of the circus ring.

Beyond this boundary, in the lugubrious liminality of Clown Alley, the masks allow incognito indulgence in a ridiculous and perverse display of toilet humour. The clowns, 'doomed to stay down below, nailed on the cross of the humiliations of this world' (120), are destined to the bodily depths of Bakhtin's degraded lower stratum. This degradation is displayed in a private dance of abjection, a 'dance of disintegration; and of regression; celebration of the primal slime' (125):

> A joey thrust the vodka bottle up the arsehole of an august; the august, in response, promptly dropped his tramp's trousers to reveal a virile member of priapic size [...]. At that, a second august, with an evil leer, took a great pair of shears out of his back pocket and sliced the horrid thing off [...]. (124)

Debased and monstrous, this uncomfortable show of slapstick horror finally strips deformity – or, at least, *male* deformity – of all its glamour. In a conflicting discourse of comedy and tragedy, both Swift and Carter's texts reveal the sordidness behind the spectacle. Swift's oscillation from jovial Rabelaisian humour to angry scorn of the Yahoos is mirrored in the clown's regression from circus-ring high jinks to perverse 'primal slime'. In Gulliver and Walser, the Brobdingnagians, Yahoos and clowns, we witness a narrative of male abjection; a deconstruction of the male spectacle culminating in the explicit phallicism – and castration – of the clowns. The following section will turn, then, to the women of the texts; discovering, conversely, a narrative of the female abject and exposing the fragility of the spectacle of femininity.

The female abject

For Mary Russo, Fevvers, with her sublime excess and face-painted caricature of femininity, is an 'exhilarating example' of the female grotesque (59). Focusing on the bleeding internal lines of abjection, Russo introduces gender into Bakhtin's original formula of the grotesque. Echoing the corporeality of the abject, the grotesque is immediately associated with female genitalia: 'Low, hidden, earthly, dark, material, immanent, visceral,' the cave-like 'grotto-esque' is a bodily metaphor for 'the cavernous anatomical female body' (1). And into this mythologized female cave are placed all the corporeal threats to the purity of the subject: 'blood, tears, vomit, excrement – all the detritus of the body that is separated out and placed with terror and revulsion [...] – are down there in that cave of abjection' (2). Bakhtin's 'material level', then, 'the sphere of earth and body' has, in a historical trajectory traced by Russo, acquired associations with the 'horror of the signs of sexual difference.' The visceral is gendered, representing – like Kristeva's menstrual pollution – the danger to subjectivity issuing from within. In this way, the viscous, leaky, uncontainable nature of visceral secretions is similarly associated with femaleness. 'It is not', explains Elizabeth Grosz, 'that female sexuality is like, resembles, an inherently horrifying viscosity. Rather, it is the production of an order that renders female sexuality and corporeality marginal, indeterminate, and viscous that constitutes the sticky and the viscous with their disgusting, horrifying connotations' (*Volatile Bodies* 195). Furthermore, 'what is disturbing about the viscous or the fluid is its refusal to conform to the laws governing the clean and proper' (ibid.); which immediately harks back to Douglas.

Through a series of encounters with Brobdingnagian females, Gulliver's observations bring female beauty under close and scathing scrutiny. These episodes range from the 'nauseous sight' of the eating habits of the Queen of Brobdingnag (109), to the spectacle of a breast-feeding nurse whose 'monstrous breast' repulses Gulliver (93). The Maids of Honour provoke the strongest 'horror and disgust', emitting 'a very offensive smell' and toying with Gulliver as a sexual plaything (123–24). Shocked by their crudeness, Gulliver cringes as the Maids 'discharge what they had drunk [...] in a vessel that held above three tuns', and turns from their naked skins which 'appeared so coarse and uneven [...] with a mole here and there as broad as a trencher, and hairs hanging from it thicker than pack-threads' (124). This discourse of deformed beauty is continued, and further magnified, in the descriptions of the Yahoos. These creatures offer Swift's antithesis to beauty, both in appearance and behaviour. The females 'had long lank hair on their heads, but none on their faces, nor any thing more than a sort of down on the rest of their bodies, except about the anus, and pudenda. Their dugs hung between their fore-feet, and often reached almost to the ground as they walked' (246). Like the Maids, they had 'a most offensive smell' (292) and their openly sexual conduct is equally scorned by Gulliver who 'could not reflect without some amazement, and much sorrow, that the rudiments of coquetry, censure, and scandal, should have place by instinct in womankind' (292). Such sweeping judgement reviles not only the female Yahoos, but 'womankind' as a whole. Femaleness, then, is made abject under Gulliver's gaze. His journey through the magic-mirror parade of Lilliput, Brobdingnag and Houyhnhnms Land has revealed to him femininity as blemished beauty; a quality which he suspects to be universal:

This made me reflect upon the fair skins of our English ladies, who appear so beautiful to us, only because they are of our own size, and their defects not to be seen but through a magnifying glass, where we find by experiment that the smoothest and whitest of skins look rough and coarse, and ill coloured. (93)

And, indeed, it is in his poetry that Swift takes up this very magnifying glass to – seemingly once and for all – discover the defects of those English ladies.

Swift's notorious 'excremental' – or 'scatological' – poems revel in the female abject and grotesque and, unsurprisingly, have created as much controversy and conflicted opinion as *Gulliver's Travels*. This group of poems comprises "The Lady's Dressing Room" (1732), and "A Beautiful Young Nymph Going to Bed", "Strephon and Chloe" and "Cassinus and Peter", which were published together in a pamphlet in 1734. Commentary has varied dramatically, from the declaration of John Hill Burton that the poems represent 'a stinging insult' to every gentleman with 'wife, daughter, or sister to cherish and protect' (qtd. in Voigt 5), to recent feminist criticism which has, claim David Fairer and Christine Gerrard, 'recuperated these poems, perceiving in Swift's intractably physical women a liberating challenge to male-constructed poetic fictions of female beauty' (72). Indeed, Claude Rawson suggests that Swift offers a damning critique of a society which 'educates women to be ornamental idiots or objects of idealised worship' (153). Common consensus, however, is that the excremental poems are 'upside-down versions of the routines of conventional love-poetry' (ibid. 151). And indeed, by taking as its subject what Gulliver would call a 'prostitute female Yahoo' (279), "A Beautiful Young Nymph Going to Bed" certainly does parody the conventional poetic heroine. Corinna, 'pride of [prostitute district] Drury Lane' (l. 1), returns home following a night's work to prepare for bed. In a horrific display of deterioration she dismantles her self, literally, revealing a decaying mass of 'scattered parts' (l. 68): she 'Untwists a wire; and from her gums/A set of teeth completely comes./Pulls out the rags contrived to prop/Her flabby dugs, and down they drop' (ll. 19–22). This 'lovely goddess' (l. 23) is reduced to a corporeal catalogue of the grotesque.

The tone changes somewhat in the other poems of this group, from the malicious scorn heaped on the Yahoo Corinna, to the more gentle mockery characteristic of Gulliver's earlier voyages. "Strephon and Chloe" witnesses Strephon endeavouring to conceal the necessities of his 'Mere mortal flesh' (l. 76) from the 'Venus-like' (l. 87) Chloe on their wedding night. Imagine his shock, however, when he discovers Chloe is filling her chamber pot: 'Ye gods, what sound is this?/Can Chloe, heavenly Chloe piss?' (ll. 177–78). Descending into the Rabelaisian slapstick of Lilliput and Brobdingnag, Strephon boldly determines 'To reach the pot on t'other side./And as he filled the reeking vase,/Let fly a rouser in her face' (ll. 190–92). "Cassinus and Peter" continues this farce as Cassinus struggles to share with his friend his abominable discovery of 'Celia's foul disgrace' (l. 112), the 'blackest of all female deeds' (l. 106): 'Celia, Celia, Celia shits.' (l. 118) Underlying these corporeal comedies, however, is a moral which nevertheless suggests Swift's sincerity: 'Since husbands get behind the scene,/The wife should study to be clean' ("Strephon and Chloe" ll. 137–38).

It is in the earliest excremental poem, however, that Celia's 'female deeds' are utterly uncovered. Relishing the exposure of the face behind the mask, Swift brews a nauseating concoction of fetid femininity in the hidden delights of "The Lady's Dressing Room". Finding the chamber of 'haughty Celia' (l. 2) empty Strephon sneaks inside, unearthing a sordid selection of 'greasy coifs and pinners reeking' (l. 53), 'ointments good for scabby chops' (l. 36) and 'scrapings of her teeth and gums' (l. 40):

> But oh! it turned poor Strephon's bowels,
> When he beheld and smelt the towels;
> Begummed, bemattered, and beslimed;
> With dirt, and sweat, and ear-wax grimed.
> No object Strephon's eye escapes,
> Here, petticoats in frowzy heaps;
> Nor be the handkerchiefs forgot,
> All varnished o'er with snuff and snot. (ll. 43–50)

Leaking 'stinking ooze' (l. 132), Celia's room brims with Kristeva's corporeal waste. 'Those secrets of the hoary deep' (l. 98) suggest the visceral viscosity of the cavernous female grotesque, while musty 'steams,/Exhaled from sour unsavoury streams' (ll. 27–28) insinuate menstrual blood – the most abject suppurate of all. The prosthetic props, filth and disarray of Celia's dressing room, then, represent saliently a 'refusal to conform to the laws governing the clean and proper'. Escaping from the carefully painted and sculpted lines of artificial beauty, bodily fluids and detritus seep across the boundaries of order, disrupting and disturbing idealized forms of femininity. Menstrual blood, 'sweat, dandruff' (l. 24) and excrement combine to concoct a 'nasty compound' (l. 41), a stale whiff of abject corporeality.

It is Celia's dressing room of disorder which takes us back to the cluttered claustrophobia of Fevvers's boudoir. In a Brobdingnagian reference, Strephon notes the presence of 'Celia's magnifying glass': 'It showed the visage of a giant:/A glass that can to sight disclose/The smallest worm in Celia's nose' (ll. 62–64). As Swift's scrutiny finally exposes, then, the 'defects' of his English ladies, so Fevvers's own mirror reveals, under the greasepaint, a countenance as 'broad and oval as a meat dish' (12). *Nights at the Circus* constructs a similar 'satire of proportion' to *Gulliver's Travels* as, in her own narrative of bodily hyperbole, Carter creates a 'giantess' (51) who boldly challenges conventional notions of feminine beauty. 'Her face', observes Walser, 'in its Brobdingnagian symmetry, might have been hacked from wood and brightly painted up by those artists who build carnival ladies for fairgrounds or figureheads for sailing ships'; indeed, 'it flickered through his mind: Is she really a man?' (35). Fevvers presents a visual defiance of femininity – an anti-Venus of extreme proportions, who rewrites the discourse of aesthetics which informed Swift's time. Leading the aesthetic debate was Edmund Burke who, in 1757, published *A Philosophical Enquiry into the Origin of Our Ideas of the Sublime and Beautiful*. For Burke, 'beautiful objects are comparatively small' (212). Furthermore, 'an air of robustness and strength is very prejudicial to beauty' whilst 'an appearance of *delicacy*, is almost essential to it'. Finally, beauty demands 'gracefulness' in *'posture* and *motion'* (218, 226; emphases in original). Thus, chugging through the air at a 'leisurely twenty-five' miles an hour (17) 'in a steatopygous perspective, shaking out behind her those tremendous red and purple pinions' (7), Fevvers exudes as much beauty as 'a hump-back horse' (19). Projecting an image in stark contrast to that of the Burkean, and Swiftian, beautiful, Fevvers shuns passive delicacy for exuberant excess, an attribute which places her firmly within Russo's category of the female grotesque. Walser's response to Fevvers, like that of Gulliver to the Brobdingnagians, is a mixture of awe and repellence; Carter has created in her heroine a descendant of Swift's race of giants: 'a *big* girl' (7) who towers 'twice as large as life' (15).

This excess is matched by an impressive appetite. Reminiscent of the Yahoos' odious inclination to 'devour everything that came in their way' (289) and the gluttony of the Queen of Brobdingnag, Fevvers attacks her food 'with gargantuan enthusiasm. She gorged, she stuffed herself, she spilled gravy on herself, she sucked up peas from the knife' (22). Walser, with a reaction akin to Kristeva's food loathing, nauseously opts 'for another glass of tepid champagne' (22). Like Celia's, Fevvers's room emits a lingering reminder of the visceral. For Fevvers continuously oozes a potent pong of corporeality; her own 'highly personal aroma, "essence of Fevvers"' (9): a 'hot, solid composite of perfume, sweat, greasepaint and raw, leaking gas that made you feel you breathed the air in Fevvers' dressing-room in lumps' (8). Her room is, in fact, an accurate reproduction of Celia's. The 'petticoats in frowzy heaps' and stained stockings of Swift's poem are here supplanted with discarded 'dirty underwear' and a 'writhing nest of silk stockings' expelling 'a powerful note of stale feet' (11, 9). Whilst Celia endeavours to keep her dressing room closed to male prying eyes, Fevvers, conversely, shows no shame in welcoming Walser into the bowels of her chamber. Swift's scandalous exposure of Celia – or 'liberating challenge to male-constructed poetic fictions of female beauty' (Fairer and Gerrard 72) – receives a gleeful response from Fevvers. Embracing the abject she makes the margins her own: visceral, moist and pungent, Fevvers's dressing room is the tabooed cave of the female grotesque, 'a mistresspiece of exquisitely feminine squalor' (9). The suggestion of bodily secretion and detritus is everywhere, from the 'few blonde hairs striating the cake of Pears transparent soap in the cracked saucer on the deal washstand', to the 'hip bath full of suds of earlier ablutions' (14). Constructing her own excremental doggerel, Fevvers's retort to Swift's warning that 'Since husbands get behind the scene,/The wife should study to be clean', is plain: politely conversing with Walser, she 'wiped her lips on her sleeve and belched,' promptly 'shifted from one buttock to the other and [...] let a ripping fart ring around the room' (12, 11).

Conclusions

'Swift's work', writes Said, 'is a persisting miracle of how much commentary an author's work can accommodate and still remain problematic' (54). Problematic, then, in the sense that his writing is at once brutally honest and utterly opaque. Seemingly deliberately, and delightedly, defying definition, Swift's status swings from misanthropist, even misogynist, to feminist: arguably liberating women from their fate as 'ornamental idiots'. Carter shares this compulsion to rouse reaction in her readers, claiming that '[p]eople babble a lot nowadays about the "unreliable" narrator [...] so I thought: I'll show you a *really* unreliable narrator in *Nights at the Circus!*' (Haffenden 90; emphasis in original). Indeed, *Gulliver's Travels* provides an intriguing – and neglected – intertext for Carter's novel. Set within the comic and superficial framework of the fairground and the circus, both texts nevertheless embark on provocative and penetrating projects of enquiry. The narrative of self-discovery, of 'people having adventures in order to find themselves', seems a challenge laid down by Swift and Carter for their characters and readers alike as the picaresque journeys become voyages of deconstruction, stripping spectacle of its glamour and exposing drives of desire and disgust in the spectators themselves. Swift aims, says Said, 'to make people more conscious than they would otherwise be of what is being put before them' (78); by transporting the fairground freaks from London to Lilliput, Brobdingnag, Houyhnhnms Land and so on, Swift is testing us, the spectators, suggesting that we do more than simply 'stare stupidly' at others (Todd 161). While Swift, as Todd suggests, is 'dramatizing the psychology of monsterviewing in the eighteenth-century' (155), so Carter exposes the contemporary and continuing desire to 'stare stupidly', exploring the fictional selves we invent to scaffold the slipperiness of subjectivity and foregrounding those monstrous others sidelined by society to 'the margins of the imaginative life.'

Moreover, gaining momentum in *Gulliver's Travels* to find its full expression in the excremental poetry is a Swiftian sub-plot of femaleness, which *Nights at the Circus* seizes and scrutinizes under its own literary microscope. Lurking beneath the passive, cleanly, contained femininity of Swift's English ladies is a rather more messy, smelly and abject femaleness. In a cast of demoted goddesses, the female becomes the ultimate other, the unknowable spectacle of both Swift and Carter's texts. Oozing Douglas's sticky secretions, these females 'disturb identity, system, order', upsetting the boundary between clean, contained, aesthetic femininity and fetid, fluid, unfettered femaleness. Representatives of Kristeva's horrifying signs of sexual difference, Celia and Fevvers embody within their visceral dressing rooms the yawning femaleness of Russo's female grotesque and, for their male onlookers, themselves embody the fundamental contradiction of desire and disgust. Swift and Carter have created their own aesthetics of abjection.

It seems fitting to end with a return to where we began – with the freaks and sideshows of the fairground. In Madame Schreck's museum of woman monsters, Carter creates a female Clown Alley: 'the whores of mirth' (119) of the circus ring are here the whores of 'jouissance,' the ultimate embodiment of abjection. This 'lumber room of femininity' (69) comprises a cacophony of boundary creatures: 'Dear old Fanny Four-Eyes; and the Sleeping Beauty; and the Wiltshire Wonder, who was not three foot high; and Albert/Albertina, who was bipartite, that is to say, half and half and neither of either; and the girl we called Cobwebs' (59–60). Further inhabitants of Bakhtin's lower stratum, these 'denizens of Down Below' (69) occupy the sticky depths of the female grotesque, assembled in 'The Abyss' (61). Accurately replicating the booths and tents of the fairground, the 'dispossessed creatures' (69) are 'made to stand in stone niches cut out of the slimy walls', with 'little curtains in front'; except, of course, for the Sleeping Beauty, 'who remained prone, since proneness was her speciality' (61). The Sleeping Beauty exists solely in a state of abjection. Her perpetual slumber is interrupted only to carry out the most basic bodily functions: she 'always *did* wake up long enough to take a little minced chicken or a spoonful of junket, and she would evacuate a small, semi-liquid motion into the bed-pan' (64; emphasis in original). Furthermore, her deep sleep overcame her 'one morning in her fourteenth year, the very day her menses started' (63). Prey to both excremental and menstrual pollution, then, the Sleeping Beauty plays 'the living corpse' (70); a beauty blemished by 'death infecting life. Abject' (Kristeva 4). This museum of monstrosity is ruled by Madame Schreck who 'started out in life as a Living Skeleton, touring the sideshows' (59). Making manifest Kristeva's 'most sickening of all wastes', Madame Schreck indeed poses the ultimate threat to subjectivity: '"Shall I open the curtain? Who knows what spectacle of the freakish and the unnatural lies behind it!"' (62).

Notes

1. For just two recent examples of essays that touch upon Kristeva's theory of abjection, see Johnson and Armitt.
2. For a detailed overview of these categories, see Grosz, "The Body of Signification"; for comprehensive summaries of Kristeva's abjection theory, see Lechte and McAfee.
3. See Eddy (57–60), for a full discussion of Rabelais's influence on Swift's work.

Works cited

Allen, Graham. *Intertextuality*. London: Routledge, 2000.
Armitt, Lucie. "The Fragile Frames of *The Bloody Chamber*." *The Infernal Desires of Angela Carter: Fiction, Femininity, Feminism*. Ed. Joseph Bristow and Trev Lynn Broughton. Harlow: Addison Wesley Longman, 1997. 88–100.
Bakhtin, Mikhail. *Rabelais and His World*. 1968. Trans. Helene Iswolsky. Bloomington: Indiana University Press, 1984.
Britzolakis, Christina. "Angela Carter's Fetishism." *The Infernal Desires of Angela Carter: Fiction, Femininity, Feminism*. Ed. Joseph Bristow and Trev Lynn Broughton. Harlow: Addison Wesley Longman, 1997. 43–58.
Burke, Edmund. *A Philosophical Enquiry into the Origin of Our Ideas of the Sublime and Beautiful*. 1757. Menston: The Scolar Press, 1970.
Carter, Angela. "The Loves of Lady Purple." *Fireworks: Nine Profane Pieces*. 1974. London: Penguin, 1987. 24–40.
———. *Nights at the Circus*. 1984. London: Vintage, 1994.

———. "A Souvenir of Japan." *Fireworks: Nine Profane Pieces*. 1974. London: Penguin, 1987. 1–13.

Douglas, Mary. *Purity and Danger*. 1966. London: Routledge, 2002.

Eddy, William A. *Gulliver's Travels: A Critical Study*. New York: Russell & Russell, 1963.

Fairer, David and Christine Gerrard. "Jonathan Swift." *Eighteenth-Century Poetry: An Annotated Anthology*. Ed. David Fairer and Christine Gerrard. Oxford: Blackwell, 1999. 71–72.

Flynn, Carol Houlihan. *The Body in Swift and Defoe*. Cambridge: Cambridge University Press, 1990.

Foucault, Michel. "The Means of Correct Training." *The Foucault Reader*. Ed. Paul Rabinow. London: Penguin, 1991. 188–205.

Grosz, Elizabeth. "The Body of Signification." *Abjection, Melancholia and Love: The Work of Julia Kristeva*. Ed. John Fletcher and Andrew Benjamin. London: Routledge, 1990. 80–103.

———. *Volatile Bodies: Toward a Corporeal Feminism*. Bloomington: Indiana University Press, 1994.

Haffenden, John. "Angela Carter." *Novelists in Interview*. London: Methuen, 1985. 76–96.

Johnson, Heather. "Textualising the Double-Gendered Body: Forms of the Grotesque in *The Passion of New Eve*." *Angela Carter: Contemporary Critical Essays*. Ed. Alison Easton. Basingstoke: Macmillan, 2000. 127–36.

Kristeva, Julia. *Powers of Horror: An Essay on Abjection*. 1980. Trans. Leon S. Roudiez. New York: Columbia University Press, 1982.

Lechte, John. *Julia Kristeva*. London: Routledge, 1990.

Matus, Jill. "Blonde, Black and Hottentot Venus: Context and Critique in Angela Carter's 'Black Venus'." *Angela Carter: Contemporary Critical Essays*. Ed. Alison Easton. Basingstoke: Macmillan, 2000. 161–72.

McAfee, Noëlle. *Julia Kristeva*. London: Routledge, 2004.

Nunn, Heather. "*Written on the Body*: An Anatomy of Horror, Melancholy and Love." *Women: A Cultural Review* 7 (1996): 16–27.

Orr, Mary. *Intertextuality: Debates and Contexts*. Cambridge: Polity, 2003.

Rawson, Claude. *Order from Confusion Sprung: Studies in Eighteenth-Century Literature from Swift to Cowper*. London: George Allen & Unwin, 1985.

Russo, Mary. *The Female Grotesque: Risk, Excess and Modernity*. London: Routledge, 1994.

Said, Edward. *The World, the Text, and the Critic*. Massachusetts: Harvard University Press, 1983.

Swift, Jonathan. *The Complete Poems*. Ed. Pat Rogers. Middlesex: Penguin, 1983.

———. *Gulliver's Travels*. 1726. London: Penguin, 1994.

Todd, Dennis. *Imagining Monsters: Miscreations of the Self in Eighteenth-Century England*. Chicago: University of Chicago Press, 1995.

Voigt, Milton. *Swift and the Twentieth Century*. Detroit: Wayne State University Press, 1964.

7
'Circles of Stage Fire': Angela Carter, Charles Dickens and Heteroglossia in the English Comic Novel

Robert Duggan

This essay considers the intertextual relations between the works of Charles Dickens and Angela Carter. Dickens the great reformer, the social critic with a journalist's eye for memorable detail that was idolized by so many Victorians, is also the writer whose work is populated by fairy godmothers, ogres, robber bridegrooms and Dick Whittingtons. In Dickens, as in Carter, the self frequently becomes a public performance, a theatrical display accomplished with brio and colour. Characters with emblematic names and atavistic qualities inhabit the margins of Dickens's narrative but take centre stage in Carter's stories and novels, as old tales such as "Bluebeard" are revisited and retold for a modern age. The apparently permeable border between character and caricature in Dickens anticipates the marvellous personages that emerge from the fairgrounds and forests of Carter's fiction. In these authors' works, the performance of self reveals by degrees the social mechanisms that regulate daily life and the search for a foundation in the course of constructing one's identity. Dickens's novels anticipate the coalescence of politics and fantasy so vividly embodied in Carter's oeuvre, particularly in terms of her novels' deployment of literary language within the tradition of the English comic novel.

As with any intertextual examination of two writers' work, but particularly in the case of Carter given the breadth of allusion in her writings, resemblances may appear between the two sets of fiction that rather than signalling a close engagement with the earlier author point instead to a common source. Shakespeare is a key intertext for both writers in this regard, with the theatrical performances of *Hamlet* in both *Great Expectations* (1860–61) and *Wise Children* (1991) arguably demonstrating the significance of the Bard for both writers, rather than Carter's direct interest in Dickens.[1] To take a different resemblance, the

manner in which *The Magic Toyshop* (1967) and *Great Expectations* conclude with   night on
its own sug   nario, an
interpretati   inn are]
escaping lik   maniac
as it might   people
alone, abou   er, given
the rite-of-p   iry tale'
(ibid.) there   revised
ending of D   ction by
fire of their   and the
subsequent   w of the
burnt house   eems to
produce a cl   mother
is dead, all t   *e Magic*
Toyshop gets   begins'
(Sage 190).   notes,
Mrs Green   novel
might be sai   to form an home feminized version of the Dickensian
bildungsroman' (254) with the protagonist Marianne leaving behind
the influence of her Professor father, discovering sexuality and finding
her place in the world as 'the tiger lady' (*Heroes and Villains* 150) ruling
over the Barbarians.

While Dickensian elements are perceptible in Carter's early fiction,
in relation to the later novels it is perhaps in the realm of the circus
that Dickens's influence may be most readily traced. Dickens's *Hard
Times* (1854), for example, presents a circus in the form of Sleary's
Horse-riding that comes to symbolize the role of fancy in the lives of
individuals and of the community of Coketown. Both the children in
M'Choakumchild's school and the industrial workers of this mill-town
are exhorted to stick to facts, the avatar of which is Thomas Gradgrind
MP who seeks to exclude all imagination from the lives of everyone in
the town and to adhere to an ultra-narrow Benthamite philosophy of
statistics and figures. The author notes that it is 'the robber Fancy' that
the schoolmaster seeks to kill in the children whom he teaches and
asks whether the schoolmaster will only 'maim [...] and distort' (53)
this faculty. The fate of Gradgrind's 'model' son, who ends being a
thief and who is discovered at the end of the novel disguised as a
clown with a blackened face, points to the danger of attempting to
suppress fancy and imagination. In the penultimate chapter, Sleary
repeats his earlier advocacy of the necessity of the circus's role in social

life when he tells Gradgrind: 'People must be amuthed. They can't be alwayth a learning, nor yet they can't be alwayth a working, they ain't made for it. You *muth* have uth, Thquire' (308; emphasis in original). Fancy at the end of the novel is thus the complement of, rather than an alternative to, modern industrial life under capitalism.

In Carter's *Nights at the Circus* (1984), Colonel Kearney's travelling circus becomes a space in which Fevvers profits from her unique physical makeup, having left behind her fairly immobile roles in Ma Nelson's brothel and Madame Schreck's dungeon-show. The troupe, with its tigers, educated apes, Beckettian clowns and its Charivari family of acrobats provides the backdrop against which Fevvers becomes the object of admiration and wonder, not a freak but the Greatest '*Aerialiste* in the world' (161). While much has been written about Carter's relation to Mikhail Bakhtin's account of carnival, and particularly the ways in which *Nights at the Circus* and *Wise Children* may point to the limits of the political potential of carnival, for my purposes it is important to note the ways in which for both Dickens and Carter the circus is depicted as a kind of theatre. Sleary's horse-riders perform a number of theatrical pieces, including a version of "The Children in the Wood" on horseback, and Carter shows the rehearsals that shape the public performances under the big-top. Just as Dickens presents the circus as a special kind of community, so Carter is always keen to show the backstage lives of performers in the circus, theatre or movie businesses, including the 'exhibits' of Madame Schreck's dungeon on their tea-break. Similarly, in *Wise Children* the magic wood set of the Hollywood version of *A Midsummer Night's Dream* permits enchantment but also exposes the tawdriness of theatrical life.

Theatre may be understood not only as a key site of textual exploration in Carter's writing and a cultural institution to be interrogated, but also as fundamental to her fictional aesthetic. Christina Britzolakis, for example, has claimed that

> [f]or many of Carter's most recent critics, her theatricalism, which dates back to her earliest work, has emerged, often by way of this body of 'gender performance' theory, as synonymous with her self-proclaimed 'demythologizing' project, the project of 'investigating' femininity as one of 'the social fictions that regulate our lives.' (43)[2]

This avenue has clearly been critically productive and could be said to have been perhaps too influential, resulting in what Joseph Bristow and Trev Lynn Broughton term 'this after-the-fact "Butlerfication"' of

Carter's writing (19). Britzolakis, however, offers a different account and aligns Carter's strategy with the petit bourgeois claiming that 'theatricalism is the language of the female "parvenue"' (53). This line of exploration, which provides Carter the author with the position of 'outsider', has also been prominent in approaches to Dickens that emphasize his own status as a lower-middle class 'outsider' and the performance of identity in his work.[3] Isobel Armstrong contends that Carter 'writes in a stylised, objectifying, external manner, as if all experience, whether observed or suffered, is self-consciously conceived of as *display*, a kind of rigorous, analytical, public self-projection which, by its nature, excludes private expression' (269; emphasis in original). And although Armstrong connects this with 'what has come to be called magical realism' (ibid.) we might, along with James Wood, instead align the 'intensely theatrical Angela Carter' (173) with Dickens, 'in particular the interest in self as public performer, an interest in grotesque portraiture and loud names, and in character as caricature' (277).

Fancy and reality

The relationship between fantasy and realism in Carter's work has exercised many critics and forms a key topic in John Haffenden's interview with Carter in 1985. Carter and Haffenden discuss Tom Paulin's suggestion that Carter's 'cerulean imagination would benefit from the constraints of the documentary novel' (19) and Robert Nye's review of *Wise Children* that Carter felt was 'grudging' and 'reluctant to concede that there had been anything more than a lot of high-falutin bluster in [her] earlier work' (Haffenden 81). These critical perspectives, together with Carter's expressions of disappointment with readers who treated *The Passion of New Eve* (1977) 'as just another riotous extravaganza' (86) and that instead of picking up on the significance of Tristessa's waxwork collection saw it as 'just part of the fantastic décor' (87), set the tone for Haffenden's recurrent focus on what he sees as a profound duality in her work.

> It is understandable, I suppose, that someone could approach the fantastic and exotic surface of your fictions and not be able to bridge the gap to the central point that your theatricality is meant to heighten real social attitudes and myths of femininity. (91)

In Haffenden's model of fiction, theatricality is opposed to 'the real' and appears to function as a potentially imperfect means of addressing social concerns. Fantasy, according to this discourse, works *against* an engagement with reality and tends, on some fundamental level, to be incompatible with an interest in the world as it exists. Haffenden ultimately presents the combination of the fantastic and 'reality' as an inexplicable paradox:

> You are a committed materialist, I know, and yet your writing unleashes what you've elsewhere called all sorts of 'imaginative gaiety'. So we're left with the paradox – since we can't explain it – that you choose to accentuate the real by writing tall stories in lush locales. (92)

The interviewer here casts the imagination as a possibly distracting superstructure covering reality from view ('exotic surface'), one that forms an antagonistic dynamic within Carter's writing. Fantasy is seen here as a force that will tend to disrupt any analysis and that, if deployed, must be used in a controlled manner.

A striking aspect of Carter criticism is how frequently both detractors (for example Paulin's 'constraint' above) and admirers of her writing are united in their concern for the author's ability to exercise the required control over her imaginative faculty. For the admirers, a dynamic equilibrium is maintained where, for the less impressed readers, fancy has run amok. Indeed the rhetoric of taming 'wild fancy' is never far away, whether in Haffenden's 'unleashes' in the above quotation or in Salman Rushdie's comment that 'Carter's cold-water douches of intelligence often come to the rescue of her fancy when it runs too wild' (xi). This tone of anxiety about the author's use of elements of fancy or fantasy is arguably present in some of her own comments in the Haffenden interview although she does not at any point take up an explicitly defensive stance, at one point remarking: 'I don't mind being called a spell-binder. Telling stories is a perfectly honourable thing to do. One is in the entertainment business' (82).

This discourse of fancy and reality has an illustrious history in relation to Dickens, with almost every critic who has commented on the author's work being drawn into the fray. *Hard Times* can stand as an especially illuminating case in its utilization of the fantastic in the narrative while seeking to address social issues to do with utilitarian politics and conditions for workers in modern industrial society. A clear example, and one of particular interest to Carter readers, occurs at the beginning of Chapter 15: 'Although Mr Gradgrind did not take after

Blue Beard, his room was quite a blue chamber in its abundance of blue books' (131). By *denying* the comparison with a fairy tale serial wife-murderer, the narrator places the reader in a rather peculiar situation. As Jean Ferguson Carr describes: 'The narrator denies that this "error" has any meaning [...] this slip of the pen provokes despite its claims to marginality. The error is allowed to stand, thereby suggesting what would otherwise be too bizarre to consider' (168). This 'disavowed' fairy tale presence simultaneously asserts and denies that Gradgrind is a domestic tyrant worthy of comparison with the Bluebeard of folklore, leaving the association as a weak presence in the novel, but one that never really goes away. Furthermore, the presence of such half-felt comparisons to ogres or fairy godmothers in the text tends to signify a symbolic pattern to the plot that is distinct from the supposedly realist concerns of Coketown and its Hands. Consequently, the narrative operates along an alternative axis of fancy held in tension with its realism. Indeed, for George Bernard Shaw, *Hard Times* marks the emergence of the fantastical Dickens:

> Dickens in this book casts off, and casts off forever, all restraint on his wild sense of humour [...] here he begins at last to exercise quite recklessly his power of presenting a character to you in the most fantastic and outrageous terms. (130)

Paradoxically, then, what is arguably the most socially concerned of Dickens's novels also marks the author's attainment of new heights (or depths) of fancy. As Shaw observes: 'He even calls the schoolmaster McChoakumchild (*sic*), which is almost an insult to the serious reader' (131).

The most famous defence of Dickens and *Hard Times* is John Ruskin's and, in common with many other nineteenth- and twentieth-century critics, as well as Dickens himself, Ruskin organizes his defence around the principle of truth:

> The essential value and truth of Dickens's writings have been unwisely lost sight of by many thoughtful persons merely because he presents his truth with some colour of caricature. Unwisely, because Dickens's caricature, though often gross, is never mistaken. Allowing for his manner of telling them, the things he tells us are always true [...] But let us not lose the use of Dickens's wit and insight, because he chooses to speak in a circle of stage fire. (47)

According to this argument, one can forgive the crudity of Dickens's treatment of reality since he offers us the *essential* truth of a situation. More recently Nancy Hill has argued along similar lines, describing Dickens's use of the fantastic and the grotesque as a means of getting people to see the world as it was. The 'corrective' of the grotesque for Dickens is in fact a step towards reality rather than away from it, Hill maintains, and quotes from Dickens's "The Spirit of Fiction" (1867) in support of her view:

> Greater differences will exist between the common observer and the writer of genius. The former accuses the latter of intentional exaggeration, substitution, addition, and has never been able in society to see the startling phenomena which he condemns in the romance as melodra   ndividual has nev   igs. (120; qtd. in F

When view   tic in the service of   militude. Realism, ar   lity, governs the fu   n seemed disordered

So how   ffered by Dickens ar   emporary approaches   n keen to emphasize   laffenden interview t   ards I've tried to ke   ou don't have to rea   t to' (87). Carter's cla   narrative signification   ificant in terms of that novel's appropriation of Dickens's "A Christmas Carol" (1843) through Finn, 'like the Lord of Misrule' (183) challenging the sway of 'Old Scrooge Uncle Philip' (160). Beneath the shop's air of 'old-fashioned charm' that an American visitor thinks 'kind of Dickensian' is a real-life tyrannical Victorian patriarch that the heroine Melanie must escape (137). While Carter, in the above quotation, presents her works' systems of signification as not strictly speaking required of the reader, the presence of such structures seems to form a solid basis for artistic value, and their identification and explication is a key objective in Carter criticism (for example, one might think of discussions of the symbolic significances of the mirrors, wolves and puppets in Carter's writing). This critical emphasis on symbolism in Carter's novels replicates the mid-twentieth-century movement in Dickens studies to read his works 'as complex and concentrated symbolic structures rather than as a series of spontaneous and brilliant eruptions' (Connor, Introduction 13). As Steven Connor argues, contemporary research on Dickens seeks to move beyond the dualism of force and form inherent in approaches of this kind. When considering Carter, it is important to examine attentively the manner in which realism and fantasy interact in the novels.

The relationship between Fevvers and Lizzie in *Nights at the Circus*, at the level of discourse, is one that has attracted some critical attention. In these two characters the reader is offered at times alternative or at least strongly differentiated perspectives on where events are leading, with the 'aerialiste' describing utopian social transformations on the one hand and Lizzie supplying a materialist scepticism on the other.[4] A key moment is Lizzie's reaction to Fevvers's hopes for herself and Walser:

'I'll make him into the New Man, in fact, fitting mate for the New Woman, and onward we'll march hand in hand into the New Century – '

Lizzie detected a note of rising hysteria in the girl's voice.

'Perhaps so, perhaps not,' she said, putting a damper on things. 'Perhaps safer not to plan ahead.' (281)

This divergence in perception is developed a few pages later when Lizzie demurs from the rosy picture of post-revolutionary bliss that Fevvers believes she may inaugurate:

'The dolls' house doors will open, the brothels spill forth their prisoners, the cages, gilded or otherwise, all over the world, in every land, will let forth their inmates singing together the dawn chorus of the new, the transformed – '

'It's going to be more complicated than that,' interpolated Lizzie. 'This old witch sees storms ahead, my girl. When I look to the future, I see through a glass, darkly. You improve your analysis, girl, and *then* we'll discuss it.' (285–86; emphasis in original)

Although this passage clearly points to a tension between two versions of social change, I believe that critics should resist the temptation to view them solely as competing accounts, only one of which can be ultimately endorsed and/or ascribed to Carter herself. Rather, the first step should be to acknowledge the ways in which the novel itself dramatizes this discord *without* resolving it, thus rendering critical attempts to amplify the materialist/utopian aspect of dubious worth.

Wise Children and comedy

If *Wise Children* is the most Shakespearean of Carter's work, then it can also be read as the most Dickensian. In combination with the Shakespearean family romance of the Hazard/Chance family, as outlined by Julie Sanders in *Novel Shakespeares* (2001) and Kate Chedgzoy in *Shakespeare's Queer Children* (1995), we also have Saskia 'the wicked fairy in *Sleeping Beauty*' (37) and Grandma Chance as 'Carter's twentieth-century version of the fairy godmother' (Sanders 47). Lizzie in *Nights at the Circus*, who is revealed as a Sicilian witch who nursed Fevvers as a baby, also has a high degree of fairy godmother potential, casting spells of discomfort on Fevvers's enemies. Fairies abound in Dickens and can be male, (Riah in *Our Mutual Friend* [1864–65]) or female (Sissy Jupe in *Hard Times*). The fairy godmother is, of course, a key figure in *David Copperfield* (1848–50) and *Great Expectations*, and Dickens is careful to show the ways in which a fairy may turn out to be either good or wicked. In *David Copperfield*, Betsey Trotwood, whose Dover neighbours think she is a witch and who was disappointed in marriage, plans to raise a girl whose heart would not be broken by men but vanishes 'like a discontented fairy' (22) on discovering that in David she has a nephew and not the hoped-for niece. Betsey, however, does become David's fairy godmother: she takes him in and looks after him although, interestingly, in terms of 'maternal' care she seeks and follows Mr Dick's counsel regarding the practicalities of caring for a young boy. In *Great Expectations*, by contrast, Miss Havisham successfully raises a girl who will break men's hearts in the form of Estella. Although Pip initially thinks of Miss Havisham as his 'fairy godmother', he eventually discovers that she is a wicked witch plotting his misery, while Mag*witch* the escaped criminal is in fact his mysterious and quasi-paternal benefactor. In *Wise Children*, Grandma Chance's 'invented' family that she created by 'sheer force of personality' (35) is also a frequent structure in Dickens where 'adoptive' families such as the Peggotys or Betsey and Mr Dick in *David Copperfield* tend to be more successful in nurturing than 'nuclear' ones. Grandma Chance may or may not be Nora and Dora's mother, but the new family of Nora, Dora and Tiffany's twins definitely owes more to 'mother is as mother does' (223) than any biological notion of maternity.

Wise Children can be read as extending the tension or potential opposition between a materialist approach and what we may provisionally term carnival present in *Nights at the Circus*. Much work has been devoted to exploring Carter's novels' relation to Bakhtin's conception of carnival.[5] However, as I argue above, our primary goal should be to analyse how the novels present such tension. Dora Chance, the narrator of Carter's last novel, reflects on a number of occasions on the relationship between the serious and the comic. She is careful to point out that 'there are limits to the power of laughter and though I may hint at them from time to time, I do not propose to step over them' (220). If Lizzie and Fevvers articulate two strands (poles would be an overstatement) of thought that differ in significant ways in *Nights at the Circus*, then Dora and her uncle Perry have an analogous relationship:

'Life's a carnival,' he said. He was an illusionist, remember.
   'The carnival's got to stop, some time, Perry,' I said. 'You listen to the news, that'll take the smile off your face.'
   'News? What news?' (222)

This passage parallels the above examples from *Nights at the Circus* in its dramatization of a tension between different perspectives. Yet, while it has been frequently read as revealing the 'limits of carnival', we might instead suggest that its chief objective is to portray the incommensurability of these two views. The two come into contact and reveal their distinctiveness without entering into a contest where there will be one winner.

Of course, the significance of the different perspectives expressed by Lizzie and Fevvers and Dora and Perry goes beyond the reader's impression of the characters and reflects on profound issues of narrative form and genre in relation to the two novels. To a large degree, towards the end of their respective narratives, both *Nights at the Circus* and *Wise Children* debate their own status as politically/socially oriented fiction and call into question the value of their specific forms of literary expression. As Dominic Head argues, *Nights at the Circus* 'makes the plausibility of its own fantastic elements a matter of internal debate, a debate that leads the reader, by analogy, to consider the principal theme: the treatment of woman as object' (94). *Wise Children* continues this trend of questioning the plausibility of its narrative, at one point emphasizing the potential unreliability of its narrator, pictured in a pub.

> Well, you might have known what you were about to let yourself in for when you let Dora Chance in her ratty old fur and poster paint, her orange (Persian Melon) toenails sticking out of her snakeskin peep-toes, reeking of liquor, accost you in the Coach and Horses and let her tell you a tale. (227)

Thus, the reader is invited to consider what fictional modes are being employed by the author, where these novels might fit into the literary landscape and what final summation of their textual trajectories might be possible. Commenting on her refusal to disclose the maternal parentage of the twins, Dora asserts:

> But, truthfully, these glorious pauses do, sometimes, occur in the discordant but complementary narratives of our lives and if you choose to stop the story there, at such a pause, and refuse to take it any further, then you can call it a happy ending. (227)

Dora's claim here, that a happy ending is a function of terminating the story at a specific point, raises more questions about how the reader is to interpret the apparent reconciliation offered at particular points of the narrative in *Wise Children*, and about whether the novel is a comedy.

Mikhail Bakhtin's exploration of Dickens's *Little Dorrit* (1855–57) provides a productive way of addressing this key question of genre. Many of Dickens's novels relish the moments when a villain or hypocrite is exposed: Uriah Heep's dispatch at the hands of Mr Micawber in *David Copperfield* is a memorable example. His later works, in their exploration of capital, focus in particular on exposing villains who are happily concealed by the torturous forms of legal and financial protocols prevalent in Victorian England. Both Christopher Casby in *Little Dorrit* and 'Fascination' Fledgeby in *Our Mutual Friend* profit from financial sharp practice but preserve a respectable reputation by employing intermediaries who are the public face of a cynical and exploitative enterprise: Casby uses Pancks to squeeze money from the impoverished denizens of Bleeding Heart Yard, while Riah the Jew is Fledgeby's 'mask'. The eventual disclosure of the puppet-master's existence and identity and his subsequent symbolic punishment is in both cases part of the happy resolution of the plot. Of comparable importance to this revelation at the level of character is Dickens's treatment of this phenomenon of revelation at the level of language. In his essay "Discourse in the Novel" (1934–35), Bakhtin painstakingly and sensitively analyses the chapters of *Little Dorrit* devoted to Mr Merdle, a man of impeccable reputation and exalted social status who is later revealed as a fraudster, becomes financially ruined and commits suicide. Bakhtin observes how the narrative brings together a variety of discourses, or heteroglossia, which coexist in the text's description of Merdle, even at the level of a single sentence. These different languages or discourses circulate in the narrative without markers that might signal who is speaking and thus without divulging any origin. The result of this is a text that has become a mosaic of apparent quotation, where what goes for 'common knowledge' about Mr Merdle is expressed. What is revealed in this linguistic process is the social construction and discursive foundation of Mr Merdle's status, of the conventional wisdom regarding his character and qualities. The most important example discussed by Bakhtin is when the narration slowly moves to the veiled source of Mr Merdle's accomplishments: 'Oh, what a wonderful man this Merdle, what a great man, what a master man, how blessedly and enviably endowed – in one word, what a rich man!' (531) All of the earlier remarks about Mr Merdle's financial acumen, penetrating judgement and fine taste are shown to issue from one 'fact' – Merdle is rich. In the society in which he lives, wealth can produce all the other effects.

Merdle's fall from grace results in his transformation, and the narrative 'chatter' about a baronetcy and a future in politics vanishes leaving the reader with the police report-style details of his suicide, where he becomes 'the body of a heavily-made man, with an obtuse head, and coarse, mean, common features' (668). Looking at these adjectives, the reader sees that even Merdle's body has now come to signify his criminal nature. Now that the glamour of wealth has been shed, 'everyone' now agrees that he was 'a vulgar barbarian (for Mr Merdle was found out, from the crown of his head to the sole of his foot, the moment he was found out in his pocket)' (760). *Little Dorrit* dramatizes the formation of public opinion and received wisdom through its deployment of different idiolects: 'common knowledge' in this situation is very far from 'fact'. Bakhtin claims that 'in the English comic novel we find a comic-parodic re-processing of almost all the levels of literary language' (301). For Bakhtin, the English comic novel, with Dickens situated squarely within it, is comic precisely through its appropriation of multiple languages and their coexistence within the same narrative, frequently in the same sentence:

> Thus the stratification of literary language, its speech diversity, is an indispensable prerequisite for comic style, whose elements are

projected onto different linguistic planes while at the same time the
intention of the author, refracted as it passes through these planes,
does not wholly give itself up to any of them. (311)

As we have seen in relation to *Nights at the Circus* and *Wise Children*,
Carter also brings together a wide variety of heteroglossia within the
warp and weft of her prose. Carnival, whether of the strictly
Bakhtinian kind or not, is always one strand among a range of linguistic registers which exist within the literary work in order that the
text may *traverse* them, rather than seek to *resolve* or *synthesize* them.
In other words, the comic novel does not merely describe carnival
pleasure or disorder but embodies the comic principle at the level of
its deployment of literary language. Carnival's existence in the two
late Carter novels is as one signifying discourse among others. Thus
Carter follows Dickens in revealing the unacknowledged kinship
between the serious and the comic, the legitimate and the illegitimate,
the respectable and the criminal. Carnival, or materialist philosophies
for that matter, is not to be revealed as a master-discourse that can discover 'reality' but rather to exist as an alternative perspective on the
world.

Looking back to my earlier discussion of *Hard Times*'s allusion to
Bluebeard, and the manner in which fairy tales haunt the characters and
plots of Dickens's novels, we may observe how, just as in Dickens's novel,
Carter presents an array of discourses without wholly committing to or
endorsing a particular one. As Bakhtin argues above, the free circulation
of and collision between discourses that he sees as particular and indis-
pensable to the English comic tradition renders any concept of authorial
intention defunct. In Carter's late novels, neither the discourse of carnival nor the discourse of materialist politics becomes the master discourse
capable of providing unproblematic access to truth. For Connor, *Hard
Times*'s analysis of Coketown society is forced to draw on the discourse of
'fact' that it has been satirizing in the person of Gradgrind:

> our firm convictions of the clarity of [*Hard Times*'s] structure actual-
> ly require the suspension of awareness of certain rather important
> internal inconsistencies. These inconsistencies have a residual force
> though, working athwart the main narrative but also, in a peculiar
> way, sustaining it. (Connor, *Charles Dickens* 105)

As Connor points out, this is not to say that the novel has suddenly
become fashionably postmodernist. Rather, it is to illuminate the ways

in which the text's deployment of 'fact' and 'fancy' as distinct and, to a large degree, opposed discourses that coexist in the narrative has repercussions affecting its capacity to offer a critique of Coketown society. Bearing Bakhtin's and Connor's points in mind, we are now in a better position to understand why critics so often disagree on, for example, the extent to which the reconciliations at the end of *Wise Children* may be taken at face value.[6] Such disagreements are apparent in Britzolakis's reading of the family reunion as issuing from a 'self-conscious and camp sentimentality' (55), while Clare Hanson, in arguing for the novel as 'ultimately an elegaic text', accuses Gerardine Meaney of misreading Carter's use of carnival (69; see Meaney 139). Although carnival may not emerge as the all-determining centre of the text, it is not then submerged or simply disposed of but, rather, persists within the reader's understanding of the novel, keeping the interpretative apparatus in (perpetual) motion.

Terry Eagleton's outline of where Dickens's realism 'ends up', as it were, is valuable here as it offers a powerful account of the impact of the kind of heteroglossia Bakhtin describes in Dickens and that I would argue can also be clearly traced in *Nights at the Circus* and *Wise Children*:

> The later 'realism' of Dickens is thus of a notably impure kind – a question, often enough, of 'totalising' forms englobing non-realist 'contents', of dispersed, conflictual discourses which ceaselessly offer to displace the securely 'over-viewing' eye of classical realism. If Dickens's movement towards such realism produces a totalising ideology, it is one constantly deconstructed from within by the 'scattering' effect of quite contrary literary devices. (154)

From this perspective, Carter is revealed as a descendant of Dickens in the great comic tradition of the English novel that stretches back to Henry Fielding and Tobias Smollett. Thus, rather than seeking to identify Carter's work very closely with specific aspects of Bakhtin's theory of carnival, we might instead follow Bakhtin as a reader of Dickens to explore how *Nights at the Circus* and *Wise Children* partake of an English literary tradition where the discourse of 'common knowledge' is the principal target for comic explosion and demolition.

Realism and the politics of vision

As discussed previously, many of Dickens's critics have sought to defend his use of fantasy by recourse to the essential realism of his literary project. One aspect that many of these comments share is an emphasis on seeing, an emphasis that Dickens himself was arguably the first to cultivate in his letter quoted by Hill above, or in his preface to *Martin Chuzzlewit* (1844):

> What is exaggeration to one class of minds and perceptions is plain truth to another [...] I sometimes ask myself [...] whether it is always the writer who colours highly, or whether it is now and then the reader *whose eye for colour is a little dull.* (9; emphasis added)

George Santayana offers a twentieth-century expansion on this in his critique of readers who may be unconvinced that Dickens offers a valid version of reality:

> When people say Dickens exaggerates, it seems to me they can have no eyes and no ears. They probably have only *notions* of what things and people are; they accept them conventionally, at their diplomatic value. Their minds run on in the region of discourse, where there are masks only and no faces, ideas and no facts. (143; emphasis in original)

It is one thing to lament the prevalence of convention, quite another to privilege an author's exemption from such convention, as we shall see. This highlighting of the visual faculty takes us back to Ruskin and Dickens's 'stage fire' and it is here that Carter's work exhibits a crucial difference to Dickens's account of his œuvre. For in Carter 'seeing is always a complex and untrustworthy business', as Pearson observes (249).

Within Carter's writing, the dissonance that Bakhtin, Connor and Eagleton attend to in Dickens but that was recouped into a more profound 'realism' by generations of critics and by Dickens himself is now out in the open. Pearson, in admirably succinct terms that stand in direct contrast to the visual model offered by Ruskin and Satayana above, contends that in Carter

> [i]t is not that an 'apparent' world of phenomenon masks a 'real' world that we could see if we stripped away its deceptive veneer. It is rather that the whole nature of reality is problematised; and radically different modes of discerning, which seem to have equal validity, are depicted. (249)

If *Nights at the Circus* is centrally preoccupied with how Walser *sees* Fevvers and *Wise Children* is centrally preoccupied with how Nora and Dora *see* Melchior, then the romance endings of the novels may be less significant as 'reconciliations' than as the subject's realization of the role of discourse in their view of someone else. Walser will have to be reborn as a human chicken in order *not* to see Fevvers as a freak or a fraud or a prize or a symbol but as an individual. Similarly, the Chance twins' most important discovery is arguably not to do with their biological origins, which are still to a degree unclear, but their growing awareness of their own role in constructing Melchior as a father. As Dora points out to Nora:

> 'And tonight, he had an imitation look, even when he was crying, especially when he was crying, like one of those great, big, papier-mâché heads they have in the Notting Hill parade, larger than life, but not lifelike.'
> Nora sunk in thought for a hundred yards.
> 'D'you know, I sometimes wonder if we haven't been making him up all along,' she said. 'If he isn't just a collection of our hopes and dreams and wishful thinking in the afternoons. Something to set our lives by, like the old clock in the hall, which is real enough, in itself, but which we've got to wind up to make it go.' (230)

The 'old clock in the hall' Nora refers to is, of course, the 'castrato' grandfather clock inherited by Grandma Chance and the girls, and Melchior presents a rather hollow and emasculated figure whose elevated status in Dora and Nora's eyes was only really an effect of the twins' hopes for a father-figure. These novels thus conclude not with the 'real' Melchior or the 'real' Fevvers stepping forth into the limelight, but with their protagonists striving to comprehend their own position within the discourses they inhabit and the shedding of illusions – which is not quite the same thing as the attainment of 'the truth'.

The shaping power of the eyes and of vision generally is nowhere more apparent in *Wise Children* than in the treatment of the woman known for most of the novel as Wheelchair, formerly Lady Atalanta, ex-wife of Melchior Hazard, who now lives with the twins on Bard Road. As the group prepares to attend the festivities organized on behalf of Melchior, Wheelchair may be the aged, unrequited lover of Dickens's *Great Expectations* who is physically and temporally confined (although now a Cockney 'Haversham' and not 'Havisham'):

In her white ballgown and pearls, she looked quite lovely, not so much Miss Haversham, more the Ghost of Christmas past.

'Got to move with the times, darling,' said Nora.

'Not me,' said Wheelchair. 'I live mostly in the past, these days. I find it's better.'... She was still eating her heart out for Melchior, after all these years, was she? (192–93)

On arrival at the party, however, Wheelchair undergoes a strange transformation as she is greeted by Melchior:

She was so light he hoisted her up easily into his arms in her white gown and her veil and she looked like a nun, or a ghost, or a very ancient bride, until, out from under that veil, she gave him a flash of her Lynde-blue eyes and he blushed [...] suddenly, she turned back into the Lady A. of long ago. (195)

If Tiffany is *Wise Children*'s new Ophelia, one who escapes self-destruction and a watery grave to new life, then Lady A. is a new Miss Havisham, one whose charms are not marred by time and whose eyes may reveal a different self to the expected. All this is accomplished not by fairytale magic but by a literal revisioning, as Wheelchair moves out of one circle of stage fire into another.

Looking at Carter's later works through the prism of Dickens, one can discern how *Nights at the Circus* and *Wise Children* adopt the linguistic play of heteroglossia that Bakhtin saw as central to the tradition of the English comic novel and to Dickens in particular. Placing Carter within this tradition is, however, not simply to recognize her novels' humour, although there is undoubtedly plenty of humour to be found. The 'circles of stage fire' that illuminate the narratives in the form of theatricality and fairytales are ultimately modes of perception of human relations. Through its use of heteroglossia, the English comic novel is engaged in moving between different ways of looking at the world and this clash of perceptions goes to the heart of Carter's literary project. From this perspective, Carter's intertextual relationship with Dickens goes beyond a common (Shakespearean) source and a series of allusions to Dickens's narratives. It extends to the adoption of the English comic novel's distinctive mixture of political critique and unashamed humorous entertainment, exploiting, in Connor's words, the novel's 'capacity, which is paradoxically intrinsic to the form, to hold together different registers of experience' (*The English Novel* 38). For Carter, Dickens provided a powerful example of how a comic novel might excel at bringing together these different registers.

Notes

1. For more on Carter and Shakespeare, see Sanders's essay in this volume and on Dickens and Shakespeare, see Gager.
2. See Carter, "Notes from the Front Line" (70).
3. 'In Dickens [...] the private imagination, comic, poetical and fantastic, was inseparable from the public imagination and the operation of conscience and rebellion. This amalgamation was possible, I think, because he felt from childhood the sense of being outside society, because he was a sort of showman, not because he was a social or political thinker with a program' (Pritchett 322).
4. As Armstrong proposes: 'Doctrinaire positions limit. This is partly why Fevvers is so often irritated by Lizzie, her loving mother figure, and her farcical eagerness to take a Marxist feminist line on everything' (274).
5. See, for example, Russo and Moss.
6. Compare the treatment of this issue by Britzolakis, Sanders, Meaney and Chedgzoy.

Works cited

Armstrong, Isobel. "Woolf by the Lake, Woolf at the Circus." *Flesh and the Mirror: Essays on the Art of Angela Carter*. Ed. Lorna Sage. London: Virago, 1994. 257–78.

Bakhtin, Mikhail. "Discourse in the Novel." 1934–35. *The Dialogic Imagination*. Trans. Caryl Emerson and Michael Holquist. Austin: University of Texas Press, 1981. 259–422.

Bristow, Joseph, and Trev Lynn Broughton. Introduction. *The Infernal Desires of Angela Carter: Fiction, Femininity, Feminism*. Ed. Joseph Bristow and Trev Lynn Broughton. Harlow: Addison Wesley Longman, 1997. 1–23.

Britzolakis, Christina. "Angela Carter's Fetishism." *The Infernal Desires of Angela Carter: Fiction, Femininity, Feminism*. Ed. Joseph Bristow and Trev Lynn Broughton. Harlow: Addison Wesley Longman, 1997. 43–58.

Carr, Jean Ferguson. "Writing as a Woman: Dickens, *Hard Times* and Feminine Discourses." *Charles Dickens*. Ed. Steven Connor. London: Longman, 1996. 159–77.

Carter, Angela. *Heroes and Villains*. 1969. Harmondsworth: Penguin, 1981.

——. *The Magic Toyshop*. 1967. London: Virago, 1981.

——. *Nights at the Circus*. 1984. London: Vintage, 1994.

——. "Notes from the Front Line." *On Gender and Writing*. Ed. Michelene Wandor. London: Pandora, 1983. 69–77.

——. *Wise Children*. 1991. London: Vintage, 1992.

Chedgzoy, Kate. *Shakespeare's Queer Children: Sexual Politics and Contemporary Culture.* Manchester: Manchester University Press, 1995.

Connor, Steven. *Charles Dickens.* Oxford: Basil Blackwell, 1985.

———. *The English Novel in History 1950–1995.* London: Routledge, 1996.

———. Introduction. *Charles Dickens.* Ed. Steven Connor. London: Longman, 1996. 1–33.

Dickens, Charles. *David Copperfield.* 1848–50. Harmondsworth: Penguin, 1994.

———. *Great Expectations.* 1860–61. London: Penguin, 1996.

———. *Hard Times.* 1854. Harmondsworth: Penguin, 1985.

———. *Little Dorrit.* 1855–57. Hertfordshire: Wordsworth Classics, 2002.

———. *Martin Chuzzlewit.* 1844. London: New English Library, 1965.

———. *Our Mutual Friend.* 1864–65. Hertfordshire: Wordsworth Classics, 2002.

———. "The Spirit of Fiction." *All the Year Round* XVIII (27 July 1867): 120.

Eagleton, Terry. "Ideology and Literary Form: Charles Dickens." *Charles Dickens.* Ed. Steven Connor. London: Longman, 1996. 151–58.

Gager, Valerie. *Shakespeare and Dickens.* Cambridge: Cambridge University Press, 1996.

Haffenden, John. "Angela Carter." *Novelists in Interview.* London: Methuen, 1985. 76–96.

Hanson, Clare. "'The Red Dawn Breaking Over Clapham': Carter and the Limits of Artifice." *The Infernal Desires of Angela Carter: Fiction, Femininity, Feminism.* Ed. Joseph Bristow and Trev Lynn Broughton. Harlow: Addison Wesley Longman, 1997. 59–72.

Head, Dominic. *The Cambridge Introduction to Modern British Fiction 1950–2000.* Cambridge: Cambridge University Press, 2002.

Hill, Nancy. *A Reformer's Art: Dickens' Picturesque and Grotesque Imagery.* Athens: Ohio University Press, 1981.

Meaney, Gerardine. *(Un)like Subjects: Women, Theory, Fiction.* London: Routledge, 1993.

Moss, Betty. "Desire and the Female Grotesque in Angela Carter's 'Peter and the Wolf'." *Angela Carter and the Fairy Tale.* Ed. Danielle M. Roemer and Cristina Bacchilega. Detroit: Wayne State University Press, 2001. 187–203.

Paulin, Tom. "In an English Market." *London Review of Books* 3–17 March 1983: 19.

Pearson, Jacqueline. "'These Tags of Literature': Some Uses of Allusion in the Early Novels of Angela Carter." *Critique: Studies in Contemporary Fiction* 40.3 (1999): 248–56.

Pritchett, V.S. "The Comic World of Dickens." *The Dickens Critics.* Ed. George H. Ford and Lauriat Lane. Ithaca: Cornell University Press, 1961. 309–24.

Rushdie, Salman. Introduction. *Burning Your Boats: Collected Short Stories.* By Angela Carter. London: Vintage, 1996. ix–xiv.

Ruskin, John. "A Note on *Hard Times.*" *The Dickens Critics.* Ed. George H. Ford and Lauriat Lane. Ithaca: Cornell University Press, 1961. 47–48.

Russo, Mary. *The Female Grotesque: Risk, Excess and Modernity.* New York: Routledge, 1994.

Sage, Lorna. "Angela Carter Interviewed by Lorna Sage." *New Writing.* Ed. Malcolm Bradbury and Judith Cooke. London: Minerva, 1992. 185–93.

Sanders, Julie. *Novel Shakespeares: Twentieth-Century Women Novelists and Appropriation.* Manchester: Manchester University Press, 2001.

Santayana, George. "Dickens." *The Dickens Critics*. Ed. George H. Ford and Lauriat Lane. Ithaca: Cornell University Press, 1961. 135–50.

Shaw, George Bernard. *"Hard Times." The Dickens Critics*. Ed. George H. Ford and Lauriat Lane. Ithaca: Cornell University Press, 1961. 125–34.

Wood, James. *The Irresponsible Self: On Laughter and the Novel*. London: Jonathan Cape, 2004.

8
Behind Locked Doors: Angela Carter, Horror and the Influence of Edgar Allan Poe

Gina Wisker

> I'd always been fond of Poe, and Hoffman [sic] –
> Gothic tales, cruel tales, tales of wonder, tales of terror,
> fabulous narratives that deal directly with the imagery
> of the unconscious – mirrors; the externalized self; for-
> saken castles; haunted forests; forbidden sexual
> objects.
>
> (Angela Carter, "Afterword," *Fireworks*)

Edgar Allan Poe is frequently acknowledged as the originator of the horror genre. His dark tales contain demonic pledges, walled in corpses, living death, curses, body horror, contagion and natural terrors turned
weird. In his study *Supernatural Horror in Literature* (1927), H.P. Lovecraft
devotes a whole chapter to Poe's horror tales, acknowledging his mastery by calling him the 'deity and fountain-head of all modern diabolic
fiction' (53). Lovecraft sees Poe as moving beyond earlier horror writers
who '[w]orked largely in the dark; without an understanding of the psychological basis of the horror appeal' (ibid.). These writers were, he
argues, hampered by the need to conform to a happy ending, side with
one of the characters and their views, reward virtue and adhere to popular standards and beliefs. Poe chooses to write of doom, decay and
death, but avoids didacticism; he 'perceived the essential impartiality of
the real artist' (ibid.). In "The Philosophy of Composition" (1846), he
talks of his awareness of effect and the importance of keeping it short:
'I prefer commencing with the consideration of an *effect*. Keeping originality *always* in view – for he is false to himself who ventures to dis-
pense within so obvious and attainable a source of interest' (480;
emphasis in original).[1]

Poe established several of the main formulae of horror and tales of terror. His well-crafted tales often begin with storytelling or an everyday opening, building up layers of suspense and horror, defamiliarizing the everyday and using a mix of psychological horror, body horror, the supernatural and the realistic. In "Never Bet the Devil Your Head" (1850), for example, an arrogant wager leads to decapitation – in his world, the devil's word should not be taken in vain. This is a typically Gothic mixture, a combination of opposites which enables readers to see the cracks and borders, lies and constructions in the ostensibly stable. Meanwhile, the boundaries between life and death are confused in "Ligeia" (1838) when a dead wife returns in the body of her successor. Poe destabilizes conventions about relationships, domestic security, family, identity, reality and time. He does this using the now well-established horror trajectory beginning with brief stability quickly troubled and undercut. As Mark Jancovich puts it in his study of the origins and development of the horror genre:

> [i]t is claimed that the pleasure offered by the genre is based on the process of narrative closure in which the horrifying or monstrous is destroyed or contained. The structure of horror narratives are said to set out from a situation of order, move through a period of disorder caused by the eruption of horrifying or monstrous forces, and finally reach a point of closure and completion in which disruptive, monstrous elements are contained or destroyed and the original order is re-established. (9)

In Poe, however, there is seldom if ever any restoration of stability and comfort; horrifying and monstrous forces erupt, but rarely is order re-established.

In his concern with perversions of power, spectacles of violence and themes of delusion, insanity and retribution, Poe's sensational horror bears the influences of Jacobean revenge tragedy. For example, his tyrants, like the evil brothers in John Webster's *The Duchess of Malfi* (1614) and the Duke in *The White Devil* (1612), as well as the various murderers in the works of Cyril Tourner, Christopher Marlowe and William Shakespeare, might meet a terrible end some of the time, but their relatively innocent victims are *not* rescued and usually die horrible deaths – poisoned, maddened, buried alive, tortured, permanently replaced body and soul by another, or already dead and only seen in a portrait. Lovecraft proposes that Poe develops psychological horror – both symbolist and, although not everyday, familiar – from the depths of our fears and dreams so that 'his spectres thus acquired a convincing malignity' (53). His characters are perverse, self-damaging bullies, drunks, tyrants, madmen; he develops 'a perverse desire to vex the self into the central motivation of his characters, removing the clutter of eighteenth-century rationalist reflection and commentary so that the self-damaging impulse stands out in sharp relief and beyond explanation' (Lloyd-Smith 114). Poe's horror fiction is underpinned by a tenuous hold on what is living or dead, augmented by a fear of social chaos. He represents time and history as processes of disintegration and loss, and many of his stories are founded upon a desire to repeat the past and move back to a state of stasis and order. So, often, time is denied or questioned through either reanimating the dead or embracing death. For example, in "The Masque of the Red Death" (1842), contagion is a metaphor for retribution following feudal lack of care for the rural populace. In a castle where the fancy-dressed rich overindulge themselves in dancing, eating and sexual entertainment while the poor die outside of the plague, Death, dressed in red, is the unwelcome guest who passes the plague between them all in a recasting of the Jacobean 'tragedy of blood'.

Gothic horror and the work of Poe are favourite sources of inspiration, atmosphere, imagery and tropes for Angela Carter. As she comments in a television interview in 1977:

> I have a kind of familial attachment to Poe. I've used him a lot decoratively, but never structurally. I don't know if that makes sense. [...] I've used a lot of the imagery from Poe. I say I've used it, I've used it as a starting point for imagery of my own. (Bedford)

Like that of Poe, Carter's work explores themes of hypocrisy, deceit, duplicity, delusion, incarceration, repression and the explosion of the unfamiliar and unpleasant from the everyday. Similarly drawing from Jacobean revenge tragedy and fairy tales, as well as Hammer studios and a range of other perpetrators, Carter concocts and nurtures her own horror scenarios – scenarios which never underestimate or sell short the violence, terror and disempowerment which Gothic horror enacts, while offering alternatives and escapes through comic undercutting and imaginative freedoms. She builds upon and reworks the expressions, images and arguments of texts to explore and expose the ways in which they feed into her and our worldviews. In so doing, she stirs together a wicked (both evil, and celebrated) mix of Gothic horror's terrifying, entrapping paralysis and the energetic agency of the imaginative and actively liberating comic, the carnivalesque.

"The Cabinet of Edgar Allan Poe", collected in *Black Venus* (1985), is a mixture of an imaginative replaying of Poe's young life, and something of a checklist of trace elements we can identify in the work of both Poe and Carter. In this story, Carter beckons us in and leads us by the hand through the influences Poe has had on her work, pulling aside the theatrical curtains of his mother's life and his fascination with performativity, artifice, the questionable, delicately constructed and maintained boundary between life and death (his mother died and rose nightly on stage) and between self and Other (marrying his cousin, Virginia, he loved and mourned a version of himself). The scenarios she conjures perfectly explain Poe's preoccupations: with premature burial and returned lovers, the grand performance of oppression and torture, the proximity of death to life and its contagion, and with mirrors which construct and replay a false self, which can hide decay, and yet reveal its insidious traces. In her short story, Carter has Poe inserting Allan in his name but does not mention the rest of the family. She details his fascination with alcohol, beginning as a pacifier whilst his mother and father acted, leading to blight in his life: 'David Poe tipped a tumbler of neat gin to Edgar's lips to keep him quiet. The red-eyed Angel of Intemperance hopped out of the bottle of ardent spirits and snuggled down in little Edgar's longclothes' (34). She also imagines Poe as a young boy spending much of his time in his mother's costume trunk, which situates him as prop, a hidden observer, while the performance goes on around him. Incarceration in the trunk becomes a source for Poe's terror of premature burial.

In the texture of her language and imagery, Carter revives Poe: the heated, threatening, nightmarish, Gothic settings, cruel deadly events, and the performativity of it all. She interprets Poe's version of artifice, his mother's nightly portrayal of dying and dead Shakespearean heroines, followed by childlike, comic parts, leaving him, upon her death, with a lingering sense of her possible return; a terror of living death, and an expectation of revival. This is the dark side of Carter's own work too: the enactment of forms of control, dehumanization and turning people into automata. But the gaiety, sawdust and gusto of the artificial world within which Carter imagines Poe's mother and the two boys, Edgar and Henry, to inhabit nightly, the paint and bawdy laughter, are the comic carnival spirit with which she balances such death in life gloom.

Carter's referencing of Poe in this story operates along a continuum, at one end of which is the title's subtle allusion to *Das Kabinett des Dr Caligari* (1920), the early German Expressionist Gothic horror movie directed by Robert Wiene. This reference indicates Poe's gruesome, Gothic taste, and the sense of surprise at opening up a cabinet of horrors, with possibly hideous revelations of incest? His cousin? Cross-dressing? Alcoholism? The latent hints of necrophilia lying behind the desire for the dead loved one? At the other end of this continuum is the deliberate referencing of themes and issues which she identifies in Poe, and which we can track in her own work – such as Puritan deceit, restraint, artifice, the close links between sex and death and deadly pressures. In particular it is those fears of incarceration and disempowerment which surface in Carter's tales in her focus on those (women) manipulated by others, often as if puppets. Carter's intertextuality references, reminds, subtly or overtly interlaces, interacts with, builds upon and re-writes works which feed into her own arguments and expression.

Carter's take on the Gothic resembles that of Poe in that she also unites realistic detail with the symbolic and excess, using the oxymoron to expose as fallacious assertions that behaviours, such as relationships of power and hierarchies, are based, in fact, in a shared reality. Postmodern Carter reveals 'realities' as versions, constructions, as does nineteenth-century Poe, but his work can ignore the pressures of everyday social and cultural institutions, while Carter, both earthy and symbolic, deals with them. As she writes in the "Afterword" to *Fireworks* (1974):

> The Gothic tradition in which Poe writes grandly ignores the value systems of our institutions; it deals entirely with the profane. Its great themes are incest and cannibalism. Character and events are exaggerated beyond reality, to become symbols, ideas, passions. Its style will tend to be ornate, unnatural – and thus operates against the perennial human desire to believe the world as fact. (133)

This essay will examine the ways in which Carter draws upon and reworks a range of related horror sources, including Poe's Gothic horror and Jacobean revenge tragedy. In particular, it will examine how, in her recasting of Poe's horror themes and tropes, she replays some of the concerns of her influences within a late-twentieth-century context and breaks the frames of the genre. Through her reworking of Poe's gothic horror, Carter rediscovers and reveals the potentially terrible consequences of domestic incarceration and family tyrannies. Nevertheless, re-working motifs linking sex, beauty and death, she frequently deploys the carnivalesque to provide endangered women with the last liberated laugh, as epitomized by the characterization of Fevvers, the winged bird-woman of *Nights at the Circus* (1984).

The *femme fatale*

"Ligeia", Poe's tale of a returned *femme fatale*, replays the promise of romantic love (the idea of eternity together), the unsettling boundary between life and death, themes of animation, stasis and reanimation, and, in particular, male terrors of women's potential for luring them into fatal attraction. In this respect, "Ligeia" provides a model for tales of returned former lovers, and undying and potentially deadly love, a common horror theme. In this tale, a husband witnesses his first wife return to life in the reanimated body of the second. Poe's ghostly *femme fatale* is fascinating and lovely. However, she has a deadly hold not only on her living husband but on the hapless second wife. Elisabeth Bronfen, arguing that a major source of pleasure and desire in Western literature concerns the dead female body, suggests that the male narrator in Poe's tale repossesses the body of the loved one: 'the resurrection assures the repossession of a lost love object, implicitly a return of the maternal body, which promised infinite knowledge and at which the child first experienced a sense of unity and wholeness' (332). David Punter questions Bronfen's reading of the text, 'that the story represents a triumph of the male over the female, of the surviving masculine over the dead female body' (107), which, he argues, remains very ambiguous, even in terms of the epigraph from John Glanville – 'And the will therein lieth, which dieth not' (310) – where the word 'lieth' could indicate either *a lie* or *remaining*. Punter's analysis, then, questions who possesses, who survives.

A typical Poe male, the self-absorbed, fallible narrator is buried in his study until awoken by the lovely Lady Ligeia. He cannot recall knowing her family name and describes this rather spectral and majestic woman as 'tall, somewhat slender, and, in her latter days, even emaciated. I would in vain attempt to portray the majesty, the quiet ease, of her demeanor, or the incomprehensible lightness and elasticity of her footfall. She came and departed as a shadow' (116). For him, she is 'faultless', 'exquisite' and 'strange'. He describes how her eyes are 'far larger than the ordinary eyes of our own race' and 'even fuller than the fullest of the gazelle eyes of the tribe of the valley of Nourjahad [...] those large, those shining, those divine orbs! they became to me the twin stars of Leda, and I to them the devoutest of astrologers' (117). Clearly, this dazzling, foreign beauty is not just the object and subject of his love but someone from another time and place – or all other times and places – but the narrator never recognizes this. Nevertheless, the telltale signs which we and he do not name but surely recognize as consumption or tuberculosis start to appear:

> The wild eyes glaze with a too – too glorious effulgence; the pale fingers became of transparent waxen hue of the grave, and the blue veins upon the lofty forehead swelled and sank impetuously with the tides of the most gentle emotion. I saw that she must die – and I struggled desperately in spirit with the grim Azrael. (118)

On her deathbed, Ligeia tells the narrator to re-read her a poem 'composed by herself' about puppets, mimes, orchestras, God, angels and phantoms – and about how in the tragedy of man the 'conqueror worm' takes all. Quoting John Glanville, the dying Ligeia shrieks against the need to depart this life: 'man does not yield him to the angels, nor unto death utterly, save through the weakness of his feeble will' (120). The staginess of this episode is echoed in Carter's depiction of Poe's mother's nightly dying and revival as she 'put[s] on Ophelia's madwoman's nightgown for her farewell' (35) in "The Cabinet of Edgar Allan Poe". The rant against death is everyone's desire not to be taken by it but somehow to cross those boundaries without the finality that seems a kind of giving in to some other power.

When the narrator in "Ligeia" remarries and generally ignores the 'fair haired and blue eyed Lady Rowena Trevanion of Tremaine' (121), he speaks of the bridal chamber in terms of serpents and melancholy. He loathes the second wife, venting his bad temper and moodiness in anger. Two months into their marriage and she is stricken with a suffering. Her mind seems as feeble as her body as she talks of movements among the curtains before three or four ruby drops fall into her wine from nowhere in particular. Spectral supernatural occurrences lead to Rowena's death. The husband mourns her briefly, but returns his mind to the compelling Lady Ligeia, whose death was much more of an event. Although he claims 'unutterable horror and awe' (124), he is clearly amazed and gradually overjoyed when the corpse by his side starts to sob and alter in a series of movements from tomblike iciness to something quite different. First with tottering steps, then more determinedly, 'the thing that was enshrouded advanced boldly and palpably into the middle of the apartment' (125), turning moments later into someone much taller than Rowena ever was with 'huge masses of long and disheveled hair [...] blacker than the raven wings of the midnight!' (125). The lovely Lady Ligeia returns. This is a powerful woman: a vampire? a ghost? She is one who lives forever, who outlasts and defies the confines of mortality. The misogyny of the tale lies in its victimization of Rowena by the narrator in life, by Ligeia in her death, and by the romantic trajectory of the tale itself. We too want her out of the way so Ligeia can return – though we might well be more troubled than the narrator by this undead eternal beauty.

Carter's "The Loves of Lady Purple" (1974) is founded on similar fears. In this short story the same tones are obvious, dated and artificial, referencing death in life and life in death through the adoration of the Asiatic professor for the puppet Lady Purple, his own product, his 'petrification of a universal whore' (30). As a marionette, Lady Purple fulfils both the fantasies of her maker who scripts her narrative and manipulates (literally pulls the strings for) its enactment, and the fantasies of the voyeuristic punters who enjoy her sexually provocative, perverse adventures and her punishment. Lady Purple's eternal life is assured when she capitalizes on the professor's undying love and drains him with a single, long bite while he hangs her up for the night. Object of male sexual admiration and terror, a deadly woman, Lady Purple, like Ligeia, is an agent. Carter's vampire marionette wreaks vengeance for being cast in the mould of *femme fatale* and manipulated by the strings of male pornographic adulation, dramatized in her every move. But, Lady Purple, the embodiment and repository of the punters' horror, *cannot* be packed away. In the end, this monster of their own making will neither lie down nor be hung up:

> she could not escape the tautological paradox in which she was trapped; had the marionette all the time parodied the living or was she, now living, to parody her own performance as a marionette? Although she was now manifestly a woman, young and beautiful, the leprous whiteness of her face gave her the appearance of a corpse animated solely by demonic will. (39)

In Carter's story, Lady Purple turns from manipulated object into vampire, acting out fears the professor did not even imagine. Nevertheless, although she escapes the role of living doll, as she marches off to wreak havoc in the village brothel 'out of logical necessity' (40) she remains somehow trapped in the professor's script as a deadly whore.

Both Ligeia and Lady Purple come back to life, both prey upon men's romantic fantasies, and both replay roles assigned to women: they are deadly and beautiful. But Carter's Lady Purple has more agency because she obtains life through killing off her adorer, leaving him 'empty, useless and bereft of meaning as his own tumbled shawl' (38). Ligeia, in contrast, only preys on another woman, the hapless Rowena, who plays little more than a walk-on part and receptacle in Poe's horror script. Moreover, Poe's narrator is not punished for his oppressive behaviour. For Poe, the returned, revivified loved one is an eternal reward, a dream come true, an exit from a nightmare. For Carter, this vilified puppet is depicted as seemingly her own woman, broken free from the romantic fantasies of others, there to wreak revenge on those who would cast her in perverse scenarios.

In Poe, there are many women with less agency than Ligeia, suffering the idolatry of husbands who desire to control and own them body and soul, rather like in Robert Browning's "My Last Duchess" (1842). In "The Black Cat" (1843), the narrator's 'tenderness of heart' (382) leads first to friendship with a big black cat, Pluto. His wife irritates him. She is a silent victim in this relationship, the main driver of which seems to be his disillusioned, downward drive to drugs and drink. His temper drives him not only to beat upon his wife and fight with others, but first to gouge out beloved Pluto's eye, then hang the poor creature. In a subsequent fire, the wall bears the imprint of a black cat. When stopped by his wife while aiming a blow at a second cat, he kills her in an act of brutal frenzy: 'Goaded, by the interference, into a rage more than demoniacal I withdrew my arm from her grasp, and buried the axe in her brain. She fell dead upon the spot, without a groan' (386). This hideously unpleasant bully, the narrator, feels only the merest qualm at his monstrous, unforgivable acts, focusing instead on the most efficient means by which to conceal her body. Walling up his wife and congratulating himself for doing such a good job of it, he deserves his fate: the detectives who he invites to take a closer look at the wonderfully strong walls of his cellar hear, as he does, the meowing of the second cat, accidentally walled up with the wife.[2] The cat is discovered, feeding on her head. This horrified narrator gets his just rewards. Poe's fascination with the terrors of life in death – of becoming paralyzed, disempowered, objectified, victim to another's power, trapped in a deadly position or walled up – resonates with that of Carter. But Carter enables those women who would in Poe be disempowered or trapped, those who would be victims or *femmes fatales*, to expose the origins of their constructions in male fantasies perpetuated by social configurations of power, as poignantly demonstrated in "The Loves of Lady Purple".

Pornography and power

Carter exposes the social configurations of power found in the horror genre as versions of pornography. When asked in an interview with Helen Cagney Watts if she was influenced by Foucault, she responded that the Marquis de Sade was the primary influence: 'my reading of Foucault has possibly influenced me to some extent [...] really, though, it had been my reading of the Marquis de Sade that has probably had more impact; it is *the* text on sexuality and power' (170; emphasis in original). In his study of Carter, Linden Peach argues that *The Infernal Desire Machines of Doctor Hoffman* (1972) is the first of Carter's books to show the influence of de Sade, representing not just pornographic scenarios but a *style* attributable to a Sadeian influence. He sees her as parodying its panoptical traditions and, by utilizing a male narrator, getting inside the mode of the male pornographer and oppressor.

> Carter as a female author is appropriating a male consciousness to expose how women are trapped, like the woman reader of this novel, in a male imaginary. [...] the narrative technique of ventriloquism – a female author speaking in a male voice – is employed not just to create pornography but an essentially sadistic version of it. (111)

In this novel, Desiderio's narrative positions the male reader as voyeur but does not actually offer him an enjoyable pornographic spectacle – again Carter is turning the tables by exposing and parodying the particularly violent and oppressive aspects of a socially legitimated pornography which relegates women to victim status.

Poe's work is not noted for its direct pornography, but the wallowing in suffering, power and torture that he dramatizes resembles that critiqued by Carter. In "The Cabinet of Edgar Allan Poe", Carter places Poe at the intersection of the years when the Enlightenment led into the Romantic grotesque. Chief of these are the French Revolution's assertion of liberation, the guillotining of thousands, and the Marquis de Sade's demands to freely enact sexual desires, while refusing to acknowledge the economic and psychological power manipulating such freedoms (for some).

> Imagine Poe in the Republic! when he possesses none of its virtues; no Spartan, he. [...] Here it is always morning; stern, democratic light scrubs apparitions off the streets down which his dangerous feet must go. [...]
>
> It was the evening of the eighteenth century.
>
> At this hour, this very hour, far away in Paris, France, in the appalling dungeons of the Bastille, old Sade is jerking off. (32–33)

In Poe's "The Masque of the Red Death", Prince Prospero hosts a masked ball while his people die of the pestilence. This Sadeian excess is a form of pornography. In the 'castellated abbey' where the partying takes place, each chamber gives way to the next with the inner chamber black, its windows seemingly bespattered with blood, signifiers of the Red Death; meanwhile, his 'bold and fiery' plans (308) and his great eye for colour operate the endless party until the fatal gatecrasher arrives, a tall, gaunt stranger wearing grave habiliments: 'the mummer had gone so far as to assume the type of the Red Death [...] his broad brow ⟨...⟩ with the scarlet ho⟨...⟩

Carter's ⟨...⟩ ower and objectify ⟨...⟩ ult alongside the Br ⟨...⟩ tion, a living death ⟨...⟩ countered by Carter' ⟨...⟩ aned, adolescent M ⟨...⟩ ld offered by her de ⟨...⟩ her wedding dress ⟨...⟩ sweetly up at her dis ⟨...⟩ s victim to her toym ⟨...⟩ t and control her s ⟨...⟩ da and the swan my ⟨...⟩ grotesque phallic p⟨...⟩ hilip's (and Melanie'⟨...⟩ the swan, beloved ⟨...⟩ l women as lucky wil⟨...⟩ descends in

a variety of guises: to Europa as a bull, Danae as a shower of gold, and Leda as a swan, inseminating each so they give birth to a mortal/god (and are cast out of their homes as whores). In her role as a 'demythologiser' ("Notes from the Front Line" 71) Carter takes on such culturally embedded and replayed myths and exposes their tendency to establish and reinforce beliefs and behaviours which demonize, disempower and victimize those cast as Others in much conventional horror. In *The Magic Toyshop*, Melanie is rescued from loss of self by Finn and Francie's refusal to continue with the music and, for us as readers, by Carter's debunking of the pompous, patriarchal control of the event through highlighting the ridiculous movements of the swan: 'Like fate or the clock, on came the swan, its feet going splat, splat, splat' (166). Thus, it is through exposing the mechanics of Uncle Philip's pornographic script that Carter parodies Poe's pompous, bullying and monstrous manipulators by directly identifying them and their preference for and equation of women as objects.

Cannibalism and incest

Amongst the horror tropes with which contemporary readers are now familiar and somewhat at ease, incest and cannibalism are the least acceptable. Both spring from a desire to be, merge with or ingest the Other, as a projected version of self. In Webster's *The Duchess of Malfi*, the latent or blatant desire of the powerful brothers, Ferdinand and the Cardinal, for their sexually-active sister, the Duchess, is exposed in images of both incest and cannibalism leading to madness, betrayal, torture and murder. Ferdinand's lycanthropy is cannibalistic: he carries a leg of a corpse over his shoulder, presumably for devouring later. Here horror tropes are deployed to expose and indict the evil Jacobean brothers and in Poe and Carter they are similarly used to make it quite clear that monstrous acts spring from abjection, from rejecting versions of self and punishing those upon whom they are imposed.[3] Poe, for example, identifies incest and madness-based disturbance eating away at the heart of a family in "The Fall of the House of Usher" (1839), a domestic horror tale focusing on inheritance and lineage, where fear of time is depicted as a process of fragmentation and loss, and the solidity of the family home, unstable and likely to implode or explode, figures the rot at the heart of the family itself. In Jacobean revenge tragedy we are more likely to have the poisoned skulls, daggers, swords stabbed through an arras, sacrificed maddened women (I include *Hamlet* here) than in Poe, but the madness, perversity, tyranny and death are much the same – and each is produced by the fears of purity and the claustrophobia of a threatened and threatening society.

In "The Bloody Chamber" (1979), the wealthy Marquis purchases his new, impoverished, beautiful wife in order to control her, to engulf and devour her innocence through perversion. Carter's language in this story recalls that in Poe's "The Pit and the Pendulum" (1842), in which a traveller is imprisoned by a dominant, absent and unseen tyrant and forced into two life-threatening scenarios. In one he is incarcerated in a cell in the pitch black, and narrowly misses falling into the bottomless pit at its centre; in another a pendulum controls the swing of a large guillotine-like knife approaching him moment by moment. The body and mind are both threatened and controlled; there is no recourse to debate or defence. However, where pleasure and pain are separated in Poe, in Carter their sexual connection is explicit; sex and torture are aligned. Although initially overwhelmed by his attention and lavish gifts, the young bride sees her husband inspecting her with 'the assessing eye of a connoisseur inspecting horseflesh' (11). To the Marquis, however, she is an object both beautiful and to be literally consumed. His books of pornography are left for her to read (accidentally on purpose) while the sexual act, replayed in mirrors, resembles the slicing and impaling of the pendulum in Poe's tale. The wife is clad only in an expensive 'choker of rubies, two inches wide, like an extraordinarily precious slit throat' (11), the 'heirloom of one woman who had escaped the blade' (17); the Marquis, like Uncle Philip in *The Magic Toyshop*, and Poe's arrogant, powerful tyrants, enjoys controlling the spectacle:

> He twined my hair into a rope and lifted it off my shoulders [...] Rapt, he intoned: 'Of her apparel she retains/Only her sonorous jewellery.'
>   A dozen husbands impaled a dozen brides while the mewing gulls swung on invisible trapezes in the empty air outside. (17)

The route to the locked chamber, 'in the viscera of the castle' (27) reeks of male power – leather, aftershave, tobacco – and is decorated with images of sexualized pain and suffering. 'There is a striking resemblance between the act of love and the ministrations of a torturer' says this Bluebeard's favourite poet (27). His way of showing his possessive love is the rack, the Iron Maiden, and other 'instruments of mutilation' which invade, warp and destroy women's bodies. Nevertheless, while in the various versions of the traditional fairy tale, the wife who crosses the thresholds of power and knowledge usually escapes being a victim, rescued by a strong man, in Carter's feminist revision, she is rescued by her warrior mother who breaks down the castle doors, reclaiming the space and her daughter.

While cannibalism is never a positive theme or figure for Carter because it exposes oppressive, engulfing power, incest (in *The Magic Toyshop* in particular) is often redefined as a way of defying such power. Carter suggests incestuous feelings in Poe's marriage to his cousin in "The Cabinet of Edgar Allan Poe", elaborating further this tightly encircled world only one step from the prop box from which he watched and adored his mother's performances. Marrying his 13-year-old cousin, Virginia, Poe married a version of both his mother and himself.

The dug was snatched from the milky mouth and tucked away inside the bodice; the mirror no longer reflected Mama but, instead, a perfect stranger. He offered her his hand; smiling a tranced smile, she stepped out of the frame.

'My darling, my sister, my life and my bride!'

He was not put out by the tender years of this young girl whom he soon married; was she not just Juliet's age, just thirteen summers? (39)

Incest is a favourite theme of horror in a society which ostensibly fears the madness and deformity caused by excessive inbreeding, but actually cannot face itself, cannot tolerate like with like and so, instead, operates through an insistence on polarities: male/female, good/bad, black/white, self/Other. And so incest, like same-sex relationships, is deemed abject, socially outcast. Incest terrifies and disgusts the conventional, and those who seek to control, because it recognizes sameness. But it can, therefore, be used as a powerful image of subversion; metaphorically, at least, incest, particularly between brother and sister, is the recognition of self in another.

Carter's "John Ford's *'Tis Pity She's a Whore*", collected in *American Ghosts and Old World Wonders* (1993), combines the terrors of John Ford's Jacobean revenge tragedy, *'Tis Pity She's a Whore* (1633), of incest and sex, with a kind of perverse Oklahoma, where 'she wore a yellow ribbon':

Blond children with broad, freckled faces, the boy in dungarees and the little girl in gingham and sunbonnet. In the old play, one John Ford called them Giovanni and Annabella; the other John Ford, in the movie, might call them Johnny and Annie-Belle. (21)

Here, the gingham world of the valorized, idealized, dreamlike American West is replayed as the Jacobean dramatist meets the twentieth-century American film-maker. Here it is deadly not so much because of the fears of inheriting family ills, as in Poe's "The Fall of the House of Usher", and family and land ownership loss, but because of internalized taboos and social punishment. The complacency of the 'grits and jowls' inbred American West hiding its secrets is replayed and referenced here in Carter's tale. Characteristics of this repressed dream turned nightmare include scalps, bullets, gun law, wife beating, and Puritan, murderous bullying of critical women suspected to be witches – all of which contribute to a small town 'take' on the high plains, and the celluloid perpetuation of these dreams and lies. Carter enters Poe's space in exposing the false beliefs of his homeland, emphasizing both the terrors Poe explored – incest, sick inheritances and threats to the body – and updates them with the ingredients from the twentieth-century film industry.

In his reading of Carter's short story, Peach notes that its representation of America 'is riddled [...] with confusion, pretence and illusion [...] Annie-Belle "cross-dresses" as her brother's wife, the community believes her to be pregnant by the Minister's son and Johnny is mistakenly regarded as a shamed member of the family' (122). When Annie-Belle and Johnny first make love, Carter gives us a stereotypical scenario:

> Imagine an orchestra behind them: the frame house, the porch, the rocking-chair endlessly rocking, like a cradle, the white petticoat with eyelet lace, her water-darkened hair hanging on her shoulders and little trickles running down between her shallow breasts, the young man leading the limping pony, and inexhaustible as light, around them the tender land. (23–24)

The tale is spliced with dialogue from the Jacobean Ford's incest and revenge tragedy: the Jacobean Annabella says 'Love me or kill me, brother' (25) and Giovanni repeats the same as a tryst and oath, on their 'mother's dust' (25). Their sad father cannot forget his dead wife. Love, sex and death are intertwined as the children embrace: 'She turned to the only one she loved, and the desolating space around them diminished it to that of the soft grave their bodies dented in the long grass by the creek' (27). Soranzo in the Jacobean Ford's tragedy is a parallel for the Minister's son whom Annie-Belle must love and marry to escape her circular fate – but who dies with her, felled by her brother's shots as they attempt to leave on honeymoon and seek escape further west. As in other American sagas, they die in the dust – a Wild West side show, for onlookers.

This tale of romance gone wrong is a tragedy based in the parallel American and Jacobean investment in social conformity. Complicity in incestuous relationships provides an entirely self-contained heaven of repetition, identicality, a heaven which becomes claustrophobic, seen as perverse by society and potentially dangerous for the self. Both tales end in revenge upon the self as betrayer and betrayed – self-destruction through the destruction of the loved sibling, beloved Other, self. As

Johnny turns the gun on Annie-Belle, he is killing a version of the self as Other. His only next route is real self-destruction. In the Jacobean Ford's play, cut into the lines from the American Ford in Carter's deadly mix, Giovanni sees his sister as a betraying whore and it drives him mad. With a Gothic turn, Carter's favourite figure, the oxymoron, builds upon the paradox and twinning of such double selves. In yoking together opposites – of self/Other, good/evil and so on – she refuses to privilege one reading, one version of self or events. Conventional horror would have it that we are dangerously split selves: the Other, or other side of self, dramatized as abject, a danger to our accepted, socially acceptab[le] [...] simplification. In [...] chniques and descri[...] [...] etaphorical, fantast[...] [...] r of what could othe[...] [...] d myth, that which [...] [...] ked away again in cl[...]

Julia Kris[...] [...] abject as part of our[...] [...] vercome the need [...] *angers to Ourselves* ([...] *of Horror* (1980), Kris[...] [...] ions and repressions [...] for racial and politic[...]

our dist[...] [...] to confront the [...] ed by the protecti[...] [...] persist in maintaining as a proper, solid 'us'. By recognizing *our* uncanny strangeness we shall neither suffer from it nor enjoy it from the outside. The foreigner is within me, hence we are all foreigners. If I am a foreigner, then there are no foreigners. (58; emphasis in original)

Carter exposes and indicts oppressive behaviour as a kind of engulfment: the destruction of the Other by killing, seen as turning it into meat to be devoured in a potentially cannibalistic act. But she problematizes the reductive depiction of incest by using it as a figure through which to critique oppressive societal and familial formulae of power. It is, rather, the sickness of society, the oppressive nature of patriarchy, which is threatened by incest, she perhaps suggests. Indeed, it can be an expression of carnivalesque liberation as is suggested in the relationship between Francie and Aunt Margaret in *The Magic Toyshop*, where the Irish family play, sing and make love as a gesture of identity, solidarity, and rejection of Uncle Philip's tyranny.

Houses of horror

'The imprisoning house of Gothic fiction', writes Chris Baldick, 'has from the very beginning been that of patriarchy' (xxii). Terrifying also, he proposes, are 'the confinements of a family house closing in upon itself' (ibid.). In both Poe and Carter, houses and homes are drawn as locations of oppression. The representation of Poe's House of Usher, for example, builds upon the conventions of its literary Gothic antecedents   (1764), later spoofe   lso fore- shadows the   ary hor- ror films, fo   r (1979) and *Poltergei*   f house or home en   of past actions, whi   In Poe's "Th   truction and exposur   age and inheritance) :   Roderick Usher's break   itimacy and hidden   ventual destruction c   narrator describes a 's   y bleak house with 'e   Gothic, lofty, with ar   oooks – although Ush   uid eye and wild silke   he nar- rator and Roderick Usher bury her with ceremony. The great terror is her- alded by some dreadful clanging; she escapes the tomb and stands in the doorway. Falling onto Usher, she turns them both into corpses. These twins die together. As the narrator speeds away over the causeway out of the place, it is lit by a red moon that sinks in to the dark tarn forever. Incest, inheritance, heredity, madness, illness, spectral visitations, entombment and Gothic setting thus define this tale of a house of horrors.

Carter takes liberally from Poe's tale in her descriptions of the 'Palladian house' in "The Courtship of Mr Lyon" (1979), as well as of Christian Rosencreutz and the Russian Grand Duke's mansions, with their Gothic doors and practices, gargoyles and leather, in *Nights at the Circus*. In Carter's narratives, however, these Gothicized interiors signify an illegitimate control of women's sexuality and power. In combining opposites and exposing the horrid, Carter's horror also exposes spatial configurations of power in the form of the patriarchal castle and the domestic home. ✶ *Grthing*

The dangers of the house of horror are poignantly foregrounded in Carter's short story, "The Fall River Axe Murders", collected in *Black Venus*. For Carter's Lizzie Borden, domestic entrapment exemplifies the repression of the Puritan neighbourhood and her claustrophobic family, where eruption is the only response to repression and incarceration. Here Carter holds us in a terrifying stasis, awaiting Lizzie's violent explosion into the ostensibly calm domestic interior. Lizzie's domestic entrapment in her undertaker father's house suggests the restraints of time and place in turn-of-the-century Puritan America. Lizzie is presented as a product of her Puritanical upbringing, and of her father's capitalist insensitivities and dominance. Her shuttered existence and dead-end future are figured in the very geography of her home, which – like Poe's sick house and Bluebeard's castle – is the locus of hidden secrets and repressed lives.

> One peculiarity of this house is the number of doors the rooms contain and, a further peculiarity, how all these doors are always locked. A house full of locked doors that open only into other rooms with other locked doors, for, upstairs and downstairs, all the rooms lead in and out of another like a maze in a bad dream. It is a house without passages. (74)

Repressive and oppressive societal constraints are thus inscribed in the very architecture of the house, from which Lizzie emerges wielding an axe. When her pigeons are killed, Lizzie turns on her hated gluttonous stepmother, carving her family up with an axe. This calm, suburban neighbourhood leaks repression and dangerous complacency. This is a Grimm house standing among 'gingerbread houses lurching' and sometimes screaming – Carter's version of the explosive urban setting of contemporary horror films. Repression shrieks from Lizzie's silences, infects the restrictive space she inhabits, and then erupts. 'Outside, above, in the already burning air, see! the angel of death roosts in the roof-tree' (87).

Conclusion

Carter's imaginative recreation of a version of Poe's life and its sources for his writing provide a key to reading much of her own horror. As close analysis of several Gothic horror tales by both Carter and Poe reveal, the two writers have much in common in their work – both using scenarios of desire and terror to explore social constraints and the deadening results of oppressive worldviews and practices. Carter's work offers a particular challenge to the underlying problems of identity construction and relations of gender and power which Poe's much earlier work highlights but cannot move beyond. In exploring and replaying some of Poe's motifs, events, characters and themes – of live burials and living dolls, of cannibalism and incest, and of domestic horrors – Carter both exposes their origins in a society dominated by male power and demonstrates how the interplay of sexuality and oppressive power which they indicate lives on. Poe's tales relish paradox, death in life and life in death, the proximity of the gaudy performance to the leprous hand of death, using the oxymoron of both Jacobean revenge tragedy and Gothic horror to highlight the fascinating glitter and beauty of pain and death, the skull beneath the skin. Carter piles on gaudy and glitter, debunks the self-satisfied pomposity of power games and celebrates the comic spirit. Her mixture of horror and farce is rather like a pantomime horse – you know this is an utterly unrealistic creature of the comic mind, its two parts sometimes in unison, most usually at odds. Carter draws back the curtain to reveal the creaking stage set and the very human hands manipulating both the paraphernalia of terror and the actors, uniting them all with the trapped audience as partners in a shared drama.

The difference, however, between Poe and Carter is that while she reprises the terrors of which Poe writes, she empowers her female figures to escape them through their own agency, their mobilization of their awareness that these are imposed and internalized constrictions/constructions, artifices, performances; and that through turning the tables on restrictive mindsets and behaviours, escape is possible, and alternatives can be brought to life and seized. And so, unlike those of Poe's imagining, many of Carter's beautiful dead, un-dead, or near dead women refuse to lie down forever. Her protagonists are feistier, empowered, twentieth-century women who narrowly escape incarceration, deification, reification and death. It is Fevvers in *Nights at the Circus* who offers an alternative to the constraints and tyrannies which are the subject of conventional horror. As a New Woman, and lived metaphor, Fevvers literally flies free of the mythic and real power games of others. She refuses the myths which would incarcerate her in her appearance, and leave her as a mythical sacrifice to the male ego and religious fanaticism of Christian Rosencreutz, or turn her into a marionette, reduced, in a Fabergé egg, for the Russian Grand Duke. This winged aerialiste is a carnivalesque figure. In her refusal of a tragic role, her energies are identified as those of comedy and thus she escapes the creaking architecture of conventional horror in which woman is positioned as *femme fatale* and/or victim, and where women's sexual energy is identified as perverse, threatening, deadly – a threat to societal and familial normality. Instead, Carter's Fevvers revels in her sexuality, literally rises above those who seek to harm and imprison her, flies free of both mythic and social constraints – and the fates suffered by Poe's women. By embracing the performative, Fevvers is able to dramatize ways of escape; it is by being and making of herself a fantastical creature that she flies in the face of the father of patriarchal structures and discourses. Thus, the powers of the imagination enable an escape from mind-forged manacles, and comedy, horror's flipside, undercuts, revealing the creaking fabrication upon which terror and oppression depend.

Notes

1. For more on the significance of 'effect' in Poe, see Tonkin (*passim*).
2. This narrative is repeated in "Heartbeat", an episode of the television show *Homicide: Life on the Street* (1993–1999), set in Baltimore, where Poe lived and died, in which revenge causes one man to wall up another as his victim. The American, twentieth-century detectives detect the crime through the usual forensics, good luck and some intertextual referencing. One of the men remembers reading Poe.
3. For more on Carter and abjection, see Hunt's essay in this volume.

Works cited

Baldick, Chris. Introduction. *The Oxford Book of Gothic Tales*. Oxford: Oxford University Press, 1993. xi–xxiii.

Bedford, Les. "Angela Carter: An Interview." Sheffield University Television. Feb. 1977.

Bronfen, Elisabeth. *Over Her Dead Body: Death, Femininity and the Aesthetic*. Manchester: Manchester University Press, 1992.

Browning, Robert. *My Last Duchess and Other Poems*. New York: Dover Publications, 1994.

Carter, Angela. Afterword. *Fireworks: Nine Profane Pieces*. 1974. London: Penguin, 1987. 132–33.

———. "The Bloody Chamber." *The Bloody Chamber and Other Stories*. 1979. London: Vintage, 1995. 7–41.

———. "The Cabinet of Edgar Allan Poe." *Black Venus*. 1985. London: Vintage, 1996. 32–42.

———. "The Courtship of Mr Lyon." *The Bloody Chamber and Other Stories*. 1979. London: Vintage, 1995. 41–51.

————. "The Fall River Axe Murders." *Black Venus*. 1985. London: Vintage, 1996. 70–87.

————. *The Infernal Desire Machines of Doctor Hoffman*. 1972. Harmondsworth: Penguin, 1982.

————. "John Ford's 'Tis Pity She's a Whore." *American Ghosts and Old World Wonders*. London: Chatto & Windus, 1993. 20–44.

————. "The Loves of Lady Purple." *Fireworks: Nine Profane Pieces*. 1974. London: Penguin, 1987. 24–40.

————. *The Magic Toyshop*. 1967. London: Virago, 1981.

————. *Nights at the Circus*. 1984. London: Vintage, 1994.

————. "Notes from the Front Line." *On Gender and Writing*. Ed. Michelene Wandor. London: Pandora, 1983. 69–77.

Ford, John. *'Tis Pity She's a Whore*. 1633. Lincoln, NE: University of Nebraska Press, 1966.

"Heartbeat." *Homicide: Life on the Street*. Dir. Bruno Kirby. NBC. 8 Dec. 1995.

Jancovich, Mark. *Horror*. London: B.T. Batsford, 1992.

Kristeva, Julia. *Powers of Horror: An Essay on Abjection*. 1980. Trans. Leon S. Roudiez. New York: Columbia University Press, 1982.

————. *Strangers to Ourselves*. 1988. Trans. Leon S. Roudiez. New York: Columbia University Press, 1991.

Lloyd-Smith, Allan. "Nineteenth-Century American Gothic." *A Companion to the Gothic*. Ed. David Punter. Oxford: Blackwell, 2000. 109–21.

Lovecraft, H.P. *Supernatural Horror in Literature*. 1927. New York: Dover Publications, 1973.

Peach, Linden. *Angela Carter*. Basingstoke: Macmillan, 1998.

Poe, Edgar Allan. *Complete Stories and Poems of Edgar Allan Poe*. New York: Doubleday, 1966.

————. "The Philosophy of Composition." 1846. *The Fall of the House of Usher and Other Writings*. Ed. David Galloway. London: Penguin, 1987. 480–92.

Punter, David. *Gothic Pathologies: The Text, the Body, and the Law*. New York: St Martin's Press, 1998.

Tonkin, Maggie. "The 'Poe-etics' of Decomposition: Angela Carter's 'The Cabinet of Edgar Allan Poe' and the Reading-Effect." *Women's Studies: An Interdisciplinary Journal* 33.1 (2004): 1–21.

Watts, Helen Cagney. "An Interview with Angela Carter." *Bête Noir* 8 Aug. 1985: 161–76.

Webster, John. *The Duchess of Malfi*. 1614. Whitefish, MT: Kessinger, 2004.

Index

Todd, Dennis, 136–37, 140, 155
Tolstoy, Leo, x
Tonkin, Maggie, 65, 197n1
Tourner, Cyril, 179
transgression, 14, 22, 25, 27, 28, 29, 30, 37

uncanny, the, 35, 101, 101n19, 103, 107n21

Vaché, Jacques, 26
vagina dentata, 30, 50
vampire, 2, 25, 30, 54, 184–85
victimhood, 4, 24, 51, 55–59, 77, 186–88, 190
Victorians, the, 1, 26, 124, 158, 164, 168
  and painting, 89, 124; *see also* Dadd, Richard; Millais, John Everett; the Pre-Raphaelites
  and representations of femininity, 124, 126, 128
  and Shakespeare, 114, 115
Vietnam War, 44, 95–96
Vigneron, Robert, 75
violence, vii, 14, 16, 25, 29, 30, 31, 33, 36, 91, 179, 180

vision, 31, 31, 43, 59, 67, 114, 127, 172, 173
Voigt, Milton, 151

Walpole, Horace, *The Castle of Otranto*, 194
Ward Jouve, Nicole, 18n11
Watts, Helen Cagney, 186
Waugh, Patricia, 9–10
Webster, John, viii
  The Duchess of Malfi, 179, 189
  The White Devil, 116, 179
Wedekind, Frank, 55, 58
Weine, Robert, *Das Kabinett des Dr Caligari*, 181
West, Mae, x
White, Edmund, 76
Wilde, Oscar, ix
Woolf, Virginia, 11n11, 18n11
  "Modern Fiction", 69
  Mrs Dalloway, 117–18, 131n12
Wordsworth, Dorothy, 65
Worton, Michael, 17

Yeats, W.B., x, 188
Youngblood, Gene, 49
Yu, Su-Lin, 96, 106n12